D1532371

DOUBLE DARE

Books by *Edward Keyes*

DOUBLE DARE
THE MICHIGAN MURDERS

DOUBLE DARE

Edward Keyes

McGRAW-HILL BOOK COMPANY

New York St. Louis
San Francisco Hamburg
Mexico Toronto

2 3 4 5 6 7 8 9 F G F G 8 7 6 5 4 3 2 1

LIBRARY OF CONGRESS CATALOGING IN PUBLICATION DATA

Keyes, Edward.
Double dare.
I. Title.
PS3561.E7694D6 1981   813'.54   80-28183
ISBN 0-07-034450-7

Book design by Roberta Rezk.

To Curtis Kelly,
who dared me on

AUTHOR'S NOTE

This book is properly labeled fiction, for a number of the characters, situations and particulars have been created wholly in the author's imagination.

Nonetheless, the essence of the story is true. Events very like those depicted here did take place not long ago. The principals involved, though disguised or presented as composites, performed for the most part as described. The outcome is pretty much the way it turned out.

There are no public acknowledgments to be made to any individuals—including some of those principals—who either provided vital information or directed me to authoritative sources. For reasons that will become obvious in the reading, not a few of those so involved would wish for anything *but* to be singled out now.

—EDWARD KEYES
New York, 1980

Reason deceives us often; conscience never.

—JEAN-JACQUES ROUSSEAU.

PART .

ONE

1

Late afternoons, when there were few customers in the restaurant, Farrell liked to come out of his windowless office in the rear and work on menus or accounts at the table near the bar. Somehow it gave him a warmer sense of belonging to Anthony's—and Anthony's to him. The restaurant was something he'd long yearned for, and he'd persuaded himself that, everything considered, he'd earned it. At only twenty-nine, he felt his life was in this place—in more ways than one.

This Monday afternoon, he'd left the office door ajar so he could hear the telephone, and it rang at a few minutes past four. On schedule, if it was the call. Pete, his manager, behind the bar, looked over to the table. "Want me to get it?"

Farrell stood. "I'll take it," he said, and walked back to the office.

Alison: "Mr. Green, please?"

She sounded cool. "In about forty-five minutes," he said.

"All right. Thank you." Click.

Choosing a key from a full keyring, he unlocked the file drawer of his desk, lifted out a small black satchel and set it on the desktop. With a smaller key he unlatched the bag and examined the contents: the two Christmas-wrapped, quart-sized bottles of Black & White were undisturbed. Snapping the bag shut, he dialed a number on the desk phone. "This is Tony Farrell. Could you get my car ready? I'll be around in five minutes."

He put on the black cashmere blazer, adjusting the open-necked soft white shirt over the jacket's collar, and checked himself in the full-length mirror inside the closet door. One night some babe at the bar had told him with melting eyes that he reminded her of Al Pacino, who absolutely turned her *on*. Now he idly searched his angular features. With a wry smile, he could only shake his head. "You're good, kid, real good—but Al Pacino you just ain't." Bogart had always been his favorite anyway.

He started out of the office with the briefcase, then turned back to the desk. From deep within the top drawer he took a small revolver in a slim black half-holster with a metal clamp attached. Withdrawing the pistol, he inserted the holster inside the waistband of his gray trousers forward of his left hip, the clamp hooking out over the top; he spun the .32's loaded cylinder once, then shoved the gun down into the hidden holster. He inspected himself again in the closet mirror, holding his jacket open wide with both hands. The bulge was almost invisible. He rebuttoned the jacket.

Farrell switched off the lights and locked the office door behind him. Several early customers were in the restaurant now, a few at tables, a couple at the bar. He beckoned to Pete. "I'm going out for a while. Be back in an hour or two. If anything comes up, call the apartment. Liz should be there if I'm not."

The manager nodded, and Farrell walked through the restaurant, acknowledging the frank attention of an attractive young woman over the head of her escort at a table by the window. Who needs Al Pacino? He stepped out onto First Avenue. It was a clear, crisp late autumn day, and he was invigorated. Around the corner on 69th Street, his tan Audi Fox was waiting just inside the garage entrance. With a wave at the attendant in the glassed-in office, Farrell tossed the briefcase onto the passenger seat and eased behind the wheel. He made sure both doors were locked before pulling out.

Driving west on 69th, he turned downtown on Fifth Avenue. As usual at this time of day, traffic was heavier on the southbound avenue, a ponderous mass of vehicles, most of them cabs and buses, inching ahead. For once he didn't chafe. Farrell felt good. It was the charged feeling of Manhattan surging: the thronged, harried traffic, the sidewalks' urgent flow, the insistent blare of sound and sight; and the smells, the musky fragrance of foliage moldering in the park, of roasting chestnuts and hot giant pretzels—it was what they wrote the song about, the New York magic, the way it should be.

That was one thing that made Tony Farrell feel well off today. The other was that he was on his way to becoming another fifty thousand dollars richer.

He made a left off Fifth at East 54th Street and halfway to Madison Avenue turned into a large open parking lot. Taking the briefcase, he walked back out onto 54th; continuing east, across Madison, he made his way against a growing tide of people.

The dour uniformed doorman threw him a tentative glance as Farrell ducked jauntily in toward the recessed canopied entrance of the Elysée Hotel between Madison and Park. He strode across the small lobby past the front desk and reception area, the stair and lone elevator to his left, the Monkey Bar with its tinkling piano on the right, direct to the glass doors of the restaurant opposite, La Veranda. Pausing at the doorway, he scanned the room, his eyes not yet adjusted to the subdued lighting. Alison was alone at the table on the left nearest him. His gaze rested casually on her a moment—young and attractive, well-groomed, ash-blond hair, good legs, a gaily colored shopping bag at her feet. She glanced at him without expression, then, looking away, lifted a stemmed glass to her lips.

Good. Still no problems. Farrell turned to the coatroom just to his right. It was open but unoccupied, as he expected; the attendant did not come on until five, when evening action would begin to pick up—which was why he'd chosen this time,

to avoid any hassle over claim checks. He swung open the
shelved half-door and set his briefcase on the floor against the
back wall. Then he strolled into La Veranda, paying no further
attention to the young woman as he passed her table.

He eased himself onto a padded stool at one end of the
three-sided bar, from which he had an unobstructed view
through the doorway out to the street entrance.

"So what's new, Tony? Still checking the competition?" The
dark, impish Celtic-handsome face of the barman twinkled at
him.

"No contest, Dan," Farrell smiled. "It's a bright new world
uptown—not like this dungeon. Like I keep telling you, you
ought to come up with me and give us a try."

"Like I keep telling *you,* make me an offer I can't refuse."
Dan slid a napkin in front of Farrell. "The same?"

Farrell nodded and, lighting a Marlboro, watched as the
barman deftly put together a tall Campari and tonic and set it
before him. In the public relations job he'd had before, Farrell
had frequented many a bar, from *21* up and down the board,
and in time had settled on La Veranda as his more-or-less
"regular" hangout. Not particularly for its charm, but for Dan.
Farrell rated Dan Mulcahy the best all-around barman he'd
come upon, unfailingly attuned to the variable humors of the
"clients," as he called his regulars.

"The joint still swinging?" asked Dan.

"Better all the time," replied Farrell, rapping the bartop
with his knuckles.

"Your uncle talking to you yet?" Dan asked with a knowing
smile. Farrell had confided in him about many things on those
darkest nights.

"Michael. Well, he's hard to convince. But he'll come
around."

Dan moved off to attend a new customer across the bar, and
Farrell contemplated Michael Palmieri. He hadn't seen much of
his uncle lately and had gotten too caught up in other things to

give him much thought. Michael, really a father to him since childhood, who had reared him in security and in a like image of sure, practical toughness . . . and who had so vehemently opposed the restaurant venture. That Farrell could have elected to chuck a blossoming P.R. career (which Michael had used his own influence to get him into!), to plunge into a go-for-broke business that had eight chances out of ten of winding up in bankruptcy had been inconceivable to Michael. And unforgivable. He had stalked away from his nephew, vowing not to lift a finger to bail him out when, inevitably, the foolhardy enterprise went down the tube. But Anthony's had survived the predicted worst, and it had been coming on big for nearly a year. And while Michael had yet to allow that Anthony's might be the exception that proved the rule, Farrell didn't doubt that, sooner or later, his uncle would swallow his stubborn pride and concede. He would have to take into account Farrell's lately conspicuous trappings of success—the custom threads, the imported roadster, the elegant East Side duplex, the bulging bankroll—and read as the bottom line that his nephew's own stubborn faith in his dream had been vindicated after all.

Which was as much as Farrell hoped he'd ever make of it. If Michael ever suspected any of the *rest* of it, he would positively go apeshit. . . .

Farrell brought himself back to the business at hand. There were only two other executive types at the bar. He swiveled to re-survey the body of the room. The cocktail area was still barely a quarter full. The dining section, separated by a baroque flowered screen, was freshly set and empty except for its claque of uniformed waiters hovering about expectantly. Okay. Deliberately he reached for his glass and took a long first swallow of the Campari.

Over the rim of the glass, Farrell watched the young woman at the table near the entrance gather her belongings and rise to go. He eyed the retreating figure appreciatively. Alison Fournier was sharp, picked right up on her cues and moved out. And he did enjoy the *way* she moved. On the surface, she didn't seem his type—more the Bloomingdale's Junior League set —but he thought he'd detected, beneath that casually decorous facade, powerful animal signals. Maybe sometime. . . . Alison disappeared into the checkroom. A moment later she emerged, paused before the glass doors to heft her shopping bag from one hand to the other, then continued out of his sight, toward the hotel elevator.

Farrell kept his eyes on the hotel lobby. No unusual activity in her wake; no sweat. He hadn't really expected any. He downed his drink in one long draught, extracted a five-dollar bill from his money clip and tossed it on the bar. Catching Dan's eye, he called: "Later."

"Have a good night, Tony." The barman nodded, winking.

Outside the hotel, the street lights were coming on. Farrell breathed deep, savoring the snap in the air, and glanced both ways on 54th. No one appeared to be loitering about. He strolled across the street and paused to browse the window of a chic wine and spirits shop; then, edging away from the bright storefront, he folded himself into shadows alongside an old brownstone directly opposite the Elysée. He checked his wristwatch: Alison and Gerard should be out in about ten minutes.

Farrell felt at ease on this street, almost as though it were his home ground. For years, while he was in P.R., East 54th had been a regular byway of his in midtown—a conduit to the corporate and media worlds he used to ply, as well as the location of several of his favored pit stops.

As for what was taking place on the eighth floor of the Elysée, he was expectant, but not anxious. The way he'd set it up, it figured to be a piece of cake. Still, when you were juggling a kilo of cocaine and seventy-five thousand dollars in cash you couldn't take anything for granted—not even with the caliber of the people involved in this deal. So he was here standing shotgun, watchful for any unanticipated fuckups when the girl and her escort would emerge from the hotel with that briefcase full of goodies for him. It was his way, seeing that all bases were covered—and it had paid off for him this past year.

He'd had good vibes about this deal from the minute Alison Fournier had brought it to him. She'd buttonholed him one night at Anthony's and told him of this very respectable dude who was in the market for a quantity of white lightning and willing to pay premium for discreet service. Farrell had learned that it could be reckless dealing with amateurs, but Alison he trusted. She was a regular patron, and he'd judged her a cool, standup kid. She also had a pedigree that he'd checked out: foaled out of the Old Westbury thoroughbred set, the only daughter of a prominent corporation counsel who was being talked up lately for a top cabinet spot with the new Albany administration—the kind of connection that, if someone could get a small lock on it, just might be useful one day.

What had really tickled Farrell was the identity of Alison's prospective buyer: a law associate of her father's in town from Chicago. She didn't say it in so many words, but Farrell deduced that they'd been balling.

When Farrell asked how much powder the lawyer was shopping for, Alison's answer almost floored him: a *kilo* the guy wanted. That was the high-rent neighborhood.

Farrell had handled dope, all kinds, this past year, but not in such quantity. He would get top dollar hustling small amounts here and there, but when it came to big orders of anything he'd always been no more than the service manager for the guys with the connections, like his "mentor," Cheech Donato.

Then, too, whenever Farrell had been involved in dealing bulk, it was always "trade" business, wholesale, where the net markup would be maybe 300 percent at best. But here, thought Farrell with a surge of anticipation, he alone stood to realize a minimum return of 500 percent—and, if everything broke right, up to 1,000 percent!

What had him pumped up about this opportunity, as much

as the richness of the score itself, was its incipient promise of independence. It was the first time he'd been in the position to make such a deal on his own. Cheech Donato had given his okay. He could hardly have done otherwise at this point: Farrell had made himself increasingly valuable to Cheech's assorted enterprises. In fact, Farrell had come to the view lately that Cheech might now need *him* as much as the other way around. That was the impression he'd gotten when he was brought up front in Cheech's blue-chip setup with the Giant as "my partner"—like a bright new account executive being showcased to reassure the prized client. The Giant had approved. Farrell could only take that to mean he'd achieved parity.

Some year! He'd had no idea, before, how much money there was floating around, accessible to any with the urge and the daring. *I've been poor, and I've been rich . . . and rich is better.* Well, he wasn't rich yet; but he'd had a taste of it, and he wanted it all. In just this brief period, he'd come from bankruptcy to relative affluence—without breaking a sweat.

So this coke deal represented to Farrell his debut into the big leagues. His planning had been deliberate and precise. He'd arranged to get the coke from Donato's most reliable Florida connection, Harry Loman, with whom Farrell had dealt often enough as agent for Cheech to have established a mutually trustful relationship. The goods were shipped north in a van loaded with produce and deposited with a packing company in Brooklyn, a mostly legitimate spinoff of the Giant's, which they'd used before. From there it was delivered across the river to the storage basement of Anthony's as part of a shipment of dry ice. Farrell separated it personally and locked it in an antique cast-iron safe to which he alone had the combination. Only then did he get in touch with Alison Fournier and instruct her to contact her friend in Chicago and set up the timetable.

The small, nestled-in Elysée was perfect for the exchange. Farrell knew that a lot of guys, when setting up meets like this, went for the mammoth, bustling convention-type hotels, with

DOUBLE DARE • 11

their mazes of wings and miles of corridors and forty-nine different exits—where, in case of a sudden jam-up, people could get quickly lost. He'd picked the Elysée for precisely the opposite reasons: for its compactness and *limited* accessibility or egress. There were just three ways in or out of the hotel, all facing on 54th Street, squarely opposite his vantage point: the main entrance; five steps to the right, the glass doors of the Monkey Bar; and another fifteen feet or so to the right, in a shallow areaway, a metal-sheeted service door. The Elysée, in the middle of the block, was a self-contained unit not connected from the inside with the buildings on either side or to its rear. For Farrell's purposes, it was a box canyon and he stood at the pass. He wanted to be sure that no one concerned with this transaction *could* get lost.

The room on the eighth floor had been reserved in advance for the man from Chicago. He was to have come in on an early plane and stayed put in the hotel until he heard from Alison. Farrell took the precaution of having the hotel staked out all day by a young fellow named Gerard who did odd jobs for him and Cheech, to confirm that the buyer arrived alone and *stayed* alone. When Gerard was satisfied, he was to signal Alison, who would take it from there. Her first task was to go up to the lawyer's room—escorted by Gerard; Farrell wanted no indiscreet hanky-panky—with a display sample (a few ounces of powder in a tiny plastic bag tucked inside her compact) and there also to examine the cash, which he had stipulated was to be in denominations no higher than hundred-dollar bills.

Gerard, last name Trantz, was a quiet blond with delicate features and arms like most other men's legs; a physical-culture freak—and also a fag—who could break human bones with one hand. Gerard also was proficient with a well-oiled, hair-trigger derringer he carried in his handkerchief pocket as well as a four-inch switchblade strapped to a calf. While Farrell didn't think Alison's "respectable" friend would pull any kind of switch, nor did he much fear police interference in a privately set-up deal like this, whenever drugs were involved, Farrell knew there was always the risk of word having leaked somewhere along the line and of some wise guys trying to muscle in for a takeoff. Gerard's presence on the inside was one defense against any such attempt, and Farrell himself, patrolling the outside, was the other.

When everything seemed kosher, Alison would leave the room to pick up the rest of the merchandise, leaving Gerard with the lawyer. What she would do actually was go downstairs to the Elysée's public phone and dial Farrell at Anthony's: If she asked for "Mr. Green," it was an all-clear and he could deliver the goods; if she asked for "Red," it meant problems, and then it would have been up to Farrell to decide what to do next. With the go-ahead, Farrell had headed downtown with his briefcase, while Alison waited in La Veranda over a drink —keeping a sharp eye on last-minute comings and goings in the hotel lobby.

The night before, Farrell himself had carefully packaged the cocaine. Weighing out half the kilo stored in his basement safe, he'd measured out an equal amount of the cutting agent lactose, a white powder derived from milk, and sifted it with the coke to make a full kilo's weight. Dividing this again in half, he'd filled and sealed two bags of durable polyethylene. Each half-kilo package then was stuffed into the false bottom of a quart bottle of Black & White scotch (chosen primarily for its dark, almost opaque glass), the top third of which, the tax stamp unbroken, actually contained whiskey. For a finishing touch, he'd encased each bottle in festive holiday wrapping, including sashes of red ribbon, and locked them in his desk.

Now it was nearly time. Any moment, Alison and Gerard should come out of the Elysée, and they would stroll west on 54th, across Madison and into the parking lot. Farrell would meet them at the Audi and they would all pile in and drive out together—just a friendly, energy-conscious car pool. He would slip Gerard two thousand dollars, a generous enough tip for being on call a few hours, and later, in private, give Alison twelve thousand five, roughly 20 percent of his profit after figuring all costs. Which would leave him, give or take a few dollars, a nice round fifty grand.

And that wasn't all. He still had that other half-key stashed, expandable to a whole kilo or more. Contemplation of it made him lightheaded. With this as a stake, if things kept breaking right, in another year or two he'd be home free. He could *retire*, for Christ's sake!—at thirty or thirty-one!—and he and Liz could split somewhere, Europe, South America, the Pacific.

At that moment there was a flurry at the hotel entrance as its doors flew open . . . out stumbled Alison Fournier . . . just behind, one hand gripping her arm, a burly man in a plaid sport jacket, propelling her ahead of him—a stranger! Farrell gaped, immobile for a stunned instant: The sonofabitch had the *briefcase!* Where was Gerard—? What in Christ—?

Hijack! The realization was explosive.

Well, fuck *this!*

The two had reached the curb as Farrell bolted across 54th toward them, groping as he ran for the bulge at his waistband. The guy, still holding onto Alison, was looking up the street and didn't see him coming. Yanking out the .32, almost upon them Farrell yelled: "Hold it, you motherfucker—!"

Alison's features contorted as she saw him. "No!" she screamed.

The man reacted instantly—dropping the briefcase, jerking Alison back and behind him, crouching and plunging his free hand inside his own jacket, all in an almost continuous motion. Farrell charged into him, driving a knee into his midsection where he thought the unseen hand should be, and with a grunt the guy tumbled backward, pulling Alison down with him. Farrell retrieved the briefcase and went for him again to break his hold on Alison. She was crying: "Stop it! *Stop* it—!"

Farrell heard screeching tires nearby and sudden shouting and pounding footsteps closing behind him. He'd started to swing about when a sharp command stabbed through him: *"Freeze* or you're garbage!"

He froze. And knew. Not a takeoff. A bust. And he'd suckered himself right into it. Daydreaming. *Shit.*

Alison was gawking at him with fearful, wet eyes. He shook his head and tried to smile and mouthed, *Take it easy, kid.* Then the revolver was being wrested from him and he was being shoved against the brick wall of the hotel and rough hands were pawing him systematically from armpits to ankles.

"You all right, Frank?" someone panted behind Farrell.

"Yeah. But who the fuck is *this* dude?" Agitated. The one Farrell had knocked over.

"We seen him across the street. All of a sudden he goes for you. Must be their shotgun."

"Maybe. Or a free-lance. He was after the bag."

"So where's everybody? How come just you and her—?"

"They're coming. We had a small accident upstairs."

"Anybody hurt?"

"Yeah—sort of. None of *us.*" The hard voice chuckled. "The one with her?—Mr. Muscles?—he makes a quick move when we bust in—goes for his back pocket like this, see. Before he can blink, Hutch hits him a shot, and right away there's this little *zap* . . . and the sonofabitch jumps three feet off the floor, holding his ass and squealing like an alley cat. Turns out he's carrying a popgun back there, a derringer. Shot himself clean through his butt! The guys fell down."

"All right, you"—brawny hand on Farrell's shoulder, pulling him around—"let's have *your* story."

In spite of himself Farrell was unable to suppress a grin. Gerard—in the *ass?* Far out!

2

If Brendan Hartnett had left his office that November evening just a few minutes earlier, it probably would have escaped his notice until the next day. And that could well have been too late for any chance of salvaging the operation.

He was about to leave when the preliminary report of the Elysée affair reached his desk. He had a seven o'clock dinner engagement for which he was already late, and this would delay him still longer. He began leafing through the report without enthusiasm: Late that afternoon, between five and five-thirty, a combined federal/city anticrime squad (dubbed JUST, for Joint Undercover Strike Team) had broken up an illegal transaction involving narcotics at a small, elegant hotel on Manhattan's mid–East Side. Four persons were arrested—three, including a young female, inside the hotel, and one male who attempted to interfere outside. Nothing to get excited about.

Then his eye caught the name of the man picked up outside the hotel. Oh good Christ, *no!*

After all the months of careful, patient setting-up, to have him blunder into their hands now!

Where in the name of God were Stabler and Thomas?

"It's me. That you?" said the familiar gruff monotone through the earpiece.

Roy Thomas twitted him, "You couldn't stand one whole day without me?"

"It was one of my best days since I know you—until just a little while ago," growled Ed Stabler. "You didn't hear?"

"Hear what?"

"We're up shit creek, boy."

"Okay, lay it on me."

"It's him."

"*Our* him?"

"Got his balls caught in the wringer. Follow?"

Thomas had a terrible sinking feeling. "Play that number again," he said slowly.

"Crashed a party," rasped his partner. "Walked in *cold,* for Chrissake!"

"Oh, *shit,* man!" Thomas groaned. "Who was it?"

"Our own bunch."

"Beautiful. Talk about Murphy's Law. Well, is it blown, or what?"

"We'll find out real quick," Stabler said. "The boss wants us downtown—like an hour ago."

"I'll bet. Is he hot?"

"Like a Saturday night special."

"Should I pick you up?"

"No. I'm in the city already. Meet you there. Just hustle your black ass."

"Up yours, honky."

The subject under observation was literally "their man." They had discovered him and established the exciting probability that they might have found at last an unsuspected entrée to the inner workings of an increasingly bold criminal machine, which JUST had been trying in vain to penetrate for over two years. They had transmitted their excitement in confidence to Assistant U.S. Attorney Hartnett, coordinator of the anticrime operations, so impressing him that he diverted them exclusively to surveillance of this single individual. Even within JUST, the pair's activities were a tightly held secret; they acted independently and reported only to Hartnett, who assessed the stakes as high enough not to invite compromise—or possibly even betrayal from within—by advising any more of his people than necessary about this sensitive new facet of the investigation. For the time being, until it paid off or failed, Stabler and Thomas were the only ones who were necessary.

The thing that confounded both Thomas and Stabler, as each hurried separately to Hartnett's office in the Federal Building in downtown Manhattan, was: how could Tony Farrell—so smooth and controlled—have let himself be scooped up like this?

Sounds echoed in the marbled corridors of the Federal Building after nine o'clock at night; an unseen door being shut, footsteps, the clank and shuffle of a cleaning person's paraphernalia, each resounded distantly.

Within the carpeted inner office of the Assistant U.S. Attorney, however, it was still. A somber Brendan Hartnett hunched over his heavy polished-wood desk, intent on the typewritten pages before him under the glare of a high-intensity desk lamp. Opposite him, erect and motionless in a straight-backed chair, sat Roy Thomas. Off Hartnett's left shoulder, Ed Stabler stood at a window, one foot on the low sill, noiselessly rocking back and forth. Chewing a dead cigar, he stared down at the city's dark outline. No one had spoken for several minutes.

At last Hartnett stirred and leaned back in his leatherbound swivel chair, clasping his hands behind his head thoughtfully. The prosecutor was a handsome man, a husky six-footer who looked it even when slouching as now, with sparkling blue eyes, unlined fair skin that turned ruddy at the slightest encounter with either the sun or sudden anger—it was pink now—and, most remarkable, a shock of thick white hair that belied his forty-four years. His hair, once a luxurious black, had turned white when he was thirty—virtually overnight, for no reason that he could think of or that any medical opinion seemed able to explain—causing him acute discomfiture at that still impressionable age. In the years since, though, having been assured by admiring relatives that the magnificent crown made him look like one of the great ancient Irish kings, Hartnett had come to accept it—indeed, to prize it, for, being no less a practical than a prideful man, he'd come to see how so distinguishing a feature could only be an asset to one in quest of an early judgeship.

Such cosmetic trappings notwithstanding, Hartnett had earned a reputation as an earnest and uncompromisingly thorough prosecutor. He gave of himself with equal vigor to any case his office was assigned or his own people developed. In this case, cooking many months now, he'd smelled something special: This could be his *pièce de résistance;* to carry it forth successfully could be for him the critical leg up to the law's upper chambers. But now the pursuit had stumbled. Recovery was possible, Hartnett had decided, but only if adjustment was rapid and sure-footed.

"Well . . ." He breathed it out as a long, contemplative sigh. It hung in the close room, like smoke. He looked across at Thomas, who returned his gaze levelly, without expression, waiting. Hartnett twisted his head in the direction of Stabler, behind him.

Without turning from the window Stabler growled: "Well . . . it's a damn shame. Look at that, down there. You can't tell the bad guys from the good guys any more. Used to be the bad guys all tooled around in big black sedans. Now . . ." He clamped his teeth on the stub of the cigar again.

"Deep. Very deep, Ed," snorted Hartnett, swinging back toward Thomas, who, eyes lowered, was shaking his head, a smile at the corners of his mouth. "*Well,*" Hartnett repeated, "we do know the bad guys in *this* case, don't we? And by the same token, we *can* recognize a—you'll forgive my directness —a *fuckup* when we fall over one, can't we? I acknowledge your prior contributions, gentlemen, by use of the singular objective noun in this reference." He paused, commanding silence like a Dickensian schoolmaster.

"You two clowns come here with your bare faces hanging out and tell me you knew *nothing* of what our target was up to tonight—and for God knows however long he might have been setting it up?"

Thomas said quietly, "We never had a clue, Bren. The guy looked like he was coasting the past few weeks."

"Gerard we know," Hartnett said, again referring to the report. "Are you familiar with this Alison Fournier?"

The detectives exchanged discomfited glances. "There is a chick named Alison," offered Stabler, "hangs out at Farrell's place. 'Now' singles type."

"She's the seller—ostensibly. First offense, and a dilly. Daddy's a lawyer, top-drawer and solid gold. That should be interesting. And how about Harmon P. Stratton, Esquire, of Chicago?"

"Never heard of him. Listen, Bren, are we sure this *was* Farrell's deal? Couldn't it have been a private setup, say between the girl and this Stratton? Maybe Farrell was just playing big brother, baby-sitting like—?"

"No, we're not *sure*. So far there's nothing tying Farrell to either the dope or the cash. The arrest team was zeroed in on Stratton, off a tip out of Chicago. They staked him out at the hotel and waited for the New York contact, and that turned out to be the girl. And Gerard. All of a sudden, out of nowhere they say, down comes this stranger—Farrell. So, all they've got is *suspicion* of complicity . . . and the gun charge. He is not, of course, licensed. And there's a matter of reckless endangerment, not to mention assaulting a police officer. Farrell claims he was just helping a lady in distress. It's possible. He *might* only have been passing by and come upon a girl he knew apparently being manhandled—or, as you suggest, he could have been acting chaperone on *her* first big date—

"But I don't buy it either way. Simply because at the heart of it is half a *kilo* of cocaine. What First Avenue bunny would have the sort of connection who could swing that big a load? No, I think a safe guess is that it's Farrell's package down the line." Hartnett regarded them. "And he slipped it right past you. My two 'ace' investigators. . . ."

The wall clock whirred. It was twenty before ten. Hartnett let them stew a few more moments before continuing.

"All right, it's a setback. But it's done. So what do we do now? Do we write Farrell off? Or can we adjust? Any ideas?"

Stabler picked a bit of tobacco from his lower lip. "We could come out of the closet now," he muttered, "and land on him—squeeze him for all he's worth. As long as the operation's burned anyway. . . ."

"Uh-huh." Hartnett toyed with a pencil. "What do you think?" he asked Thomas.

Thomas shifted restlessly. "I don't know. How much *is* he worth to us at this stage? Sure, if we open our file on him we could send him away for a long time . . . but that misses the whole point of this exercise. He was going to be our master key to the big guys. We're not close to that yet. We might make a case on Donato, but for the other crowd—Farrell's only just got his foot inside the door. There have been signs the Giant digs the kid, might throw a lot more action his way, but for our purposes there's a way to go before they're *tight.* So, I don't know."

"Anything's better than sucking wind," insisted Stabler. "Anyway, what choice do we have? He sure as hell won't be doing us no good up in the joint! Himself, neither."

Thomas shrugged his doubt. "I suppose . . . but then, there's also the risk of blowing everything we've put together so far. We lean on Farrell to cop a plea, and that tips the Giant, Donato, all of them, to just where we're at. They just change all the locks, and we come away with a few nickels and dimes."

"All right," cut in Hartnett. "You're both right and both wrong. Now listen. We've put too much patient time and effort into this fellow to lose him, and maybe the whole ballgame, on a freak. I think we have no choice now but to go for broke. Hit him with everything we've got." He paused. "And turn him."

Thomas and Stabler looked at one another. "Bring him over

to us—all the way?" Thomas said incredulously. "Jesus! Have we got enough to trade for *that?*"

"I believe we have. If we need sweeteners, I should be able to swing it."

"Immunity?"

"In all probability. Full VIP accommodation would be justified, considering the payoff here, wouldn't you think?"

"Shit!" groaned Stabler. "Sucking up to a goddamn stool!"

"Not just a stoolie, Ed," Hartnett corrected. "A 'special employee.' A full-time operative, under rigid supervision. I want to keep Farrell inside—*working* for us. He produces, or he goes."

"That's one hell of a tough order, Bren," said Thomas, "on both ends."

"My end is less difficult. I've already started laying the groundwork with Justice. The brunt is on you two. However, as I see it, you do have a certain edge. One, Farrell may be as vulnerable now as we're ever apt to find him. A fairly big caper was blown out from under him; and he suckered himself into the bust in the bargain. Whether it was his own setup or he was playing somebody else's stake, the people he travels with don't figure to be very impressed. Two, I'm persuaded he has no idea whatever of the book we've compiled on him these past months. This seems plain from his consistent behavior recently —loose as a goose, as you've put it, still confident he's 'invisible.'

"So when you come down on him with the full force of what we have got on him—I'd say it adds up to, in round numbers, a good thirty to forty years of his life, less time off—he may have to seriously re-examine his options.

"I don't say it will be easy. We dare not underrate this subject. Tony Farrell is intelligent, composed, resourceful. He's not your standard hoodlum. He must be made to understand that we are not bluffing. We're playing it strictly down and dirty."

"And if he does stiff us?" asked Stabler.

Hartnett shrugged. "We lose a good prospect. Maybe we have to start from scratch with the Giant. That's a sizable risk. But suddenly it's the only game in town." He sat back, thoughtfully. "Prospects come and go. *We'll* be around."

The three fell silent. Then Roy Thomas spoke up: "When do we start?"

"Now," Hartnett said. "We don't have much time."

"He's probably already got his lawyer making bail," Stabler said.

"Not yet. He hasn't been able to make his call yet—a 'communications problem.' And he won't be arraigned until morning. Bail will be set then. So you've got tonight—all night."

"Terrific," grumbled Stabler. "Where're they holding him?"

"Right down the street. The Tombs."

"The Tombs! You're letting it go as a *local* collar?"

"Who does the honors doesn't matter here," said Hartnett. "It's only paperwork. Frank Casanova happened to be heading the detail—made the arrests himself. He asked for it, said the Department needed it."

"*Frank* needs it," Stabler declared. "He's tired of lieutenant. This could get him captain."

"What's *our* story over there?" asked Thomas. "How do we move in on Farrell without attracting attention?"

"I've arranged that," Hartnett replied, "with the assistant D.A. He's straight; I trust him. I said Justice wanted to check him out on the firearm violation—in possible connection with a multistate gun-running operation. Of course, Farrell's not into anything like that—so far as we know—but it's enough to give us time with him . . . we can only hope *enough* time."

"So what's the drill?"

"You go down to Manhattan Criminal and get a pass from the A.D.A."—Hartnett scrawled on a pad, pronouncing "Chris . . . Adamowski" as he wrote—"and then you go to the Tombs and collect your package." He handed the note to Thomas.

"Then where?"

"Bring him back here. You can use an office down the hall where we'll have him to ourselves."

Thomas and Stabler gathered themselves, and Hartnett saw them to the outer door. As they moved off down the long corridor, the prosecutor called after them: "Be sure he's had his 'rights.' "

Stabler's mutter echoed back: ". . . fucking stool pigeons don't *have* no rights!"

The two walked through deserted Foley Square in silence.

There was only one way to describe Ed Stabler: a bulldog. He could have been a character drawn by Dashiell Hammett. At thirty-nine, a compact, brawny man beginning to give some ground to flab ("Muscle at ease," he would crack), Stabler had the jaded yet coldly intimidating air of a bouncer in a Third Avenue saloon. An only child whose parents had separated early, he was by preference a loner, not given to easy partnerships. He'd married once and had one daughter; but his young wife found it impossible to compete with his absorption in police work, and they were divorced after only two and a half years. He had lived for several years in an efficiency apartment in Queens, not far from LaGuardia Airport and the abundance of on-the-go airline stews domiciled nearby. What time he allowed himself for recreation he gave to an occasional sexual sortie. Nothing, with the trivial exception of big-league base-ball, held his attention for long outside his job.

Stabler had been a cop in New York since the age of twenty-one, without ever having been a city policeman. He passed the Police Department exam, but, discouraged by the several thousand applicants ahead of him on the appointments list, he signed on as a patrolman with the para-police of the Port Authority. It didn't take Stabler long to decide there was too little challenge, and perhaps less future, in that job, and next he tried the State Police. This was better—but, for a city boy, not much. A couple of lonesome years upstate left him homesick for the urban grit and clamor, so he returned and joined the Housing Authority Police—where he found a niche that, if not completely fulfilling, afforded his restless, prowling nature a continuing source of "action."

Stabler soon recognized that Housing cops were at least as well trained as, and possibly more versatile than, the run of NYPD regulars. Experiencing and learning to cope with every known human failing, seaminess and barbarism that eroded the city at large, Stabler developed an extraordinary sensitivity to evil. He trained himself to trust only his instincts, and they proved uncannily trustworthy. He could "feel," almost without seeming to have noticed, a prospective rapist lurking, a ripoff in the conception stage, a furtive junkie on the make . . . and his arrest record bore that out. One of the most decorated Housing officers in ten years, he'd plowed ahead to unchallenged rank of senior detective. Which was where he was when tapped by Brendan Hartnett for detached duty with the JUST unit. It was the highest mark of recognition in Stabler's professional life, but he took it in stride as fitting.

Ed Stabler's acquired partner within JUST was unlike him in several notable ways. Roy Thomas, five years younger at thirty-four, was college-educated (an accounting major) and, as a law officer, not street- but FBI-trained. He was taller and athletic; well-groomed; soft-spoken, gentlemanly. What really set them apart, though—in Stabler's view, at any rate—was Thomas's blackness. Instinctively, Stabler viewed blacks with mistrust. It was thus a source of some wonderment to Stabler that in a year's forced association with Thomas he should have, without any conscious accommodation on his own part, acknowledged a growing respect for this able man—even, he could not deny, a genuine affection. Yet this unlikely new bond had in no way blurred Stabler's perception of Thomas as a *black;* somehow, it only made him see the other more clearly as "different."

Thomas, one of the large family of a hard-working Yonkers

carpenter, had made it to college through a basketball grant-in-aid. Accepted to the Bureau soon after graduation, he'd since done the standard apprenticeship time at FBI field offices in Seattle, Detroit and Atlanta, before his last assignment—with some promise of permanency, he hoped—to the prestigious New York bureau. Back "home," he'd completed night courses at the John Jay College of Criminal Justice and then gone on to NYU for a master's degree in Contemporary Urban Sociology. A precise, scrupulous agent both in the field and administratively, Thomas was seen by his superiors in the Bureau as an excellent prospect for command responsibility—his added showcase value as a minority representative hardly escaping official attention. His ultimate goal was to teach at the college level.

Thomas was married to a beautiful young woman he'd met four years before in Atlanta. Camille Dubois, American-born of Haitian parentage, had been a fashion consultant in a large department store. She was strong and vibrant, and they'd fallen thunderously in love. After their living together there, when he was summoned to the New York post, she'd soon followed —though not solely to be with Roy, for Camille was driven no less by her own career ambitions—and they'd resumed their passionate relationship. Finally, although neither had felt it necessary, there being no thought between them yet of institutionalizing their union with children, the couple had bowed to convention (and some gentle prodding from Thomas's family) and taken one another ritually. For the past year and a half they'd lived in a 3½-room apartment in New Rochelle overlooking Long Island Sound.

It was a good marriage, if not without some sharp edges. Camille had not found it an easy transition, once wed, to acclimate to the often unpredictable, sometimes volatile life of an active policeman; while able to immerse herself by day in the zeal of her own pursuits, there were too many empty nights —and frequently, many nights on end—without Roy. At the same time, though she was an assertive woman who had long since shed herself of both sexual and racial restraints, in the depths of Camille's black heritage dwelt a sore she found difficult to heal, as much as she loved her husband: an intrinsic distrust of and antagonism toward police, the timeless symbol and instrumentality of white repression.

Roy Thomas was not insensitive to this and, as in his relations with the outspoken Stabler, could only try to make the best of it. It had occurred to him more than once that, though their passions were at different poles, his wife and his partner were not unalike. Odd, Thomas thought now, he'd been with Stabler almost a year, and the detective had yet to meet Camille. Well, maybe not so odd at that—and probably for the better. . . .

"Okay, how do we work Farrell?" Stabler broke into his reverie. "He don't know us, right? How about *I* play Snow White for once, and you be Grumpy?"

They'd started up the steep, broad steps of the Manhattan Criminal Courts Building. Thomas looked at Stabler and shook his head: "We'd better stay in character. Farrell would never go for *you* in drag."

3

Tony Farrell had run a decathlon of emotional responses the past six hours, leaving him woolly-eyed and with the beginnings of a headache.

After the initial shock then anger then dismay, his mind had remained a turmoil of anxiety and self-reproach. Even so, for a while he'd been buoyed by a certain fascination with what was happening to him, as though he were an outsider observing a performance by others. He'd never been involved in an arrest situation before, and he'd followed the exhaustive procedure with curious interest—for a while . . . until he was shuffled from one location to another, from questioner to questioner with yet another set of forms to be typed, for what seemed the tenth time. All he knew was that he'd been dragged this way and that for hours, like a dry bone between a couple of bored dogs, finally only to be discarded without a backward look in a dank hole that stank of urine and mold. He hadn't seen Alison or Gerard or the man Stratton; he hadn't been given the opportunity even to call a lawyer, or anybody—he was going to scream bloody murder about that!

And then into his troubled night had come the two new dicks, the stony-jawed white one and the tall, smooth black. Now, locked alone in a small gray windowless room—vacant except for a bare metal desk and three wooden chairs, and a square mirror embedded in a wall—he was disoriented and cranky.

In the darkened office, the three watched him from the other side of the mirror. Hartnett had not seen Farrell in person before, knew his features only through tiny black-and-white contact prints or grainy blowups of shots taken with a long lens through rear windows of surveillance panel trucks. Farrell sat motionless by the desk now, slouched in one of the hard chairs, one leg over the other, arms folded, eyes closed, the brows knit and forehead creased. Except around the eyes, his face appeared placid, betraying no inner strain, although a dark shadow beginning to show up across the jaws and chin made the skin look unnaturally sallow in the harsh light.

"He shaves twice a day sometimes," grunted Stabler.

"Well," said Hartnett, turning to face them, "he's had fifteen minutes to get spooked. Want to give it a go? You've got about eight hours before we have to get him back to the Tombs."

The only movement by Farrell as they entered the room was his eyelids flicking open; the dark pupils were red-rimmed, but his gaze was unblinking as he gauged the two intruders. Thomas, giving him a polite smile, seated himself easily in one of the chairs by the desk. Stabler spun the other chair around and straddled it, arms crossed over the backrest.

"Anthony Farrell—" Thomas began.

"Tony," Farrell corrected evenly.

"Okay. It is my duty to advise you that you have the right to remain silent—"

"—and also to have counsel present," Farrell cut in, still matter-of-factly. "Six, going on seven hours, and I still haven't had my call. You people are making big trouble for yourselves."

"You mean nobody—?" Thomas displayed astonishment. He looked to his partner. "What is *wrong* with those people, Ed?"

Stabler shrugged, unmoved: "Coordination gets screwed up sometimes. Nobody's perfect."

Thomas turned back to Farrell with an expression oozing

concern. "Of course you're right. And we'll straighten that out, I promise you. But first . . . so we all have a clear understanding of what this is all about . . . maybe we could talk a little."

"Name, rank and serial number—that's all you get."

Thomas smiled appreciatively: "Your Army training."

Farrell's eyes narrowed. "What are you guys, feds?"

"Well . . ." Thomas considered. "Yes and no."

"The team don't matter," Stabler picked up flatly. "What matters is the score. And we got you down as a heavy loser, mister."

"For what? Come on! I'm not some kid in the street, you can't jive me. I've never been arrested in my life before—never come *close*."

"So *you* think. . . ." Stabler let it hang there.

"Now, now," Thomas put in soothingly. "Let's keep this simple and peaceable. I think we're getting 'way ahead of ourselves. As to identification: I'm Roy Thomas, special agent FBI, detached. This is Ed Stabler, detective first grade, New York City police." Thomas omitted "Housing Authority" as unnecessarily confusing. "Obviously, we're working jointly on this."

"Yeah," Farrell said, looking them both over. "But what *is* 'this'?"

"Right now it's you, pal," taunted Stabler.

"Take it easy, Ed," Thomas said. "Even if Mr. Farrell—" He hesitated. "Mind if we call you Tony?" Farrell just looked at him. "Even if Tony chooses to exercise his Constitutional privilege, he does have the right to know why he's here." Thomas opened the folder he'd placed on the desk, then looked up at Farrell. "It should become clear if we start at Point One and take it step by step."

"I'm not starting anything," Farrell said, "without an attorney—"

"Not even name, rank and serial number?" smiled Thomas.

Farrell breathed out. "Name: Tony Farrell. Age: twenty-nine. Residence: one-one-one East Eighty-fourth Street. Occupation: restaurant owner. My place is called Anthony's, and it's at thirteen-thirteen First Avenue—and it's my *only* occupation. Period. End of statement.''

"Tony Farrell . . .'' Thomas was reading from the folder . . . "born Ravenna, Italy, March twentieth, nineteen forty-five. Parents: Martin Francis Farrell of The Bronx, New York, then a tech sergeant, U.S. Army Signal Corps; mother, Elena Teresa Graziano, Italian citizen. Emigrated to the United States nineteen forty-seven . . ." He paused, reading on silently. "Orphaned at age six . . . both parents . . . died in a fire." He glanced up. "Tough."

Farrell said nothing.

"A couple named Palmieri took you in," Thomas went on, "and they've been your family ever since." He looked up again. "Are you beginning to get the drift?"

"I get it," Farrell cracked; "I'm part Italian, so you've got me down as Mafia."

Stabler pushed forward on his chair back. "These Palmieris: they're relatives? Of your mother?"

Farrell sighed. "*He* is. Distantly. Look," he shifted restlessly, "so you've done some homework. Now just what has any of this to do—?"

"That's the operative word: homework," Thomas broke in. "Think he's starting to get it, Ed?"

"He will. Michael Palmieri," Stabler returned to Farrell. "He's some kind of financial consultant, right?"

"Something like that. I don't know much about his business. He's independent."

"But you and he," asked Thomas, "have had a pretty close relationship over the years?"

"Sure. What the hell, he raised me."

"More than that. He's been your closest advisor in all aspects of your life, including business affairs—is that right?"

"I suppose. Not that much in business."

"Did he stake you in the restaurant?"

"No."

"You've done it all by yourself?"

"Right. Well . . . I've had help, but not from Michael."

"I see." Thomas and Stabler exchanged glances, then Thomas looked back down at the folder.

Farrell studied them both. "Why all this about the Palmieris? You're not really trying to drag *them* into this?"

"Into what?" barked Stabler.

"Into anything," Farrell shot back. "They have nothing to do with whatever it is you're after."

"They have a lot to do with *you*, Tony," Thomas put in quickly. "Practically your whole life. The kind of person you've become. You call that 'nothing'?"

"Of course not. Like you said, they're family: I owe them. That's not what I mean. They're there, and I'm here. My life is my own."

"Mmm . . . maybe so. Maybe not," amended Thomas.

Farrell eyed him. "Meaning what?"

"You've heard the expression 'No man is an island'? Think about it." With arched eyebrows and a gesture of his hands, Thomas conveyed inevitability—unpleasant, perhaps, but unalterable. "Lives do have a way of . . . getting involved—much as we sometimes might wish otherwise," he added, almost apologetically.

These bastards! seethed Farrell. So cocksure, so fucking smart—! Yet, how much of this might be a game of bluff? The white guy acted like he was begging to lean on him, trying to scare him—but maybe *too* anxious? The fed was playing it cuter, lots of smug hints that they had all the answers; but then, why this cat-and-mouse routine? . . . No panicking—yet; stay cool. Let them string it out, see where they lead him. . . .

He'd forgotten about a lawyer.

"What is most extraordinary about your background," the black one was saying, "is that it's so *normal*—in the traditional sense of the word. I mean, in view of what you've since got into."

"Yeah? And what *am* I into?"

"Respectable family"—Thomas, ignoring the question, had gone to his notes—"nice home in Westchester . . . parochial schools, good Catholic prep . . . above-average grades, no indications of any delinquency, in fact an all-star high school athlete—football and baseball . . . athletic scholarship to Duke University. Two years' college, before dropping out—to enlist in the U.S. Army. Three-year hitch . . . mostly in Germany. Cleared for cryptography—FBI seal of approval," he appended wryly. "Three stripes, spotless service record, honorable discharge." Thomas looked across at him, shaking his head. He read on: "Then home and into a career—starting at the bottom, in the old-fashioned American way . . . and in public relations, no less!—probably the most uniquely American of all honorable professions! And the rapid rise toward the top: In no time at all, a vice-presidency, twenty-five thousand a year. Stature. Freedom. You invest in a restaurant. All this before you're twenty-seven years old! The makings of a classic modern American success story. . . . Remarkable!"

"A regular Jack Armstrong," muttered Stabler.

Farrell sat still, taut.

"So with all that going for him"—Thomas's words were measured now and a little sad—"how could such a man change so *completely?*—renounce and betray everything, and everybody that had shaped him? . . . to run with the wolves?"

"It's got to be a death wish," Stabler echoed.

Shaken, but determined not to show it, Farrell tried the offensive: "All right, you can knock off the Abbott and Costello bit. What do you think you've got?"

"We *know* what we've got, mister," Stabler bored in on him: "The scale, from gambling and shylocking to peddling hot merchandise and moving dope in quantity—and that's *aside* from tonight's caper. We've got a book on you that would give any red-blooded prosecutor a hard-on. In fact, the one we're working with is already talking numbers like forty years. . . ."

Farrell's stomach knotted, but he didn't blink.

"We've been on you for months, Tony," said Thomas, "almost from the time you hooked up with Cheech Donato. Without getting into particulars just at the moment, take my word for it: It's all in here, fully documented and ready to go."

"Take your pick," said Stabler. "Four Class-A felonies, minimum, all solid as rock. We've got you locked—up, down, and sideways. So the question is not what we've *got*. The only question now is do we throw away the key, or—" Stabler cut off abruptly and looked to his partner.

When Thomas, contemplating Farrell, did not speak, Farrell finally asked hoarsely: "What do you want, then?"

Thomas said: "We want the Giant."

The words thundered in his ears. "You want—?" he fumbled.

"The Giant," Stabler repeated. "Aaron Luke Brothers himself. And company."

"Including your friend, Cheech Donato," Roy Thomas threw in.

"You're putting me on." Farrell said it without flipness.

"No joke, Tony," Thomas said. "We're out to close down their whole setup, chop it into little pieces. And you're our entrée."

"Why *me?*"

"Because you're in with them," exclaimed Stabler irritably. "Because the Giant likes you—you're his fair-haired honky. You think we been sitting around all these months with our hands up our ass?"

"We are aware of your association with Brothers," Thomas resumed, "and of your increasing position of trust in his operations—so please, to save us all some time, let's not quibble over basic truths." He regarded Farrell contempla-tively. "It's a tight organization, very difficult to get close to, as you doubtless know. At first we thought Donato might be the link—a white man, and a kind of renegade Sicilian at that, doing business with these people. Cheech is cagey, but it looked like our only play. Until *you* came along.

"We just kept an eye on you for a while, until it became clear that Cheech was grooming you. Then we took a harder look. We *really* got interested when Cheech showed how much he needed you by bringing you to the Giant. Remember that evening last summer when you and Cheech drove up to the clothing factory in the Bronx? We were right behind you. And we said to ourselves: *There* could be our hole card. . . ."

Farrell swallowed. He knew he had to try at least to make a stand here, but they'd come at him too fast, from all sides, and he was rattled and couldn't think what defensive position to take first. "So I met the guy a few times," he tried. "I meet a lot of people in my business. Now you pull me in off the street and tell me I'm supposed to hand him over to you?"

"Forty years says you should think about it very seriously," snapped Stabler. He reached over and brought a slab of hand down on the bulky dossier between them. "What do you think we got in here, chopped liver?"

"I don't know *what's* in there," Farrell persisted. "I hear a lot of tough talk . . . but I wonder. Like I told you, before tonight I never had a single rap against me. I've never *seen* a cop close up. So how—?"

"You'd be surprised how much live evidence cops can put together without ever showing their faces." A hard grin creased Stabler's features, and he sat back smugly. "You were this close to *me* one time—closer. I made a speed buy off you one night, around the corner from your joint—nice buy, couple of hundred grams, cost the government a wad." He waited as Farrell searched his face. "Remember, a guy your friend Augie recommended? Of course the street was dark, and I had myself fixed up a little different than now. The point is, *I* could send you away for a good stretch all by myself. We got the stuff marked for exhibit and my sworn complaint, we got an expert eyewitness—my partner here—and infrared pictures and tape to top it off. And I'm just *one*."

Farrell looked to Thomas. "We do have a number of such documentary records," Thomas corroborated. "Incriminating tapes—all legal. Also depositions from reliable witnesses, and even some *participants* in some of your dealings . . . who, let's say for certain practical considerations, have decided to tell us under oath some things that go down quite badly for you —though we never let on exactly *who* it was they were helping us finger. All very intricate, but in the end, we think, solid." Thomas paused to let it sink in. "Effectively, to be honest, the bottom line for you might not be as much as *forty* years; but—"

"Okay," amended Stabler quickly, "so twenty-five . . . the way the courts are these days, maybe even only twenty—but that's rock bottom. Some guy going on thirty now . . . when he got out he'd be in his fifties, at least." His eyes glinted at Farrell. "A guy's pecker could shrivel up and fall off by then."

The room fell quiet. Farrell's mind raced, his head throbbed. The silence grew intense.

Thomas broke it. "Why don't we give Tony a few minutes to sort it out—by himself," he suggested to Stabler. He rose, stretching. "We could use a breather ourselves. Come on, let's take a walk around the block." Stabler looked like he would have preferred to keep the pressure at full-throttle, but at Thomas's insistent look he got to his feet. At the door, Thomas turned to Farrell:

"We can bring you back something—coffee, milk, soup? It's from a machine. . . ."

Farrell looked at him dumbly. "Yeah . . . okay. Coffee. No, make it milk."

"Sure. We'll be back in a few minutes."

The door clicked shut and was bolted.

4

Jesus! Who dealt this mess?

Alone in the airless room, Farrell tried to focus on when exactly he'd crossed over—to "run with the wolves," as Thomas had put it. Odd, but he'd not thought of it in those explicit terms before; not, at least, of his having "crossed over"—for that really had not taken place in a single, sharply realized step from one threshold to another. It had come about gradually, through an accumulation of factors and forces—new experiences, needs, stimuli, challenges, satisfactions—all "different," surely, yet absorbed not in a stunning rush but by almost imperceptible degrees, so that the pattern of a new life had taken shape without his being conscious of a dramatic transformation. It had just been the way things had turned out. . . .

The restaurant had been, of course, the catalyst of change, if not the imperative. But he could not be sure now that the stirrings of chain reaction had not in fact been set off even before that, out of the public relations job. *Fast rising young executive . . . vice-president, twenty-five grand a year . . . stature.* Stature! To an outsider, maybe; but to him it had become little more than white-collar prostitution. What it had taught him was how to ass-kiss and hustle at the same time.

Oh, he could have been good at it—he *was* good at it—and it did have its perks: expense account, travel and entertainment, running in tony circles someone like him wouldn't have otherwise have easy access to. But none of that had been worth Edgar Stelman.

Edgar Stelman Associates, Public Relations: Chrysler Building, 57th floor. Three long-term, firmly-entrenched, well-paying accounts: an expanding savings and loan association; a popular brewery; and, *numero uno,* a giant realty combine that seemed to control half the commercial property in New York (and which itself was persistently rumored to be financed by the syndicate, although the most diligent inquiries by both law and media had failed to turn up a shred of evidence in that connection), whose major "public relations" concern accordingly was—for a six-figure retainer—to keep *out* of the public eye. All ruled imperially by Edgar Allen Stelman.

Stelman was a total, unmitigated shit. Out front, smooth as a snake-charmer with the clients he cultivated and stroked so tenderly; behind the doors of his tower domain, he turned into the cobra with his subjects, who had to make good on his bullshit. Suspicious, treacherous, he would suffer no imagined threat from any of his bright young so-called vice-presidents; challenge Edgar in either imagery or expertise, and you walked down fifty-seven flights. Farrell wouldn't have stood it as long as he had if it hadn't been that he'd been recommended by Michael Palmieri. He couldn't let Michael down, Farrell had told himself, so he'd tried to make a go of it . . . until it was just no use.

The restaurant finally had been his means of escape from that bondage. And yet even now he could only wonder whether he would have taken that gamble, or something else as unconventional, had it not been for Liz. Liz, and her infectious vitality and encouragement. She was at least one good thing in his life he could thank Edgar Stelman for. . . .

They'd been drawn together at, of all unlikely places, a topless cabaret.

It was after a cocktail buffet arranged by Stelman Associates for the savings and loan client, with financial analysts and journalists. Later, some of the more spirited guests insisted on carrying their glow elsewhere. Somebody suggested one of the ribald go-go joints on East 53rd. Farrell groaned to himself at the prospect, but he was bound to cater to the whims of his corporate clients.

The place, called The Oda, was dark and strident and raunchy. It featured a long, low spotlighted bar over which were served outrageously priced and watered drinks and a nonstop fare of "exotic" grinders wearing only G-strings. Farrell's group took two small tables jammed together in the rear. It wasn't far enough from the raucous "action" to suit him; he was anything but a prude, but such places embarrassed him. He'd never hated his job so much as just then.

When the "featured" performer pranced out to the deafening recorded beat of "The Stripper" and began her gyrations, Farrell lit a cigarette and looked away impatiently. His eye caught the most dazzling smile he'd ever seen. A slim young woman, seated at the adjacent table, her smile directed full upon him. In the gloom he could barely distinguish her features, but she appeared to have high cheekbones and a firm jawline; her hair, which could have been spun of old gold, flowed to her shoulders, and she wore large tinted pilot-type glasses. And though he could not quite make out her eyes, he felt they were warm—her gaze telling him she perceived exactly what he was feeling—even, it seemed, embracing him appreciatively. He grinned over at her with a shrug of affinity.

Farrell could not imagine how he had missed her earlier. The chair beside her was unoccupied, and he thought of moving to her table but decided he'd better not: She could be with one of his clients. The two of them shared their secret mutely, eyes locked, ignoring the gaudy exhibition thundering across the room.

After, when the group finally had had its fill of The Oda and was outside, splitting up, Farrell saw that she stayed off to one side, evidently not escorted. She beamed across at him again, and he went over to her. She had in fact, she said to his polite inquiry of whether she was alone, been the date of the bank's advertising manager; but he'd been taken, ah, ill, she explained delicately, soon after their arrival at the cabaret. Bombed out, Farrell guessed, knowing the man. She only smiled.

Her name was Elizabeth Anne Melville—Liz. And, yes, it would be very nice of him to accompany her home.

She lived on East 36th, just off Park Avenue. At Farrell's suggestion they walked, talking easily. She was an artist with the advertising firm representing the savings and loan account and had designed several of their recent print ads, which, Farrell recalled, he had especially admired. She was from Boston originally, had been graduated from Wellesley, and had been in New York just over a year. She was unmarried and uncommitted. Farrell persuaded her to stop for a nightcap at a little bar in the sedate Sheraton-Russell on Park, and over cognacs they chatted for another hour. They both liked dancing. She liked ballet, art museums and books. Except for long solitary walks through the city, she was not outdoorsy, and she didn't care much for spectator sports. He dropped her at her apartment half a block from the hotel and asked her to dinner the following evening.

He took her back to La Veranda, where they dined by candlelight and sipped wine and could scarcely hold a conversation with one another for all the fuss made over them by the incorrigibly romantic host, Luigi. Then Dan Mulcahy sent over a note on a paper napkin: *This looks serious. Need any help?* As they were leaving Farrell threw the grinning bartender a breezy kiss. They'd decided they wanted to dance and strolled along 54th Street to Jimmy Weston's, where a combo played after nine o'clock.

It was old-fashioned mood music, slow, rhythmic ballads spiced alternatively with a soft, upbeat jazz tempo, the lights dimmed as the dinner crowd thinned out, and they were up on the dance floor almost from the moment they'd ordered. She came into his arms, fitting her body firmly into the contours of his, and they swayed together, thighs meshing snugly, not speaking much. Her fingers played lightly at the back of his neck, and her mouth, dewy fresh, was at his ear. His skin began to tingle.

She said very softly: "Are you taking me home with you tonight?"

If either of them had thought in terms of a one-night stand or even just a casual affair, to their deepening mutual pleasure it had proved otherwise.

That had been two years ago, and they were still together. Shortly, at Liz's invitation, Farrell had moved out of the cramped upper East Side apartment he'd been sharing with a friend, Georgie Scanlon, and into her place on 36th Street. Without yet having talked about it openly, they accepted implicitly the idea that, some day, they probably would marry.

Georgie Scanlon was the proprietor of a bar Farrell had frequented on the singles trail. Young, about Farrell's age, and inexperienced, Scanlon had sunk all the resources he could scrape together into trying to transform what had long been a neighborhood workingman's-type saloon into a facsimile of the hip "swingles" bars that attracted the fast-moving younger set to the East Side strip. Called The Gin Mill, it had fallen far short of Scanlon's expectations, and he'd begun to hurt financially. When Farrell earlier had decided to move down from Westchester and get a place of his own in the city, Scanlon's offer to share his apartment and rent had been a help to each of them.

With his move to 36th Street, Farrell had not forgotten Georgie. Once or twice a week, he and Liz would make a point of stopping in to The Gin Mill for a nightcap. Sadly, the bar had continued to languish, and Georgie Scanlon seemed to grow more despondent by the week. He was just about tapped out of resources and was beginning to wrestle with debt. Liz's artistic eye conceived the true potential of the place, and they would sit there extemporizing schemes of redecoration and dramatic new touches of ambience—all lost on poor Georgie, who no longer had either the wherewithal to afford major changes or much stomach left to start over if he could.

The idea, however, had begun to sprout in Farrell and Liz. They would laze around the apartment bouncing ideas off each other about what *they* would do with The Gin Mill if it were theirs to play with. At first it seemed a harmless, if intriguing, amusement. But in a short time they'd taken to sketching out rough visual concepts of "their" place and drafting checklists of *Must Haves* and *Do Withouts*. Imagine being proprietors of another Friday's, or a Maxwell's Plum! It was a notion that had long teased Farrell. The dream excited her as much as him, maybe more so; to Liz, this could only bind them closer together.

And so it had seemed no more surprising than the next chapter in a book that Georgie Scanlon announced sadly to them at The Gin Mill one night that he'd decided at last to get out. If he didn't sell soon, he saw himself in hock the rest of his life. He doubted he could get much for it any more; he just wanted enough to pay off his suppliers and few employees and satisfy a couple of his larger personal obligations.

Farrell had suddenly asked, "How much would you let it go for, Georgie?"

"Why? You know somebody looking?"

"Could be."

"No joke?" Scanlon said. "Well, if I could get thirty thousand. . . ."

"How about twenty-five?"

"I really need thirty. I'd throw in the inventory."

"What kind of shape is that in?"

"Pretty low," admitted Scanlon. "But it's a start. Who do you have in mind, Tony?"

Farrell and Liz had looked at one another, eyes gleaming. He'd said: "Right here, Georgie. Liz and I."

They'd been able to raise over fifteen thousand in cash by pooling their savings, selling stocks, borrowing against insurance, and tapping a modest trust fund set up by Liz's grandparents, which she'd come into on reaching twenty-five; the balance was remortgaged. And, once the sale was consummated, they'd set about vigorously to remake The Gin Mill —christened, by Liz, "Anthony's." With Georgie Scanlon having offered to stay on to keep the place running during the transition, for weeks Farrell and Liz gave every spare minute to the arduous—(but for them, exhilarating)—tasks of renovating, cleaning, painting, refurbishing; except for the most technical work that required professional skills, they attended to everything themselves.

The demands on their available time and energies became enormous, however, with each still holding a fulltime job, and Farrell soon decided that the moment had come for him, at least, to devote himself entirely to the new enterprise. He would leave Stelman Associates—and, at long last, good riddance! he told himself. But when he went to Edgar Stelman to tender his resignation, the P.R. chief had a surprise for him. Eyeing Farrell with that brittle smile, Stelman informed him of disturbing reports from several clients of Farrell's mysterious unavailability and apparent loss of interest lately; in the best interests, therefore, of both the clients and the firm, he had no choice but to let Farrell go—at once! Farrell was taken aback at first, and then ecstatic; he almost laughed in the other's face. He'd been prepared out of usual business courtesy to give Stelman two weeks' notice; now, fired out of hand, not only would he save those two precious weeks, which could be better spent at Anthony's, but he would also be entitled to severance pay—no less than two thousand dollars for four years' service, which also would be put to good use in the restaurant! Thank you, Edgar Stelman—you sonofabitch!

Within a month's time, Anthony's was about ready for its gala reopening. Two bartenders had been hired, a waiter and waitress, a cook, even two strolling minstrels for late evenings.

Georgie Scanlon, having tutored them as well as he could on the mechanics of food-and-beverage operation, bade them luck and went off to nurse his own failure. It was only after Georgie had gone—to parts unknown, Farrell would discover to his dismay when he sought him out—that one giant, immovable stone was found left unturned: Anthony's was notified by the New York State Alcoholic Beverage Control Board that, in transfer of ownership, the new establishment was required to endure a six-month waiting period for re-issuance of a valid liquor license!

Six months. Good old Georgie had neglected to mention that little contingency to his neophyte successors. Appeals to the ABC Board were in vain. Yet they couldn't just ride it out for half a year, trying to hang on practically empty-handed; with their limited capital, they'd be out of business before they had ever really gotten it started! They had to chance it; maybe, somehow, they would luck out.

At first, the place had actually done well without booze. Within weeks, however, interest in the new place had dwindled noticeably. There was no *action.* It was deadsville.

Farrell had to let the musicians go first. Then the night barman. The waitress quit, leaving the waiter, a young graduate student. Liz gave her notice at the ad agency, against Farrell's protest, and came to work, helping in the kitchen, waiting tables. Farrell and Liz were spending most of their waking hours at the restaurant, desperately struggling to keep it above water, and themselves as well.

By the time the probationary period governing the liquor license was nearly up, it was too late. Their every available resource had been exhausted. Debts had piled up insurmountably, and creditors were drumming at them. They were on the verge of losing the place, their dream. . . .

And then, as if on cue: Enter Cheech Donato.

Farrell had seen him around the East Side hangouts a number of times but had never known his name, even after he'd started

coming into Anthony's. He was not the sort Farrell particularly
cared to get to know. Everything about him, from appearance
to manner, pegged him as "connected," and that was a league
that interested Farrell only from a safe distance. Farrell also
thought the guy faintly ridiculous. A squarish man of middle
height, probably a few years older than Farrell, he always
seemed to be trying too hard to fit into the hip scene and
invariably overshot the mark: the stylized blown-dry hair,
tinted shades, diamond pinky rings, and the flamingo-pink
Lincoln he tooled around in. Still, he always seemed amiable
enough and spent money freely. He tipped well, and Farrell
could only be thankful for his patronage.

Then one night, just before closing, as Farrell, in despair,
was lost in a stack of invoices at the bar, Mr. Mod ambled over.
"Hey, bro'."

Farrell looked up in surprise. "Hey, how you doing?"

"Another day, another dollar, huh?" the man eyed the
paperwork.

Farrell managed a smile. "That would be a *good* day. What
can I get you?" He glanced up at the clock.

"Nothin'. I wanted to talk to you—got a minute?"

"I guess."

"You're Tony Farrell, right? I'm Donato. Everybody calls
me Cheech. Look"—he twisted around on his stool, surveying
the nearly empty room—"I can see you got a problem here,
right? They got you hung up on that liquor license, and that's
death in this town."

"So I've discovered," said Farrell.

"I kind of like this place. It's nice, quiet, got class to it. And
I been watchin' you and your lady friend—she your old lady or
business partner, or what?"

"Some of both," Farrell said; "sorry for her, I guess."

"Naw, naw, that's where you're wrong," Donato declared.
"I told you, I been watchin' you. And you got a style I like. I
think with a break or two, you could make this place go."

"We thought so. But . . ."

Donato leaned confidentially over the bar. "But you got no breaks, and you're runnin' out of time and, worst off, bread —am I right?"

"More or less."

"You still want to keep this place?"

"Well, sure . . . but there's just no way, man." Farrell was growing a little tired of the man's aggressive nosiness.

"There's a way. You listen." His deepset eyes bored into Farrell's. "Hey, can you still get me some of the espresso?"

"Huh? . . . oh, sure, why not?" said Farrell, caught off stride. He came out from behind the bar and went into the kitchen thinking, What the hell is this character getting to?

Back in a few minutes with the thick coffee in a demitasse, he straddled a stool alongside Donato. Cheech reached into his coat pocket, withdrew a thin, polished silver flask, and poured a dollop of clear liquid into the espresso. "Like I was sayin', you need help? I can help."

"That's really generous," said Farrell, "but we barely know each other."

"You don't listen. I been sayin', I like the joint and I like the way you handle yourself. And I happen to have a few beans lyin' around just now."

"Are you saying you want to invest in the place?"

"Naw," Donato said. "I come here to enjoy, I don't need the hassle of worryin' about it. 'Course, if it worked out and you wanted to put aside a little piece for me, like a silent partner, you know, I wouldn't complain. All I mean is, I got some cash handy you could probably use." He put up a cautionary hand. "No gift. Strictly business—I expect to get paid back. Now, how much could you use right away?"

Farrell cleared his throat. "Well, I need about five thousand, just to hang in a couple of weeks more."

"That's when you'll have your license, right? Then how long after that?"

"To turn things around? Two–three months, probably."

"All right." Donato did some mental finger-counting. "You

need five now, plus a little cushion . . . suppose I let you have seventy-five hundred?"

Farrell's head was spinning. There had to be a catch. "What do I have to do—?"

"Come on, it's a *loan,* among friends. We'll make it you can pay me back, like . . . a hundred seventy-five a week, how's that?"

Farrell computed swiftly. The guy obviously expected high interest. But even if it was *double* the usual bank rate, at $175 a week, with any luck he could repay the whole amount in a year! God! Was this possible?

"I'll have it for you tomorrow," said Donato.

"Don't we have to sign papers or something?"

"It's just between me and you. Friends, right?" Donato unscrewed the top of the flask again. "Get yourself a glass."

Next day, Cheech Donato delivered the money—seventy-five hundred-dollar bills in a tan manila envelope—and told Farrell he didn't have to begin repayment for a month.

Tony and Liz threw themselves with fresh energy into regalvanizing Anthony's. They distributed letters and fliers to apartment buildings in the surrounding neighborhood, announcing the celebration of the liquor license. With the arrival of the license, business began to pick up again almost at once. Even so, the young proprietors were still on precariously thin ice when time came to start paying off the loan from Cheech Donato.

After a month of such payments, Farrell began finding it more of a strain each week to scratch together $175. And Cheech—or his courier—was there on schedule every Tuesday to collect. It was handled quite amicably, with no suggestion of pressure, and indeed, Farrell had every intention of making each payment on time without fail.

There came a Tuesday, however, when, having to choose between the regular installment and disposing of one particularly longstanding obligation so as to avert another judgment, Farrell had to beg a week's indulgence from Cheech's courier. The man, small, dark and ratfaced, gave him a shrug and went off. Farrell heard nothing from Cheech the rest of that week, so he assumed there was no problem. But then the following Tuesday he was due to pay $350, and he could scarcely put together $175. Again he asked Ratface for an extension, and once more the fellow departed without comment. Thus, again the next Tuesday, Farrell was liable for $350. He simply didn't have it; and, rather than face the discomfort of yet another plea, he made himself scarce and was not at the restaurant when the collector came around.

The next afternoon, Donato himself showed up. Farrell greeted his benefactor brightly, trying to mask his embarrassment: "You haven't been in for a while, old buddy."

"I was here yesterday, Tony," said the other dourly.

"Yesterday . . . ? Oh, right, I completely forgot. I had so many errands."

"I thought maybe you was duckin' me. So, there's no sweat over the payment?"

"Well . . ." Farrell turned to the barman. "Pete, let me have a beer—Beck's. How about you, Cheech?"

"No. Tony," Cheech pressed, "I got places to go, people to see. I'm double-parked outside—"

Farrell could see the pink Lincoln through the front window. There were two men in the front seat. The one he could make out, on the passenger side, was large-boned and flat-faced.

"—so just hand over three-fifty," Cheech was saying, "and I'll be on my way."

Farrell put down his pilsener glass and faced him squarely. "It's been rough, Cheech. The place is picking up, but it's slow. It's going to take time. . . ."

"Aw, Tony, Tony . . ." Donato was the picture of long-suffering disappointment. "I know you got problems, kid —that's how come I advanced you. I even give you a whole month free. But everybody's got to make a livin'. When I loan out money, I expect to get paid off—I told you that up front, right? Now it looks like you're takin' advantage, you know?"

"Not true, Cheech, I swear," Farrell protested. "You'll be paid back every dollar. It's not like you're the finance company and I'm some deadbeat trying to stiff you . . ."

"But that's just the point, Tony," said Donato with a long face. "I *am* the finance company." He looked around the empty restaurant. "This operation is not comin' on as good as I thought. So I got to worry that I *could* get stiffed, see what I mean? And that I wouldn't like. *You* wouldn't like it."

Hairs prickled on the back of Farrell's neck. "But what can I do, Cheech? I just don't have it right now. All I've got is about a hundred bucks."

"A hundred bucks," said Donato disdainfully. He shook his head. "That don't even make one week's vigorish."

Farrell stared at him, for the first time beginning to realize how deep he was in. "Vigorish?"

"My return on investment. Interest—hundred and a quarter a week."

"Out of one seventy-five? That's more than two-thirds interest, for Chrissake!"

Donato shrugged. "You could've went to the other finance company. Anyway, I give you a break—'cause I liked you. Other people pay more."

"You'll be sucking my blood for three more years at least! A goddamn shylock!" Glaring, Farrell snapped: "Well, you can just fuck off, *paisan*. I'll pay you back what you loaned me and *legal* interest, and not a dime more!" He slid off his stool and towered challengingly over the squat Donato. "If you don't like it, sue me."

Donato appeared undisturbed. "*Madon'*, I finally met somebody who was born yesterday." Shaking his head, he walked slowly to the front door, gestured, then returned to the bar. "I want you to get acquainted with a friend of mine."

The big man from the car filled the doorway. He was wearing a suit without a tie, and his body inside seemed to be straining to get out. He was six-foot-four, about thirty, and he could have been a fighter or wrestler. "Goomba, say hello to Mr. Farrell. He works for me. I'll tell you what he does for me: He breaks things. Goomba, Mr. Farrell is gettin' antsy about our business arrangement. Show him how easy something can get broke."

Goomba, impassive as a stone, glanced about and settled on one of the heavy wooden chairs at a table. He plucked it up, took hold of one of its solid legs and, with a single powerful yank, tore the leg free. Dropping the mutilated chair to the floor, he displayed the leg, then, gripping it with both hands, cracked it down against an upraised thigh, breaking it in two. He brought the splintered halves over to Donato.

Donato examined the pieces with satisfaction. "Ain't that somethin'?" he said to Farrell. "He can break just about anything. And it don't matter to him what—things, people —women—just so he makes an impression. You get my point?"

Farrell nodded. The message needed no deciphering.

"Keep your hundred," Donato said. "Next Tuesday you own me five hundred and twenty-five clams. Goomba will be around to collect. If I was you, I would make sure I had it for him." Donato paused in the entranceway to toss the two chunks of wood clattering across the floor. "Write that off as a late-payment charge."

Farrell didn't tell Liz any of this; he couldn't bear for her to contemplate the possible consequences of Donato's disaffection —on either of them.

By Tuesday he could raise only $300—shy $225. He tried to quell his panic. There had to be some way to work this out.

Farrell nonetheless was jittery awaiting Goomba's arrival Tuesday afternoon. He sat in his office trying to concentrate on work, in vain. He smoked a lot of cigarettes and, though normally he seldom drank before evening, took a couple of belts of scotch to calm himself. Then the massive figure was in the doorway. "Cheech sent me," he said unnecessarily.

"Come in," Farrell said as briskly as he could manage. "Close the door, will you."

Goomba came to the desk, looming over it like a great Matterhorn. "You got the payment?" he rumbled from high above.

"Most of it," Farrell said evenly. If he held steady, he still might be able to finesse this. "But I've got an idea, and I'd like to talk to Cheech about it—personally."

Goomba looked perplexed. "Cheech said for me not to leave without the full payment. . . ."

"You don't have to leave," Farrell reassured him. "We'll wait for him together. I just want to discuss something with him. Would you call him?" He rose from behind the desk. "Here, use my phone."

They waited in heavy silence until Donato breezed in. "Okay, Tony. What's your story this time? I'm tellin' you straight, for your sake it better be good. Goomba," he said, "you can wait outside."

"Look, Cheech, I'll be honest with you," Farrell began when they were alone. "There's just no way I can hack these payments." He spread his hands in a gesture of helplessness. "So, you'll either have to satisfy yourself by busting me up . . . or we've got to think of another way."

"Yeah. Whatever," Donato said. "I'm listenin'."

"You said once if the place hit it big you wouldn't mind having a piece of it. Suppose we applied the seventy-five hundred loan toward a part-ownership? Then you could keep tabs on income and when we do start to score, it should be worth many times your original investment."

Donato examined his fingernails. "That idea don't send me," he said, "for a lot of reasons. One: I don't have to put up dough to know how this joint is doin'—I see what I see, and I can find out what I need to know. Two: I ain't sure it's so great an investment any more. Three: Even if you do score, whatever I might sweat out of a percentage might not be as much as I could make off our present arrangement. So, who needs it?"

Farrell eyed him bleakly, knowing he was probably right about that last: Simple arithmetic had showed that in the approximately three years it would take Farrell to pay off the $7,500 loan, Donato stood to *net* close to $19,000! It was a hard argument to debate.

"What else you got?" Donato said.

"I don't *know* what else," murmured Farrell.

"Well, I'll tell you what," said Donato crossing his legs comfortably. "I been thinkin'. There might be a way." He studied Farrell. "You could do some work for me."

Farrell bit. "What?"

"I been thinkin' of opening like a branch office. . . ."

5

That was it: the turning point, thought Farrell. Or, his point of no return.

Donato said he thought Farrell might be in a good spot to generate some additional "trade"—money-lending at places along the strip, where he was a recognized member of "that crowd," as Donato lumped the East Side singles arena. "You're their kind; you talk their language . . . and I think you got some con in you, kid, that could line up a few customers. All you do is hang around and keep your ears open for prospects. Anybody starts leanin', you just tip him over to me. Then I do my thing. If we connect, you're in for a percentage—and we credit that against your bill.

"Who knows?—dependin' how you do for me, you could maybe work off your whole nut. You might even come out with a few beans for yourself."

The prospect deeply troubled Farrell. And yet, thinking of Goomba . . . and of Liz . . . he was able to argue with himself that it was really a small price to pay.

Farrell told Donato he would try.

He told Liz nothing.

His first prospect fell into his lap almost immediately: Georgie Scanlon reappeared. He showed up at Anthony's dispirited, out of funds, in need of a stake. With little sympathy in light of his own position, which he attributed in large degree to Scanlon's having left him holding the liquor-license bag,

Farrell smoothly referred him to "this really terrific guy, an independent businessman. He's helped Liz and me a lot and I'm sure could work out something for you, Georgie . . ."

Donato hooked his fish, and true to his word deducted five hundred dollars from Farrell's own balance due.

Within a matter of days, Farrell was able to shunt three more "customers" to Donato—all people he didn't know well, or whose respect he cared nothing for. The loanshark was impressed. And after only six weeks, so pleased was Cheech with the amount of return directed to him by the efforts of the glib, convincingly low-key Farrell—and with the relative lack of aggravation in collections—that he decided to pardon Farrell's remaining debt and, as a bonus, assign him a regular commission on each "account" he brought in. So, by little more than two months after his unpromising confrontation with Donato, Farrell had not only escaped from seemingly hopeless indenture, but was learning to accustom himself to the unexpected pleasure of anywhere from two to four hundred dollars a week, free and clear.

This much, in time, he'd had to tell Liz, for he'd immediately begun plowing most of this windfall back into Anthony's. On the one hand, she acknowledged the need; but on the other, she was apprehensive. Cheech Donato was not one she would have chosen to be associated with, much less beholden to; no permanent good could ever come of it, she knew in her soul. Farrell's deepest instinct told him the same. Yet, what he persuaded himself—and Liz—was that the new infusion of capital into Anthony's was beginning to show results: Life had sparked again in the place; that indefinable magnetic charge that drew people was in the air—they couldn't afford to let it escape again. They *needed* to stay with Cheech . . . for a while, until they could manage on their own.

It amazed Farrell how much potential there was to be mined by a well-set-up and enterprising usurer. He'd never realized before how many ordinary people had their lives so screwed up that illegal loans, even at intolerable rates of interest, were their only recourse. Cheech Donato might not be a deep thinker, but Farrell quickly realized that in Street U., he was practically a Ph.D. Cheech knew how to exploit and turn to profit every fault of human greed and self-indulgence. And loansharking was only one facet of his operation.

Cheech commenced the further education of Tony Farrell one night at Anthony's when he took him into the back office and handed him a package, about the size of a shoebox, wrapped in brown paper. He wanted Farrell to stash it securely until a certain guy came by to retrieve it. Farrell, bemused, locked the package in his desk. The next day the individual Cheech had spoken of came for the box. That night, Cheech came in and with a wink passed Farrell an envelope. Later, in the office, he opened it . . . and counted out ten hundred-dollar bills. He got goose bumps.

Farrell didn't have to ask himself what could have been in a package that was worth a thousand-buck tip: It had to have been dope. And he was mildly surprised that this realization should generate so little guilt. But after all, what had he actually done here? Just hold somebody's package in safekeeping until its owner called for it, and accept a gratuity for the service—he hadn't been directly *involved*.

Cheech's interest in Farrell seemed to grow, as did the number and variety of "favors" he began to ask of him. Cheech came to him with a book full of airline ticket blanks, saying he had set up a private travel business and that good bucks could be made writing up trips for selected customers at discount rates. If Farrell wanted to act as his "agent," Cheech would send the preferred customers to him and the two of them would split the proceeds. Farrell suspected, of course, that the blanks were stolen, but what was to lose?—the only ones who could get hurt were some airlines, and they were fat enough to absorb an occasional loss.

Then Cheech thought Farrell might help him organize

parties for after-hours bars and gambling parlors he had interests in on the Upper East Side. He might also steer well-heeled patrons to certain massage parlors across town. None of this seemed "criminal" to Farrell, even if technically illegal. Another step. And each step came easier.

When Cheech proposed that Anthony's become the "bank" for his receipts from a numbers franchise, Farrell saw no objection. Cheech promised him he wouldn't have to handle any slips, only quantities of cash delivered at designated hours by respectable bagmen.

Anthony's was fast becoming Cheech's cover; and Farrell, now pulling down as much as a grand a week for his cooperation and services, was caught up in a current that he could no longer resist. By degrees so imperceptible that he could not pinpoint when or how, he'd come to crave not only the abundance but the games that produced it. Consideration of crime and punishment came into his mind only occasionally but did not occupy him for long; such conceptions just did not seem to have any realistic application to *him*.

Cheech next invited him into a deal where they could make a handsome profit on quick disposal of a haul of hijacked merchandise—in that instance, a truckload of booze. The next time, it was bootleg cigarettes. Later it would be furs; then a shipment of gems.

By then it was plain to Farrell that Cheech was no hit-and-run hoodlum; the sonofabitch was a veritable mini-conglomerate! He was into just about every scam Farrell had ever heard of, and not least profitable was the movement of narcotics. Cheech had grown rich trading junk. A more prudent, discriminating man, Farrell told himself, ought to do at least as well and better.

For cautionary reasons, Cheech had so far shielded Farrell from more than tangential participation in his narcotics trafficking—limiting him to handling occasional drops. Now Farrell suggested to Cheech that he'd like more—more of the real action and commensurate reward. Cheech started him off as a courier, transporting packages from one drop to another. Then Farrell was permitted to supervise whole transactions prearranged by Cheech, from pickup to packaging to exchange of cash. Eventually, he was encouraged to engineer a modest deal or two of his own. A few ounces of grass or hash for a few regulars of Anthony's, some speedballs or coke for preferred customers. Off these individual efforts, his own take went up to three grand each week.

He reveled in it. In one week he bought the Audi and moved himself and Liz from the little apartment on 36th Street to a twelve-hundred-per-month, two-bedroom duplex on East 84th.

Liz was torn between delight and deepening concern over this new aspect of Farrell. His way of minimizing her anxieties had been to tell her as little of his extracurricular pursuits as he could get by with. But Liz was not naive, and she worried. Vestiges of Puritan ethic told her that what he was doing now would have to be paid for in the end.

Having observed with satisfaction how smoothly Farrell had developed his private little action, Cheech let down his latest barrier and took Farrell to meet Aaron Luke Brothers. In the previous months, Farrell had heard about this huge black man with the hairless skull and penetrating eyes—referred to, almost in reverence, as "the Giant." In only six years, it was said, Brothers, a native West Indian reared in the South, had built an organization already beginning to surpass the power and influence of some of the established Sicilian families. His network (a black Mafia, some called it, for its inner core was made up of young, lean, stone-hard Muslim types) already dominated hard-drug traffic the length of the Atlantic seaboard, from New England into the Caribbean; it controlled an increasing proportion of the numbers action in the Northeast; and it virtually had a lock on contraband smuggling, especially of gems, through Florida ports. As sidelines, it also specialized in multimillion-dollar dealings of stolen or counterfeit stock certificates, plus routine shylocking and random extortion. On top of these occupations, Aaron Luke Brothers—who, though arrested and indicted a dozen times or more, had been convicted only once, for an assault somewhere in his obscure past—owned a number of legitimate businesses, including a Bronx wholesale clothing outlet, a Brooklyn meat-packing and carting firm, and night spots in Atlanta and Philadelphia. He lived like a lord, with fine, expensive clothes, a fleet of custom automobiles, a small yacht, even his own Learjet. He kept luxurious homes or apartments at several locations in the New York area as well as women to go with them. Larger than life, he was becoming widely viewed as unassailable.

Brothers had been doing business with Cheech Donato for quite some time. The Giant needed Cheech—or had, when starting up his ambitious new organization. Notwithstanding the black mob's expanding influence in large-scale narcotics trafficking, the major sources of *supply* then still were largely controlled by the entrenched syndicates, and Cheech had provided vital contacts to that sector. Though ostensibly a free-lance Mafioso, who seemed to go about his affairs unbound by any strictures, Cheech must have maintained a strong tie with one or another of the powerful families, for such impunity could only have been sanctioned by *somebody*. (Farrell suspected Cheech's connection was his wife, who perhaps was closely related to somebody big enough to countenance a maverick in-law.) However he managed it, Cheech had been able to breach the closely guarded pipelines of dope supply and divert significant quantities for use by his black clientele—who were beginning to flex their muscles at the increasing expense of the established order. Cheech may or may not have appreciated the irony in the fact that this situation could not go unchallenged indefinitely, or that when the inevitable showdown came it well could be over *his* body.

For the moment, though, Cheech still had the driver's seat as long as he could produce for the Giant. But it was evident to Farrell at their first meeting that Brothers and Cheech were complete mismatches in style. The Giant was awesome, not just in his physical size (he was all of six and a half feet tall, with the massive frame of a defensive end), but in his cultured manner, with his modulated bass voice, expressive, mobile features, piercing yet slightly amused eyes. Brothers suffered the lumpish Italian solely for the precious commodity that, so far, only Cheech could afford him. Cheech must have sensed a growing disaffection; this was why he was bringing Farrell into the picture. He introduced Farrell as his "new partner." With his easy confidence and range of mind, Farrell would lend a note of class to the operation. Farrell did not resist this tide of favor; he was flattered, and expectant: He felt as though he had almost reached the mountaintop and Satan was about to show him all the world's riches for the taking below.

Thomas and Stabler watched him through the two-way mirror. It was past 3:30 A.M. now; less than four and a half hours left before Farrell had to be present in court—regardless of their success or failure with him.

It was impossible to guess, looking at him alone in the cubicle, what Farrell was thinking. He was drawn and obviously uncomfortable; but it had been a long and unusual day for him and he had to be spent. As they themselves were. Stabler's eyes were stinging and his stomach had turned sour. "*I* should've had milk instead of that shithouse coffee," he grumbled, eyeing the half-pint milk cartons Thomas held. "I'll never learn."

He got up a belch.

"Okay, let's bring our little playmate his milk and cookies."

Farrell sipped thoughtfully. "What is it exactly you're asking me to do?" he asked.

"We're not asking," drawled Stabler, "we're telling."

"No," Thomas amended. "We think you would be very unwise *not* to cooperate, but we can't make you. We can only try to make you see that it will be to your advantage to take your chances with us."

"Like how?"

"By providing us the information we need to put the Giant out of business."

"You keep saying that," Farrell replied, frowning, "but I'm really not so close to that whole thing, you know."

"Not yet, maybe. But we're betting you will be."

Farrell's face darkened. "*Will* be—are you saying what I think you're saying?"

"You stay in place," Thomas said. "We send you back out, and you go right on doing what you've been doing. Only now you're *our* man. You feed us till we've got enough, then we knock them out."

"Dynamite, huh?" added Stabler with a hard grin.

"That's the *advantage* you're offering me? To *spy* on that crowd? Jesus Christ! Why not poison the milk? Or take me up to the roof and push me off? My chances would be just as good!"

"No one's suggesting it'll be a waltz," said Thomas. "But it *is* your only chance."

"For what?" Farrell broke in hotly. "To trade a stretch in the can for the death sentence?"

"It's the one opportunity you'll get to reduce your own liability," Thomas continued, laying a hand on the dossier, "and quite possibly to walk away from all this clean. You see, the real balance here is between your future and how much you're willing to risk to *have* a future."

"Some future!" Farrell lapsed into brooding silence. The detectives waited, Thomas raising a quizzical eyebrow at Stabler, who remained expressionless.

At length Farrell stirred: "You're saying I could get amnesty out of this?"

"No guarantee," Thomas said. "It depends. If everything works out—you go a hundred percent for us, we'll break our butts plugging for you. Right, Ed?"

"Hmph."

Muscles worked in Farrell's face. His eyes were bleak. "I have to go to the john," he said.

Farrell hunched miserably over the commode, his head spinning, stomach writhing, trying to quell the nausea. He'd always prided himself on a cast-iron stomach, and this weakness now somehow was degrading. He hadn't eaten since early afternoon, and that milk was a curdled lump in his gut. He hadn't slept either, in damn near twenty-four hours. He shuddered from a fleeting chill; he was sweating.

Four o'clock in the morning, squatting in a locked john in some strange, gloomy public building, with a black federal cop outside guarding the door.

Farrell could suppress the gorge no longer. Heaving to his feet, he bent over the dank commode and vomited.

Roy Thomas, waiting outside, looked at him with concern when he emerged unsteadily. "Are you sick?"

"Something I ate," Farrell said. His face was ashy.

"Come on," Thomas urged, taking his arm, "let's move around a bit."

They walked slowly down the long deserted corridor, only their footsteps breaking the silence. They stopped at a water fountain and Farrell rinsed out his mouth. "Tastes like the Polish army marched through in sweat socks."

"I know the feeling," Thomas said, as they moved on. Thomas halted at a closed door, opened it and switched on the lights inside. "Come on in," he invited Farrell, smiling, "and we can relax."

It was a small, bright room with walls filled floor to ceiling with books. An oblong conference table flanked by sturdy leather chairs took up the rest of the space. "Grab a seat," Thomas said, flopping into one himself. He spun a glass ashtray across the table's polished surface. "Smoke if you want." He nodded toward the formidable collection of bound volumes. "This is one of the U.S. Attorney's law libraries. A memorial to all the mischief of the past."

"And the solutions?" parried Farrell, lighting a cigarette.

"There's always hope," Thomas grinned. "Much study of the human miseries is done here."

"But not all."

"No. Not all knowledge is gained from books. Or *by* the book. Fortunately." Thomas made a steeple of his long fingers and sat back regarding Farrell. "We have some things in common, you know."

Farrell looked at him doubtfully. "Yeah?"

"For one, we both come out of Yonkers."

"I never said I was from Yonkers."

"Well, Crestwood—that's part of Yonkers."

"To Yonkers, maybe. Not to Crestwood."

Thomas laughed. "You have a point. Well, then, we both went to college on athletic scholarships. Mine was for basketball. . . . " He paused, studying Farrell. "Tell me something: What happened at Duke?"

"Duke? What do you mean, what happened?"

"I mean, there you are with a free ride at a fine school . . . and you walk away from it after only two years. Why?"

Farrell half closed his eyes, considering. At last he blew out a puff of smoke and snorted: "You want the truth? I went down there a big hotshot jock, and I couldn't make the squad—first string, anyway. Football *or* baseball. And it got my ego twisted all out of shape, so I just said screw it. Simple as that."

Thomas shook his head sympathetically. "And so you joined the army."

"I joined the army. I was *itching* for a fight about then. Vietnam was getting hot. . . ." Farrell dragged on his cigarette and smiled with self-mockery. "So they sent me the other way."

"Then you came home. And then . . ."

"And now," Farrell amended, ". . . here we are."

Neither spoke for a minute. Then Thomas asked quietly: "And what do you think?"

"About this?" exhaled Farrell. "I don't know. I—it's all too sudden. I need some time."

"Time is growing precious," the FBI man said. He checked his watch. "It's after five. You have to be in court in a few hours."

Farrell's eyes widened. "Are you saying we only have till *then* to—?"

"Today you'll be arraigned on the current charge. You'll no doubt be bailed out, and that means you'll be roaming around loose, perhaps subject to . . . let's say to unhealthy influences or pressures. And we want you committed—one way *or* the other—on the strength of your own gut response and intelligent instincts, not by outside forces." He measured Farrell. "Frankly, I can't see that you have but one reasonable choice."

"So *you* say. It's not your life."

Thomas considered. "All right, I'll give you forty-eight hours. Somebody will be on you every minute, I guarantee you. You let on in any way what's happening, and you could have more trouble than you think you've got now. Within forty-eight hours, you let us know what it's going to be."

"And if I don't?"

"If you don't, we'll have to assume you've decided to take your chances with them, and we'll proceed accordingly—as promised."

After several moments, Farrell spoke up: "Can I make my call now?"

"Right." There was a beige push-button telephone next to Thomas, and he placed it in front of Farrell, then stood. At the door, he said: "I'll be just outside. Knock when you're finished." Then: "Tony, when you're deciding, I hope you'll give a lot of thought to your family—the Palmieris."

Farrell looked up sharply. "What does that mean?"

"What it could do to them . . . finding out about you."

He'd been staring immobile at the phone before him. Whom to call—at nearly five-thirty in the morning? There was only one person, of course. Lifting the receiver, he took a long breath and poked the buttons mechanically.

Liz answered, foggily, after several rings.

"Hi, babe."

He could picture her snapping erect in the bed: "Tony? God almighty, where *are* you?"

He didn't know just how to get into it. But there was no kid-glove way around it. He sighed. "I got myself busted."

"Oh, God!" she breathed. "What—?"

"Take it easy," he went on evenly. "It's not that serious. I have to appear in court this morning, but if I can make bail I should be home in a few hours."

"Bail . . .?" She was flustered. "What should I do? How much is it?"

"Hey, it's all right. Don't flake out on me now. Look, get my address book, will you—in the night table."

"Yes, yes . . . hold on." He would have to tell her about everything, he knew, if they were going to face it together. But he could only do it later, when they were alone.

". . . Okay, I'm back," she said.

"Okay. Look up Donato."

She made a barely audible "Ugh."

"I know, but please. There are a bunch of phone numbers for him. Under 'Personal' there are two. One's his private line at home, the other his girlfriend's place. Try the second one first. If you woke his wife and he wasn't there, there'd be war. Tell him I need his bail bondsman at Criminal Court, downtown, at nine o'clock this morning. I don't know what amount they'll set. Tell him I got in a fight with a guy who happened to be a narc staked out on a bust, and . . . well, I happened to have a piece on me."

"Oh, Tony, that *damned* gun! I *knew* something like this . . ."

"Okay, Liz, okay. It happened. Scold me later. Now listen, when you're through, take that address book and hide it somewhere. Understand?" It had occurred to him that this conversation might well be monitored. And he wasn't prepared to give anything away for free—yet.

"I understand," Liz murmured. "Tony, you are all right?"

"I'm fine. Just bushed, and a little gamey. And sore as hell at myself. And wishing I was there next to you."

"Oh, honey, so do I."

"In a little while . . ."

"Call me," she said huskily.

"Soon as they turn me loose. I'm counting on you."

"I love you," she said.

They put Farrell back in the interrogation room, alone, and then Thomas, at six o'clock, telephoned Brendan Hartnett at home. The prosecutor, roused from sleep, was not overjoyed with the leeway given Farrell to make a decision; but, assured by Thomas that the subject was "leaning," Hartnett grudgingly approved. "But not a minute over forty-eight hours," he growled. "And you fellows make damn sure he's covered 'round the clock!"

Thomas went back to the darkened office where Stabler stood observing Farrell through the two-way mirror. "He still don't look too good—pale," Stabler said without stirring.

"You don't look that pink-cheeked yourself," Thomas commented.

Stabler turned to regard him. "Neither do you, boy," he grinned.

"Let's get him back to the Tombs," Thomas said.

Close up, Farrell looked even more drawn; his rich black jacket sagged, the soft white shirt appeared slept in, and the trim gray slacks were wrinkled and stained. Expensive clothes always suffered worse for overwear, Thomas thought, than the knockabout stuff he usually wore. Expensive tastes, too.

"All right, Tony," Thomas said, "it's been a long night. We're taking you back. I hope you're not tied up in court too long—but there's nothing we can do about that. Get some rest. You've got a hard decision to make. Remember, forty-eight hours, that's it."

Farrell stirred, but said nothing.

Thomas took out his notebook and pen. On a blank page he carefully printed a telephone number, tore out the sheet, folded it and handed it to Farrell. "This is the safest way to contact us. It's a private line, guaranteed 'clean.' Only *we* can be reached on it—no one else—any time of the day or night."

"By the way, there's one other thing you can be thinking about while you're making your great decision," threw in Stabler. "If you *don't* play ball with us . . . we'll see word gets around that you *did*. Okay?"

Glaring at the burly detective, Farrell rose quickly, color flushing back into his face. Thomas shot to his feet at almost the same instant and stepped between the two. Farrell stood rigid for a long moment, then slowly subsided.

"Come on," he muttered, straightening his shirt collar, "take me back to jail—where the smell isn't so bad."

6

It was close to one in the afternoon before Farrell was released. Cheech's bondsman, a dour, balding little man who called himself Sherman, hadn't shown up in court until eleven, and by then Farrell's turn before the judge had come and gone and he'd been returned to the detention cage while a dozen other defendants shuffled out ahead of him. Though bone-tired, he'd remained sharply wakeful. Being among that collection of human flotsam . . . derelicts, hoodlums, half-wits . . . had filled him with distaste and self-reproach. The only one he'd felt any sympathy toward was a begrimed, scabrous old bag lady, who could not comprehend why she was there and probably shouldn't have been. But when he'd tried to befriend the pitiful creature, he was rebuffed suspiciously. He withdrew, and studied her the more, and when it came to him that, somehow, inexplicably, she reminded him of *himself,* he was repelled almost beyond endurance.

When his turn finally came, he pled Not Guilty, and as they waited for the judge to order him to return for hearing ninety days from this date, Farrell hissed frantically to the bail bondsman, "Where the hell've you been?" The man cocked a fish eye at him and said without apology, "I work for you? You wanted to pay this yourself?" and at the dismissing rap of the gavel, he slapped a fedora on his scalp and scurried off without another word.

Farrell found the first available phone booth and dialed Liz.

She sounded faint with relief. She had an art class at 86th Street at one, but she would cancel, wait for him at the apartment. He told her no, he'd meet her afterward at a pub they liked on 85th; he wanted a little time alone, to freshen up and get his head together.

In the shower he turned over and over in his mind what he should tell Liz, what parts maybe should she *not* know, for her own safety, for her peace of mind, for her regard for him. But when he left the apartment to join her he was still undecided.

It was as he walked north on First Avenue that it occurred to Farrell for the first time that he was probably being shadowed. Not that he'd become aware of anyone observing him—he stopped once to inspect a corner shop window, but spotted no one—but those two cops had made it plain that he would never be out of their sight, or somebody's. He'd never had this peculiar feeling of self-consciousness before, and it was unsettling. There had been a certain sense of furtiveness in the dealings with Cheech and the Giant, but he'd found a kind of excitement in that, a challenge to alertness and ingenuity —because then it was *he* making the key moves, watching, anticipating, adjusting for the deceits of others, with scarcely any thought of being similarly watched himself. Now he was the target. Moreover, the humbling awareness had sunk in that he had been watched for months without the slightest suspicion of it. That irked him.

Was this how it was to be from now on? Could he possibly live like this indefinitely, amid shadows?

Could Liz . . . could he expect her to?

He *had* to lay it all out for her. It would be grossly unfair to her to try to diminish any of the enormity of what they faced. *She* had to have a chance to run, even if he didn't.

She didn't press him while they were in the pub, and not until they were outside, where there was no chance of being overheard, did he begin talking about it. It was late in a crisp, clear autumnal afternoon, and they walked, Farrell's arm about her shoulders, hers circling his waist, he looking down at her, gauging her response in her expression as he spoke. Her eyes were steady upon him, wide, frightened, liquid, by turns mirroring incredulity and doubt and compassion . . . and fear . . . and yet, he thought, resolve.

When he'd finished telling her of the progressive evil he'd allowed himself to be caught up in, and the crushing decision now thrust upon him, they walked a long way in silence.

They were on Fifth Avenue, alongside the park, nearing Grand Army Plaza, and daylight had faded and streetlights and distant windows were twinkling on. Liz said: "Honey . . . do you think it could help if . . . if you went to your uncle and—?"

He stopped and faced her: "Michael! Liz, have you any idea how he would take this? He'd blow sky high! He's the last one I'd ever lay this off on!"

She took his hand. "Tony, wasn't he the first to come to you when you were alone in the world? Doesn't he *deserve* your trust now? He above all—surely as much as I, if not more. . . ." She squeezed his arm and started them walking again. In a little while, Liz added gently: "Michael *loves* you, Tony. If there's any way he could help you, you know he would."

He didn't speak again until they were by the fountain in front of the Plaza Hotel. He turned to her then and said: "Look, I'm going to put you in a cab, do you mind? I've just got to wrestle this by myself for a while, you know?"

"You mean about Michael?"

"Yes."

"I understand." She reached up and kissed him lightly. "Come home soon." Then she spun away and hurried out onto Central Park South, waving for an eastbound taxi.

Farrell watched her go, then turned and made his way through the square to the Plaza. In the Oak Bar he found a small table vacant, overlooking the park, and ordered an Irish coffee. And, absently stirring the mound of whipped cream into the steaming liquid, he thought of Michael.

Michael was not really his "uncle"—their genealogical relationship was so distant they might have been strangers—but in every practical sense other than birth he was truly Farrell's father. When his natural parents died Farrell had been too young to retain more than a scattering of yellowed, fading images of them. His only family had been the Palmieris —Michael, acquiring the "son" he'd always wanted, and his wife, JoAnna, a fair, handsome woman of Scandinavian descent, whose Nordic reserve inhibited outpourings of "motherly" warmth, but who, to a bewildered orphan, had provided comfort and stability so desperately needed. And then, of course, coming later, the girls, their daughters, his "sisters": lovely, vivacious Terri and pert, independent-minded Linda. Farrell had never felt shunted aside, an outsider or pretender, with the birth of the Palmieris' own children; rather, their arrivals only made them more a family. He adored the girls; and, growing up—eight years older than Terri and eleven over Linda—he'd been their fiercely protective "big brother" and they'd idolized him. Those were times he would cherish forever.

Farrell was not sure just when, or why, the Palmieris' marriage had come apart; the rift must have started and grown wider after he'd gone away to college and then the army, for he could not recall any distressing problems while he'd been at home (although there could have been things a flighty teenager wouldn't have noticed). He only knew that when he'd come back from Germany the family was in disarray. Michael and JoAnna were separated, on the verge of divorce, Michael having already moved to bachelor quarters in Manhattan. Michael had turned sour and JoAnna bitter (it became clear that she suspected him, and had accused him scathingly in front of their daughters, of having kept another woman in New York), with the girls buffeted cruelly between them, confused, fearful, angry.

Returning to be caught up in this swirl of unhappiness, Farrell, whose aim had been to strike out soon on his own, had felt obliged to remain in Crestwood with JoAnna and the girls as man of the household, for a while at least. But with time the situation had only worsened, as he found himself mired in a crossfire of disharmony between people he loved and powerless to mediate. For two years he'd stuck it out, commuting between New York (where he would often visit the dispirited Michael) and a suburban home become as forbidding as a minefield. JoAnna had grown ever more shrill and intolerant with her daughters, venting much of her frustration on them, and waspish toward him, as though seeking to punish Michael through his alter ego. The unpleasantness was constant, and exhausting. And finally, when JoAnna arranged to bring her widowed mother east from Illinois to live with them, Farrell had decided it was time to separate himself from the battle. That was when he'd moved in with Georgie Scanlon.

In the three years since, things seemed to have settled into an armed truce. Terri, now twenty-one, had managed to survive and even blossom into an admirable young woman of quality and grace; perhaps her advantage had come in having been sent away to college and out of the direct line of fire. Linda, however, at eighteen, was showing disturbing signs of turning into quite something else and had become an increasing source of concern to both her parents. Linda had changed unattractively in her last years of adolescence: from pert to impertinent, irrepressible to willful; irreverent—tough. Michael kept getting troubled, anxious reports from JoAnna about Linda's growing unruliness, late hours, unsavory associations (she'd taken up with an older crowd, according to JoAnna, of "leather-jacket hoodlums"), and she'd urged him to talk with the girl—Linda was just getting to be too much for her mother to handle alone. And Michael *had* made special efforts to get through to his daughter, showing remarkable patience, for him, in trying to draw her out, to get to the source of her waywardness (sensing all the while, to his deep remorse, where the roots lay), only to receive for his pains little other than Linda's further withdrawal behind a thickening wall of sullen mockery.

Farrell gravely considered all these factors, and he pondered: Could he bring himself now, could he be so unfeeling, to
trouble Michael still further out of a selfish need to unburden
himself of his own baseness? He didn't see how—but then
something Liz had said kept coming back to him: Could
Michael ever forgive him if he *didn't* share his trouble? Was he
no longer worthy, Michael would think, of Tony's trust, his
confidence, when it was needed most—no matter how despicable the transgression? Michael would rant at him, but he would
not be overcome. He would grip the dilemma and shake out the
right answer . . . and leave it on the table between them, for
Tony to take up or not, as he would. And Michael would stand
by him—if only because Tony had felt bound to come to him
directly.

The worst thing he could do, it came to Farrell at last, would
be to try to keep Michael out of this—have him shocked and
outraged by first learning of it elsewhere. That would be the
ultimate indignity, far more unforgivable than any disgrace
confessed to him now.

The first two times he dialed the apartment, five minutes
apart, the line was busy. He ambled about the hotel lobby,
scanning the newsstand, looking into boutiques. He didn't
know whether he would feel relieved or not if the impulse
deserted him. He'd give it one more try.

This time Michael picked up on the first ring: "Yes!" he
almost demanded.

"Michael. How're you doing?"

There was a half-beat's hesitation before Michael responded, "Oh, *Tony,*" as though he'd been preoccupied. "Sorry. It's
been a rough day."

"Hey, are you tied up?"

"No, no—I was hoping to hear from you. I tried to get you
last night." He sounded terribly fatigued.

"I didn't know. I was tied up kind of late myself." He
swallowed. "Look, I was wondering. Could I drop by?"

"I wish you would, kid." The tone was strained and somehow imperative. He paused with a sigh that was almost mournful, and Farrell's heart tripped: *He already knows!*

"When can you make it?" Michael asked.

"Well . . . I guess now's as good a time as any. Fifteen minutes?"

"I'll be here."

It was impossible to find a cab, so Farrell walked east, apprehension perversely driving his legs harder toward a confrontation that he would have given almost anything to avoid. How could Michael have found out so soon? The cops! They were using Michael as a safety valve against him! The way they'd kept getting back to the Palmieris . . . he'd *suspected* something devious like this, but he'd let himself believe they wouldn't really play that dirty. Reflexively, he began to peer about him for some giveaway sign of a tail. They were there somewhere, he was convinced. And, in his mind, he thrust the middle finger of his right hand above his head. *Fuck yourselves,* you miserable bastards, wherever you are.

At Michael's building, the doorman rose from his closed-circuit television monitor in the vestibule with a smile: "Evening, Mr. Farrell. Nice to see you again." He pressed the intercom button next to 17E, announced him to a rasp of static from the speaker, and said cheerily, "Go right up, sir." In the elevator, Farrell reflected how often he used to drop in on Michael here, especially after Michael had moved in permanently. Following the divorce, Michael had given up his longtime office in a modest commercial building down in the Wall Street district for this more centrally located and spacious pied-a-terre. Out of this command post in solitary comfort he conducted his business over a battery of telephones from early morning until often well into the evening. It occurred to Farrell that even now he would be hard put to define just what Michael's "business" was. He knew only that it had to do with money—capital investments, corporate financing, sales and transfers of stocks, that sort of wheeling and dealing of which Farrell understood little—and that Michael seemed to be a highly regarded counselor or broker. Although Michael seemed consumed by the work, however, he never discussed it.

Michael's apartment, on the seventeenth floor, was at the end of a long corridor. Just as Farrell reached the door it opened—Michael having learned to judge within a pace or two, depending on elevator time, how long it should take his long-legged ward to get from the lobby to the threshold. They used to make a game of it—

No games now. Farrell was not prepared for Michael's grim appearance. The man looked haggard—eyes heavy and streaked with red; face drained, pouchy, unshaven, even the dapper mustache turned bristly. His graying hair, customarily so neatly brushed and groomed, was tousled as though his hands had been through it again and again. Normally the most fastidious of dressers, Michael now seemed unaware of what he wore—rumpled, soiled beige cotton shirt and uncreased, shapeless brown trousers; nondescript scuffs on bare feet. Farrell accused himself: Is this because of me?

Michael wearily closed and locked the door behind him. "You haven't been up in a while," he said.

"I guess not. You know, busy . . ." He glanced about. Big, warm living room, richly carpeted and filled with green plants and subtly lighted paintings and deep, soft couches; the brightly lit fish-tank divider separating the main room from the L-shaped mahogany bar in one corner: the imitation wood-paneled fireplace, the wall of glass doors to the terrace and the fascinating collage of city lights beyond. Essentially it looked the same. But now there was an untidiness about the place: newspapers scattered about, notes carelessly strewn over the glass coffee table; here and there plates with scraps of unfinished sandwiches, and assorted beer and soda cans; and everywhere ashtrays overflowing with butts. The occupant might have been on a weeklong binge.

Michael had shuffled behind the bar. "Scotch?" he asked without looking up.

"Huh? Oh . . . no, thanks."

"Well, *I'm* having one," the other grumbled, "so you might as well. We both need it."

Michael put the drinks between them and leaned heavily, arms folded, on the bar. Farrell looked at him, waiting. Michael snorted wanly:

"Nice mess, eh?—me, the whole joint," he waved his arm. "All since last night."

Farrell flushed. "Michael, I—"

"Have you spoken to anyone else in the family?" The older man had turned stern.

"No. Not recently." He hoped he could take this.

"Then you don't know?"

"Know—?"

"About Linda." Michael's face was a taut mask.

What was this? "What about Linda?"

"She was picked up last night"—the gruff voice broke a little—"on a . . . narcotics charge."

"*Narcotics!*" Farrell was stunned. "For what? Possession? Selling?"

"Everything." Michael shook his head dismally and a sob tore from his throat. It was a full minute before he gathered himself. "Heroin. Goddamned filthy junk. She's a pusher—a beautiful eighteen-year-old girl . . . *pushing shit!*" He fought again to control himself. "And then, today, they tell me she's on the stuff herself. An addict . . ." Farrell's heart was breaking, listening to him.

Early Monday evening JoAnna had called from Crestwood, nearly hysterical. She'd just heard from the Westchester District Attorney's office in White Plains: Linda was in custody, along with two others, for a felony offense. Michael had made some fast calls, then raced to White Plains. He was allowed to see her briefly—and hardly knew her. She was wild-eyed, abusive, battling her captors, screaming obscenities. He'd never been so shocked in his life. He'd left, shaken to his soul, and driven to Crestwood, intending somehow to comfort his ex-wife. But she was already under sedation, and Michael had made his way back to the city. He'd tried to reach Tony, then spent the rest of the night alone, replaying all the scenes of a lost child's life.

He'd been on the phone all day Tuesday, back and forth with White Plains and his lawyers and Crestwood and the observation center his daughter had been removed to in Valhalla. The D.A.'s office said Linda and a small group of friends ("all amateurs") had been under surveillance by a sheriff's intelligence squad for months. From small quantities of marijuana, they'd turned to dealing pills, and then, somehow, had picked up a heroin connection—identity as yet unknown. The felony charge was serious, but the penalty could be watered down as far as Linda was concerned because of her age and first-offender classification. Michael's legal counsel assured him they would try for a suspended sentence with strict probation; but the Palmieris had better also prepare themselves for the possibility of Linda's having to serve some time—perhaps eighteen months to two years. . . . Michael had tried to impart these things to JoAnna as gently as he knew how, but she collapsed again.

And then, late this afternoon, he'd received the word he'd dreaded—from the hospital: Linda was found "moderately" addicted to heroin. It was recoverable with continuous treatment and supervised rehabilitational therapy—*if* the patient were both willing and determined to be cured. Michael hadn't yet told that part, the most terrible part, to JoAnna. He didn't know how he could, *when* he could.

"I figured that's why you were calling," Michael finished, "that you must have heard something about it." He took his first sip of the drink in front of him—a long, contemplative swallow. "Sorry. I've been doing all the talking," Michael said at length. "I haven't been thinking about much else. What was on your mind?"

"Me? Oh, nothing that can't wait. Just some advice . . . about Liz and me."

"Problems?"

"Not that big. We're fine." He took a sip of scotch. "What are you going to do, Michael?"

Michael lit a cigarette. "Naturally, I'm going to stick with Linda," he said, "do all that's necessary to bring her out of this, whole. That's priority number one." He ticked off priority number two: taking care of JoAnna and his other daughter, Terri, especially now. "They'll need looking after until we're out of the woods." He paused before continuing: "And one other little thing. Starting now, for however long it takes . . . the rest of my life if I have to . . . I'm going to be looking for the scumbags who turned my girl on to this. And I'll find them, sooner or later, that's a promise. And then we will have . . . full satisfaction." He smoked quietly, looking out across the terrace into the city.

Farrell shivered inside. "Can I help, Michael—with Linda, the rest of the family?"

"Sure you can. I expect you to. You are part of the family, after all—we've all got to stick together." He came around the bar and laid a rough, affectionate hand on the young man's shoulder. "I've got to get some sleep, organize my head. Then I'll be calling on you, okay?"

Walking Farrell to the door, he asked briskly, again the skeptical auditor: "How's your business holding up?"

"Solid now—practically runs itself," Farrell replied, without feeling the satisfaction he once might have. In the doorway he faced his uncle. "Liz and I keep hoping you'll come in. It is all in the family, you know," he added, summoning a smile.

"I will—one of these times. I'm glad I was wrong. What the hell, only the Pope's infallible—and I'm not too sure about *him* lately. Take care, kid. We'll be in touch."

Anthony's was barely eight blocks from Michael's apartment, but it took him an hour to get there.

He wandered the East Side streets, whipping himself with shame. He accused himself of having been as responsible as anyone for the tragedy of Linda Palmieri. He knew that wasn't logical, yet he could produce no convincing rebuttal. It was just *true,* in a way that perhaps was meaningful only to him. *He* might just as well have sold her her first joint, her first uppers, her first nickel pop of smack; he might just as easily have seduced her into the thrall of predators like Cheech and the Giant . . . and himself. His own baby sister. A scumbag was just what he felt like.

He could no more have laid himself bare to Michael tonight than he could have cut both their hearts out. Now, could he *ever* tell him? Even if he could somehow make up for Linda, could Michael possibly ever embrace him again? Probably not, no matter what. He could only try to do something positive now that at least might balance the negative, even if that could never be outweighed. And of course, now there was no question about what he must do.

A sudden scuffle of feet behind him, and in the next instant Farrell was grabbed roughly by an arm around his neck and being muscled down steps toward the sunken entrance of a darkened townhouse. Half falling, he twisted sideways to stay upright and caught the glint of a knifeblade—just before a hand slapped his face hard and he was slammed face first against a brick wall. "Don't look at us, man!" a harsh Negro voice hissed close to his ear. "You just stay still, move quick when we tell you, and maybe you'll walk away from here. You read me?" The point of the knife pricked his neck. Then his jacket was being stripped off him, and rude hands were clawing into his trouser pockets.

There were two of them. The one who must be going through his jacket let up the pressure on Farrell's back just a bit. He didn't hesitate to consider. Propelling himself off the wall, in the same motion he heaved himself around and flung the jacket into the mugger's face. The other one went for the side pocket of his Army fatigue jacket. Farrell kicked out as hard as he could at the groin. His foot connected solidly with the soft flesh, and the other yowled and doubled over, dropping to his knees. With an animal growl the first one, flinging away the jacket, charged at him with an underhand swipe of the knife; but he was off balance, and Farrell twisted and ducked away. He brought his right knee up, aiming for the groin again, but it landed high, in the lower abdomen. His attacker grunted and slashed wildly with the blade, and Farrell wrestled him against the wall and sprang to the steps. He turned as the mugger charged up after him, and he kicked the youth in the face with all his might. He heard bone splinter as the knife-wielder toppled back with a scream and landed in a heap at the door of the house.

Farrell stood there, panting, looking from one to the other. Neither moved. He retrieved his jacket, which did not appear torn anywhere, and hunted about until he found his wallet. Straightening himself, he resumed walking east, faster than before.

A chilling thought stopped him in his tracks: Suppose those two were goons of the Giant's, sent out to work him over, to find out what had gone on between him and the cops? No doubt the Giant would have found out by now what had happened, from Cheech; maybe he—no, it was ludicrous. Aaron Luke Brothers wouldn't handle it like this. Well, he *would* . . . but with street hustlers, not with someone like Farrell. With him the Giant would be more subtle—and thorough. He wouldn't send a couple of stupid young pig-stickers after him arbitrarily, without first digging around for more incriminating information. No, these had to be just two stray hyenas on the prowl. He hoped.

Anthony's was more than half-full at 8:45, and loud. Farrell edged to the bar, nodding at regulars, but not stopping for conversation. Pete looked at him quizzically, but asked nothing.

"Sorry I hung you up last night, Pete. Something I couldn't get out of." The barman just nodded and gave him a familiar wink. Farrell smiled wanly to himself. "Anybody looking for me?" he asked.

"Mr. Donato called a while ago."

"Right." He sighed and made for his office, closing the door behind him. Hanging up his jacket, he caught a glimpse of himself in the closet mirror. There were no evident signs that he'd been in a row, except perhaps for slightly mussed hair. He combed it and looked himself over. His eyes were deeply shadowed, as though he hadn't slept in some time—which he hadn't, he abruptly realized; this was his second full day without rest.

He slumped behind the desk, all at once aware of how very tired he really was. From the large bottom drawer he took out a bottle of Black & White and a tumbler and poured himself a full measure. He downed it in one swallow, cleared his burning throat, and reached for the phone. From his wallet he extracted the folded slip of notepaper and dialed the number.

"Yes?" a hollow voice answered after four rings. Probably had to hook up the recorder, Farrell said to himself.

"It's Farrell."

A short pause. "Yes?"

"Okay."

"You're sure?"

Farrell couldn't tell the voice. But he said, "I'm sure. Now what?"

"Right on. We'll be in touch." Roy Thomas, he thought as the connection was cut. He couldn't say why, but he was glad.

We'll be in touch. Michael's parting words, too. A tremor went through him, and he reached for the scotch again. He had one more call to make.

Liz answered right away, as though she'd been waiting by the phone.

"It's the moment of truth for you, babe," he said. "Maybe your last chance to get out of this. I just turned the corner."

"Tony, Tony," she crooned into his ear, "just come home. I want you tonight. . . ."

PART .

TWO

7

They had consumed one another long into the night, urgently, before they'd sunk into deep sleep, still in each other's arms.

Farrell's dreams were turbulent and disturbing. Several times he had the sudden sensation of falling into space, jarring him half awake. He relived the old nightmare of trying to run, to flee some unidentified terror reaching out for him, and his feet turning to stone. He kept trying to scale a high wall, climbing torturously again and again almost to the top, only to find it just beyond his reach . . . falling, straining, groping desperately for a handhold. A bell ringing far off . . .

He started, awake. For a second he tensed, uncertain where he was. Then he saw Liz beside him. The bell jangled close by. It was the phone. He squinted at the clock in the half light: nine o'clock. Morning or night? He fumbled with the telephone receiver. "Hello," he rasped.

"Good morning," a soft male voice said. "Did I wake you?"

"It's all right." Farrell cleared his throat. "Who is it?"

"Mr. Blackman. We had a long talk the other night."

"Who the hell—?"

The fog parted in Farrell's brain. Black man. "Oh . . . yeah."

"Now, are you awake?"

Farrell pushed himself up so that his back was against the headboard. "Yeah, I guess so. . . ." Liz stirred, turning onto her side but not waking. He lowered his voice, "What's happening?"

"I want to set up a meet," said Thomas. "But first: You haven't been in touch with your business associate yet, have you?"

That had to be Cheech. "He left a call at the place last night, but I missed him. I figured to look him up today."

"The sooner the better. It'll look funny otherwise."

"I know. He's usually not available till around noon."

"Okay. When's the last time you had a haircut?"

"A haircut? Hell, I don't know . . . a month, month and a half? Why?"

"You still go to the hotel barber, right?"

"Yeah . . ."

"Make an appointment this morning. For eleven. Call me back to confirm. You still have the number?"

"Of course."

"Leave your house about ten," Thomas went on. "Walk down First Avenue to the restaurant, as you normally do. Leave word you're going to the barber's for an hour. Stop off at your garage and say you want a tuneup on your car—you'll pick it up at the end of the day. At ten forty-five, hail a cab, westbound, at the corner of Sixty-ninth." Thomas paused, as if that were all.

"Then what?"

"Then you'll go for your haircut."

"That's it?"

"Not quite. You'll see. Let me know when the time is set." Thomas clicked off.

Farrell hauled himself out of bed, went into the bathroom, then put on a terry robe and shambled down the carpeted stairs of the duplex to the kitchen. He started heating water for coffee, poured himself a glass of juice and slumped at the dinette table, bleakly contemplating what lay ahead. Code names. Ducking around corners. Peering over his shoulder at every step. He felt as sodden and lifeless as if he were hung over.

On the kitchen extension he called the barber at the Barclay and then "Mr. Blackman," confirming his 11:00 A.M. appointment.

Before leaving the apartment, just before ten, he scribbled a note to Liz: "LOVER: If anybody asks, I'll be at the barber at 11, at the restaurant by noon. Play it by ear from there. Don't worry. Luvya."

At 10:45, Farrell came out of the garage on 69th Street and walked to the corner of First Avenue. No sooner did he look around than a yellow Checker drew up alongside. Farrell climbed into the back and said, "Barclay Hotel."

"You got it, boss," the driver, a black, said to him in the rearview mirror.

Something in the voice made Farrell peer into the mirror. The face looking at him, deadpan, was Roy Thomas's. "For Chrissake!" Farrell exclaimed.

The signal changed and they started moving west. "Surprised?" Thomas asked sidewise.

"Why all this hocus pocus? Aren't we being a little melodramatic?"

"Not really. We figure our first responsibility is to protect you. I could have come to your place to talk, but my partner, the old bird dog, said maybe we ought to see first if your friends might be keeping an eye on you."

"And—?"

"He tailed you from the apartment to there. Nothing. I'll check one more time." Thomas leaned forward to retrieve something from under the seat. He straightened and brought a handset to his mouth. "Blackman to Whitehead. Are you with us? Over."

A voice crackled back: "Whitehead, roger."

"What's the picture now?"

"Looking good. I make it all clear."

"Roger. You'll stay with us to destination?"

"That is affirmative. Over and out."

Farrell smiled tightly. "Blackman and Whitehead," he said. "Cute."

"Normally we avoid using names at all in communication," Thomas said. "But in this particular situation we decided it best if each of us is able to identify one another without mixup. From now on, you're 'Specs.' "

"Specs? How'd you come up with that?"

Thomas grinned. "Actually, it was Stabler's—excuse me: Whitehead's—idea. For 'special employee.' Or, 'on speculation.' Either way it fits."

They turned south on Lexington Avenue. "A special employee, huh?" Farrell repeated with distaste. "What is that, your polite way of saying fink?"

"Don't you go sour on me," Thomas shot back. "A fink's a fink. You're going to be working with us fulltime. It's a job—a big one."

"You're putting me on the payroll?"

"Well . . . in a way, if it works out. Compensation will be put aside for you. Later, when you might need it, you'll be paid regularly. For now, with the kind of bread you're pulling down, we don't have to use up the taxpayers' money."

"You'd better run that past me again," Farrell said. "Are you saying you're really going to let me go on doing what I've *been* doing?"

"Absolutely. That's the whole point of this operation. Nothing changes."

"There's got to be a catch."

"Of course, it's loaded with hooks. The better *you* do, the better our chances of bagging *them*. Then, too, we keep a running tally of what you're into . . . and if you ever should think of going back on our bargain—"

"So what you're really letting me do is set myself up for a super bust."

"If you don't play by our rules—sure, that's our insurance."

Farrell was silent for a moment. They were coming out of usual heavy traffic in the Fifties near Bloomingdale's and Alexander's. "All right," he said, "how do we begin?"

"First, as I say, pick up the normal routine. Just be sure you smooth it over with Cheech and the Giant. They must be convinced your rap was just a dumb mistake that's not about to make any waves."

"And if they won't convince—if they hang me out to dry? Where does that leave us?"

"Negative thinking," Thomas said, shaking his head. "Make *sure* you're convincing—for your own sake."

"Terrific. Just the pep talk I needed," grunted Farrell. "Okay, what then?"

"Regular communication with us. We'll have you covered, but check in every day or two. If we don't hear from you, *we'll* be in touch. Remember the IDs; if any of us uses any other name, it'll be a tipoff something's not kosher. If you spot us around anywhere, don't give a second look unless we let you know we want to talk."

"And what am I supposed to be doing, beside running a restaurant and building my crooked pile on the side?"

"Now what do *you* think?" snapped Thomas out of the side of his mouth. "Don't start playing dumb with me."

"I'm your pipeline. Feed you everything about—what's going on."

"That's better. Yes, *everything*—names, places, numbers —anything that goes by you, and especially anything connected with the big man. In a few days—after we get the feel of how it's working out—we'll sit you down some nice quiet place and let you tell us everything we don't know about what's been going on up to now. So you also give *that* some hard thought in the meantime."

"I was wondering what I'd do with my leisure time," Farrell grumbled.

"We're here," Thomas said.

The cab went by the back entrance of the Waldorf Astoria and pulled over at the corner of 49th and Lexington, outside the Barclay. "I almost forgot," said Farrell as he riffled through the cash in his wallet: "What's happened with the others—the girl, and the other guy?" He passed Thomas a five-dollar bill.

"Alison's daddy scooped her up," Thomas said. "He's throwing a lot of weight around to keep it quiet. She'll probably be under wraps for quite a while. And your pal Gerard, he's locked up in the infirmary with a very painful fanny." Thomas handed back a couple of singles, some silver and a folded slip of white paper. "There's our new number. We'll change it periodically.

"Listen, about Gerard: I'd advise you to think about arranging his bail when the time comes. You don't want him badmouthing you out loud for leaving him hanging. That might get cops nosing around you and queering our main action."

Thomas flipped the meter flag up. "Good luck, Specs."

He'd been in the chair hardly five minutes when the barber was interrupted by the telephone's ring. "For you, Mr. Farrell." The barber brought the phone to the chair.

"Yes?"

"Antonio! My *paisan!* Where you been?" Cheech.

"Hey, how you doing, buddy! I was going to call you in a while. Figured it was a little early yet. What's happening?"

"That's what I'm wonderin'. I couldn't even sleep, worryin' about you. So I call your pad, and your old lady says you went to the barber! Like a friend of ours was sayin', that Tony, a pretty cool cat. Not a worry in the world, right?"

"Oh, it's been hectic enough," Farrell said. "This is a good place to unwind."

"You got to tell me about it."

"Yeah, I was meaning to. When can we get together? I'm going back to the restaurant from here."

"No. You come and talk to me," Cheech said. "I'll be at Sal's. You remember the clam house?"

"Sure. Downtown."

"Come around noon. We'll eat. And talk." He rang off.

Farrell left the barbershop at eleven-thirty and went to a pay phone in the hotel lobby to inform Liz of his change in plans. He asked her to cover for him during lunch and to monitor the private line in his office. If either a Mr. Blackman or a Mr. Whitehead tried to reach him she was to tell them where he was. She sounded anxious, and he tried to reassure her there was no problem.

Next he dialed the number Thomas had given him. A recorded voice responded: "Casualty Mutual. We are sorry, but no one is in the office at this time. If you wish to leave a message, please wait for the beep, and then—" Farrell hung up. Casualty Mutual?

At the same corner where Thomas had dropped him off, he hunted for a taxi—vaguely wishing he would find Thomas again behind the wheel.

Where the cab took him was just a few blocks north of where he'd spent the long night two nights before, within a stone's throw of the Tombs. The several square blocks of Little Italy was one of the safest enclaves in New York City. Every Italian neighborhood was, these days—neighborhood bastions holding out against the swarming "minorities" that had in fact become the majority in most of the rest of the city. The Italians kept to themselves and took care of their own. Outsiders were permitted entry or to pass through, but anybody who went into an Italian stronghold and messed around got a quick response. If you came and went and minded your business, it was as safe as a stroll in the park. Safer, these days.

Sal's Seafood was on a corner. It had two entrances, the one in front under a green-and-white-striped awning and an unadorned side door around the corner. He'd yet to come upon any place *they* favored that didn't have at least two ways in and out. The interior was long and narrow, with a small bar just inside the entrance and a double row of red plastic-covered tables the length of the well-lit room, many already occupied, mostly by men of middle age and older. The air was rich with marinara.

Farrell found Cheech alone at a corner table in a rear alcove screened from the back door. He pulled out a chair. "Breakfast?" he smiled, measuring the table laid out before the other.

Cheech, mouth full, nodded. He was attacking a bowl of steamed mussels, sopping up the spicy juices with chunks of Italian bread. Waiting was a large green half melon draped with pink prosciutto, and alongside that a pot of espresso and a newly opened bottle of anisette. Cheech ingested his mouthful and poked at his lips with the napkin that was tucked into his collar. He took a sip from the demitasse. "I always eat light first thing," he said. Signaling for a waiter, he asked Farrell, "What'll you have? Fish? Pasta? It's the best."

"That melon looks good," Farrell said. "And coffee. American."

Cheech instructed the waiter in Italian. He swirled bread in the mussel broth and looked at Farrell. "So, tell me something," he said.

"Thanks for making the bail. I owe you."

Cheech eyed him. "Just give me my money's worth."

With a rueful shrug, Farrell said: "What can I tell you? I played amateur night." He gave Cheech a blow-by-blow account.

Cheech studied him speculatively, waiting for more. When Farrell did not continue, he demanded: "So? What's the breakdown, f'crissake?"

Farrell shook his head. "It had to be a setup. The narcs had the deal made. Most likely out of Chicago, because they had this guy staked out at the hotel, but I'm pretty sure they were shooting craps at this end until the people showed up. That's what frosts me: When they'd bagged Alison and Gerard and the other guy upstairs, they thought they had it all! They didn't know who the hell I was or where I fit! I could have walked away from the whole thing—a little poorer, but with nobody the wiser. Instead, like a dunce, I walk right into it!"

"Yeah. Then what?" Cheech asked with narrowed eyes.

Farrell showed no concern. "I played Johnny-the-Pork-Chop, naturally: 'Who, *me*? Involved with *criminals?*' I said I was just passing by and saw this nice young lady being threatened by this mean-looking man, and like a good citizen I flew to her rescue. How could *I* know he was a police officer? Crap like that."

"And they bought that?" asked Cheech skeptically.

"It didn't go down easy. They wanted to connect me, you know, because I'd used muscle with them and that ticks them off. But they spent all night working at it and came up blank. I stuck to my story. I've got no record. Nobody knew me from anywhere. All they could make me for was a guy with an unlicensed gun—that and attempted assault. I doubt they can make the last part stick, though. So it'll probably come down to just the gun."

"They were city bulls, then, not feds?"

"Looked strictly local to me."

"Get any names?"

"Of cops?" Farrell shook his head. "Too much coming and going. I didn't pay any attention to who was who, I was too busy being pissed at myself. Why, what would you do with names?"

"Oh, maybe we could check out a little more what outfit they're with, what they're into— Never mind. So you gave them a snow job and got away with it. All right—so far. But somethin' else bothers me: What about the other three?"

"Well, the guy from Chicago—I figure he's on his own. You pay your money, you take your chances. Besides, he's a lawyer—he'll find some way to take care of himself. The main thing is, he doesn't know about me or where the merchandise came from. Gerard? Did I tell you he got wounded during the bust?" Farrell described Gerard's "accident."

Cheech gagged on a mouthful of melon. "That silly fuckin' homo!" he sputtered.

"It's funny," Farrell said, "but we still ought to see he gets

taken care of, don't you think? We wouldn't want Gerard
feeling neglected, maybe start crying—"

"Gerard knows better," growled Cheech. "He knows what
could happen to him. We'll do what we can, but . . . he goes
away, he goes away, that's the game. It won't be his first time. I
think he even likes it up there. He gets to be queen of the
cellblock." He laughed.

"How about you?" Cheech was serious again. "How do I
know *you* won't bust out cryin'? You got a lot more to trade
than a stiff like Gerard."

Farrell steeled himself. This was the test. He leaned forward
on the table, pushing close to Cheech, boring into his eyes, and
in a lowered voice said: "Don't you say that to me, you guinea
fuck."

He waited while Cheech's face changed colors. "You should
know better," Farrell went on in the same grave tone. "I'm not
a goddamn flunky any more. I'm *with* you. And you can take
that to the bank!"

His stomach churning, he sat back to let it sink in. Cheech
gaped at him, half in astonishment and half in fury. For one
awful instant Farrell couldn't be sure whether or not the brawny
figure was going to explode. But then, gradually, Cheech
subsided.

"Hey, you got balls, kiddo," he said "—and the luck of the
Irish. Not a bad mix." He poured anisette into both their cups.
"Salut'."

Farrell only lifted his an inch or two off the saucer in a token
response, because his hand was shaking too much. "Like you
say, you win some, you lose some. How tough could a gun
charge be? Only months, maybe, and I'm out and back in
business. And with a sharp lawyer"—he looked significantly at
Cheech—"I might even end up with a suspended. So why
should anybody get their balls in an uproar?"

"We'll see you get a defense," Cheech responded as hoped.
"When are you up?"

"The hearing's in about three months."

"Okay. I'll talk to somebody." Cheech sat back, arms folded. "We got everybody accounted for," he said, looking questioningly across at Farrell, "except one: the girl."

"I understand her father sprung her. He's loaded. Alison shouldn't be any trouble. She's a class kid."

"It's the 'class' bit—and her rich old man—that worries me," Cheech mused. "She figures to get hit the hardest in this whole deal. And if she does, *he* does. He's a fancy lawyer, right? Big political hopes? You think he'll sit still for her standin' trial, takin' the full rap, with all the bad publicity that's sure to come out?"

"Well, he'll pull all the strings he can to keep the noise down," Farrell said.

"No way he could cover this up," insisted Cheech. "The daughter of a big public figure caught sellin' a kilo of dope? That's major, man! Front-page news. It would dirty him down to his socks."

Farrell considered. "You may be right at that. It could be rough," he said, thinking of Alison and meaning it.

"*If* it happened," Cheech said. "But he ain't about to let that happen, see."

"What do you mean? You just said—"

"He'll pull those strings of his so she gets to cop a plea. That he can control—it'll be kept nice and quiet. And what does he give in return? Information the heat would love to have. He knows, *they* got to know, his little girl ain't no kilo-class dope retailer—she got to be a shill for somebody heavy in the business. So he turns the screws on her, scares her . . . and all of a sudden it's a different ballgame—and you're in it."

"I know Alison," Farrell said curtly, "she's not the fink type."

Cheech raised his eyebrows. "Who knows *who's* the fink type? Don't be sure about nothin'," Cheech snapped. "That's when you can get suckered—like you did. You got to learn from your mistakes, my friend. Figure what *could* happen. You're dealin' with a civilian here. Now if this chick folds on you, you got trouble." It was Cheech's turn to lean close and drop his voice. "And for *you* to get that kind of trouble, it could make certain *other* people kind of restless. Get my drift?"

The drift was plain enough; but Farrell couldn't quite grasp the end point. "All right," he said, "but what can we do about it?"

Hoods dropped over Cheech's eyes. "That's the question. You better give it some more thought. And fast."

On the way back uptown, Farrell slumped on the back seat of the cab, leaden with fatigue. It had been a grueling test for him, but he felt he'd cleared the first hurdle without serious mishap. He could only wonder how long he might have to sweat out the next qualifying heat. Should Aaron Luke Brothers turn "restless," as Cheech had put it, he would be several more handfuls to grapple with than the Italian had been—there would be no boldly facing the Giant down as a "nigger fuck."

One thing Cheech had said, or started to, could be of interest to Blackman & Company, if he'd interpreted it right: that bit about checking on who'd collared him. The inference was that Cheech, or somebody, might have a conduit into the police department. Odd, he thought, that he'd never had an inkling of that before this. But it did make sense, could well be the prime reason why Cheech, to say nothing of the Giant, had survived so long—having dependable access to police intelligence.

One other thing Cheech had said—or rather, *how* he'd said it—left Farrell disturbed: about the Alison Fournier situation, his shadowy implication that something might have to be done to neutralize her as a potential threat. It was a consideration that had not occurred to Farrell, and he did not want to believe it was real.

For the first time he questioned himself: Was he really tough enough to see this all the way through?

8

Aaron Luke Brothers maintained three domiciles and women with each. His legal residence was a high-rise cooperative in Englewood Cliffs, New Jersey, with a magnificent view of the Hudson, the George Washington Bridge and the New York City skyline. He spent little time there, however; it was only an occasional retreat, where he could briefly put out of mind the demands of business while dutifully visiting with his wife of record and four young children who lived there. New Jersey was a convenient place to file both them and, because of the state's low tax structure, his reported assets, but most of his other interests remained on the New York side of the river.

Where he actually resided was in a spacious home in Fieldston, a wooded parklike preserve within the fashionable Riverdale section of the North Bronx. Here, spaced generously on winding lanes canopied by sturdy century-old trees, the houses all were quietly elegant, many in the Tudor or chalet styles favored in the 1920s, when most were built. It was a community of almost courtly reserve, where neighbors rarely fraternized, a consideration of particular appeal to Aaron Luke Brothers. His house was a solid, squarish two-story Georgian of red brick with white trim, set back from the street behind a ten-foot-high brick wall and heavy iron driveway gates. This was Brothers' refuge, where he lived without ostentation and serenely with his common-law wife, her teenage daughter by a prior marriage and their own two-year-old son. Except for rare occasions, no one was ever invited here for business.

The third place Brothers kept, his operation control center and where he spent the greater proportion of his days, was a Manhattan townhouse on West 104th Street, just off Riverside Drive. This was convenient to Harlem, where much of his business was conducted. The building, four stories tall, was gray and un-notable. The street entrance, always locked, showed no name by the bell, nor was there any house number visible, although it was in the 300 block. The front windows on all floors were usually shuttered or heavily curtained.

Inside, the ground floor had a rather clinical air. Facing the entry, a burly black man with close-cropped hair sat behind an L-shaped desk, with two telephones, an intercom box, and a large loose-leaf register. On the extension to his left a compact television monitor showed the front entrance and street immediately outside. The rest of the lobby contained only a row of straight-backed chairs, generally occupied by intense-looking men waiting to bring tribute or proposals to the Giant.

A mahogany staircase behind the "receptionist" led to the second floor, where the Giant and his people conducted business. The parlor overlooking 104th Street was furnished like a boardroom, with wood paneling, an old-fashioned hearth with mantelpiece, leather easy chairs, and an oblong conference table covered with green felt. The large windowless adjoining room, probably once a dining room, was partly office, with partitions on one side forming three little alcoves with tables and telephones for the Giant's lieutenants. The remaining area was a lounge, with overstuffed chairs, card tables and a television set; a bar and refrigerator were recessed into a wall. To the rear, at the end of a narrow corridor, was a fully equipped kitchen with a fulltime cook.

The third floor was the Giant's private apartment. Old walls had been restructured to create two huge rooms, a front living room and rear bedroom, separated by a smaller den/office and a sumptuous bath and dressing room with walk-in closet. Brothers seldom stayed overnight here, but when he did he lacked no creature comfort. Among the latter was the woman in residence on the floor above, his current mistress, who had her own luxurious apartment and wanted for nothing—with the possible exception of freedom of movement, for her obligation was virtually permanent so long as Aaron Luke Brothers remained pleased with her.

This, then, was the core of the Giant's growing empire. It was patterned on his conception of how the most powerful Italian godfathers would have it. But that was only his imagination: He had never been close to any of the Mafia elite. Those who *had* been came away shaking their heads in bemusement over the extravagant pretensions of the black entrepreneur. ("That big-assed cat thinks he's the fuckin' king of Ethiopia!")

One who did know how the Sicilian crimelords really lived, but who neither scoffed at nor resented the Giant's studied opulence, was Cheech Donato. Cheech had shrewdly balanced his action between the old gangs and the aggressive newcomer, gradually tipping his weight to the side of Giant, having concluded that black organized crime was the wave of the future. He didn't know how far this particular black powerhouse would go before his supremacy would be challenged, but Cheech calculated there were untold fortunes to be made in a hurry as long as he could keep their interests mutual and profitable.

Cheech was at the townhouse on West 104th Street now to discuss with Aaron Luke Brothers some of those mutual interests. Brothers received him in the second-floor conference room. As usual, the Giant was in the company of his right-hand man, Abou Jamal, whom he called "Boo." He was almost as tall as the Giant but lean and hard as a ramrod. Like Brothers, he kept his head shaved smooth, but instead of the stylish clothes the other affected, he wore only severe black suits, white shirts and thin black ties. Cheech could not recall ever having seen the man's eyes, for Jamal always wore dark, wire-rimmed lenses. He seldom spoke, but it was plain that he held whites in icy contempt—although Cheech had observed that Jamal was hardly less stony around his black brothers.

"Cocaine. Truly a phenomenon," the Giant was musing aloud in that cavernous baritone. "I chide myself for having failed to anticipate its enormous potential. Still, by no means do I feel it is too late for serious investment into this field. Don't you agree, Francesco?"

Cheech winced inwardly, as he always did at the sound of his given name. He hated it, and he'd long ago adopted the obscure diminutive "Cheech" from a bartender who used to call every customer that whose name he couldn't remember. Donato would not suffer many people to address him as "Francesco" these days, and especially not with the faintly mocking intonation this big coon always seemed to give it. But this was not *just* another coon; Cheech would suffer it. "I wouldn't mind havin' a steady cut of that action," he said, "but the Latinos got it locked by now."

Brothers smiled. "Only because they have yet to be challenged."

"It's their turf," insisted Cheech. "You deal coke, you got to deal with them. It ain't like H or grass."

"What you say is true—up to a point. So long as the essential resource is confined to the mountains of South America, they will control it, at least its production. But there are other ways to enter the competition. One is the matter of distribution. There we are geared to provide certain refinements that could be mutually advantageous."

"Hell, they got their own supply lines. What do they need anybody else for?"

"They may not, at first glance, *think* they need outside support," Brothers granted. "But I have something in mind that could persuade them it would be to their own best interests to welcome us as working partners."

"War?" asked Cheech.

"We would hope not," said the other. He pursed his lips. "In your estimation, what prerequisites would be required for us to establish a substantial foothold in this allegedly 'exclusive' market?"

"You gotta have somethin' to offer they don't got."

"Exactly. I've mentioned distribution as our forte. How do you suppose the South American lords of cocaine would respond to an exclusive arrangement whereby we could guarantee a virtually foolproof system of transporting their product into the United States?"

"Foolproof?" echoed Cheech. "All I can tell, them spics already use every gimmick in the book. And they still get bagged regular."

"Just so," Brothers grinned in triumph. "For all the Latins' ingenuity, all too many deliveries these days are being intercepted. Why? Because the opposition are not fools. International detection agencies have grown more sophisticated. And as they become more difficult to deceive, the toll of loss and waste rises."

"So what can *we* do about it?"

"The answer is so simple, Francesco, as to sound improbable." Brothers paused for effect. "By seeing that the hazards of direct confrontation between the antagonists are effectively removed. *Bypass* their regulatory controls, and the opposition is neutralized."

"You talkin' about them old bootleg routines—offshore boat landings, private airfields, all that? That ain't any new idea."

"No. And not new to the police, either. They are increasingly watchful for illegal entry."

"So then how—?"

The Giant grinned. He was enjoying the game. "*All* risk would be eliminated, would it not, if it could be arranged that the merchandise were transported into the United States proper *not* from foreign originations but between points *within* the

United States itself? That would obviate any *need* of perilous clandestine operations. Do you follow me so far?"

"Yeah . . ." muttered Cheech tentatively. "Well, not exactly . . ."

"I can appreciate your puzzlement. Let me sketch it out plainly for you. It is important that you fully understand, for your old connections in the Caribbean will be indispensable in making this plan functional. . . ."

When the Giant finished, Cheech was excited. "Terrific!" he exclaimed. "It's a cinch. When do we start?"

"It's in your hands. I would hope as soon as possible."

"Give me a day or two to double-check the different setups. If everything's still copasetic, I'll hop down there and plug each one in personal."

"Excellent!" boomed the Giant. He thought a moment. "I think our young friend Farrell could fit nicely into the operation, don't you agree? His particular image of respectability . . ." A change of expression on the other's face made him pause.

"I'm glad you brought that up," Cheech said with a frown. "I don't know now. This beef he got into. . . ."

"Are you saying," Brothers asked, "that you have cause for mistrust?"

"Not of *him*." Cheech then traced his analysis of the Alison Fournier situation essentially as he had earlier with Farrell.

"Ah! Then what you propose is some defensive measure against the girl—to forestall the possibility of ill consequences."

"Yeah . . . like that."

"And what did you have in mind?"

"I ain't sure yet. What do *you* think?"

The Giant got up and went to the window, where he stood with his back to the room. After several minutes he turned to Cheech.

"You do what you feel you must. But make it clean."

Cheech glanced up into the flinty eyes riveting him and nodded.

"Think positively, Francesco," Brothers exhorted, hearty again. "Turn your full attention to the pleasurable prospects lying open before us—the great fruits of our Caribbean harvest. The sooner you sow, the greater we shall all reap!"

"Okay." Cheech hauled himself up. "Should I tell Farrell the deal?"

"Mmmm . . . perhaps not quite yet. When arrangements are complete, we'll all go over it together." Brothers waved a hand of dispatch without rising.

When the stocky figure was gone, the Giant sat quiet for a while, then turned to Abou Jamal. "We should have a talk with Tony Farrell."

Michael Palmieri had asked Farrell to accompany him up to Valhalla that afternoon to visit Linda. The twenty-five-mile ride north passed mostly in introspective silence, eased by soft background music from an FM station and the scenic charm of the Bronx River Parkway. Valhalla, a few miles north of White Plains, was a relatively pastoral setting in which Westchester maintained its county jail and medical center. The spacious complex of brick structures, scattered over a small rolling valley, with its tree-lined lanes and manicured lawns, could almost be taken for a condominium park or a small college. The jail section, administered by the sheriff's department, consisted of several separate buildings, one of which is reserved for women. It contained both cellblocks and a hospital section. Michael and Farrell checked in at the visitor's desk, and finally, after a half-hour's wait, were escorted to the third floor. In a small room, behind Plexiglas paneling through which she could be observed constantly, Linda lay in a hospital bed, drowsing.

The two men tiptoed in and stood at the foot of the bed. She looked awful—drawn, pallid, eyes recessed in sickly shadows. Her eyes fluttered open and she peered at them without recognition, as though focusing. Her gaze settled on Farrell, and after a moment of puzzlement, her dry lips slowly parted in a wan smile. "Hi, big brother," she murmured.

"Hello yourself," he said, managing a grin. He moved around the bed and took her hand; it was as inanimate as plaster. "What's a nice girl like you doing in a place like this?"

"It's a trip, man," she chortled huskily. "They've got me all doped up—" Her laugh turned into a spasm of coughing.

Farrell squeezed her hand. "We've got to get you out of here," he said, "get you well."

"Out? Where to? In here, at least I get my fix every day—free."

"You're *not* an addict!" burst out Michael.

Linda's bleak eyes drifted to him, as though only then noticing his presence. "I'm not, Daddy? I sure tried hard enough. Anyway, by the time I get out of here, I ought to be." She raised an arm to display a series of pink needle pricks.

"We're doing everything we can. . . ."

Linda surveyed her father a moment, then asked flatly: "How's Mama?"

"She's . . . Well, it hit her pretty hard, you know?" Michael cleared his throat. "The lawyers think there's a chance you can get off with a suspended sentence, a couple of years' probation. First offense and all . . ."

She snorted. "And what do I have to do, rat on my friends?"

Farrell glanced quickly at Michael. His face was a clenched fist.

"What friends?" Michael fired. "The garbage who got you here? You need them like you need cancer. Besides, it isn't the ones you were hustling with—they're already in the same boat. It's the creeps who put you on to this. The greasers still out there, who couldn't care less whether you live or die. I'll find them someday," Michael said tightly, "and when I do—"

"I wouldn't, Daddy," warned Linda, "you'd be outmatched. *They're* not gentlemen." She looked up at Farrell, and he could see she was withdrawing into a hard shell. "And *I'm* no fink," she said.

His skin prickled, as though she were seeing inside him.

Nothing more was said. The men lingered a few more minutes. Finally they said clumsy goodbyes and left Linda, her face turned from them, blank eyes on the window, or perhaps on the bars beyond.

On the drive back Michael talked with renewed determination of how he was going to see to Linda's recovery and well-being at any cost. Farrell was grateful that he didn't speak again of his promised vengeance on the ones responsible, talk that tied him up in knots inside.

It was after seven that evening when Michael dropped him in front of his apartment building. As the LTD moved off and Farrell turned to go inside, a car horn behind him sounded insistently. He looked around and saw a black man in a conservative dark suit get out of the driver's side of a gray Imperial and beckon to him. Farrell stared at him; he was wiry and his shaved head glistened in the street light. He wore dark lenses and he was unsmiling. It was the Giant's man. Farrell walked to him.

"The Man wants to see you," Boo said tonelessly. He opened the rear door.

"Now?" Farrell looked at his wristwatch.

"Now," Boo repeated, motioning him into the car.

Farrell hesitated a moment, exploring the stony features, then ducked into the Imperial. His heart was pounding.

9

Abou said nothing to him on the way across town, through the park and up to the building on West 104th Street. He led Farrell straight upstairs to the third floor.

Farrell had a fleeting impression of bookshelves and lighted paintings on cream-colored walls, before the Giant's imposing frame rose from a white divan to command attention. He was coatless, wearing dark trousers and a pale blue shirt with white collar and a striped regimental tie.

"Tony! Welcome!" he boomed. "Come, join us," gesturing to an armchair. "Thank you, Boo," he said to his aide, who, thus dismissed, promptly returned down the stairs.

A young black woman sat in another armchair across a teak coffee table from the divan. She was very attractive, with smooth café-au-lait skin, stylish, close-cropped hair, and luminous eyes. Her beige suit was chic and finely tailored. She sat easily, legs crossed, smoking, a delicate stemmed glass half full of what looked like sherry on the table before her. Farrell wondered if this was the fourth-floor mistress he'd heard talk of.

"Hello, Aaron," he said as evenly as he could manage. "Your warm invitation"—inclining his head toward the stairs descended by Abou—"was, you might say, a bit abrupt."

"Ah, the trusty Boo." Brothers grinned. "Unpolished, perhaps, but in all important respects a gem of efficiency. Tony

Farrell," he said, taking his arm, "I'm pleased you could meet a charming memory of mine from Atlanta: Millie Dubois."

She held out a hand: "Hello, Tony." It was silken, but firm.

"A drink, Tony?" Brothers asked.

"If that's sherry the lady has, I might try a scoop."

"Excellent. La Ina. Imported from Spain," Brothers moved to his sidebar set into a wall of the bookshelves. "Be seated, Tony, relax," he called back.

"About all I know about Atlanta," Farrell said pleasantly to the woman, "are the Braves—Hank Aaron—and the Falcons."

"And *Gone with the Wind*?" she added with a smile.

"Right," he grinned. "You still live there?"

"No. I've been in New York several years now," she said.

"A newly discovered fact," Brothers interjected, handing Farrell a small glass of pale sherry, "which I hope to turn to Camille's and my mutual advantage." He lowered himself onto the divan and sat back expansively. "Millie is a designer —women's fashions. She has been recommended to me as a young woman of highly innovative ideas, some of which we've just been going over. You know my clothing outlet, Tony. I've been thinking of expanding into women's fashions . . . but only if I could produce a distinctive imprint, something unique, yet tasteful. I think the lovely Millie may have brought me exactly what I've been looking for." He sat there obviously pleased, projecting the stature of a benevolent potentate.

Farrell well remembered that Bronx "clothing outlet" where Cheech had first taken him to meet the Giant. A tacky warehouse under the el—damp and drafty, with cement floors, probably once an auto repair shop or garage—where a score or more of shabby women sat around long tables cutting and stitching rolls of fabric. He remembered their faces, hollow-eyed and unsmiling, some very young, others of indeterminate age, blacks and Latins, toiling at the only work they could get, no doubt, probably at below-minimum wages and off the books—an old-fashioned sweatshop turning out garments whose under-the-counter sales helped make their employer a potentate indeed. Farrell wondered if Brothers would ever show Millie Dubois his factory; would it be what *she* was looking for . . . ? But that was no concern of his.

"Are you interested in fashions, Tony?" Millie Dubois smiled.

"Not really," he grinned back. "But I know a few ladies who might appreciate some inside tips."

She and Brothers exchanged amused looks. "In due time, Tony," the Giant chuckled. "Millie and I have much to work out yet. Perhaps later, when all is ready, we may have a sneak preview for some of our most trusted friends—eh, *ma petite?*"

"I hope so," she said.

"Well now," Brothers said, rising, "Millie must be off, and Tony and I have a few items to discuss. Don't despair, Tony, I'm sure you'll get the chance to learn more about the fashion business as time goes on."

"I'm already developing an interest," Farrell said lightly, shaking her hand. "Good luck to you."

"Make yourself comfortable, Tony," Brothers said, "while I see Millie out."

Farrell sipped at his sherry; he could feel its warmth all the way down into his empty stomach. So she was not the mistress in residence—not yet. He wondered idly how she and Brothers had known one another before. When he was in Atlanta, the story went, he wasn't the high flyer he'd since become; and she looked like her class was built in—they didn't seem to match.

He wandered about the room. Examining some of the books—American and world history, encyclopedias, volumes on the law, a few classics and an occasional bestseller—he could see that they were read, not merely on display.

He still had no indication of why he had been brought here. He poured himself another sherry. It figured that the Giant wanted to talk with him about the other night's bust; but what his slant would be, Farrell couldn't tell. Brothers' manner while the young woman was present had given no suggestion whatever of distrust; on the contrary, he'd seemed almost proprietary toward him. Farrell told himself he could not afford to be lulled by such artful shows of comradeship: He knew how skilled the Giant was at seducing antagonists into a complacent sense of well-being before he struck.

Odd how one's outlook could be turned around practically overnight. Only a few days ago, he would have been elated at finding himself in these inaccessible rooms; it would have been a powerful expression of the Giant's confidence in him, of the rich promise of closer association. Tonight . . . he could only wonder. And steel himself.

"Antonio! Forgive me." The Giant's basso filled the room from the stairwell. He glided across the carpet and resumed his place on the divan. "I see you've been examining my library," he smiled. "A source of considerable comfort to me. I had little exposure to books as a boy. Now I can scarcely get my fill. Come, Tony, tell me what you've been up to. Would you care for another drink?"

"I already helped myself," said Farrell, seating himself.

"So . . ." He appraised Farrell with a benign expression. "I'm told you found yourself in an, ah, altercation with the law recently."

"Yeah. I've been meaning to fill you in. I figured Cheech would brief you. . . ."

"Your associate was unfailingly prompt," Brothers said.

Farrell recited the details of the incident, much as he had to Cheech, realizing he was becoming quite adept with the lines. "It's really not that big a deal. I don't see why Cheech is whacked out about it."

"His concern is understandable. It unsettled him to contemplate your confederate turning on you in her own defense and thereby initiating the downfall of us all." He grinned, as if to dismiss exaggeration. But then he added: "However, why would she *not,* if it served to ease her way? But the larger question is, what would be the likely repercussions of that act?"

"If she fingers me, I deny it. So then what? The kid's just freaked out. She's got nothing to hang me on, I made sure of that, down the line. There's just no place they can run with it."

"Perhaps you're right. Still . . . giving the devil his due, let us examine all possibilities. You assume that by your flat denial of the accusation, her inability to provide any substantiation, and the absence of any recorded precedent of wrongdoing in your past, the police would be put off. Not necessarily so. From the official standpoint, there could be too much at stake —considering the political influence of the girl's father, as well as the appreciable quantity of contraband and cash involved. No, it is at least as likely as not that they *would* feel bound to pursue it further."

Farrell shrugged. "All they'd come up with is a fistful of air. I'm not worried."

The Giant eyed him appraisingly. "I wonder if you may be taking this *too* lightly. You must be aware that determined authorities can find access to other corridors of intelligence independent of a subject himself?"

"Such as?"

"The streets, my friend. *Informers*. The law knows all too well the uses of duplicity—the police could scarcely function without their informants! And they are everywhere."

Farrell hoped his face did not mirror the sudden panic in his breast. He swallowed and said: "I can't believe anybody *we* deal with—"

"Oho! You cannot be so naive! Let me pose a set of circumstances: For the sake of argument, you are betrayed. The police swoop down on you with incontrovertible evidence, sworn testimony, of your various illegal activities. They promise you conviction and X years in prison—*unless* . . . unless you see the wisdom of 'cooperating,' of leading them to others with even greater stakes than your own."

"I—"

Brothers held up a hand to silence him. "Now you, Tony, I do not imagine you would be moved by spite, nor excessive greed. But your instinct for survival—how deep does that run in you? That has yet to be tested. Could you withstand the forbidding prospect of canceling all the remaining years of your youth in harsh captivity . . . while those others, no less sinful than yourself, whose lives could have provided you reprieve, remain at liberty? Consider, Tony. How do you suppose you would deal with that?"

Wow, socking it right to me! thought Farrell. The Giant was not being whimsical. No faltering here, he exhorted himself. He looked Brothers dead in the eye: "Aaron, if you're really asking me that, I might as well get out of here right now." He moved to rise.

"Sit down, Tony. I'm still interested in your response," Brothers said, his scrutiny unwavering.

"You want an answer? Okay. There's no way I would ever stiff you. Are you convinced, or do I have to get *in* that kind of pickle before I can prove myself?"

"How can you be so positive?"

"Two very basic reasons," said Farrell with intensity. "One, I'm just not built that way—which you can only take on faith, since obviously you haven't sized me up the way I figured you must have by now. And two, because I'd be scared shitless ever to cross you. I'd rather be in a cell in Attica than in a six-pack of dog chow."

The Giant measured him a long moment. Then the eyes crinkled and white teeth flashed. "Splendid, Tony, excellent! As I'd noted, you do have perspective." He regarded Farrell appreciatively, then stretched across the coffee table for the other's glass. "Here, let me freshen your sherry."

"No, thanks, I'm fine," Farrell said, placing his palm over the glass.

"Have no doubts, Tony: You do have my confidence, and I in turn acknowledge your good will. However . . ." Brothers paused, as if choosing his next words. "We have yet to resolve the question of the girl. It remains, as your associate obdurately points out, that she could represent a most unfortunate inconvenience. Some precautionary tactic should be taken to ensure against that."

Farrell tried to read his eyes.

"If you," the Giant said, "can devise an equitable solution to the dilemma, without resort to . . . shall we say, extreme measures . . . do so by all means. I would submit only that you see to it before too much more time elapses."

With that he glanced at his wristwatch, which looked to be solid gold. "Speaking of time—I'll be blessed: It's well passed eight. I'd planned to dine out. Won't you join me, Tony?"

"Eight?" Farrell consulted his own watch. "God, I'd better get moving, too. My lady must be in a frazzle. I haven't checked in all day. Can I make a call?"

"Of course. There, on the sideboard." Brothers rose and went into the next room.

Farrell pulled himself erect. It had been a day of unremitting tension, and he felt sapped. He wanted just to be with Liz, the two of them—the hell with everything else.

Absently he picked up the receiver—

". . . *all the bodies you need, right?*" came over the line, causing him to start.

"*Could've had twice as many for this job, man,*" a throaty voice answered with a chuckle. Farrell thought he recognized the voice. "*Everybody wants in on the gravy,*" the second one added.

"*Okay. Friday. Remember, don't get 'em to the hospital no earlier than six. It's quiet around there then, and you don't want to get no static about a bunch of dudes hangin' out that time of day, dig? Still plenty of time before the payroll— Hey, you got somebody on another line there?*"

Gingerly Farrell replaced the receiver. He'd been too preoccupied before to notice that one of the buttons was lit.

Somebody downstairs, no doubt, on an outside call. Talking about what sounded like an organized hit somewhere—a payroll stickup? A hospital. Friday, probably morning. *This* Friday? *Where?* He would try to sort it out later. He pressed down another button and reached for the receiver to make his call—and then halted. If he picked up now, *that* button would light downstairs as well. No, better to wait until he got outside. He sat down, his legs rubbery. Already he was behaving like a spy. . . .

Brothers returned wearing his suit jacket. "Mission accomplished?" he asked breezily.

Farrell, who had been engrossed in the lit telephone button, started as it abruptly went off. "What? Oh, yeah. My old lady is steaming. I've really got to hustle."

"Let me drop you."

"No, no. It's 'way across town. I'll scrounge a cab."

"Nonsense. In *this* neighborhood?" Brothers smiled. "A compromise, then: You can drop *me* uptown, and Boo will deliver you. I insist. After all, it *was* I who disrupted your schedule."

In the Imperial, Brothers did not refer to the earlier discussion. Instead, he chatted about several of his legitimate businesses, of plans he had for expanding some of them and for investing in other areas—"as the Italians have so wisely and successfully done." It amused him to anticipate diversifying his meat-packing enterprise with the addition of a purely kosher line, for which he was on the verge of signing an exclusive supplier's contract with a chain of local Jewish-oriented supermarkets. He returned with enthusiasm to the new fashion concept he would develop with Millie Dubois. Millie reminded him of Atlanta, and that got him reminiscing of his youth there after having emigrated from Jamaica—a hard youth evidently, the earlier days consumed with backbreaking farm labor on dusty sharecropper spreads beyond the city, later hustling to claw out an existence in the still forbidding streets of the metropolis. With pride he mentioned the two prosperous clubs he owned there now, as well as other commercial interests. He still visited Atlanta every so often, he said, and it was different for him there now. He had conquered the past.

In Harlem, on Columbus Avenue, Farrell began to see why the big man's mood was so hearty and expansive. The car slowed at 118th Street, then, deliberately, was inched along by Boo the length of the next block, although there was no excess of traffic impeding them. A look out the side window told Farrell what was happening: Along the littered sidewalks, people were gathering—young and old, men and women, almost all black—moving alongside the car in growing numbers, jostling for position, waving to the Imperial as it made its way regally up the avenue. It was a procession. Here Aaron Luke Brothers, the West Indian peasant by way of Atlanta niggertowns, was royalty.

The car eased into a space magically cleared in front of a canopied place whose marquee glittered: *The Gold Tree*. The crowd clustered around, filling the sidewalk and spilling into the gutter, as Boo—unremittingly austere in manner and dress —got out and came around to open the rear curbside door. Glancing out the rear window, Farrell spotted another car pulled up and double-parked behind them; a stern-faced young black with shaved head got out of the passenger side and stood behind the opened door, eyes darting over the scene before him like a Secret Service agent—the Giant's security detail, no doubt. It would be tough for any antagonist—much less honky cops—to get close to the Giant.

Farrell resisted the impulse to survey the street at length. How many undercover police were out there, observing the Giant and wishing they could nail him? And right now wondering, perhaps, who shared the big man's limo. Farrell suddenly was thankful for the anonymity of the car's darkness.

The Giant made a grand exit into the midst of his admirers, smiling genially, exchanging palm-slapping repartee with a few (effortlessly switching from the accustomed elegance of his private discourse, Farrell noticed, to cool street jive: "Hey, brother, you gittin' it all down?"). Many in the crowd peered around him to see who his favored passenger was, and Farrell could hear the murmuring upon recognition of the young, well-groomed white man. Brothers was aware of it too, and he turned and bent to the open window:

"Leave me, then, in the bosom of my flock," he said, adding with a wink, "go and sin no more." Reaching a paw into the car, he gripped Farrell's hand, urging him closer to the window where he could be seen more clearly by those standing by. "I trust our earlier discussion will be acted upon duly, and with dispatch." Straightening, the Giant boomed: "Boo, take good care of m'man, you hear!"

As the Imperial pulled away, the great man, bodyguards around him now, benignly moved through the exuberant crush to disappear into The Gold Tree. The king.

Farrell sank back in the darkness of the limousine and let out a long, slow breath of satisfaction. He felt he'd cleared a major plateau with flying colors. Not only had the Giant not indicated any displeasure with him but, indeed, he had seemed to make a point of showing him off as a favored ally. If that were so, Farrell considered, he might be further ahead in this uncertain game than he'd imagined.

Then his eye caught the rear-view mirror and Abou Jamal's opaque lenses. He was transfixed with the conviction that those unseen eyes were glued on him. And not with admiration or trust, only malevolence. Chauffeuring a smart-ass white man! Farrell's satisfaction evaporated.

10

Roy Thomas had arrived home early for once, hoping to surprise his wife. But the apartment was dark. Deflated, he wandered the rooms vacantly, wondering what to do with himself. In the living room, he flicked on the television and slumped in an easy chair. The seven o'clock network news was just going off, and some loud, inane game show took its place. He snapped off the set and went to the kitchen for a beer.

The telephone clanged in the empty apartment. That would either be Camille or Ed Stabler. He hoped it was his wife, but he had to bet on Stabler.

"It's me," the rough voice greeted him. Naturally.

"What's doing?" Thomas asked.

"I been touring. Uptown, West Side, near the river. You with me?"

Thomas sighed. Stabler and his doubletalk games. "I'm hip," he said. "The powerhouse. So he paid his call."

"Not exactly. He got invited. The man's number-one honcho picked him up personally."

"Uh-oh. What do you make of that?"

"Can't tell," Stabler said. "They been in there over half an hour. Everything's quiet. I'll hang out till it breaks. Where'll you be?"

"Right here. I'm waiting for the madam. Keep me posted."

"Yeah. Enjoy. Tomorrow night's my turn."

Thomas hung up and took a slug of his beer. He returned to the living room and sprawled on the couch, trying to imagine the scene being played in that building on West 104th Street. If Farrell could come away still in the Giant's confidence, they had a foot in the door. *If* Farrell was not playing both ends against the middle.

His eyes grew heavy, and he let himself nestle deeper into the cushions. . . .

He snapped awake at the sound of the apartment door opening. Camille stood in the tiny foyer, peering at him with a look of surprise on her face. "Hi, sugar!" he greeted her, sitting up.

"Well, hello," she said with a little smile. "Imagine finding *you* here at this hour."

"Just passing through," he smiled back, stretching. His watch read 8:30. "How about yourself?"

"Oh, I drop in regularly." She put her things on the foyer table that served as their dinette. "Usually I don't run into anyone else." Her tone was light, he noted gratefully.

He watched her remove her gloves and then the top of her trim beige suit. As she placed the jacket on a hanger at the closet, he admired the way her sleek white blouse clung to her body and her thighs were outlined against the tailored skirt. She was some kind of put-together female!

He went over and put his arms around her waist from behind, drawing her firm, rounded fanny against him. "I made a deal with the boss." He nuzzled her ear. "More nights off."

She twisted around, unloosing his clasp, and kissed him lightly on the lips. "I'll believe it when I see it two nights running," she said, turning into the kitchen. "Did you eat?"

"No. I wasn't in the mood," he said from the doorway.

"Well, I'm starved." She opened the refrigerator and examined the meager contents.

Thomas reached out and pushed the refrigerator door

closed. "You don't want to cook. Why don't we go out—some place nearby? We can relax and celebrate."

"Celebrate what?"

"Our homecoming."

Guido's was an unromantic but dependable Italian restaurant at one end of a small shopping center within walking distance. It was not crowded, and they took a table in a corner farthest from the bar and its throbbing juke box. Thomas ordered veal piccante for Camille, hot antipasto for himself, and a bottle of red wine. Sipping the wine, they looked at each other quietly, then began to talk.

"It's been a while since we've done this," he said.

"It's been a while since . . . for a lot of things," she said looking into her wine.

His eyes roamed her face. "We've lost something, haven't we?"

She toyed with her glass, then glanced up at him. "Contact, I think."

He nodded. "I guess that's as good a way of putting it as any. I'm to blame. Or, rather, the job. I know how rotten it's been for you. For both of us. It won't go on like this forever, hon. Pretty soon—"

She was shaking her head. "Roy, there's no blame. You *are* your job. How could I blame you for being *you?* You never deceived me—I knew what to expect . . . or thought I did. The job won't change, you know that. *I* know it, now." She shrugged. "So, the choice for me is either to accept it, reject it, or . . . adapt my own life around it."

"And?"

"I think," she said after a moment, "I've done all three." She paused, thinking it out. "I've accepted it in the sense that it's the way it is, but I do *not* accept it unconditionally, so in that sense I've also rejected it. And I've adapted. I'm remaking my life independent of yours. I'm creating a need for myself other than just as a policeman's standby wife."

"You really hate my being a policeman that much?" he asked.

"Do any wives *enjoy* it?" she challenged. "But it goes deeper than that. I've thought a lot about it. . . ."

It was going to come out at last, Thomas thought. He'd known it must, some day, and now he wasn't sure how he would handle it. "You mean my being a *black* cop," he said.

Camille studied her wine without expression.

"Black or white, law is important—surely you can see that? If we want any kind of liveable society—"

"—somebody has to do it," she finished for him, eyes suddenly flaring. "But what society, *whose* law? The white man's! They make the law and build *their* society on the sweat and shame of our people!"

"That's nigger talk," Thomas snapped.

"Sure it is. 'Cause I *am* a nigger! And so are you. But you're trying to forget that!"

"I'm not forgetting anything. Being black—and if anybody else can't handle that, that's their problem—doesn't make me any less responsible. As long as I stay my own man . . ."

"But *are* you? Can you, in their world? You do it their way, or you wind up back in the ghetto—just another 'colored boy,' itchin' 'n' scratchin'. So you accommodate. You become their enforcer!"

"Why must you put it on such an adversary basis," he protested, " 'us' against 'them'? What kind of world is that? It doesn't *have* to be that way! We *can* all live together . . . or at least side by side . . . under the same rules. I'm enforcing, as you put it, the same rules for everybody. And blacks need rules—law, *and* policemen—as much as anybody."

"There are rules for them, and rules for us," she hissed. "*That's* what you don't see, or won't anymore. You can work for whitey and take his crumbs. But *I'm* finding out if you go your own way you can open up a whole new beautiful world for yourself. A beautiful *black* world . . ."

They ate in moody silence. After a while, he poured them more wine and gently slid his glass across and clinked hers. She looked up, and from the depths of himself he said: "Just don't give up on me completely—please."

She had to melt at his boyish intensity. "Sometimes I wish I could," she said with a wistful smile. "But it's really not that easy." She raised her glass to his.

"Tell me about *your* work," he said.

A sparkle appeared in her eyes. "Today I had the greatest stroke of luck. I've had this idea for a line of women's apparel patterned after authentic African dress—casual, right up to ceremonial formal. It could be sensational. I made sketches, but I just couldn't get the idea across. Anyway, today my boss finally gave a little and sent me uptown to see this fabulously rich black businessman who owns a clothing outlet—one of those discount, plain-piperack places, you know, but very successful. Who did it turn out to be but a fellow I used to know back in Atlanta! And he *loved* the idea!"

She was all animation as she went on to tell him how this black tycoon was talking about investing in her designs. Thomas listened, charmed by her enthusiasm, eager to get home where they could be alone.

They strolled back to the apartment hand in hand. Upstairs, Camille went straight to the bedroom, while Thomas poured a cognac. Carrying his brandy, he walked to the bedroom. Only the small lamp on the night table was lit, but he could see her vividly in the dim glow. She lay naked on the bed, coffee and cream spilled gracefully over soft white percale. "Oh, God," he breathed, "you are beautiful!"

She held out an arm to him, and he went around and sat beside her, his heart pounding. She raised herself a little and led his hand with the glass to her lips. She sipped, eyes holding his, then lifted her mouth to him. As they kissed, her lips parted and a trickle of brandy entered his mouth. He thought he would explode.

They made love fiercely: He couldn't get enough of her, and she responded to him each time. It must have been after two when they finally released each other into contented sleep.

Tony Farrell had fallen asleep early, and alone.

Arriving at his apartment, Farrell had intended to freshen up before heading down to Anthony's. He telephoned Liz at the restaurant to tell her he was all right and would be in shortly. She said the Fournier girl had been trying to reach him. Farrell had hardly hung up when he got a call from "Mr. Whitehead," demanding a recount of his session with "numero uno." Stabler's reaction was disappointing; the detective's enthusiasm, if any, remained closely guarded. Farrell considered telling him about the overheard phone conversation, but decided to hell with it.

He made himself a sandwich, then dialed Alison's Manhattan apartment; there was no answer. He considered trying her home on Long Island, but discarded that notion for fear of running afoul of her father. Switching on a soft-music FM station, he stretched out on the living room couch, just for a few minutes.

". . . Tony. Tony!" A hand was tugging at his shoulder. He opened his eyes and looked about dazedly. "Telephone," Liz said, "Mr. Blackman."

He looked up at her. "You just get home?" he asked thickly.

"Hardly," she said. "It's eight A.M. Did you hear me? Mr. Blackman is calling you."

He got up and shuffled toward the kitchen.

"Sorry to wake you." Roy Thomas sounded chipper. "What are your plans this morning?"

Farrell tried to clear away the fog. "Can't think of anything special."

"Well, get yourself together," Thomas said. "We're going to discuss Phase Two. Is Liz busy?"

"I don't know. Probably not. Why?"

"She can come with you. I want you to meet me at the Cross County Shopping Center in Yonkers. You know where that is?"

"Sure."

"Take Liz shopping. Drop her at Wanamaker's, then you drive up to the Red Coach Grill. Go in and have a cup of coffee. Then, after about ten minutes, go back outside and sit in the car. Bring a newspaper to read."

"What time do we do this?" asked Farrell.

"How about ten-fifteen?"

"Sure."

Thomas said, "Now listen: Wait for me no more than fifteen minutes. If I *don't* show by then, something's come up and we scrub the meet. Drive back to Wanamaker's and hunt up Liz and head home. I'll contact you later."

Liz was standing in the kitchen doorway. Farrell sighed wearily and said: "Want to go shopping up in Westchester?"

"I hadn't planned on it," she said, "but sure."

He looked at her with regret. "I'm sorry, baby. I'd rather not be dragging you into this. . . ."

She came over and kissed him. "Hey, I'm with you —remember?"

"Yeah. Your tough luck." He frowned. "Well, we've got just over an hour to get moving. You want to make some coffee while I shower?"

He was luxuriating in the hot streams of water, his face turned up into it, eyes closed, when the glass door to the stall opened and closed and she stepped in next to him. She took the soap from him and began to lather his chest. "It'll take a while for the coffee," she said. She was soaping his stomach, sliding down to where he was already erect. Gently she massaged him there. Looking up, she said, "We haven't time for separate showers," and handed him the soap.

He washed her body in the same way. And then they were

together, and he lifted her, and she wrapped her legs around him.

They drove up the FDR Drive to the bridge and over onto the Major Deegan Expressway north, past Yankee Stadium, along the bank of the Harlem River up through the Bronx, Farrell relating to Liz what had transpired the day before and how he assessed his prospects in the treacherous enterprise as of last count. They got off the highway just past Yonkers Raceway, and a few minutes after ten turned into the sprawling Cross County Shopping Center.

In front of the John Wanamaker department store, Farrell said: "Just browse. If you see anything you like, feel free. We'll meet in the coffee shop. From what he said, I shouldn't be much longer than forty-five minutes at most."

Farrell watched her disappear into the crowded mart, then drove on to the Red Coach Grill and went in and had coffee. Returning to the car, he sat back and opened the *New York Times*.

He was into the sports section when the passenger door opened and Thomas slid in alongside, laying a black attaché case on his lap. "Morning, partner."

"Partner, eh? I'm coming up in the world pretty fast."

"Faster than most. If you can get Ed Stabler to think positive, you've got to be doing something right."

"Him? On the phone last night he was nothing but grunts and growls."

"That's just the way he is. Look," Thomas said, snapping open the latches on the black case. Inside was a tape recorder. "Our boss, the man running this case, wants everything you can give us about the Giant and his operations." He clicked on the machine, which had a self-contained mike. "So let's go for it."

Farrell sank lower into the car seat, feeling heavily laden. This part he did not like; it was demeaning, distasteful; spying was one thing, matching wits for survival, cataloguing the iniquities of those he was forced to betray—even *them*—was something else, somehow ugly and contemptible. If only there were some other way. . . . But he was hooked, committed. Them or him. He let out a long, resigned breath and began.

Slowly, haltingly, groping back through his memory of dealings related to the Giant and his organization . . . for half an hour Farrell talked, in flat, deliberate tones, interrupted only occasionally by specific questions from Thomas.

He lit a cigarette and inhaled deeply and sat quiet at last, gazing out the car window, feeling a little sick with himself, not only for his recitation but for the jarring recognition it had brought to him of the filth he had allowed himself to become part of.

Thomas waited a moment, then snapped the attaché case shut. "Okay, that's not bad," he said. "We'll have to run through it again later for the boss—for the formal depositions. Having done it once, maybe it'll jog your memory even more."

Farrell looked at him. "You'll never convict them on this kind of crap. Especially *him*."

"No, this is just framework. To lock up this crowd, we've got to fill it out and top it off. Nail them with something specific—something *solid*, with no cracks in it.

"The big reason nobody's been able to touch him," Thomas went on, "is that he's been so careful not to expose himself personally to actual criminal acts. He's like the old dons, maybe even wiser than a lot of them: *Nothing* ever seems to go through his hands directly; he's shielded by layer after layer of understudies. Some of *them* may go down, but never any near enough to the big man to bring him down with them.

"But nobody is perfect, as my partner is fond of saying. There have got to be times, certain deals, where top dollar and intricate negotiations are involved, when Aaron Luke Brothers *does* dirty his own hands. No crook in the world has ever been able to avoid it at one time or another. And that's what you've got to smell out for us, and then cue us so we can grab him, all of them, up to their elbows in shit. . . ."

"What *kind* of shit?"

Thomas shrugged. "We're not particular. The smellier the better. You just dig it up for us."

"Sweet," grunted Farrell. "The trouble is, I don't know of anything hot in the works right now—not the kind of thing you're talking about."

"It'll come."

Farrell was silent for a moment. "I came across something last night that could be of interest."

"Don't leave me in suspense. Let's have it!"

Farrell told him about voices he'd heard on the Giant's extension.

"That is interesting," the other commented, making notes. "A hospital payroll, eh? It might be to finance something they've got coming up. The cops should be glad to hear about it."

"Whoever you give it to," Farrell urged him, "just be sure you don't say where you got it."

"Don't worry. I'll let Ed handle it. He knows how to deal with the department. Okay, I guess that's it for now then," Thomas said. "You have our number. I forgot to mention before, if you get a recording when you call, don't sweat it. Just give your message straight out, like you were talking to one of us. It's on scramble, and we're the only ones can unscramble it."

"I already tried, and got the machine." Farrell squinted at him. "What's that all about?"

The agent smiled. "Casualty Mutual Insurance. Cute, huh? Considering the line we're in? Stabler's idea. He has his moments." Thomas glanced at his watch. "It's almost eleven. Drop me around the side of the restaurant and go pick up Liz."

Farrell backed out of the space and maneuvered the Audi through the aisles of parked vehicles. "Are you married?" he asked abruptly.

"Yes, why?"

"How does your wife take all this—what you do?"

"Well, she doesn't know much about what I do—it's better that way. In general, though, we have our ups and downs. I guess it can be rough—the constant uncertainty. Why, are you getting trouble from Liz?"

"Not trouble. Uncertainty, yes. I'm not sure how much of this she'll be able to take." He looked at Thomas. "I wonder how *their* women hold up—Brothers, and Cheech?"

"Forget it," said Thomas. "*Their* women are completely different."

"I guess." As Farrell swung the car around the Red Coach he thought of something else: "I didn't tell you about the chick with Brothers when I got there last night." He whistled appreciatively.

"One of his harem?"

"Not this one—although I think it's crossed his mind. Pure silk. Sexy, cool, beautiful dresser—expensive clingy outfit, Gucci boots—the whole class number, but just oozing animal energy. Aaron's got fine taste."

"What was she doing there? Was he buying?"

"He might have been, in his way. But she left soon after I came." Farrell braked the Audi alongside the restaurant. "An old playmate from Atlanta, he said. Evidently a fashion designer. She had Brothers all pumped up about some new line he said was just the thing he was looking for to expand his clothing business—that operation he's got up in The Bronx? The way he was talking he plans to keep her around awhile. Millie Dubois was her name."

Thomas had opened the car door, and Farrell turned to him. The agent looked like he had just been slapped across the face.

11

Ed Stabler did not personally communicate Farrell's tip about an imminent hospital robbery to the New York Police Department. To mask the source, as well as his own position as receiver of such information, Stabler had an old friend, a senior detective of the State Police, pass it on to a counterpart in the city's Criminal Intelligence Division: no attribution was given, only a warranty from the State Police that the informant was considered reliable. This was enough for the CID to take it seriously.

As rare as it was for police to be alerted in advance of a planned crime, they still were left with some problems. First, it was Thursday, and the projected stickup was to be early Friday. Which Friday had not been specified, but they had to operate on the assumption that it would be the next day. Second, they didn't know exactly *where* the target hospital was located; but, as the information suggested the holdup men were likely to be blacks, it seemed a reasonable conjecture that it was in an urban location—where a group of blacks loitering might not be conspicuous. There were scores of private and public medical facilities in the five boroughs. Each would have to be checked —in less than a day's time—to pinpoint which customarily had payroll delivered on Fridays between 6:00 and 7:00 A.M.

The investigators were luckier than they could have hoped. Only two hospitals in the entire city were found to have regular payroll delivery at that hour on Friday: The Mount Sinai

Medical Center on Fifth Avenue at 100th Street, and the sprawling Bronx Municipal Hospital on Pelham Parkway and Eastchester Road. Brinks armored trucks serviced both hospitals, bringing the week's payroll to Bronx Municipal between 6:30 and 7:00 A.M. each Friday and to Mount Sinai "precisely at seven" a spokesman there said. The Bronx facility expected a shipment of $250,000, higher than usual because of a recent wage settlement; Mount Sinai would not disclose precise figures except to say that the amount to be delivered was "substantial."

Emergency security plans were quickly drawn up and teams of ten detectives each assigned to the respective hospitals from 4:00 A.M. on Friday. A quarter of a million dollars seemed a nice round sum to get out early for.

Still unable to raise Alison Fournier at her flat in Manhattan, Farrell finally tried her family home on Long Island. The voice that came on the phone was so hushed and taut, shrunken, that he wasn't sure he'd gotten the right number: "Yes? Who is it?"

"Alison?"

There was an uncertain pause. "Tony . . . ?"

"Are you all right? I hardly recognized your voice."

"I've been trying to reach you," she said, her voice now full in his ear, urgent and husky, as though she didn't want anyone else to hear. "I must talk to you."

"I know. I'm sorry, it's been kind of a scramble. What—?"

"Not on the phone," she said quickly. "Can I come by the restaurant?"

"Any time. Just take it easy. Don't let it get you."

She's coming unglued, Farrell thought, putting down the phone. Was it too late to put the pieces back together? A flush of new guilt swept him.

It was late afternoon and Farrell was at his favorite rear table leafing through paperwork when she came in. He could hardly have expected the appearance she presented. In only a few days her cheeks had become hollow and pale, her normally well-brushed flowing hair unkempt; she had a hounded, almost furtive look. Farrell rose to meet her and put a friendly arm around her waist. "Let's go in the office. Are you hungry? You want a drink?"

Alison shook her head. "Nothing, thanks."

"So how's it been going?" asked Farrell when he'd closed the door behind them. From the look of her, it was clearly a gratuitous question.

"Tony," she quavered, "it's been a nightmare. My father . . . the police . . . like the Inquisition. Hammering at me all the time, to . . ." Her voice trailed off, her eyes beseeching him.

"To what?"

"To . . . tell who . . ." Alison breathed deep. "They say I've been 'used.' That they *know* somebody else was behind it, and if I tell them they'll see it goes easy for me—maybe even probation. Otherwise . . ." She looked hopeless.

"That rough, eh?"

"My father, he's the worst. It's like *he's* been attacked!" She reached out and clasped his hand. "Tony, what should I do?"

He regarded her, thinking of how to spell it out for her without seeming callous, wondering if he could be direct and gentle at the same time. "Look," he began, giving her hand a squeeze, "they've got you scared, and they're clanking the chains. Frankly, I don't think it will go to a trial. Your daddy, if you'll excuse me, would see to that—to spare *him* the exposure. They'd accept a quiet guilty plea."

She swallowed but said nothing.

"All right," Farrell went on, "what then? I think you'd stand a good chance of leniency—especially if the judge is in the same political crowd as your father, which could well be the case. Your age, background, a first offense—you might even get a suspended sentence. And that would *still* leave them with somebody to come down heavy on: Gerard."

Alison's eyes widened. "I'd almost forgotten him. But why would he take that? Wouldn't he talk?"

"Gerard will take it." He leaned toward her intently.

"Look, I'm not going to pull any punches with you. Gerard is no innocent. Nor am I. He's connected in certain areas, and so am I. Gerard won't say anything because that could seriously inconvenience certain people, and they're the kind who can be very unforgiving about being inconvenienced. . . ."

She stared at him.

"I don't mean to frighten you, but if there *was* an investigation involving me, and some of their interests got messed up, they might decide to take steps." He studied her. "The last thing I want is for anything to happen to you." He raised a hand and lightly fingered her tangled hair. "Do you follow, Alison?"

They were close, and her aroma was musky sweet. It wrenched his heart. If only he could keep her from harm. He kissed her cheek and gently pulled her to her feet.

Liz was at the end of the bar with Pete when they came out of the office, and she watched them silently as he escorted Alison through the restaurant. At the car, he asked her: "Where to now?"

"To the apartment. Maybe I'll sleep over. Try to sort everything out." She looked blank, drained.

With a wan smile, she turned her face up to him and kissed him lightly. "I'm sorry, Tony," she said. Then she was gone. He stood at the curb and watched as she drove off. Then he joined Liz at the bar.

"The kid's in some muddle. I still don't know which way she'll go." He took her arm. "Come on inside."

Pete watched them into the office. Then he moved to the telephone behind the bar and, eyes on the closed door, dialed a number. "Is Mr. Donato there?" he said.

Farrell rang Cheech later that afternoon, saying he'd had an interesting conversation with "the girl" and wanted to fill him in. He tried to sound enthusiastic. Cheech said sure: they could meet that night up at the Royale on Cheech's rounds, say around eleven. As a matter of fact, Cheech had something he wanted to talk to Farrell about, too.

The Club Royale was one of a number of peripheral estab-
lishments, from the quasi-legitimate to the outright illicit, in
which Cheech had varying degrees of vested interest.

It was the classiest of three covert gambling spots, located in
a stately old townhouse on East 74th Street just off Fifth
Avenue. The club itself occupied the second and third floors
—the first floor kept unused so as not to attract attention from
the street—and the decor and furnishings were a tasteful mix of
traditional richness. It drew a faithful clientele of well-heeled
patrons, from business-executive types to "beautiful people" of
the international jet set.

Admission was not easy, requiring personal references
either from other patrons known to the management or from
someone connected with the management itself. Steely-eyed
doorkeepers, well-groomed and polite but unyielding, scrutinized all newcomers and turned away any who could not supply
acceptable credentials. For those who were admitted, though,
the Royale provided only deluxe hospitality. New customers
were welcomed with three free chips. Attractive, gracious
hostesses circulated, offering liquor, soft drinks, coffee, cigarettes; each room had a well-stocked buffet of hot and cold hors
d'oeuvres, meats and simmering chafing dishes. Guests were
encouraged to post their own betting and credit limits, which
the house would strictly enforce so as to minimize problems
growing out of excessive individual losses. Club employees were
available as escorts to winners from the time they left the
premises until they reached their cars or were safely in waiting
limousines or cabs.

When Farrell got to the club at a little past eleven, he was
advised that Cheech had already come in and, as was his
custom, gone straight to the accounting office on the third floor
to check the take for the night so far. While waiting, Farrell
beckoned to a pretty young hostess wearing billowy haremlike
pajamas of silk and ordered a scotch; then, from a vantage
point at one end of the room, he idly scanned the play.

Farrell's gaze drifted to one blackjack table where four

women played, all fashionably coiffed and glittering with jewelry. One, a middle-aged blond, well turned out though not particularly attractive, seemed to have become the center of attention. As Farrell watched the deal with interest, one of the club's security men came alongside and whispered, "That one's down about forty-five hundred. She's only good for five. After this play, we might have to shut her off."

She was dealt a trey, a six, another trey—twelve points. The dealer impassively produced sixteen, with the hole card down. She said "Hit." A deuce—fourteen. A film of moisture broke out on her forehead, and she dabbed at it with a tissue. "My husband will *kill* me," she said with a nervous laugh, looking about at the others, imploring encouragement. After a breathless moment of indecision, she slapped the table with her palm for another card. The dealer flipped out an eight.

The knot of people moaned. The man beside Farrell signaled the dealer with a finger across his throat.

"Let's go, let's go," demanded the distraught woman at the table. "I'm in again. Give me another chance—"

"I'm sorry, ma'am," said the dealer quietly, looking from her to the security man behind her as he reshuffled the decks. "You're over your limit."

"*Limit?* I don't care about limits!" Feverish, she screeched: "I can afford *twice* this much! You've got to give me a chance to win my money back! My husband—"

"I'm sorry, ma'am," the dealer repeated, holding onto the cards. "You'll have to give way to another player. If you'd care to speak to the manager—?"

"Give way?" she cried, half rising. "I'll talk to the manager, all right!" With that, she reached across and, with a sudden thrust of her arm, swept chips and a handful of the cards from the table.

The security man leaped forward to restrain her. Grabbing her roughly, he started to wrestle her from the room.

"Edgar!" she screamed. "Eddie!"

Farrell took two strides and got a hand on the security man's arm. "Hold it! Not so rough."

The man spun around, eyes blazing. "Who the hell—?"

Farrell stared him down. "Just take it easy." Farrell dislodged the man's grip on the blond, then took gentle but firm hold of her arm himself.

There was a sudden flurry behind him, then a man's arm was thrown around Farrell's neck. "Get your filthy hands off my wife!"

Farrell whipped his right elbow back as hard as he could into the man's ribcage and heard a pained "Ooof!" In a continuous motion he spun and stamped viciously on one of the man's black tasseled slip-ons. Farrell braced himself for a new attack. Then, staring at the man, his muscles relaxed and he broke into a broad smile. It was Edgar Stelman, his old public relations chief! Every cloud did have a silver lining.

Stelman looked up at his tormentor, and his mouth dropped open in astonishment. "*You!*" he cried.

"I never thought of you as physical, Edgar," Farrell said lightly.

"You!" Stelman repeated.

Farrell turned from him to the gawking spectators gathered about them. "It's all right, ladies and gentlemen," he called, "just a little misunderstanding." The patrons, buzzing, began to drift away, and Farrell returned his attention to the Stelmans.

"All right now, Edgar," he said, "suppose you just collect yourselves and call it a night."

"Who the hell are you to—?" demanded Stelman. "I want to speak to the management!"

"I represent the management," Farrell replied.

"Then I'll have your job!" the other sputtered.

"You had my job once before, Edgar. And I never did thank you. Now I'll return the favor, by inviting you and your" —Farrell cocked an eye toward Stelman's wife—"your lady to leave the club quietly before anybody becomes impatient." He glanced meaningfully around at the hard-faced security men looking on.

Livid but impotent, the couple were escorted to the stairs. Farrell watched them down. He hadn't felt so pleased with himself in a long time. He looked about for a hostess and a soft hand was on his arm. He turned to find Randi Hollander smiling at him, her eyes bright.

"Honey, you were *super!*" she gushed. Her fingers squeezed his bicep sensually. "So strong! I didn't know you were such a tiger!"

Randi looked sensational—maybe a shade too much so. She was wearing a clingy knit dress that accentuated every line of her extraordinary body and set off her lustrous red hair like a burst of flame. She was Cheech's favorite playmate, and Farrell was reasonably sure she was a nympho. He remembered the first time he'd met her. Cheech had brought her into Anthony's late one night, taking a booth in a candle-lit corner, and when Farrell came around to say hello he could tell right away that she was giving Cheech a hand job under the table. She wasn't at all flustered by Farrell's appearance. Smiling at him as though it was a sunny day in the park, she didn't miss a beat.

"And a *hungry* tiger," Randi smiled wickedly.

Farrell realized his eyes had been absorbed by the heave of her breasts against the knit. He looked up and grinned. "I confess, you are delicious to look at."

"Good enough to eat?" she purred. Her fingers played on the inside of his arm, giving him goose bumps. "Why don't we have dinner together some time?"

"Let's keep it open," he said. He wasn't about to mess with Cheech's woman. "You want anything—to drink, I mean?" He smiled.

She asked for a brandy alexander. When the hostess left, Randi entwined her arm in his again, moving against him, but Farrell eased out of contact. "Let's cool it," he said quietly. "I don't think it's smart playing footsie in this place, do you?"

"Nobody's watching," she pouted. "They're all gambling. Don't *you* ever gamble?"

"Only when I like the odds. And right now—Listen, Cheech said he had something to tell me tonight. Any idea what?"

She shrugged. "He never tells me anything." Looking across the room, she said: "Ask him yourself. Here he comes."

Cheech bounded down the stairs from the third floor. He spotted them and hurried over. "Hey, what happened before?" he asked Farrell, his brow furrowed.

Farrell described the incident, not bothering to explain the identities of the offenders.

"Well . . . I guess you handled it okay," said Cheech, considering. "It just ain't good to have no scenes in a place like this, you know? As long as you got them out quick. . . . Look, let's go in the back, sit down and have a talk."

They walked through the room to a quiet corner where a settee and wing chairs were arranged around a Sheraton coffee table. "Okay," Cheech said to Farrell, "gimme what you got first."

Farrell blinked from him to Randi and back.

"Aw, Randi's all right," Cheech said. He smirked. "She don't care about nothin'. Except one thing—right, toots?" He turned and pinched her breast, hard.

"Ow!" she yipped, recoiling. "You hurt, honey!"

"Come on, baby, that wasn't nothin'. Don't get sore."

"I *am* sore," she complained, pulling away from him.

"Well, go take a walk, then!" Cheech growled. "Lose yourself in the crapper."

"I just came from there!" Randi protested.

"Well, go back. We got serious things here."

She flounced off, hurling "Bastard!" back at him.

"Cunt," muttered Cheech after her. But then he grinned. "But what tail! Fucks like a mink. Okay, so?"

They took a table and Farrell began. "I had a long talk today with Alison Fournier. I gave her the facts of life, by the numbers. I think she got the picture."

"Yeah?" Cheech regarded him in that hooded-eye manner of his that meant he was calculating. "Did you get it in writin'?"

"She's not stupid. A little scared maybe, but not blind."

Cheech looked thoughtful. "Okay. It's your ass. You wanna let it ride, I ain't gonna argue with you."

Farrell studied him. While relieved by Cheech's easy accommodation, he'd hardly expected the matter to be settled without heat. Was he really persuaded that Alison could be written off as a threat to them? Or was the wily sonofabitch up to something else?

"What else you got?" asked Cheech.

"That's it."

"Good. 'Cause I don't want nothin' worryin' you the next week or so. I'm goin' out of town, and I want you to look after the business for me. Okay?"

Farrell raised an eyebrow. "Sure. Where are you going?"

"South."

"Catching some rays?"

"Some of that too, maybe. But it ain't a vacation." Cheech leaned forward and lowered his voice. "It's a deal. Maybe the biggest yet. The big guy put it together and I'm settin' it up. If it comes off like it's laid out—" He put the tips of his fingers together and waggled his hand. "*Mamma mia!*"

Farrell's pulse raced. "What is it, for Chrissake?"

Cheech glanced cautiously about before bending closer. "Coke. Not nickel-and-dime stuff, like we been into. We're gonna move in on the spics and show 'em how to do it!"

Farrell blew out a silent whistle. "When are you leaving?" Farrell asked.

"Tomorrow. And I'm takin' Goomba with me. So I need somebody around I can trust." Cheech reached into his jacket pocket and handed Farrell a folded sheet of lined yellow paper. "Here's a list of all the people you should be in touch with. Watch nobody fucks off on me. When I get back, you can buy yourself the Empire State Buildin'."

"How can I reach you if I have to?" Farrell hoped he wasn't

pressing too hard, but Cheech's itinerary could be meaningful.

Cheech mulled it over. "I'll be on the move pretty much. In and out of some of the islands. I can't give you none of the details yet. The less people knows what's goin' on right now, the less chance of anything gettin' screwed up. When it's all set to go, then you'll get the word."

"But still, if there's any problems I can't handle while you're gone—"

"Don't let there *be* no problems," Cheech snapped. Then he hesitated. "You could check in with Randi. I might give her a call to see how things are. She's got the only phone I ain't sure is hot."

Maybe not now, Farrell thought. "Okay then," he said. "Well . . . good luck. I'll mind the store as best I can."

Farrell saw Cheech's eyes squint beyond him, and he turned to watch the remarkable figure of Randi undulate across the room toward them, drawing the attention of many at the tables. It took a powerful force to distract dedicated gamblers at play.

"Here comes the mink," Cheech said, eyes glittering.

Farrell was struck by one more thought. "What about the Giant? Am I supposed to know anything about this?" he asked quickly.

"Naw, let him tell you when he's ready. You know how he likes to make a big deal out of everything."

Cheech rose, arms spread wide. "Baby doll! I thought you fell in!"

By 6:30 Friday morning, the restlessness of the ten detectives staked out around the Bronx Municipal Hospital had quickened to a fine edge of alertness.

They'd arrived in the pre-dawn darkness and unobtrusively taken up their positions—some dressed in the starched white of hospital personnel, some in the blue-helmeted work clothes of a Con Edison maintenance crew.

At 6:15, an automobile appeared cruising slowly past the hospital carrying four men including the driver, all blacks. It circled the building and returned at the same deliberate pace, this time trailed closely by a second car with only a driver. As the detectives watched from their borrowed ambulance and Con Ed utility van, walkie-talkies relayed the alert.

The second auto stopped just beyond the main entrance to the hospital, the driver remaining in place while the other vehicle made a third circuit around the facility. Finally, at 6:45 that car braked to a halt at a pavilion at the side of the main building. The three passengers, each wearing medical green, got out and slipped through a door into the pavilion; the driver stayed put at the wheel. Security information specified that that entrance was locked at all times, indicating that the holdup men had help on the inside.

Once they were inside, the stakeout team moved in quick, successive thrusts; three officers pounced on the car in front of the hospital, and the driver was hustled inside the Con Ed van. Moments later the other driver was subdued almost as quickly by a second group, and locked inside the ambulance. Then the detectives entered the hospital in three waves—through the main entrance, the pavilion door, and a third entrance on the far side of the building. From separate corridors, they converged on the basement office containing the vault to which the Brink's delivery was expected momentarily.

Inside, the bandits had a badly frightened custodian covered with pistols. They were relaxed, cocky; their plan had gone like clockwork.

The policemen, eight of them, in their whites and blue jeans, walked in with weapons drawn and told them the clock had stopped. The gunmen surrendered without any resistance.

When the Brink's truck rolled up to the hospital minutes later, the messenger and armed guard who alighted carrying the $250,000 payroll thought nothing of a Con Edison truck and an ambulance pulling away one behind the other. Con Ed never slept.

12

When Abou Jamal got the news about the hospital, he was enraged. The motherfuckers were planted there, just waiting for somebody to show up! They had to have gotten word in advance. From somebody who knew what was going down and where and when. The Giant would demand retribution, no matter how long it took. It wasn't just that that quarter of a million was meant to help finance the big new coke deal; an example had to be set. Whoever had finked had to pay the maximum price.

Roy Thomas felt as though he'd been led into a maze of distorting mirrors and stranded there to find his own way out. When Tony Farrell had told him about Camille with Aaron Luke Brothers, he thought he might faint. His wife, in league with the scoundrel that he'd dedicated himself these long months past to destroying? The irony, in its suddenness, had been very nearly overwhelming. "In league" was no doubt imprecise and unfair to Camille—that was Thomas's one consolation. There was no question in his mind but that she was unaware of the notoriety of her proposed benefactor. Reflecting on her remarks over dinner about this promising new connection (which, damn him, he'd barely listened to at the time), Thomas concluded that her manner had projected only innocent enthusiasm. It was a golden career opportunity waiting to be seized.

He dared not warn her about this man. Any abrupt

withdrawal from cooperation with Brothers would be bound to excite suspicion in him; and his discovery of her true position could provoke harsh defensive action. The only course left to him was to let the charade be played out as contrived—and pray to God that he could keep Camille untouched by the time it ended.

Thomas could not stop wondering just what their actual relationship amounted to. They'd known one another in Atlanta, evidently, but she'd never talked of him before. (In fact, he realized, she had yet to mention her wealthy friend's name to him.) That she'd not spoken of him could mean either they'd been no more than casual acquaintances, or that they'd had something on together once. But if the latter were the case, would she have told him about their meeting so openly? Thomas kept going back to Farrell's description of Brothers's open admiration for her, and of his oblique references to exciting future plans for the two of them.

Cheech's revelation about major expansion into the cocaine trade had excited Farrell. And it had provoked an intense debate. There could be a *fortune* to be made under the auspices of an organization like the Giant's! Should he just turn his back on what could be the chance—maybe his last—of a lifetime? If he could get in a few deals, without letting on to the cops, he could squirrel away a pile of bucks for Liz and himself, and then— Then *what?* Cut out somewhere and hole up? The odds were long against. *Everybody* would be looking for him. All right, but what if he pocketed a nest egg, *then* tipped the cops about what was going on—what he'd just "stumbled across"? If he could cover his tracks, it would be like he still was keeping his bargain with them, but he'd have the stash too. But if they found out . . . he'd be finished, on both sides. Was it worth that big a gamble? He guessed not. . . .

He'd bounced this back and forth for a couple of hours after leaving Cheech at the Club Royale, before finally putting in the call he had to make.

"Casualty Mutual," the mellifluous programmed voice responded. "No one is in the office at this time . . ."

Farrell waited out the standard message and at the beep said tersely: "The proposition you've been sitting on, the *big* one, looks like it's in the oven. Got that?" There was no sound at the other end. He cradled the instrument.

Ed Stabler rang the apartment a little after eight the next morning. Farrell, who had not slept well, was in the kitchen sipping coffee.

"You got the message?" he asked.

"Just now. How big *is* it?"

"It sounds like a super operation—the kind of thing you've been looking for."

"And numero uno's involved?"

"From the top, the way I get it." Farrell hesitated. "Should we be doing this on the phone?"

"Maybe not. What's your schedule?"

"I'll be here for a while."

"Okay. Stay put," ordered Stabler. "We'll get back to you." He clicked off.

Farrell went upstairs, taking care not to disturb Liz, and showered, shaved and dressed. He was back down in the living room, restlessly anticipating a return call, when the doorbell startled him. He padded to the door and squinted through the peephole. "Jesus H. Christ!" he swore. Hurriedly he unlatched the door.

It was Roy Thomas. "Good morning," he said pleasantly, stepping inside.

"For God's sake, you had to come *here*?"

"It sounded important," Thomas said. "This seemed the safest place in a hurry."

"Safe! Why not Macy's window?"

"Relax. It's a big apartment building, anybody can come and go. Besides, we have a watchdog outside—Ed."

Farrell shook his head doubtfully. "Well, sit down. You want coffee or anything?"

"No, thanks." Thomas smiled. "Just the facts."

Farrell related tersely what Cheech had told him of the ambitious aim to corner the booming cocaine market. He watched Thomas's eyes light up.

"But that's all I've got so far," concluded Farrell, "just the bare outline. They're keeping the lid on tight until Cheech wraps up the preliminaries, I guess."

"It's enough to keep the heat on downtown," said Thomas. He looked thoughtful. "I sure would love to know where he's going. Think: He didn't give you any more specific clue?"

"Only what I said. I make it the Caribbean—but where?"

"And he was leaving today? Maybe there's still time to spot him at the airport. For the Caribbean, he'd have to leave from JFK."

"If Cheech sticks to form, he won't be going anywhere before noon. But you've got a mess of ground to cover out there. How many different airlines do you suppose fly to the Caribbean? Which terminals would you stake out?"

"Good point," conceded Thomas. "We *don't* have all that much manpower available. If we could get a team on his house before he goes, tail him from there. . . ." The agent was full of electricity. "You know, with a little luck this might be the first time we'll be able to track one of their major operations from the start right up to the payoff! There's no question in your mind that the Giant himself is running this show?"

"Not from what Cheech said."

Thomas turned grave. "Still think you can cut it?"

"Suddenly I've got a choice?"

"We told you up front: You've *always* had a choice."

"Yeah." Farrell brooded. "Listen, when this gets down to the short hairs, it could get *very* hairy. If they ever start getting ideas—I think I ought to have something to protect myself."

"A gun?" Thomas considered. "I don't know. That could be more dangerous than protective. I'll take it up with the boss." He rose. "Anything else now?"

"Just one more thing. Cheech sort of gave me his key to the executive washroom. He wants me to run things for him while he's gone. Can you keep the cops off my—"

Farrell was interrupted by the doorbell's ring, long and insistent. "Who the hell can *that* be?"

"Maybe Ed." But Thomas unbuttoned his coat.

Farrell went to the door. "Yes?"

"Tony Farrell?" a deep muffled voice called.

"Who is it?"

"Police officers. Can we speak with you, please?"

Thomas held up a cautioning hand, and looked to the stairs behind him, raising an inquisitive eyebrow. Farrell nodded. Thomas turned and went up the stairs two at a time. Liz came out of the bedroom onto the landing, gaping at the black man hurrying up toward her. Farrell put a finger to his lips and motioned to her to show Thomas out by the second-floor exit to the corridor above. In two little steps she was at the door, fumbling with the lock. With a silent nod, Thomas went out and the door closed behind him.

"Mr. Farrell?" called the voice from outside.

He peered through the peephole. Two men, white, wearing suits. "Will you show me some identification, please?" he asked.

One of them pulled a small black case from an inside pocket and flipped it open to reveal a gold badge and an ID card with a small photograph on it. Detective. The man's face seemed familiar, Farrell thought. He unlocked the door.

"Hello, Tony," that one said with a small, crooked smile. He was burly and dark-complected. The other was leaner, fairer, and younger.

"Have we met?" asked Farrell.

"Why, sure—head-on, you might say," the man chuckled sardonically. "Lieutenant Casanova. How could you forget?"

Casanova—of course—the dick he'd brawled with outside

the Elysée! "Oh, yeah," Farrell said uneasily. "So . . . what can I do for you?"

"We just want to ask you a few questions, Tony," Casanova said. "This is Sergeant Hurley."

The detective took in the apartment appreciatively. "Nice layout," Casanova commented.

Farrell shot a look at the landing and was grateful that Liz had retreated from view. "It's home," he said.

"Anybody up there?" inquired Casanova.

Farrell bristled. "Yes. A lady."

"Not Alison Fournier, by any chance?"

"Alison Fournier?" Farrell said incredulously.

"We're looking for her," said Casanova.

"Why, what's wrong?"

"We don't know yet. She's dropped out of sight, you might say. Her daddy is worried about her."

"But I saw her just the other day."

"We know," said Casanova. "That's why we're here. Far as we can tell, you're the last one talked to her. Fournier had a P.I. on her. Tailed her from your place to her apartment. But then he lost her. She went in, he didn't see her come out. But she ain't there. Neither is her car." The detective peered at Farrell. "Where is she?"

"How the hell should I know?"

"Mr. Farrell," Sgt. Hurley spoke up for the first time, "this is a matter that could be more serious than you seem to realize. I'm from the district attorney's office. Miss Fournier is facing a serious felony charge. Half a key of cocaine and forty thousand dollars is no casual score. Now, suddenly, the principal is missing. If she's decided to skip . . . or if anybody is harboring her . . . it is a major violation and will go down hard on whoever might be involved. Do you understand that?"

Half a key of cocaine and forty thousand dollars . . . Farrell's mind raced to sort that out. Either the guy had the numbers wrong, or somewhere between the Elysée and the police property office somebody had cut a half-kilo of marketable coke and thirty-five grand in cash to boot!

"You *do* understand what's at stake?" Hurley prodded.

"Oh . . . yeah. I was just surprised at the amount. . . ."

Casanova chortled, "You had no idea your little girl friend was such a big operator, eh, Tony? It surprises us, too. So maybe if you thought a little harder . . . ?"

Farrell settled himself. "I don't have to think any harder. All I know is what I've told you. Now, if you're through with me, gentlemen . . ." He moved toward the door.

"Through with you?" snorted Casanova. "Not by a long shot. You still got your own beef coming up, remember? At *least.* No, we'll be seeing you again, Tony boy."

Farrell opened the door without comment. Before going out, Hurley said: "Be sure to let us know if you hear from Miss Fournier. Here's my number." He handed Farrell a card.

Farrell closed the door behind them. Then he slowly climbed the stairs, and in the bedroom he and Liz held one another in close silence until they were both calm.

13

Ed Stabler was in his car, across the street and up the block with a clear view of Farrell's building entrance, when Thomas came out and rejoined him. "Did you bump into Frank Casanova in there?" Stabler asked.

"So *that's* who it was! Somebody came to the door—who was with him?"

"I didn't get a good look, but I don't think I know him. Younger guy, light hair."

"I wonder what it's about," mused Thomas. "I hope they're not about to queer our act—not *now*."

"Farrell's poop—is it good?"

"The jackpot, maybe." As Thomas summarized it, Stabler whistled in delight.

"Lov-er-ly!" he whooped. "They're finally playing our song, partner!"

"Sounds like it. Look, I've got to get to Hartnett right away. He has to put somebody on Cheech. You watch for them to come out."

From a luncheonette at the corner of Second Avenue, Thomas reached Brendan Hartnett on his private line. The prosecutor's enthusiasm was evident despite the austere office manner he affected. He was curious about the unexpected intrusion of Lt. Casanova, inasmuch as Casanova, while essentially a unit commander of the NYPD's Narcotics Division, also happened to be a member of Hartnett's own JUST task force. He wanted to look into it.

"Oh, by the way," Hartnett said. "That hospital robbery Farrell tipped Ed to? It went down this morning, up in the Bronx, and the PD was waiting for them. Five solid arrests. The CID is very impressed. They're hoping their mystery informant doesn't plan to go into any other line of business. It appears we've made a sound choice in our new employee."

"I think so," agreed Thomas. "Did you listen to the tapes I did with him?"

"Yes. He didn't seem to be holding anything back, judging by the intelligence we already had."

"I felt the same. You wanted to be sure of him before showing any of our cards . . . well, I think it's time to make your play. The stuff I got from him, without witnesses, is no good as evidence. *You* need to tap him, officially."

"I'm inclined to agree," said Hartnett thoughtfully. "We'll have to be very circumspect about where to interview him. There must be no risk of exposing the relationship."

Thomas came back to the car, and Stabler said: "They just left, drove off in an unmarked."

"Not with him?"

"Just the two of them."

Thomas returned to the phone booth and dialed the apartment. "Blackman. What'd they want?"

Farrell told him laconically. "You know who one of them was?" he concluded.

"Your friend Casanova. Who was the other one?"

"From the D.A. He gave me his card. Sergeant Vincent X. Hurley, special investigator."

"D.A.'s squad, eh?" pondered Thomas. "Don't know him. What do you think: Might the girl have gone underground?"

"It's possible. She was pretty bummed out that day. But I really didn't think she'd run."

"Damn!" exhaled Thomas. "If she *is* fugitive, it could turn a spotlight on *you*—just what we wanted to avoid."

"Something funny came out while they were here," Farrell

interjected. "And not funny ha-ha. They're telling me how serious this all could be, and Hurley points out that *half* a kilo of dope and *forty* thou is not chicken liver. And Casanova—who *knows*—let that slide right by!"

Thomas waited a beat. "Yes. So?"

"What, 'yes, so?' It was a full kilo. And seventy-five—You didn't know . . . ?"

Farrell was on his way out of the apartment when the telephone rang again. Liz called out, "Tony, it's Michael."

"I'm glad I caught you," the gruff voice greeted him. "I just had a call from an old friend of yours."

"Who's that?"

"Edgar Stelman."

"Oh, shit," Farrell breathed out.

"Oh shit is right," Michael said sternly. "What the hell was that scene all about?"

"Edgar was being his usual obnoxious self. I just set him straight." Farrell remembered it was Michael's influence that had gotten him the job with Stelman's P.R. firm. "No damages," he added.

"That's not what bothers me. What does bother me is where it happened. The Club Royale! What the hell were you doing *there?* Stelman says you acted like you owned the place."

"I drop in there now and then for a little action. I get a kick out of it."

"You do, eh? And do you know what kind of place that is?"

"You mean the gambling?" Farrell chuckled quizzically. "Well, that's what it's all about, Michael."

"I mean who runs the place."

Farrell cleared his throat.

"I'll tell you. It's one hundred percent mob! You didn't know that? What'd you think it was, the Holy Name Society's Tuesday night Bingo?"

"I never thought about it. What are you so hot about anyway?" Farrell asked defensively.

"Because of *you* playing with fire, boy! You start mixing with that crowd, one of these days you're liable to find yourself tarred with the same brush. And it's not so simple to get rid of that stigma."

Farrell didn't know what to say.

"Did you ever hear of a guy named Donato?" Michael asked.

Farrell jumped as though pricked by a live wire. "Donato? I might have heard it around."

"In the rackets from top to bottom. Strictly a lowlife, but has a hand in everything, from dope to shylocking, *and* the Royale. Let somebody like that get next to you, and you'll wind up in the gutter."

"You—you've had dealings with this Donato?" Farrell stammered, heart pounding.

"I wouldn't walk on the same side of the street with a bum like that!" spat Michael. "You don't have to know people personally. It's enough to know *about* them." He paused, and his tone turned softer: "I'm only thinking what's best for you, Tony."

"I know, Michael. I suppose I *should* be a little more careful. . . ." He wanted to change the subject. "How's Linda coming along?"

Michael sighed. "They say she's making some progress. But I don't know. It seems so slow."

"She'll come around, Michael, I know it. She's got good stuff in her, deep down. Look, I do appreciate your calling. I'll be in touch real soon, okay? And give Linda a squeeze for me."

"I will. And you remember what I told you."

"That's a promise." Farrell put down the phone. *Oh God, please don't ever let him find out!*

Brendan Hartnett had been hard-pressed, on short notice, to piece together a stakeout on Cheech Donato, but he'd managed it, and by 11:00 A.M. a pair of agents was positioned near Donato's Queens home. They were to watch for a

flamingo pink Lincoln sedan; the racketeer never went anywhere without it.

At 12:35 P.M., the garage doors rose and the pink sedan
emerged. They followed it onto the Long Island Expressway,
westbound. Approaching Exit 22, its directional tail-light
blinked on. This was the cloverleaf connecting with the Van
Wyck Expressway, the expected route south to Kennedy
Airport. But the Lincoln took the first, northbound ramp onto
the Van Wyck and proceeded in the opposite direction from
JFK! And a little farther on there was another surprise: Skirting
Shea Stadium, the pink sedan bore right on the Whitestone
Parkway and continued leisurely northeastward towards the
Whitestone Bridge and the Bronx! Then, just before the
approach to the bridge, it continued right again onto the Cross
Island Parkway, and back toward Little Neck where they'd
started. They were making a complete circle.

When the occupants of the Lincoln stepped out in front of
the Donato house, Cheech was not among them!

What Cheech had done was take simple precaution. He'd
had Goomba drive out from the city in another car, a rented
green Chevrolet, and park it on the street behind the house, a
block away, to wait for Cheech. Ten minutes later, May
Donato, with "Ice" Faccialati, Cheech's wheelman, and a
cousin of May's, Sal Fusina, a journeyman member of the local
crime family, had driven off in the Lincoln. Cheech had stayed
inside the house for another fifteen minutes. Then he'd made
his way out the back, through a neighbor's yard, to the street
behind and the green Chevy.

He and Goomba followed the same route as the Lincoln had
minutes earlier, except that at Shea Stadium they went *left* on
the Whitestone Parkway and then onto the westbound Grand
Central Parkway—to LaGuardia Airport. Parking the car in the
extended-time lot, they followed the concourse to the Eastern
Airlines waiting room. There Cheech went to the cocktail
lounge while Goomba checked their bags and picked up the

tickets (reserved the previous day by telephone in the names of "F. Torre" and "G. Franco"). By 1:30, the pair were relaxing over drinks with more than enough time to kill before their 2:00 P.M. flight to the sun.

They were already airborne by the time Brendan Hartnett, returning to his office from a Justice Department luncheon meeting, was informed of the failed surveillance. The Assistant U.S. Attorney did a slow burn. It was a personal slight: to be outmaneuvered by a cretin like Cheech!

Loosening his tie and rolling up his shirtsleeves, Hartnett summoned Roy Thomas and Ed Stabler to his inner sanctum on the double. The three of them were going to spend the rest of the afternoon, and into the night if necessary, on the phones trying to pinpoint Cheech's destination. With some industry and a generous helping of luck, maybe through some airline's passenger manifest they could locate him and still pick up his trail before he lost himself altogether.

Using the Official Airlines Guide, they narrowed their field of inquiry to those carriers serving the Caribbean from New York. The field proved not to be all that narrow: No fewer than ten airlines offered direct service to a discouragingly large selection of islands. On examination, however, the possibilities were thinned out by the presumed time of departure: early to mid-afternoon (although admittedly that was but fingers-crossed conjecture, since Cheech *could* have flown out earlier for all they really knew, or indeed he might not even have left yet). Within that time range, the number of destinations considered most likely was reduced to five: the Dominican Republic, Haiti, Jamaica, Puerto Rico, Trinidad; there were seven afternoon flights to those places on six different carriers.

What made it a gruelling exercise in patience was the standard airlines' ban against releasing passenger information to just anyone who called in, whether or not he identified himself as a certified law-enforcement officer or even a crusty federal prosecutor. One or the other would have to state his name and position and the telephone number of the United States Attorney's office; then he would wait for the airline to return the call for verification. Each return call went through one of Hartnett's secretary's phones; then generally the one making the request would have to answer corroborative questions from the airline representative before the information was transmitted.

After two hours, all their inquiries were exhausted and they'd come up with a total blank. No two men of the identities sought had booked a flight together from JFK to any of the suggested destinations. The three, weary and dejected, slouched about Hartnett's office.

"Well, if at first you don't succeed," yawned Stabler, "forget it."

"Too bad," grumbled Hartnett. "I guess we'll just have to depend on Farrell to find out the details later."

The prosecutor's interoffice phone buzzed. "Yes?" Hartnett responded curtly. Then he pressed a lit button and held out the receiver to Thomas. "Eastern Airlines," he said, lifting an eyebrow. As the FBI man took it, Hartnett flicked another switch that put the call on the speaker.

"Roy Thomas here."

"Mr. Thomas, Jack Landau, Eastern Airlines security."

Thomas remembered Landau as the one who'd taken time earlier to reminisce about his own prior twenty years as a federal agent, with the U.S. Customs Service. "Yes, sir. Have you got something for us?"

"I think maybe. After we spoke before, I decided to recheck all our reservations and manifests for the destinations you'd mentioned. And—just dumb luck, I guess—this time I noticed something curious. The thing was, it was in a place I wouldn't have expected to find it."

"How's that?"

"A two-o'clock flight out of LaGuardia, not Kennedy."

"LaGuardia? You don't fly to the Caribbean from there, do you?"

"No. This was a nonstop to Miami. But what caught my eye was this party of two with Italian-sounding names, late reservations, who were booked through *via* Miami to San Juan, Puerto Rico, on Pan Am. Our people made the forwarding reservations for them, that's why it was on this sheet. Now, it struck me as odd anybody should go to San Juan that way, because we've got a couple of direct afternoon flights out of JFK, and so does American. . . ."

"Maybe they had business in Miami first," suggested Thomas politely.

"I thought of that. But if that was so, they sure didn't give themselves much leeway. Our flight gets into Miami around four-forty, and the Pan Am departure is scheduled for six! See what I mean?"

Thomas grew more interested. "What are their names?"

"Not the ones you gave me. A 'Torre' and a 'Franco.' Anyhow, I looked into it a little further, and I think we just may have hit paydirt!" By the rising tone of excitement in the man's voice they could tell he was savoring this account of his detective work. He was a government agent again. "The reservations were made by phone in New York City just yesterday. The tickets were picked up at LaGuardia today not long before departure, and—this is interesting—paid for in cash! They were booked first-class all the way, so we're talking about well over five hundred clams shelled out. That's unusual in itself these days; for such large amounts we usually get credit cards or checks . . ."

"I understand," Thomas prodded. "Go on."

"Well, I got to the agent at LaGuardia who wrote up these tickets, and she gave me an ID—partial, anyway—of one of the two. He'd be hard to forget, she says: a great hulk of a guy, Caucasian, maybe six-foot-six and built like a mountain with a face to match . . ."

Thomas broke into a smile, to Hartnett and Stabler his mouth silently forming the word *Goomba*.

". . . and if that wasn't enough," Landau went on, "paying for the tickets he pulls out a roll that could've gagged an alligator, she says. Never saw anything like it: peeling off fifties and hundreds like picking lint out of his pocket!"

"Which one was this," asked Thomas, " 'Torre' or 'Franco'?"

"He didn't say. Just took the tickets and left. And she never did see the other one."

"Did you check with the people at the security checkpoint, or at the boarding gate?"

"I did," Landau said, a tinge of disappointment entering his tone, "but I couldn't really get any eyeballs there. They see so many people coming and going all the time, thousands a day, it gets so they don't notice anybody in particular—unless there's some kind of trouble, of course. The best I got was there *might* have been two men of those descriptions who boarded that flight. What I did do, though," he added quickly, "was telex Miami to have the flight attendants contact me as soon as the aircraft disembarks there. *They* certainly should be able to confirm the IDs, especially in first-class."

"Good thinking. Let us know the minute you hear back," Thomas said. He considered a moment. "When reservations are taken by telephone, doesn't the airline normally ask the caller to give a return phone number, where he can be reached in case of cancellation or some other problem?"

"That's right. I didn't think of that. I'll try to dig it out and get back to you."

It was almost 4:30 P.M. The New York-to-Miami plane would be landing in another ten or fifteen minutes, so there was not enough time to arrange coverage of the arrival there. And it was likely to be another twenty minutes to a half-hour after that before Landau's flight attendants could get to a phone and attest that passengers "Torre" and "Franco" in fact matched the descriptions of Cheech and Goomba. While Thomas and Stabler prowled the office fretfully, Hartnett put in a call to Miami to set up surveillance of the Pan Am aircraft bound for San Juan, pending verification of the subjects.

At 5:10, Landau reported back. He was excited. The Eastern crew's descriptions of the two men seemed to fit.

Hopefully, Thomas asked, "How about that phone number?"

Landau gave him the number of a Queens exchange.

It was all the FBI agent could do not to whoop. Instead, grinning, he said: "Mr. Landau, you've been a great help. We'll take it from here."

"I'm sure happy if I contributed," the airlines man said. "After all my years in the service . . ."

"Of course. It's a lifetime experience," Thomas concurred, winking at the others.

When Thomas had hung up, the three in the office leaped to their feet and danced one another joyously around the office.

Stabler summed up their common wonder: "I'll never get over how these wise guys, with all their smarts, can be so fucking dumb sometimes!"

The number left with Eastern they practically knew by heart. It was Cheech Donato's home telephone.

"Too much funny goin' on all at once," Abou Jamal said in the mirror to Aaron Luke Brothers. "It give me the itch."

The Giant, solitary in the rear seat of the Imperial, only hmmmm'd distractedly.

They were returning to Manhattan from Brooklyn, where Brothers had just settled a most favorable contract with a consortium of buyers from local specialty-food markets to supply them kosher meats at "discount" prices. (Since kosher foodstuffs commonly were priced, even at the wholesale level, on a par with or above comparable non-dietary products, cornering a significant portion of this market promised appreciably lucrative returns.) It had been no simple enterprise, requiring a carefully orchestrated campaign of intimidation and sabotage of competitive meat packers—including certain calculated personal violence, and even selected introduction of unsanitary materials amongst some competitors' shipments, the resultant chain of outrage among retailers doing much to clear the path for Brothers' company to step in unchallenged. And, since many, if not most, of these buyers had never before considered, much less experienced, procuring kosher from a *schwarze* purveyor, it had also taken the influence and stature of Brothers' versatile attorney, Arnold Weissberg, to seal the deal, along with his presence of mind to award an accommodating rabbi a generous honorarium.

So, with Brothers' plant—a sprawling, one-story stone-block structure in Brooklyn's decayed Williamsburg section, which previously had turned a steady but comparatively modest profit out of processed meats of indeterminate Italian suggestion—already geared to convert to all-out Jewish, the Giant should have been at ease, relishing his latest triumph. But the savor had been muted by these disagreeable considerations from other spheres, which his lieutenant was alluding to. Even the crowning touch, which he had anticipated with ironical whimsy, of concluding the negotiations on a Saturday—the Hebrew Sabbath—seemed to have fallen flat.

Word on successive days that two of his most reliable conduits for drugs and other valuable merchandise, in Florida and in Virginia, had abruptly been put out of business in raids by Federal agents had been unsettling. Then the irritating report that the Fournier girl had "disappeared," and concomitantly that Tony Farrell's relationship with her—and with a sizeable consignment of cocaine—was being reviewed. The timing was awkward. But perhaps most galling had been the fiasco at the Bronx hospital. Those other setbacks and improbable turns *could* have been coincidental. But this patently could only have been the work of an informer.

"That is a great deal of useful capital to squander," the Giant said aloud but as if to himself. "A costly loss for us—and so it must become for the one responsible. Boo," he said to his driver, "you say our man downtown has *no* clue as to the source of the police information?"

"Not yet. He say it go through another division. He gonna ask around, but . . . he don't know. Anyway, that what he *say.*"

"Keep after him." The Giant fixed his gaze on the impenetrable opaque lenses in the rear-view mirror. "What are your own thoughts, Boo?"

"We got us a fink." Jamal replied slowly, "Else some dumb mother with a mouth too big—puffin' hisself up to some fox."

"Hmmm. That last *is* possible," considered Brothers, "but only, I think, up to a point: A slip of the tongue, a boastful hint of an adventure soon to be undertaken, would be one thing —stupid, yes; human, even understandable, though of course unforgivable nonetheless. But I really can't imagine any of our people *so* stupid as to recklessly blueprint the *entire plan* to some outsider—a 'fox,' if you will—merely to gain attention or favor.

"No, the police obviously were primed beforehand by someone in a position to know, who gave the information quite deliberately. The only question, then, is *who?*"

"We find that out," Boo offered, "maybe we find out more than that."

The Giant smiled. "As always, we are in perfect accord, my friend."

14

In the hiatus of Cheech's absence, even as all relevant action was suspended until his return, Farrell felt the pressure on him grow rather than ease. It was like watching a gripping motion picture, getting into it as the suspense built toward what all anticipated would be a shattering climax, only for the film to snag at a most critical point, freezing on a single frame . . . leaving the audience hushed and anxious, on pins and needles waiting for what came next: then beginning to squirm with impatience to get on with it, with their mounting restlessness creating a new, different sort of tension that inevitably turned ominous.

Strangest of all for Farrell, with the time to consider it, was trying to pick up "routine" where it had been so jarringly interrupted. It was not the restaurant that gave him much of a problem, for there, with Liz backing him up, his perspective had not been so materially altered—although even at Anthony's now the familiar did seem to waver a little out of focus sometimes. What *was* unreal, the most unnerving, was his ordered resumption of those other arcane pursuits he'd involved himself in with Cheech, now that he was so acutely aware that his every move had been known and recorded for God-knew-how-long. He felt like a small boy engrossed in acting out a fantasy drama in some most private place, secure in the assumption that he was sealed off from a prying world, only to look about suddenly and realize with abject mortification that his intimate performance had been observed all the while.

It seemed hardly possible to continue his play-acting with the same intensity of concentration, as though nothing had changed, once his own audience had revealed itself. Yet this was what he was expected to do, what he *must* do for self-preservation, without the slightest telltale hint of self-consciousness.

Overseeing Cheech's assortment of illegal enterprises was not a role Farrell had essayed directly before, and he found it more intricate and demanding than he'd imagined. It was one thing to have played the executive functionary, so to speak, close to the center of power and sharing many of the perquisites without bearing material responsibility for administration, and quite another to assume that responsibility even temporarily. Cheech's affairs were diverse, to say the least, and since he operated essentially out of his hat without a tangible organizational structure, Farrell could only marvel at how so primitive a one managed it all so effectively. Successful racketeering was a full-time, consuming occupation; he could never—he realized with a certain sense of self-justification—have undertaken it on his own.

Aside from the demands of familiarizing himself with operational intricacies and the constant supervisory attention required, Farrell actually was not all that uptight about handling the numbers receipts and payoffs, processing loan agreements and collections, and looking after the illicit pleasure joints ("Ice" Faccialati being a helpful guide in such everyday matters), even under the known scrutiny of his watchdog JUST agents. These things by now hardly even rated to him as "criminal" activities; somehow they seemed practically accepted—"accepted" in the sense that everybody knew that the law recognized all this action going on and yet that little or nothing was going to be done to shut any of it down. Local cops mostly looked the other way, on the one hand in tacit acknowledgment of a flawed side of the human condition as ineradicable as the cockroach, and on the other in the undeniable perception that their more primal concerns stalked the streets. As for the feds, they didn't much care one way or the other because, after all, these *were* essentially "local" matters, and their mission was in their view infinitely more cosmic.

But to go right on blatantly procuring and trading for profit in stolen goods? And worse, dealing drugs, however modest the quantities—*now,* right out front, with that infrared spotlight full on him? He couldn't help it, *those* things made him very self-conscious indeed, the dispensation granted him notwithstanding. There would be enough of that to squeeze his gut when the crucial time came, when he would *have* to perform under direct supervision.

So he drove himself all the more during this trying waiting period, keeping always on the go, intent on outdistancing any possible opportunities for such damning transactions. This led Farrell through a succession of seemingly endless days, at times as long as eighteen hours without letup, a grind that left him virtually no respite for himself or Liz.

They scarcely saw one another, with little chance to exchange much more than passing words: Liz spent most of her time at Anthony's—with her few spare hours given, at Farrell's urging, to keeping up with her art studies—while in what random visits he could afford the restaurant he would usually find himself occupied with the books or tied up on the office phone. At the apartment, often as not either Liz was not there when he would rush in at odd hours to bathe and change, or by the time he got home nights she was already asleep, and when he awoke late most mornings, she would be gone.

It was dispiriting, and yet from one standpoint Farrell was almost grateful for the gulf separating them just at this time; for if they had been left to themselves to contemplate and discuss their situation, as it now seemed to be nearing decision, Liz might have only become more apprehensive than she already was, more afraid than he ever wanted her to be. And so, for that matter, might he.

It was better for both of them to keep busy, trying *not* to think, than just to wait.

Cheech and Goomba proceeded to confound their trackers. Though under constant watch the next few days, the pair was not detected behaving in any way suspiciously. Even to the trained eyes of undercover observers, they appeared to be but a couple of northerners taking a sojourn in the sun. At the Puerto Rico–Sheraton they spent hours by the pool, or in the hotel's bar and nightclub. Afternoons they visited some of the area's tourist attractions. Once they enjoyed the company of two young women (identified as top-drawer local hookers), who later returned with them to spend part of the night in their rooms. A check of hotel telephone records determined that the only calls either made were local: a half-dozen or so to the Pronto Taxi Company, others to various restaurants, and one to Pan American Airways.

After three days they checked out of the Sheraton and took a cab to the airport, where they boarded a Pan Am flight to Port-au-Prince, Haiti. They did not dally long in Haiti, only two nights and a day—including dinner with a middle-level government official, and a daylong tour of the north shore of the Golfe de la Gonâve and the mountains beyond.

Next they flew to Santo Domingo in the Dominican Republic where, due to a mixup in surveillance, they lost themselves for almost a full day. Less than twenty-four hours later they boarded an Eastern Airlines plane back to San Juan.

On arrival, the two went to a bar in the hotel adjacent to the Isla Grande terminal, ordering drinks while Donato made a call from a pay phone. Then they parted, Donato leaving the terminal and Goomba taking the next flight to New York.

Donato took a cab to an expensive-looking apartment tower in a residential section of San Juan, where he stayed the night. The following day, he boarded an Eastern jet back to Miami.

There, he rented a car and drove to a condominium on Key Biscayne. That evening, he emerged in the company of a Latin-looking man, and in the latter's brown Cadillac they cruised into Miami and had a night on the town.

During the evening, a check was run on the vehicle

registration; it was traced to a Raúl Santiago of the Key Biscayne address. Information about him immediately available was that he was an enterprising Cuban expatriate who in a few years had built a flourishing business dealing in marine supplies, mostly in the Miami area and south. He operated several boatyards and also rented small craft, from runabouts to power cruisers, to fishing or party groups. The Miami and Dade County police had him on file as having been investigated on at least two occasions for possible association with known or suspected criminal elements amidst Miami's teeming Latin population, but nothing directly linking Santiago had yet been uncovered. Nor was there any record of his prior association with notorious racketeers from the north.

By 3:00 P.M. the next day, Donato was on a National flight to New York's LaGuardia Airport. But not before he made his promised call to Randi, picked up by the police wire. He didn't tell her where he was. She told him all had been quiet. She'd missed him, she said, and asked poutily if *he'd* had a good time, as though she'd been locked in her tower just pining away (which at least gave the bored eavesdroppers a chuckle in their dank basement listening-post two blocks away, for by their reckoning, Randi had entertained different men up there at least three nights during Cheech's absence). He said he'd be back that night and to keep herself open for him—if she knew what he meant. She squealed, knowing.

The only other call Cheech made to New York, at least so far as could be documented, immediately followed that one. It was to his wife, May, at their Queens home, which of course was continuously wired. Without indicating to her, either, where he was speaking from he told May to expect him in *two* more days.

Cheech finally showed up at Anthony's looking fit and pleased with himself. He closed the office door and lowered himself into a chair with the air of a tycoon at ease.

"Talk about the fat cat," Farrell commented. "So . . . ?"

"So . . . we got it made, pally."

"It's all wrapped up?"

"Like a Christmas present." Cheech couldn't screen his beaming with cool. "All we got to do now is pick it up and take it home."

"So what's the drill?"

Cheech grinned. "You'll find out. It's beautiful. We'll have a sitdown with the Giant tomorrow night."

"Okay. Where?"

"Don't know yet. He'll pass us the word tomorrow, he says." He got up to leave, and turned at the door. "Hey, you done okay takin' care of things. You want the job permanent?"

"No, thank you. What happened to the Empire State Building?"

"What?"

"That's what you said."

"Oh yeah." The other grinned again. "Soon, baby, soon."

After Cheech had left, Farrell sat for a while. So this was it—or coming close to it. Could he hack it? Would he fold, or crack, in the crunch . . . ? And what about this place? He got up and stood in the doorway, scanning the restaurant, now starting to take on life. They'd have to give up the place once he'd fulfilled his part of the bargain. What would happen to it?

He returned to his desk and dialed Casualty Mutual.

Blackman answered. "Specs here," Farrell said. "Looks like we're in business. The big powwow is on."

"When?"

"Tomorrow night."

"Good." The agent hesitated. "Where are you?"

"At the restaurant."

"Stand by. I'll get back to you."

In five minutes the phone rang.

"Do you ever go to museums?" asked Blackman incongruously.

"Museums! Not much. What kind of museums?"

"Art museums specifically. With Liz into art, I thought—"

"Yeah, well, *Liz* does."

"Do the two of you have anything on tomorrow morning, say around tennish?"

"Nothing special."

"Tomorrow at ten," Thomas instructed, "you take Liz to the Museum of Modern Art. Leave time for at least an hour there, maybe two. Inside, let Liz go her own way, and you browse. Head up to the third floor. There's a sculpture exhibit you may find interesting."

Farrell waited. "Yeah, and?"

"Then you're going to meet the boss."

Shortly after ten o'clock Farrell and Liz separated at the open garden at the rear of the museum. He made his way, without hurrying, to the third floor. The sculpture exhibit Thomas had referred to was a wall-long display representing a collage of American history from 1880 to the present. Doing his best to give it serious attention, he was up to a grouping dated 1915–1935, when a soft voice off his right shoulder said:

"Interesting era, wasn't it? From doughboys to bootleggers."

Farrell hadn't noticed him approach. Thomas was wearing shades, an ascot, several strands of beads and a red-and-white checked tam with a red pompon on top. "*There* you are," Farrell said, looking away from him. "Aren't you coming on a bit loud?"

Thomas smiled at a piece of statuary. "The secret of anonymity in the Big Apple. The more conspicuous you look, the less anybody looks directly at you."

Farrell smiled. "You might have something at that. Okay, now what?"

"Take the elevator to the fifth floor," he said. With that, he meandered off.

Farrell stepped out on the fifth floor. Sitting in an armchair across from the elevator, thumbing what looked to be an illustrated art publication, was Ed Stabler. Dressed neatly, for once, in a dark suit and tie. Farrell must have shown his surprise.

Stabler stood and came over. "What's the matter, you in culture shock?" he chortled.

"I guess. In a way." Stabler, in or out of a suit, was just not the museum type.

"That makes two of us," said the detective. "Come on."

He led the way along a quiet, carpeted corridor to a closed door of dark wood with ornamental brass fittings. Stabler knocked, three little taps with one knuckle. In a moment the door opened a crack, noiselessly. A woman with auburn hair and horn-rimmed eyeglasses looked them over without expression. Then the shadow of a smile flickered across her face; she said "Hi, Ed" and swung the door open, closing it softly behind them as soon as they were inside.

The room could only be described as sedate, dominated by a modest-size round conference table not quite in dead center of the room. Seated alone at the table, back to the sunlit window, was a handsome man with a lordly shock of almost white hair.

"Welcome, Tony," the man said with a small but warm smile. He rose and held out his hand. "I'm Brendan Hartnett. Please, have a seat."

Farrell sat at the table where indicated by Hartnett. There was a tape recorder between them. The man was younger than his hair suggested; his face was ruddy and smooth, the eyes quick and alive.

"I am Assistant United States Attorney for the Southern District of New York," Hartnett declared. "Detective Stabler you know. The lady"—he nodded across the room, where the auburn-haired woman had seated herself in a straight-backed chair, a stenographic pad open on her lap—"is Sheila Carbone, my good right hand, *and*," Hartnett smiled, "frequently my crutch when I stub a toe."

Hartnett sat back and sized up Farrell. "You know why we're here, of course," he said at length.

"I know *why*," replied Farrell, looking about the room, "but I sure as hell can't figure out why *here*."

"Fair enough. It was essential that you and I get together, but equally imperative that we in no way risk compromising you by bringing you into the office downtown. I'm sure you can appreciate that. This is private, and unlikely—and I am a member—so we can exercise maximum control and security.

"Now, a while back you and Agent Thomas made a tape. It was helpful. But I want to do it again. Cover the same ground, perhaps in more detail, *plus* all that's happened since —anything you've seen or heard or taken part in from the time you, ah, joined forces with us, up to the present. And then we'll discuss the future. Okay?"

Farrell nodded, impassive.

Hartnett opened a sheaf of notes and fingered the recorder switch. "In addition to the tape," he said, "Mrs. Carbone will transcribe everything said here." His blue eyes held Farrell's. "This is official. It all goes into the book." Then he flicked on the machine.

They were at it close to an hour. Hartnett was good. He asked pertinent questions, and he knew how to draw out of his subject more detail than Farrell himself had thought he had to give. Farrell could see how the government attorney was building an infrastructure enclosing the Giant and his machinations. "Let's get back to the officers who questioned you that day. You told Roy Thomas they shortchanged the amounts of both the cocaine and the cash involved in the Fournier case."

"By about half."

"Which one did you say made the misstatement?"

"The D.A.'s man—I forget his name."

"Hurley. And the other, Casanova?"

"He didn't even blink. And I looked right at him, because who should know better?"

"Is it conceivable that *you* are in error about the actual numbers?"

"Are you putting me on? It was *my* deal, remember?"

Hartnett riffled through the papers in his folder and withdrew one. "The official report of the arrests at the Hotel Elysée states that seizures at the scene included approximately one-half kilo of cocaine—packaged in bottles of scotch whisky —and forty thousand dollars in paper currency." He glanced up at Farrell.

"That's a crock!" Farrell snorted. "Why would I tell you there was more than there was? Whoever wrote that report either can't count, or—or something else!"

"Is it possible that Miss Fournier and her accomplice could have doubled on you, held out a quantity of both the merchandise and proceeds for their own later use? That might well account for her sudden absence now."

"Mr. Hartnett, that just doesn't make any sense," Farrell retorted. "Did they know there was a bust coming? What would she have told me about coming out short?"

"She could have claimed they were ripped off."

"I think they *were*—we all were. What does the guy from Chicago say?"

"Unfortunately, nothing. He's pleading Not Guilty, so he's staying buttoned up."

"May I ask who wrote that report?"

The prosecutor's brow furrowed as he considered. After a long silence, he said "No," and returned the report to his folder.

"I think I can guess," Farrell challenged.

Hartnett answered only "The matter is being investigated further." He slid the folder across the table to Stabler, then sat back, hands clasped behind his head, regarding Farrell. "So . . . we approach the end of Act Two. Tonight."

"Yeah. Tonight . . ." murmured Farrell.

"When you find out where the meeting will be, try to let us know. That will be much more convenient than if we must shadow you to the location."

"But you *will* be around?" inquired Farrell, glancing toward Stabler.

"You can count on it," the detective said.

"I can't overemphasize the importance of what could come out of this affair tonight," said Hartnett. "Number One, what's discussed there could provide us with the firm base needed to establish major criminal conspiracy. Two, we could learn the salient details of this new operation, which would enable us to take the necessary steps to smash it when the time comes —hopefully, thereby to bring down the Giant and his top henchmen. And for you, Tony, of course all this could represent a long stride in your own passage to redemption."

Farrell sat thinking. "How will you know," he asked finally, "if I don't give you the right information?"

Hartnett showed him a tight smile. "Because we'll be *listening*, Ed." He nodded to Stabler.

The detective reached down to a briefcase at his feet and held up a small black plastic case, about the size of a miniature transistor radio, which he laid on the table. Unsnapping it, he removed what appeared to be a thin black belt with several clothlike pouches attached.

"This is actually a radio, believe it or not," explained Stabler, "a remote sending device, called a Kel unit. A mini microphone and three batteries," he said, displaying each item in its individual pouch. "You strap it on under your shirt. Take off your jacket," he told Farrell, "I'll show you."

Farrell stood, and Stabler fastened the belt around his upper torso under the arms. "To turn on the mike, you just press this button here, and again for off. And don't waste it: The batteries are powerful, but they have short lives."

Farrell undid the Kel and weighed the belt in his hand. "Where will it—I—be sending *to*?"

"To a recorder," said Stabler. "In our car. And like I said, we'll be pretty close by. We have to be, because the one problem with this gizmo is the range is limited—you can't depend on it much more than a few blocks away, then you start to lose it."

"Swell. So you can hear me getting carved up in living color," grumbled Farrell.

"Just act natural and you won't have no problem," admonished Stabler. "Sometimes guys get stage fright and start acting jerky. *Then* people begin to wonder."

"One last thing," Hartnett said. "We'd like you to get as many *names* as you can of those attending this meeting."

"How will I know if you're picking me up?" Farrell asked Stabler.

"You won't. Not till later. But don't think about that. Figure we're hanging on every word."

15

Tony Farrell had been correct in his unspoken guess about who had written the Elysée arrest report: It was signed *Frank L. Casanova, Lt., NYPD, Narcotics Div.*

Frank Casanova had been a capable and effective cop for twenty-two years. The past four of those years, however, he had been other things as well. Thief; extortionist; and, most significantly, double agent. As a specialist in narcotics, he was occasionally called on as an undercover operative by Brendan Hartnett's JUST unit. And simultaneously he was in the employ of one Aaron Luke Brothers.

Casanova had been recommended to Brothers by Cheech Donato, who had heard about him from a Mafia acquaintance who was related by marriage to Casanova. Disgruntled by a third rejection for promotion to captain, after eighteen years on the job Casanova had decided to hand in his papers, despairing for further opportunity for advancement in the Department. He was only forty then; he could still get a decent-paying civilian job, then in two more years start collecting his half-pay pension. He'd damned well earned it. He had four citations for heroism and other outstanding service beyond the normal call of police duty, plus one knife and two gunshot wounds as mementos. Little good any of that had done him, though, when it came to *material* recognition. He'd a wife and a mortgage and a couple of kids almost ready for college; but as far as the

Department was concerned he'd gone as far as they were going to let him go.

Then this cousin of his wife's had taken him aside and talked to him. Why quit, the guy said, when your experience and contacts on the job could be worth two, three times what you're making? You wouldn't be the only one, Frank. Lots of cops are living better this way. Think it over.

He'd thought it over. And next he was talking to this shylock Donato. Then Donato set him up to meet the big black racketeer they called the Giant. And as he'd begun his nineteenth year in the NYPD, he was on two payrolls—his retirement papers, unsigned, in a metal box on a closet shelf at home, his eldest child enrolled at a fine college in Virginia.

Casanova had increasingly become a valued asset of the Giant's; he had contributed in significant ways to Brothers' success in having so far eluded major entrapment by the law. At the same time, in the eyes of the Department he'd displayed a noteworthy regeneration as a working cop. It was this burst of renewed zeal that had in fact brought him to the attention of Brendan Hartnett.

Casanova was driven almost entirely now by greed, however. He'd learned how to use the authority of his badge, along with acquired street psychology and knowledge of the power of fear, to bleed felony suspects for all he could squeeze out of them (his old moral values having been redefined by rationalization: *What the hell, these bums had only taken it from some other poor suckers!*), including appropriation of their illegal wares for his own disposition. Usually he confined his extortion and pirate attacks to hard-line offenders; but he was not above victimizing the merely vulnerable as well, where opportunity was too ripe to resist. Which is how he had come to cut out for himself roughly half the spoils of the Elysée affair.

The young preppie daughter of a local civic leader and a "respectable" corporation lawyer from another state: pushovers! *They* weren't about to complain—if they even realized what he'd done—and he'd made sure nobody else in the arrest detail knew. So he was able to bury thirty-five grand in cash and half a key of highly marketable snow. What he wrote up in his report was enough to make it a pretty-good-sized bust as it was. Nobody need ever be the wiser.

Pure chance had led Casanova to the realization that the brash young man who'd barged into him outside the Elysée that evening was somehow associated with the Giant. He'd considered Tony Farrell only a wise-ass punk until the call had come from The Man himself inquiring into the nature of the charges against Farrell. The Giant had indicated no awareness that Casanova himself had led the arresting party, and the lieutenant chose not to enlighten him immediately, until he could think on it a little. The first thought he had was that the Giant would be sore as hell to know that it was Casanova who had messed up somebody he evidently had some interest in. Then Casanova's vision had lengthened, and he thought that filing this bit of information away for now might just prove useful one day—he wasn't quite clear yet just how.

He'd only started to feel some concern when the D.A.'s office informed him they'd "lost" Alison Fournier. That could be a problem. If she'd skipped, she was running around loose with information that could hurt him if it ever came back to the wrong people—the Giant *or* the Department.

And then had come this summons from the Giant to a meeting. No hint of what about. Hush-hush made Casanova uneasy. Of course he couldn't back out. But he'd go prepared for anything.

Farrell and Liz had got back to the restaurant just ahead of the lunch crowd. Pete had a telephone message for him from Cheech; it was simply to "stay handy," and Cheech would get back to him.

He waited all afternoon for word. He'd locked the microphone device in his desk drawer, not wanting to put it on until the last minute. Twice in the late afternoon he put in calls to Casualty Mutual to report he'd yet to learn where the night's meeting would take place. Each time he got only the recorded voice.

Around seven, as the cocktail business began to dwindle, he went out and took a breather down First Avenue a few blocks. Re-entering the restaurant about twenty minutes later, he stiffened just inside the doorway. At the bar, talking with Pete, was Cheech. Instinctively Farrell looked for Liz. She was across the room chatting with a table of customers. He braced himself and went up to Cheech.

"Hey, buddy," he scolded lightly, "I thought you were going to get back to me."

"I am," Cheech said. "I'm here. Ready?"

"Now?" Farrell thought of the little black case in his desk. "Well—sure, I guess. Just—give me a minute to go to the john. Have another drink."

Cheech looked at his wristwatch. "We got to be there in half an hour."

"I'll be right with you," he said, starting for the office.

"That ain't the crapper," Cheech said after him.

"I need my shaver," Farrell said over his shoulder. "Got to look my best for the party," he threw back.

"Well, hustle up," Cheech said.

Farrell went into the office. He fumbled with his keys at the desk, watching the doorway out of the corner of his eye; finally he got the drawer open and took out the black case. He went into a stall in the men's room and latched the door. Hurriedly stripping off his jacket and shirt, he sat on the seat and removed the Kel unit from its case. He adjusted it snugly, positioning the batteries against his upper ribcage just below his left armpit and the tiny microphone on his breastbone about at his shirt pocket, which was where he normally kept his cigarettes. He stood and flexed his chest and back muscles for any discomfort; it felt strange, but not constricting. He slipped on his shirt and was buttoning it when the men's room door was pushed open, and he quickly sat down again.

"Hey, what're you doin' in there, the fuckin' crossword puzzle?" roared Cheech. "C'mon, willya! It's seven-thirty already!"

"I told you," Farrell called as he finished buttoning the shirt. "When you gotta go, you gotta go. I'll be right out."

"And you still hafta shave yet?" the other grumbled.

Farrell rustled toilet paper. "No, I guess I can get by the way I am."

"We ain't goin' out dancin', y'know," Cheech gibed. He flushed the urinal and said, "I'll be outside. Move your ass."

When Farrell came out, Cheech was nowhere in sight. Liz was sitting at the corner of the bar by the register. "Where'd he go?" he asked her.

"He said he'd be outside and for you to hurry up." She looked at him anxiously.

He kissed the tip of her nose. "I don't know how long I'll be. A couple of hours, maybe."

She reached up to put her arms around him and suddenly her eyes opened wide, questioning. Her fingers traced the thin strap across his chest beneath the shirt.

"My truss," Farrell said, attempting a smile. "I wear it kind of high." He took her hands, slipped a piece of notepaper into one of them, and folded it into a fist, clasping it lovingly. Looking past her to be sure Pete was out of earshot, he said, "Listen. There's a phone number on that. After I'm gone, go inside and dial it. They should answer 'Casualty Mutual.' Say you're calling for 'Specs'—got that?—that I've just left with my friend, and I still don't know where, but it's set for about eight o'clock. That's all. Hang up. Then get rid of the paper. Okay?"

Liz was bewildered and frightened now. " 'Specs' . . .?"

He pressed her hands between his and kissed her tenderly. "Don't worry. It'll be all right." Then he turned and left.

Cheech met him outside and said, "We'll take your wheels."

"Sure, I don't care. What's wrong with your load?"

"Nothin'. It's just too easy to spot sometimes."

They were about to pull out of the garage when Cheech said, "Hold it." Two figures came out of the dark and climbed into the back seat. Farrell twisted around to see Goomba and Ice.

He turned to Cheech. "They coming to the party?"

"Yeah," the other said. "Now we got our whole delegation. Okay, get on the East River Drive, downtown."

Farrell obeyed, wondering if the agents were with them. Cheech directed Farrell to get off the Drive at Houston Street. "I grew up around here," Cheech said as they headed west. They turned into a narrow street and after a few blocks came out at Delancey Street. "Okay, go left again and keep goin'," Cheech instructed.

Farrell looked at him. "Over the bridge, to Brooklyn?"

"Right." Cheech grinned. "We're goin' to the Giant's kosher meat factory. It's right on the other side. Ain't that a pisser? That big black sonofabitch even got his own fuckin' rabbi!" Goomba and Ice laughed in raucous appreciation. Even Farrell had to smile at the incongruity of it.

Their destination was practically within sight of the old Brooklyn Navy Yard. It was a gloomy industrial area of squat one- and two-story factory and storage buildings in varying stages of blight, on deserted, poorly lighted streets cluttered with litter. The Giant's place, a low-slung stone-block structure, appeared to be one of the better maintained. Several other cars were already parked in the fenced loading zone alongside the packing plant. A single low-watt bulb burned over a sheet-metal door at the top of a ramp. As they got out of the Audi, two figures emerged from the darkness on either side of the door. They were black. "It's Donato," Cheech announced.

Goomba stayed in the Audi's rear seat to act as sentry, and Cheech and Farrell, trailed by Faccialati, climbed the ramp and went through the scarred metal door into the plant.

The place was in semi-darkness, the only source of light

streaming from the open doorway of a room at the far end. It was cold. As they drew near, threading their way among bulky wooden chopping blocks and long metal tables, a huge silhouette appeared in the doorway, all but obscuring the glow. It could only be one man.

"Welcome, my friends!" the Giant boomed out. He stood aside for them. "Now we can begin," he said heartily.

They filed into a surprisingly well appointed office with wood-paneled walls and carpeting. A number of men sat about a table, looking over the new arrivals. Farrell glanced around at them. Abou Jamal, of course. Two dark-complected Spanish types he didn't know. And—his mouth dropped open—the cop, Casanova!

Suddenly chilled again, Farrell quickly looked for the Giant. *Did they know who this guy was?* Brothers caught the startled look and peered curiously from him to Casanova. He came over to them.

"You two have met?" he asked softly.

Farrell's throat dried up. The Giant didn't know it was Casanova who'd arrested him! He looked down at the swarthy detective, who was squirming. Surely they did know he was a cop. Then why—? He decided to play along for a while, see what happened. "We've run into each other, around," he answered Brothers.

"Yeah," said Casanova quickly, "once or twice."

"And neither of you knew of your mutual association," smiled the Giant. "Interesting."

He brought the meeting to order. "Gentlemen, let us be seated."

As the rest were busy shuffling chairs, Farrell reached into his shirt pocket, and, in withdrawing his cigarette pack, pressed the button activating the Kel. His fingers trembled as he lit one of the cigarettes.

The Giant took charge. "If you'll allow me, gentlemen, we'll go around the table one time. To my left, my invaluable chief of staff, Abou Jamal. To his left, Lieutenant Frank Casanova, of our estimable New York City Police Department. The lieutenant has proven himself a most valuable contributor to our growth." Brothers moved on. "Next to him, Mr. Francesco Donato, of whose reputation you are already aware, a most productive and dependable ally. His own associates: Mr. Charles Faccialati—known as 'Ice,' I believe; and of course Mr. Tony Farrell, a highly versatile young man of whom I have come to expect many good things. And lastly, the two gentlemen on my right, our new partners, Señor José Colón, and Señor Guillermo Vasquez." The two men nodded and smiled around the table.

Are you getting this, you guys in the car? thought Farrell. *Christ! the whole cast, right at the top of the show!* He reached to his cigarette pocket to adjust the microphone against his chest. There was a stinging sensation under his armpit. . . .

"All right, then," the Giant resumed, "as most of you know, Mr. Donato recently conducted an organizational expedition to several islands in the Caribbean. He has informed me that the mission was an unqualified success. So, Francesco, without further ado, the floor is yours."

"Okay." Cheech cleared his throat and leaned forward on the table solemnly. "Pure and simple, we figured out how to lick the number-one problem's been holdin' coke back: gettin' it into the country without any hassles from the law! And now we're ready to roll!"

Farrell arched his shoulders in discomfort. That stinging underneath his arm was getting worse, beginning to burn.

Thomas and Stabler had been picking up loud and clear. In fact, it would have surprised Farrell to know they had been tuned in from the moment he and the others had left 69th Street.

The stroke of fortune for the agents was that the Audi had been chosen for transport. For the Audi was monitored—in two ways.

The day Thomas had had Farrell leave his car in the garage for a "tuneup," JUST electronic specialists had gone to the garage in the guise of city fire inspectors and proceeded to wire it. In the trunk they had installed a directional homing device, which would transmit radio sound waves to a matched receiver, enabling trackers to calculate the location of the target car without need for visual contact. And under the dashboard they attached a tiny remote microphone, not unlike the Kel now worn by Farrell, except that it was voice-activated and therefore always "on" when needed.

So Thomas and Stabler had stopped worrying about losing Farrell and his companions. As it turned out, they'd managed to keep the Audi in view for most of the ride downtown anyway. The agents did lose sight of it briefly, after it had left the Drive and turned into the maze of streets off Houston. In fact, the Audi's precise destination might have eluded them, following its unexpected turn onto the bridge approach to Brooklyn, if not for a few chance words that came clearly through the hidden radio! *". . . the Giant's kosher meat factory. It's right on the other side."*

They drove slowly past the plant. Two blocks away, within sight of the target, they found an alley, wide enough for their car and inky black. They pulled in, killed the engine, rechecked the Kel receiver, and slumped down in the darkness to wait. Now they could only will the Kel to behave.

Both tensed as one when, after what seemed an interminable silence, the receiver clicked on. They heard random coughing . . . then the Giant's unmistakable *profundo* in introduction. He was mentioning Farrell—

And Frank Casanova. Casanova was *there,* actually sitting in with the presidium of conspirators! Thomas and Stabler stared at each other grimly, each with a measure of sadness in his heart. "It is Frank. . . ." muttered Thomas disconsolately.

"That slimy prick!" breathed Stabler in helpless rage.

But almost at once they put aside their brooding over the

renegade cop as Brothers began naming all present. "Hot shit!" Stabler exclaimed. "He's running down the whole lineup for us!"

Then it was Cheech's turn. They bent forward, scarcely breathing. "The fucker's giving us a blueprint! Quick, make sure the tape's running!"

"It's okay," said Thomas. "Quiet down. Listen."

It was during Cheech's preamble that the crackling began and the sound became distorted. They would catch a few sentences distinctly, then the crackling would obscure the reception. They were beginning to lose the thread of what Cheech was saying.

"God*damn* it!" burst Stabler, pounding a fist on his knee. "Is Farrell screwing with that thing, or what?"

"I don't know," said Thomas. "It could be the set's going."

"Hang in, baby, hang *in!*"

It was only with concentrated effort that Farrell prevented himself from swearing aloud. The smarting at his upper left ribcage had intensified, searing the skin as though a lighted cigarette were being held very close. Straining to keep out the pain, he tried to focus on what was being said.

". . . but not if the shit gets brought in the country *legitimate,*" Cheech was explaining, "not from some foreign country but from some place that's already part of the U.S. Get it?"

Colón and Vasquez looked at him intently.

"The answer is Puerto Rico," Cheech pronounced triumphantly. "You load up with the stuff *there,* and fly it home, and it's like goin' from Miami to New York."

Colón said something in Spanish to his companion, then turned back to Cheech. "There still is the question of how will the materials get *into* Puerto Rico."

"A perceptive observation," the Giant interjected. "And here, I think, lies the really distinguishing beauty of our plan. Francesco?"

"Okay. The gimmick is we go into the tourist business. We ship people out on cruise ships—them regular Caribbean cruises you see in the ads, strictly legit. The thing is, wherever else they go, they gotta hit either Haiti or the Dominican Republic, and then Puerto Rico after. They pick up the shit in one of the first two places—it don't matter which—and P.R. is the drop.

"Here's how it'll work: The boat stops at Haiti, say, where the passengers can get off and catch some of the local color for a couple of hours, right? Now our passengers do like everybody else. And they come back to the boat loaded with packages same as everybody, only they got stuff in them that nobody else got.

"Okay, so they ship out again, and the next stop, or whenever, is Puerto Rico. This is U.S. territory, right? So they get off—American citizens, no bullshit there—takin' their souvenirs with them—and whattaya know, when they come back this time they got different packages than the ones they got off with!

"Get the picture? Don't worry about where they drop the stuff; we got it all worked out, okay? Now, from there it's even simpler. In San Juan, we got people waitin' to fly to the States—maybe locals comin' up for a visit, maybe somebody we sent down, it don't matter—and they just shove the stuff in their suitcase, get on a plane, and when they get here they just walk away and bring it to us. No Customs, no nothin'!" Cheech looked around the table, beaming. "Neat, huh?"

"In point of fact," interjected the Giant again, " 'neat' seems hardly adequate to the implications. Let me suggest why. As we envision it, our basic party of cruise passengers, our couriers, should be four—preferably mixed, I think, although this is of small matter at the moment. As we refine the technique, of course, I foresee no difficulty in dispatching multiple groups—eight, twelve, or more, on single cruises or several, simultaneously or successively. But let us confine discussion here to the minimum unit, four. Each of these couriers should be able to deliver to Puerto Rico from four to five kilograms of cocaine apiece. Ten pounds of powder packaged in bulk ought to be neither too onerous for one individual to manage nor apt to excite any suspicion among port authorities, who, as Francesco has pointed out, are quite used to cruise passengers in the islands returning to their ships laden with purchases of native craft.

"Thus, from our basic foursome we may expect forty pounds or more of merchandise per voyage—approximately twenty kilos. Now, project: Were we content to dispatch *only* this minimum group at conservative intervals—let us say no more often than just once a month—even then, in less than one year's time we could anticipate accumulating a volume of cocaine worth, at today's wholesale rates, easily two and one-half million dollars! As for the *retail* value of even so modest a quantity, after processing and so forth—well . . .!" He sat back grandly, surveying his admiring retinue.

"Thirty million on the street, easy," submitted Cheech. "And remember, that's just the *ground floor!*"

Farrell was perspiring; he could feel it running down the small of his back.

"Something troubles you, Tony," he heard the Giant say to him. "You have a question?"

"Well . . ." He did, in fact, though he would just as soon have tabled it for now. "I'm just wondering how we get the coke into Haiti or the Dominican Republic in the first place. Are they that wide open?"

"Ah, quite to the point," said Brothers. "As with most civilized countries, they do have their laws and restrictions. Nonetheless, such formalities tend to be, ah, somewhat more flexible in these particular countries—provided one has the means and influence with which to bypass the usual restraints. These we have, gentlemen. Haiti and the Dominican Republic are in effect our exclusive franchise. Now, as to precisely *how* this has been accomplished—well, better, I think, that all intimacies were not generally known or discussed.

"Satisfied, Tony?"

Farrell nodded.

"One point I *shall* clarify now," Brothers added, "with regard to our method of shipping product: Primarily, we expect to employ chartered aircraft, contracted in the United States and flown to the various depots in South America, whence the cargoes will be ferried to Hispaniola. This last is, of course, the vital area of concern of Señores Colón and Vasquez: coordinating traffic, organizing our purveyors—in short, keeping the supplies moving, the planes filled." He looked around the table.

Everyone sat quiet. Colón and Vasquez exchanged some words quietly in Spanish, then Vasquez said to the Giant: "We like what you have said. We are with you." He put out his hand and Brothers took it warmly.

"I never doubted it." The Giant beamed around the table. "Now, gentlemen, before we proceed to matters of organizational structure and responsibility, I propose we seal our pact by raising glasses together. Who will do the honors?"

Helpless to do anything about it, the agents in the car were choking on their frustration. Very little had come over the Kel since Cheech's summation.

Then, as they were straining to hear through the static, they had a scare. In the rearview mirror Thomas caught a glimpse of a shadowy figure—a man, very large, who had been walking slowly, as if prowling, then had halted and seemed to be peering over toward the alley. In one motion Thomas flicked off the receiver and slumped far down into his seat. "Bury yourself. I think it's Goomba!"

Stabler ducked. "Where is he? Did he spot us?"

"I couldn't be sure. He was across the street, looking this way. He must be patrolling."

They waited, their breathing faster. Stabler whispered: "If he makes us, what do we do—blow him out?"

"We might have to jump him and then take off like big-assed birds," Thomas said.

"What do you mean 'we'?" Stabler growled. "You expect me to play knuckles with that gorilla? Buuull-*shit!*"

They listened. Still no movement outside.

At last, Thomas cautiously raised his head and searched either side of the car. "He's gone."

Stabler expelled a long breath. "Good thing for him."

"We'd've moidered d'bum," Thomas said. He switched the receiver back on. Nothing.

Thirty-five minutes had passed since they'd heard anything intelligible. Thomas sighed. "I'm afraid we've had it for good."

"Yeah. Well, we got some pretty good stuff. Farrell will just have to fill us in on the rest."

Farrell drove in silence most of the way back into Manhattan and uptown, where he dropped Cheech and the others. He wasn't sure he would make it to his apartment from the elevator. Inside, he locked the door, then tore off his jacket and the shirt beneath. Grappling with the strap around his body, he flung the Kel unit to the floor. The shock of cool air on his wound took his breath away. He peered down at his side. There was a round lesion about the size of a silver dollar under his arm, raw and festering, as though he'd been branded. Then he realized what it was: battery acid. Leaking, eating at him for two merciless hours. He made his way to the liquor cabinet, and poured out an old-fashioned glass full of scotch.

The phone. He reached for it laboriously.

Whitehead. "Are you all right?"

"No, I am *not* all right!"

"What is it?" The tone was alarmed.

Farrell felt himself swaying. He took a long breath. "Sorry. I'll survive, I guess."

"Can you talk?"

The room was moving on him. "Tomorrow . . ." He put the receiver back onto its hook. Sitting dully on the arm of the couch, he raised his glass and bolted down the scotch. His senses began to reel, and then, as all the sustained tension and resolve and pain oozed out of him, he sank backward onto the cushions and blacked out.

He was lying that way, bare-chested, arms thrown back from the ugly burn on his side, when Liz came in much later. She had to stifle a scream at the sight of him.

16

Liz cleaned and dressed the sickening wound while he was still out. When he came to and found her there, his head in her lap, he held her close as though he had been away a long time. He couldn't bring himself to tell her about how it had happened, and she didn't press him. She brought him something to eat and took him up to bed.

Farrell awakened very sore, his body stiff as though he'd overdone a long day of manual labor. With a start he remembered the Kel discarded on the living room floor. Liz calmed him. She'd found the contraption, and had wrapped it in a plastic bag and stuffed it into the back of the crisping drawer in the bottom of the refrigerator. She didn't think it was the sort of thing to leave lying around the house for visitors.

The doctor told him it was very nearly a third-degree burn. He praised whoever had tended to it. The doctor's manner suggested he was dying of curiosity to know how one managed to burn himself with acid so uniformly on that part of the body, but Farrell didn't bother to offer an explanation. He couldn't think of a lie that was plausible.

Later that morning Farrell took a cab to the New York Hilton in midtown. Brendan Hartnett waited there in a suite on the twenty-seventh floor. Thomas and Stabler were with him, along with a tape-player, and of course Sheila Carbone and her notebook. All apologized profusely for his freakish mishap.

They listened to the tape, such as it was, Farrell filling in the gaps as best as he could remember and clarifying parts that were garbled or ambiguous. Obviously the "tourists" landing at Haiti or the Dominican Republic would pick up their consignments of cocaine at preordained local gift shops; their locations should not be hard to uncover as the operation proceeded. Not yet clear was how the dope would finally be switched at San Juan. As for the transportation of the contraband by air from South American points, the odds were on somewhere in Colombia. Home base for the chartered aircraft mentioned by the Giant might be Florida. This surmise was grounded in new information compiled on the contact Cheech had visited in Key Biscayne, the Cuban Raúl Santiago. Santiago had recently acquired franchises at several general-aviation facilities dotting southern Florida, and was in a position to provide a variety of aircraft types, from sporty two-seaters to refitted DC-3's.

For the rest, Abou Jamal would supervise allocation and distribution of the cocaine when it did start flowing in. And Farrell's own assignment seemed a particular stroke of fortune: The Giant had named him, with a touch of whimsy, "tour director"—to administer actual movement of the couriers by sea and air. It could hardly have been better, the lawmen exulted, if they'd planted him themselves!

Farrell brought up the question of Frank Casanova. Hartnett said there seemed little doubt now that it was Casanova who'd dipped into the Elysée seizure, although proving it conclusively might be something else again. Moreover, there were now strong indications that he'd engaged in such practices for some time, hiring himself out to people like Cheech and the Giant. "Judging by how close he seems to them," Hartnett concluded, "he must have been on the payroll quite a while."

"He could be real trouble," Farrell warned, "their eyes and ears inside your task force."

"Possibly—but not so much as long as we *know* he's playing both sides of the street. It can work both ways, you see. We can see that Frank gets certain information to pass along that will be misleading with respect to our direction and progress. So, on the one hand we can erode his credibility with them, bit by bit, and at the same time, at this end, keep maneuvering him until we've got him in a box, airtight. And *then* . . . well, we'll put him to the wall and lay out the facts of life. Frank might just get a whole new perspective of where his best interests really lie."

"In other words, turn him into another renaissance man —like me," Farrell said drily.

"With a vital difference: Rogue cops *never* get off the schneid," Hartnett declared. He eyed Farrell a few moments thoughtfully. "All right now, is there anything else troubling you, anything we can try to set straight before the going really gets heavy?"

"I've been thinking about my restaurant . . ."

"What will become of it?"

"Yes. I wouldn't want to just abandon it. If I could sell it, Liz and I at least would have some cushion."

Hartnett thought, brows knit. "One way might be to quietly transfer ownership to us now—I mean, a dummy corporation that we can set up—and then later, at an appropriate time, we'll arrange a legitimate sale and deliver the proceeds to you. How does that sound?"

"I guess it's the only way."

Hartnett rose, signaling the discussion was ending. But he added earnestly: "Please believe that your continued well-being is a fundamental concern of ours. We'll do everything possible toward that end."

"In that case," Farrell said, seizing the opening, "there is something else. After last night, I would feel easier if I had something to protect myself with. If they'd found out what I had on me, I wouldn't have had a chance!"

"A gun?" the prosecutor cut in. "Roy mentioned it to me. I'm sorry. That would be illegal."

Farrell glowered around at them and thought, *Well, you can just shove that. I'm no clay pigeon. If I can't get it from you, I damn well know where I can!* But all he said was "Okay, then, I'll see you," and headed for the door.

"Of course," Hartnett said, "if you did happen to come into possession of such a piece of equipment, and we didn't know of it—"

Hartnett's expression was as innocent as an altar boy's at midnight mass.

Picking his way through the busy hotel lobby toward an exit, Farrell was not aware of a pair of eyes following him from behind opaque lenses. Abou Jamal stood in a corner of the lobby with two other conservatively dressed black men just arrived from out of town. Distractedly, he watched Farrell out into the street, thinking again how he could not bring himself to trust that one, despite the Giant's partiality. Jamal felt the same about Casanova, but him he could rationalize—*he* was The Man, no matter which angle you looked at it from, and a turncoat on top of it. Farrell—somehow he just couldn't find a handle on him. . . .

A few minutes later, as the discussion with his associates from Philadelphia and Baltimore was about to break up, Jamal got another surprise. Striding briskly through the lobby, with a woman at his side and a couple of aides behind, was a robust man with a thatch of white hair whom Jamal recognized instantly: Hartnett, the hotshot federal prosecutor. The party went out the same doors Farrell had used.

Farrell did his homework on the Caribbean cruise picture before reporting back to the Giant. A half-dozen major shipping lines made the run regularly, with the biggest —Cunard, Holland-American, and so on—generally featuring weekly departures. The standard trips were from one to two weeks; from the standpoint of economy he concentrated on the shorter cruises. Ports of call varied, and he found the selection of cruises that included an early stopover at either end of Hispaniola and later at San Juan to be relatively limited, just three or four a week. The majority by far originated in Miami, with some others out of New Orleans and only a few direct from New York. Most common from the Northeast (and the Midwest) were fly-cruise package plans—plane to Miami, ship from there.

It was not inexpensive. Studying the seemingly infinite variety of shipboard accommodations and fares offered, Farrell telescoped his preference, considering both costs and availabilities, to the lower-range double rooms—priced roughly between $600 and $700 per person on a seven-day sail out of Miami. Multiplying a mean fare of $650 by a party of four, as the Giant had termed the "basic unit" of couriers, costs would average $2,600 per voyage, give or take a couple of hundred dollars. There would also be the additional air fares for those flown from New York or wherever; while round-trip fares offered by some participating airlines were discounted, the typical rate between major northern cities and Miami was $125 per person, adding $500 to the tab for a party of four. This would bring the total transportation cost per trip to something over $3,000.

Of course, these were mere cosmetic expenses, essential but, on the overall balance-sheet, literally small change. Contemplating the significant numbers projected in this operation, Farrell could not be but awed by the enormity of it all:

First, the price to the South American producers for the raw cocaine, which he estimated to be currently around $3,500 a kilo. Based *only* on the Giant's proposed "bare minimum"—a single cruise a month, bringing in roughly 20 kilos each—in one year perhaps 250 kilos would be an order. One bulk shipment of that relatively meager amount alone would cost in the neighborhood of $900,000. Add the costs of hiring aircraft and pilots, plus miscellany such as payoffs to assorted functionaries down the line, and total expenses probably would exceed $1,000,000.

But those were only paper figures. Naturally, the big nut,

the whole price of the bulk cocaine, would not be paid up front; there would be a down payment, maybe 10 percent, with the balance to be payable in installments later out of profits—so, $90,000 in cash, say, for the goods on consignment. Neither would individual payouts for service be made in full; probably half now, the rest when the job was done—maybe another $60,000 cash, then. Total initial outlay: about $150,000, give or take a few thousand. (Pro-rated over a year's time: effectively, $12,500 a month.)

And that was like spit in the ocean measured against the return anticipated. At the least, each kilo brought in could be dealt to other wholesalers for two to three times the purchase price; at retail it could go, as is, for *ten* times its cost. But it would hardly be sold that short. It would be "processed" —adulterated, multiplied—so that up to three-and-a-half times more product eventually would be put into circulation than had originally existed: 70 kilos instead of 20. And with the going market price for coke up to the equivalent of $35,000 a kilo—in such demand, though in smaller quantities, on the college campuses, in the plush offices and clubs, the swank townhouse and suburban sets—what was really at stake here, against a contingent investment of $1 million, was a liquid *net* profit of close to $30 million! Or, from Farrell's own narrower view-point: For each foursome a month he sent out on a $3,000 cruise, there would be a likely return of almost $2.5 million!

Now they were ready to roll.

The Giant told Farrell to book four reservations on the next available ship—a Holland-American liner scheduled to depart Miami nine days hence. All Farrell needed was the bodies. The Giant handed him a folded sheet of paper. There were four names on it, two couples. The addresses given were in Camden, New Jersey, and Towson, Maryland.

"They've been carefully screened," Brothers said. "For this maiden voyage, we thought it prudent to avoid employing anyone locally. The couples themselves are not acquainted. The fewer interlocking relationships, the safer for us all."

"Do I deliver the tickets to these addresses?" Farrell asked.

"No. All travel documents are to be routed through here, to Boo. He will see to the rest."

"And paying for the bookings . . .?"

"Cash—*only* cash. This is your bank. You advise Boo how much is required in each instance; he will advance the precise amount. Keep no permanent records, but submit all notes of your computations. Naturally, we shall expect scrupulous accuracy."

"Naturally. Okay, so I guess we're just about in business." Folding his papers neatly and putting them into a pocket, he asked, trying to make it sound offhanded: "I assume the stuff, the merchandise, is stashed and ready for pickup?"

"Not quite. One vital link remains. Being the most precarious, it has awaited the consolidation of all the others." Brothers turned to Cheech. "Your man in Florida is prepared to move?"

"Santiago? All he needs is the word. And the down payment," Cheech amended hastily.

So it *was* to be Santiago, Farrell thought. Another loose end added to Hartnett's web.

Michael Palmieri got out of the Fugazy Continental and surveyed his old neighborhood. It had been years since he'd been back to 187th Street. "Arthur Avenue" was how the neighborhood was familiarly known as a whole, for the core thoroughfare of the several-square-block area—the Bronx's version of lower Manhattan's "Little Italy," smaller but just as compact and self-sufficient and essentially unchanging. There were a few more buildings here and there that stood apart from Michael's boyhood memories, but overall it looked—and smelled—as it always had to him: the rows of three- and four-story tenements, old and mostly gray but still kept neat and uncrumbling, and scattered among them the fragile little frame houses, scarred and some dowdy but scrubbed clean like fussy old ladies; and the shops—the Italian food markets, sidewalk fruit or fish stalls, coffee shops and pizza counters and restaurants squeezed in between buildings; and of course the church the most prominent structure, gloomily ornate, almost forbidding in its austerity and yet at the same time reassuring and inviting in its ageless solidity.

The influence of the Mafia here was largely unseen but always sensed. None of the leaders had resided in the old neighborhood in some time, having long since upgraded their personal lives by relocating to the affluent, respectable suburbs of Westchester, Long Island and New Jersey. Councils of the "association" were still held regularly, however, within the limits of Arthur Avenue, in the back room of one or another unprepossessing little restaurant favored by the older dons. One could tell when they were meeting from the sleek limousines double-parked outside such a place. The police, who routinely cruised these streets, knew when they were there as well, of course, but kept their distance. Why make waves? Tranquillity was nothing to be tampered with these days.

The limousines were there today, outside The Grotto, a corner restaurant with an old-fashioned striped-canvas awning, and red burlap curtains hanging from a brass rod inside the front window. It specialized in home-cooked Northern Italian dishes and fish, and it was a place where the dons could feel easy when discussing business. Today, for the first time in many years, their distinguished financial expert from downtown had been asked to attend.

Michael wasn't sure whether he was pleased or not. It was a mark of respect to be invited to a council. It undoubtedly meant there were matters to be decided of high-level concern. At the same time, the shabbiness of Arthur Avenue reminded him of a hard early life he'd fought diligently to surmount. He'd grown used to conducting his affairs in the luxurious detachment of his apartment office, or across a fine linen tablecloth with individual "clients." This was like coming back out into the streets. It gave him a gritty feeling.

Michael entered The Grotto into a small bar. He looked around. The place, always unpretentious, had changed little: tile flooring, walls painted a muted green, framework and the few booths opposite the bar of sturdy dark wood; the only concession to "atmosphere" consisted of a few heavy fishnets hung randomly overhead in halfhearted simulation of a fish "grotto." And the pair of great illuminated fish tanks flanking an archway to the dining room in the rear. Michael remembered those tanks and shuddered.

The dining room was closed off now by a drapery of carmine velvet drawn across the archway, standing in front of which, arms folded, was a muscular young man wearing a leather coat. There were two old men at a table and two younger ones at the far end of the bar, all eyeing Michael.

Behind the bar was a fat, balding man in rolled-up shirt-sleeves, polishing glasses. Michael knew him to be the owner, Paulie Tedone.

"Hello, Paulie. Do you remember me?"

Tedone kept wiping as he searched Michael's face and examined his well-cut clothes. "Maybe," he grunted at last. "I think I seen you. Who are you?"

"Michael Palmieri." He inclined his head toward the back room. "I was invited."

Tedone inspected him a few more seconds, then turned to the one by the velvet curtain and called over: "Palmieri." The sentry gave Michael a long look, as if memorizing his appearance, and ducked behind the curtain.

From the bar, Michael's gaze was drawn inevitably to the fish tanks. These, in their own way, gave The Grotto its one truly distinctive touch. The tanks contained live piranha, the little razor-toothed flesh-eaters from South America's Amazon. Regulars at The Grotto liked to amuse themselves some nights by tossing chunks of raw meat to the piranha, then betting on which of the frenzied creatures would devour its prize first. The thought of it both repelled Michael and fascinated him: showcasing these deadly cannibal fish *here,* in this fish restaurant where the councils sat. A trenchant warning to all who entered here to be of good faith.

When the messenger came back out, his expression showed a courteous deference. Michael ducked through the arch.

Seven men sat at a long table covered by a crisp white tablecloth. There was wine on the table, and pots of espresso and a bottle of anisette, and bread and pastry. All the men wore suit jackets and ties. Most appeared to be about Michael's age, a couple younger. He didn't know most of them, though a few were familiar.

The one who had invited him was seated at the head of the table: "Michael! Welcome home!" called out Giuseppe Bucceroni. "Come and sit—here by me."

Michael went around to him and shook hands. "Nice to see you again, Joseph."

Giuseppe Bucceroni—also known as Joseph Butcher (and to some as "Joe the Butcher")—was in his fifties, of medium height and a once husky frame, grown slack since Michael had last seen him. He had a full head of hair, still as black as ebony, which he brushed straight back without a part—the classic look of an Italian peasant. But he was no peasant. He was smart, as shrewd a tactician as Michael had ever encountered. Bucceroni was a boss. He himself did not head one of the major "families," but he had succeeded in earning the trust and respect of the heads of each of the existing families, even those factions that often were at odds with one another, so that in effect he was recognized as a surrogate for all, authorized to speak or act for any.

Bucceroni introduced each of the others—Michael missed some of the names, recognized others: Nicotra, Cabrini, Terraciano—and the warmth with which they all responded to him confirmed his expectation that he was to be a key participant at this meeting.

Once past the amenities, Bucceroni got right down to business. "Michael," he began, "everybody here knows you by reputation, so we don't need to waste time running down your credits. What we're here for is to talk about a situation that some very important people think something should be done about. You know about this big nigger, Aaron Luke Brothers —the one the spades call the Giant?"

"Ah, yes," said Michael, "I understand he's becoming quite a power."

"Not becoming—is," corrected Bucceroni. To the table at large, he said: "This guy's built himself one of the top organizations in Harlem. We got word on good authority what this Brothers and his crowd are up to. They got a deal worked out with the South Americans to set up like a new distribution franchise for a big chunk of all the coke shipped into this country. They're guaranteeing a way to move the stuff in without any trouble from the law—Customs, D.E.A., nobody! And from what we hear, it'll work! They don't have all the nuts and bolts lined up yet, but I got to hand it to them, they put together a beautiful framework. I wish we'd of thought of it first. But we didn't. So what we got to do now is pick their lock and walk in and take it away from them.

"And you," he said to Michael, "are going to be our lock-picker."

Everybody's attention on him now, Michael said to Bucceroni: "You'd better spell it out, Joseph."

"All right. We got to latch on to somebody who's high up in that outfit—somebody who'll give us the combination without a fuss. So, who we got? Brothers has got a lot of them bald-headed goons around him—mean bastards, and no way they're about to come over to us. But there also happens to be some white guys working with this outfit, of our own blood even. Now, the fact is, one of these is the guy with the contacts they needed to set this whole thing up. Some of you might even remember him: Frankie Donato—they call him Cheech."

Michael remembered warning Tony about Donato. He'd

known the man was a hoodlum and trouble, but he was surprised to hear about his teaming up with the *black* mob.

"He's no fucking good," one of them spoke out, "but he could be the key, all right. He'd sell anybody out to make his mark."

"That's the problem with him," said Bucceroni. "You can't trust him. And you have to be careful about leaning on him because he's got a rabbi. Not him, his wife. She's a niece of the Ippolitos. They're not too happy about that, but as long as she's married to him— So, put Cheech aside for the time being. There could be somebody even better. A young guy, new, hasn't been around long, but he's tied in pretty close to Donato. And not only that, the word is the Giant's adopted him—like a pet monkey! Now I think *he's* our real key . . . because not only is he one of us, he's actually part of the family! Eh, Michael?" Bucceroni smiled. "Your own nephew, who you raised from a kid—!"

Michael was staring at him, speechless. Bucceroni's exuberance vanished before the stricken face. Then his eyes narrowed, and Michael could read what the Mafia boss was thinking: *You didn't know?*

17

Farrell had offered to drive Cheech to LaGuardia for the flight to Florida. Most of the way, Cheech was uncommunicative. Unlocking the bag on his lap, he occupied himself riffling through the cash—Raúl Santiago's "down payment." Stealing glances, Farrell could see about ten stacks of bills bound with rubber bands—all twenties, it appeared, and well used. He asked himself how many of these might have come into the Giant's treasury straight from the hands of pitiful junkies. That thought drew Linda Palmieri into his mind all at once, and he stirred in discomfort. Who was *he* to turn self-righteous? he swore silently to himself. . . .

"How much is there?" he moved himself finally to ask Cheech.

"Ten."

"Ten thousand doesn't seem like much on deposit."

"He don't need more now," Cheech said distractedly. "Just for front-line expenses. He'll do all right later."

"What *is* Santiago's deal?" Farrell prodded. "In round numbers." He wanted to ask if Cheech had his own percentage of the Cuban going for him, but decided not to push it.

"He gets the balance of his expenses when the stuff is delivered—then half a point of our take."

Farrell did some rapid calculating and whistled. "Then he figures to clear about a hundred and fifty big ones, maybe more! Not bad for just renting one airplane."

"And crew, don't forget," Cheech said. "They don't come cheap. Also, it's a high-risk business. Ray's got a lot sunk in it." He sounded almost defensive, as though this was how he'd presented the case for his friend Santiago to the Giant.

"Okay, so how does it work now?" Farrell asked, pressing his advantage. "You and he pick out a plane, he signs up somebody to fly it, and away they go—into the wild blue yonder?"

"About like that. There's one catch, though."

"What's that?"

"Nobody knows *where* they're goin'."

"They don't—" Farrell exclaimed, incredulous. "How can that be? They've *got* to know, so they can figure the fuel load they need for distance, adjust for weight—"

"Not till they're practically there."

Farrell scrutinized him. "I don't get it. What do they have, sealed orders—like in a war movie?"

"Close. Them spics, Vasquez and Colón, they're pretty cute. One of them goes along on the plane, see. *He* has the map showin' where to go—*but* he don't show it till they're long gone. All these guys know before takeoff is what they *have* to know—like, yeah, how much gas and that. But they could be goin' anyplace. This way, see, there's no leaks beforehand."

"Don't they have to file a flight plan?"

"They do or they don't, it don't matter," shrugged Cheech. "You can say you're flyin' anywheres, you don't have to go there. Nobody pays no attention. It's a fuckin' game."

"Not bad," mused Farrell. "Except—the pilots *will* find out the destinations, obviously; and when they get back Santiago will too. So what's to stop them, and him, from using that information for their own ends later on? Can we really trust all these people?"

"I don't trust *nobody* a hundred percent," Cheech growled. "But you gotta take *some* chances to get anyplace in this world, right? Anyway, that ain't the point. So what if they know where the stuff gets picked up and dropped off? First, that's just *this* trip. The South Americans got lots of different places. And they might see where we dump it, but they ain't gonna see what we do with it *after*. Second, so they know; what're they gonna do about it? Go into business for themselves? No way—cut off their own noses? They got a good deal goin' here, why fuck it up for nothin'? And the last thing is, anybody does try to fuck us—Santiago or whoever—they're gone, and they can bet their ass on that! Like *splat*," he said, whipping a hand across his throat. "You never seen them bulletheads of the Giant's pull the plug on somebody."

"Have *you?*"

"Not personally"—Cheech blessed himself—"but I heard. I don't even like to think about it."

They rode in contemplative silence for a while before Cheech said absently: "Me and Santiago go back a long ways. He's all right—our kind of guy. He's too smart to do anything stupid."

Farrell stole a quick glance at him, and returned his attention to the road ahead. "Then I guess there's really nothing to be concerned about," he said.

On his return to Anthony's, Farrell was surprised to find among his messages one, marked "important," from Frank Casanova. He dialed the number given. It was answered "Manhattan South, Homicide." When the lieutenant came on he sounded breathless. He said they should get together right away, something had come up that Farrell ought to know about. Farrell said he'd been out much of the day and really should attend to restaurant business that had piled up, and proposed that Casanova come to Anthony's. The detective said he didn't think he ought to be seen there just now and asked him to think of some more neutral place. Farrell then suggested La Veranda at the Elysée—an appropriate touch, he thought, considering. Casanova agreed.

It was Farrell's first time at La Veranda since that fateful evening weeks before. He slid onto the same corner stool and waited for Dan Mulcahy to notice him. When Dan saw him he broke into a broad smile.

"Hey, stranger!"

"How's it going, Dan?"

"Could be better. It's been worse. How's by *you?*"

"You shouldn't ask," Farrell said in a mock Yiddish dialect.

"What'll it be?"

"I'll have a beer. You got any imported German?"

"Sure." Dan poured a Beck's for him, then leaned on the bar and lowered his voice confidentially. "Did you have a little trouble last time you were in?"

Farrell eyed him. "Where'd you hear that?"

"Are you kidding? I know everything goes on within two blocks of this joint. A couple of dicks were asking around the hotel right after that." He paused, then asked: "So what's the story?"

"No big deal. A little misunderstanding. I'll tell you about it some time. Right now—" He checked his watch.

"I'll be damned!" Dan said. He'd turned to look toward the doorway. "This looks like one of the bulls who was nosing around!"

Advancing toward them was Frank Casanova. Farrell said quickly: "Could be. Don't say anything, okay?"

"I don't even know you," Dan said, moving away.

"Hiya, pal." Casanova climbed onto the stool next to Farrell's. He ordered a V.O. and ginger ale and waited until Dan had set it before him and moved away again. "I wanted to get to you before somebody else did," he said *sotto voce.*

"About what?" Farrell asked.

"About the girl—Alison Fournier. They found her."

"Oh, Christ, I'm glad. Where?"

"I don't know if you'll be so glad. It was in twelve feet of water, out in Great South Bay."

Farrell stared at the swarthy detective.

"She'd been there a long time, they say," Casanova added. "She couldn't have been very pretty."

"Drowned?"

The other nodded. "In her car. Ran it off the road. The Suffolk cops don't know if it was an accident or . . ."

Farrell tried to clear his head. "Or—?"

"Maybe suicide?" Casanova put it as a half-question. "The autopsy may tell us. Tough way to turn out your lights."

"My God!" breathed Farrell numbly.

Casanova took a sip of his drink and leaned toward Farrell earnestly. "Look, because of her old man there'll be questions. You're on the D.A.'s list, and I thought you oughta be prepared—especially *now,* you know what I mean?"

Farrell suddenly remembered something that chilled him. "When I called you before—they said 'Homicide'!"

"Any death like this where there's an autopsy goes through Homicide. They called me in because she was my case." Casanova looked at his watch and downed his drink. "I been here too long already. If I hear anything new I'll clue you."

"Thanks for the tip," Farrell said as he left.

He sat morosely, eyes fixed on the bottles lining the back bar and seeing only Alison's distant image. Dan approached him and he looked up. "Make it scotch this time, Dan, on the rocks, double."

The bartender served him, then leaned on the bar close to him. "Tony, I couldn't help hearing some of that. *Are* you in some kind of jam? You haven't got yourself wired up with—you know, any of the wrong people, have you? I know that cop's a narc. . . ."

Farrell looked at him bleakly, then tossed down the double scotch, shook his head and left.

Later, at Anthony's, Liz turned her face to the back bar and wept soundlessly when he told her about Alison. He didn't know what else to say and retreated, with only a glance at Pete, who'd overheard, to keep an eye on her. Oddly, it seemed to Farrell, Pete himself all at once looked very ill at ease.

In the office there were new messages: one from Michael, another from "Mr. Blackman." He dialed Casualty Mutual first.

Thomas himself answered. He had not yet heard about Alison and swore softly in commiseration with Farrell's brooding sense of guilt. But what exercised him more was the source of the information. "Casanova!" the FBI man exclaimed. "That's what I was calling you about—to steer clear of him, in fact. He's about to get himself busted."

"Busted! What for?"

"Dealing narcotics. Our undercover people have a dead make on him, and tonight they're pulling the plug. It's what we've been waiting for. Frank might be a big help to us."

"Hey," Farrell cut in quickly, "I hope you're not going to tell him about me!"

"Oh, no. We don't have *that* much faith in him. It'll be interesting, though, to see if he tells us about you."

"What do you do then?"

"As far as he's concerned," Thomas said evenly, "we will start keeping an eye on you."

"Getting back to the other thing," said Farrell, "he told me I might get a visit from the D.A.'s people. That could be a complication I don't need right now."

"Mmmm . . ." the agent considered. "You may have a point. I think all you can do is roll with the punch. No fancy footwork."

The call from the D.A.'s office came the next day. Sergeant Vincent Hurley asked if he would mind coming downtown at his earliest convenience to make a formal statement on the subject of Alison Fournier. Farrell protested that he'd already told all he knew, but Hurley said there'd been a new development on which Farrell might be able to shed some light.

Farrell had a half-hour wait in the anteroom. Among the nine or ten visitors seated about in varying states of anxiety or expectation the subdued air seemed like an employment office or doctor's waiting room.

Finally called inside, he found himself blocked by a tall man coming out. Farrell looked at him: tall, graying, face drawn, jaw clenched, eyes strained and hard. Farrell sensed both deep distress and anger in the man, and sidestepped to let him pass.

He was received briskly by a pudgy Assistant District Attorney named Jacobson. Sgt. Hurley was present, and a third man Farrell sized up as another detective. Jacobson wasted no time: "You've heard about Miss Fournier?"

Farrell nodded gravely. "It was on the news last night." The early television reports, as well as accounts in the morning papers, had said only that the young woman had drowned as the result of an automobile accident on eastern Long Island; most of the story in each case was devoted to the prominence of her father. To Farrell's relief, there had been no references to Alison's arrest on a narcotics charge, nor of any other of the incidents at the Elysée Hotel weeks earlier. Significant, too, it had impressed him, was the absence of any speculation in the news media over the question of suicide.

Jacobson first asked him to relate again the circumstances of their meeting that afternoon at Anthony's. Then he switched to the Elysée, and Farrell once more mouthed his account of his inopportune intrusion into the affair.

"To your knowledge, was Miss Fournier regularly engaged in the sale or exchange of illicit narcotics?"

"Not to my knowledge."

"Would you say she was given to the regular use of drugs herself?"

"No . . . I wouldn't say that."

"Occasionally, perhaps? Now and then?"

"I couldn't say. I didn't keep tabs on her social life."

"I see." Jacobson frowned at the folder in his lap. "Then you would have no way of knowing that Miss Fournier might have been into anything more lethal—say heroin?'' His eyes came up sharply.

Farrell bristled. "I wouldn't believe it if she'd sworn it to me herself! Alison was just not that type."

"I see," said Jacobson again, studying Farrell with half-closed eyes. He tapped the folder. "The autopsy report we've just received tells a somewhat different story. Her death was officially caused by drowning. But she probably would have been dead soon in any event—from a massive overdose of heroin."

Farrell was thunderstruck. "I just can't believe it! Why would she—?"

"What makes this especially interesting," Jacobson went on in the same flat tone, "is that nowhere on her body are there any signs to indicate she had injected herself with any regularity —none of the needle tracks of the habitual user. So, to that extent at least, your appraisal of her would seem justified.

"However, you can see how this makes it even more puzzling. Was her running the car off the road the unintended result of an overdose? Or had she administered the drug with the full, premeditated intent of destroying herself? Or . . ."—Jacobson paused—"*was* the heroin self-administered?"

Farrell involuntarily shuddered. "You're saying she could have been—?"

"I'm not *saying*. I'm asking."

"Well, if you're asking me, I can't help you."

"What was she running from?" asked Jacobson crisply.

"I don't know any more than what I've told you—the same as I told him," Farrell said with a tilt of his head toward Sgt. Hurley, "the first time. I wish I did."

Jacobson frowned. "The fact remains, you are the last person known to have been in direct contact with her."

"Come on!" said Farrell. "That was a couple of weeks ago. Surely somebody—"

"Ah, yes," the other broke in, "that what's so curious. You

see, I neglected to mention, according to the autopsy, Miss Fournier's death occurred just about two weeks ago . . . within hours, perhaps, of your meeting with her!"

Farrell was speechless.

With a glance at Hurley and the other detective, the Assistant D.A. said to Farrell: "So, if we can go back to square one . . ."

Farrell came out of it with a jolt. *Wait a minute, here!* "No," he said. "That's all there is. I came down here—voluntarily—to help. Now you're putting me on the griddle. Well, forget it. Either you charge me with something, or I take a walk—*now*."

Hurley spoke up. "There's no need to get upset, Mr. Farrell. We really only want to have a friendly discussion."

"Yeah, friendly. Well, you've got my statement. Now I've got other things to do. So, if you'll excuse me." Farrell got up and started for the door.

"You do have an attorney, Mr. Farrell?" Jacobson snapped after him.

Farrell turned to him coldly. "If I need one."

"I'd say you will." The A.D.A. scanned his notes. "Your day in court comes up quite soon now."

Farrell refrained from slamming the door as he went out. He was halfway across the anteroom before becoming aware that the tall gray-haired man stood in his path to the elevators. They appraised one another for a moment, then the man said: "So, you're Farrell."

It came to him then who he was. "Mr. Fournier," he said, "I can't tell you how sorry I am. Your daughter was—she was a nice girl."

"Oh, yes, a nice girl." The voice was laced with bitterness. "But you—I wonder how nice *you* are?"

"I don't know how to answer that, sir."

"Perhaps not. Or maybe you know very well! What was your relationship with my daughter?" he demanded, voice rising.

"We were friends," he said. "I'd give anything to—"

"Just friends? Or was there something more? Some sort of *business* relationship?"

Farrell could not prevent a flush. "Please, Mr. Fournier . . . I understand how upset you must be. I just—I'm sorry, that's all I can say." He held the older man's eye a moment, hoping to transmit some sense of earnestness, then stepped around Fournier and walked toward the exit.

The wretched man hurled after him: "You haven't heard the last of this!" Farrell kept going, out to the elevators.

18

Farrell walked dejectedly through Foley Square, his mind in a turmoil. Accident? Or suicide? Could Alison actually have meant to take her own life? She might have been that close to the edge. But still, why that way? Try as he would, he simply could not picture it. But if not that, and not an accident, then . . . was it possible?

The fact was, it might be one of the surer ways to eliminate somebody with a minimum of fuss or likelihood of detection. A bullet in the head, a rope, a hit-and-run—all left too many questions of directed assault. But this: The girl is quietly kidnapped, driven by night far out to a remote part of Long Island, and there. . . . It would have taken only two persons, one to hold her secure, muffling her, as the other injected her with a massive dose until the pestilence flooded her veins, ravaging her strength and will. Then, when she was insensible, they would drive her to the water's edge, throw her car in gear, and—

Farrell shivered. His mind went back to a submerged memory. That night at the Club Royale with Cheech, attempting so earnestly to convince him that Alison posed no threat to them. And Cheech hearing him out quietly, just sitting back as if the matter was no longer of any real concern to him: *Okay. You wanna let it ride, I ain't gonna argue with you no more.* And then the very next day, being told that Alison was "missing."

Was it possible? Yeah, it was, he concluded grimly. There

was probably no outrage he could safely put past one such as Cheech. Farrell suddenly flayed himself. Who was the one who must bear the ultimate guilt? No one but himself.

Shrill whistling somewhere close by finally pierced his consciousness. He looked about. A yellow cab was slowly cruising alongside. The driver gestured to him. Roy Thomas!

"Where to?" the agent said when Farrell got in. Thomas twisted around to study him with concern. "What's wrong? You look shellshocked."

Farrell slumped back. "I am, in a way," he muttered. "Let's just ride a while. Uptown. Anywhere."

"That *must* have been a kick in the ass," was Thomas's response to Farrell's morose account of his session in the D.A.'s office. "But I don't see how they have a prayer of tying you to—" He glanced into the mirror. "Murder—that *is* pretty far-out."

"I wish I could think so. . . ."

"What do you mean?"

Farrell dully related his morbid speculations about Cheech.

"Hmmm. I suppose it is possible, but—" The agent considered. "It's still pretty remote. Not that I'd put anything vicious past your buddy. But this doesn't really seem his style. Too slick."

"Slick?" cried Farrell. "You call *that*—?"

"Hold on, don't pop your cork. I mean, he's more basic —wham, bam, breaking heads. Now, if this *was* planned, it's more like . . . well, how the Giant might have handled it."

Farrell thought about that. It hadn't occurred to him, because after all it was Brothers who had seemed to be trying to moderate the difference of opinion over Alison; he had even cautioned Farrell to settle the matter agreeably before Cheech might take any rash action on his own. Yet . . . if Cheech could be capable of anything, was the Giant any less so, just because he showed more polish? Still dissatisfied, angry, he grumbled, "Maybe . . ."

Thomas was eying him in the mirror. "Listen," the agent said sharply, "listen good. If you're thinking what I think you're thinking—forget it! I can understand how you feel about that girl, but you've got to put it aside. It's over. It's a shame, but there's nothing you can do for her now. You think only about helping yourself, period. Let yourself get sidetracked now by remorse, or retaliation, whatever, and *you're* going to wind up the loser. There's only one job you've got to do. Keep your mind on that and *only* that."

Neither spoke for several minutes as the cab made its way north on the East River Drive. Thomas finally asked sideways: "Did you happen to notice any black dude hanging around the D.A.'s office, or in the lobby?"

"Not especially, no. Why?"

"One came out of the building right after you. He watched till you got in the cab, then I saw him jump in a car waiting across the street. He and his buddy have been on us ever since."

Farrell turned to peer out the rear window.

"Don't look too long," Thomas commanded. "A dark blue sedan, two or three behind us. They're cool."

"Who are they—D.A.'s cops?"

"Don't know 'em," Thomas shook his head. "Maybe privates of Fournier's?"

"Jesus!" swore Farrell. "Already?"

"I *would* like to avoid anybody making the two of us together," the agent said, "whoever they are."

"You want to let me out somewhere now?"

"I'll drop you where you'd naturally get off. You say when."

"The restaurant'll be fine," Farrell said.

The blue car was still behind as the cab pulled up in front of Anthony's. "Just act normal," Thomas said as he made change. "Go inside and see what happens. I'll stay close by."

Farrell got out, and Thomas flipped on the "Off Duty" lights atop the cab and moved away down Second Avenue. Farrell crossed the sidewalk and was about to enter the restaurant when a voice hailed him: "Hey, Tony! Wait up."

The blue car had drawn to the curb. A black man wearing a jacket but no tie leaned from the driver's window.

"You in a hurry, man?" he called out.

Farrell peered in at the car's occupants. There was something familiar about the driver, though he couldn't quite place him; he couldn't make out the other one. "What do you want?" he called back.

"Come on over, man. Somebody wants to talk to you."

After a moment's hesitation, Farrell approached them slowly. "Who's 'somebody'?" he asked.

The man waited until Farrell was alongside before answering. "Somebody *big,* man. Over on One-oh-four Street—you dig?"

Now he recognized them. A couple of the Giant's honchos! A thrill skittered up his spine.

"Anything wrong?"

The man's eyes were pinpoint hard. "You just wanna climb in?"

Farrell opened the rear door and got in. As they drove off, he looked toward the restaurant again. Liz, her face drawn with anxious questions, watched from the front window.

Roy Thomas, who had pulled into a vacant loading zone in the middle of the next block south, gave them a short head start, then pulled out and followed—across Manhattan to the west side and uptown.

It gave him a turn when he realized that the pair who'd tailed them from Foley Square belonged to the Giant. To think that Farrell was being watched so closely—as closely as to the D.A.'s office! Was this something recent, Thomas had to wonder, or . . . had it been the case all along? The latter possibility made him shudder: So many times in the past weeks Farrell could have been compromised if spotted in a clandestine rendezvous with the agents! But, Thomas made himself reason, if Farrell *had* been detected, surely something would have been done about it long before this; it was unimaginable that he would have been allowed access to so much detail in the cocaine setup, for one big thing, had he been suspect.

Continuing around the block, he found a space close to a hydrant on the far side of Riverside Drive, which afforded him a relatively unobstructed view into West 104th Street. Turning off the engine, Thomas slumped behind the wheel, the peak of his cap lowered to eye level, and became the tired cabbie making a rest stop.

Rationalizations be damned, he just did not like this. Could Farrell persuade them of the actual reason for his visit to the D.A.? If they were not easily convinced, would they turn the screws on him? What if, under extreme pressure, he cracked? Conceivably he might never come out of that building again, at least not freely. What then? Brendan Hartnett had once estimated that if this investigation could be developed to conclusion without a major setback, Farrell's *personal* testimony would put the chances of finally nailing the Giant as high as ninety to ten; without him the odds would soften, maybe to sixty-five to thirty-five—still a pretty good shot.

Yet cold calculation was no substitute for the man. Thomas tried to think what to do. He contemplated calling in for backup . . . then discarded the idea. What would they do, storm the building, have a big shootout? That would be foolishly, and wastefully, reckless. It would blow everything apart before it was time. There *was* nothing he could do, except sweat it out.

The Giant was deep in a discussion with two visitors when Farrell was ushered upstairs. One was the chic young black woman Farrell had met there before; the other was a tall, lean white man with modish black hair and an expensively tailored look of utter assurance.

Brothers looked up. "Ah, Tony." But there was no warmth in the greeting, and he remained seated. "You remember the lovely Miss Dubois, of course."

"Definitely," Farrell said, taking her hand with a smile.

"I don't believe you've met this gentleman: the esteemed counsellor, Arnold Weissberg. The timing would seem fortuitous, don't you think?" Brothers added with a significant glance at Farrell.

Weissberg half rose and gave Farrell a cursory hand.

"Why don't you go inside, Tony," Brothers proposed, indicating the adjoining room, "and fix yourself a drink, while we conclude our business. Arnold is explaining to Millie the technicalities of incorporation. We shouldn't be but a few more minutes."

"Sure. Nice to see you again," Farrell said to the woman. He went next door. Lighting a cigarette, he was surprised to find his hands trembling. He tried to concentrate on calmly reasoning out the Giant's state of mind. First the almost furtive manner of his interception; now the relative chilliness of his reception here—it seemed vaguely ominous, as though he might suddenly have fallen into disfavor—or, for some reason, distrust? But why? Could it simply be alarm at his having been called before the District Attorney just as the big cocaine operation was about to be inaugurated? Or had he unknowingly slipped up somewhere else, somehow tipped off the double part he was playing? He wracked his brain to recall anything he'd done or said lately that could have sparked doubt. Just stay cool, Farrell exhorted himself. As the Giant had noted once, self-created problems tended to snowball and become self-fulfilling.

He hoped Roy Thomas knew where he was.

The meeting sounded like it was breaking up, and soon the three of them appeared in the doorway. "Millie is leaving," said Brothers. "I knew you'd want to say goodbye."

She was lovely in a creamy suede pants suit, a tan mohair coat over her shoulders. "We hardly said hello," Farrell said with a rueful smile.

"We do seem to meet and run." Millie smiled back.

"Surely there will be other opportunities for the two of you to become better acquainted," Brothers said. "If all goes well."

"I'll look forward to that," said Farrell, asking himself if the Giant had intended any significance with his last remark.

Brothers walked her to the stairway. "Transportation is waiting for you downstairs. Forgive me if I don't escort you," he said with an explanatory tip of his head toward Farrell and Weissberg.

"I understand. Aaron, I can't thank you enough for all you're doing. . . ."

"The gratitude is mutual, my dear, I assure you," Brothers purred. "We complement one another."

Watching her go, Farrell wondered again if the bright-eyed young woman really suspected whom she was getting herself mixed up with.

The Giant returned looking somber. "Well, Tony, I gather you've managed after all to attract some unwanted attention."

"You can hardly say I 'managed' it," Farrell said. Defensive and nettled at the same time, he explained. "The kid turns up dead, and they insist I was the last one seen with her. She was loaded up with horse."

Brothers raised an eyebrow at that but showed no alarm. "How unfortunate this should have come to light now, of all times."

Farrell shrugged apologetically.

"Who talked to you downtown?" Weissberg spoke out.

Farrell told them, summarizing the interview.

"Jacobson, eh?" the lawyer said. "He'd like to be a hardnose, but he can be handled. Definitely not first-string," he said to Brothers.

The Giant had been observing Farrell intently, as though from a long distance. "The larger question that persists in my mind," he said at last, "is whether Tony has supplied us with the most accurate interpretation of what has transpired."

Farrell stirred, about to object, and was stilled by a raised hand.

"That is to say," Brothers continued, "might there yet be

some unstated meaning here that we fail to recognize? Might the District Attorney's true purpose be more covert, might he in fact be probing deeper than the cause of one young woman's quite possibly accidental death—however unfortunate and, ah, unusual that may have been?"

Farrell gave him a blank look. "That's all they seemed interested in. I got the feeling her old man must be pressuring them—the way he was hanging around there."

"Just so. Undoubtedly he *has* been pressuring them. I can only wonder: Could the influential Mr. Fournier be playing the role here of cat's-paw—with or without his own knowledge?"

Farrell measured the other two. "Remember, they do know she was in the middle of at least one big dope setup. And they know what can—happen to people, sometimes. . . ."

"I think it's time now I absented myself," declared Weissberg, rising, "before we start bandying names. Aaron, I'll set that other business in motion at once. Mr. Farrell, I understand your court appearance comes up shortly. In your situation, able legal representation would be advisable, regardless of the charge; but now, in light of the District Attorney's untimely new interest in you, I think it essential—in the interests of all concerned here—that you have the best possible representation. Here's my card. Call me. We'll sit down without distraction and discuss your case thoroughly. Then I'll decide what steps are required."

When Weissberg was gone, Farrell and Brothers settled back in moody silence. It occurred to Farrell that for once Abou Jamal had not been in evidence. Usually it was Jamal's baleful presence that he found unsettling. But today he didn't need the hatchetman to make him feel uncomfortable.

"Francesco is due back later tonight," the Giant said, returning to the subject obliquely. "He has completed the arrangements, and the enterprise is activated. In just another week . . ." The expression on his face registered with Farrell: In effect, don't screw things up now by giving outside forces any more cause to pry than they already have.

Farrell nodded resignedly, but had to relieve himself of one last brooding shot: "I just hope this hasn't opened up a can of worms it was intended to bury."

The Giant gave him a sharp look. "Intended or not, what's done is done. Let the worms lie. They have a natural tendency to bury themselves."

Brothers walked Farrell to the stairs and had a parting shot of his own: "You will keep us informed should the District Attorney contact you again?"

Farrell turned and looked up at him, searching for any irony. "You'll be the first to know," he said, and continued out.

The Giant picked up the telephone and pressed an intercom button. Almost at once it was picked up: "Yeah."

"You got everything, Boo?"

"From the top."

"What do you think?"

Boo hesitated, then said tonelessly: "We should keep an eye on him."

"Yes. It would also be well to have somebody look into his visit downtown."

"We already on that."

The effect of watching his wife emerge from the Giant's headquarters and drive off with one of those forbidding Muslim types had left Roy Thomas shaken. His first inclination was to bolt from the cab and— Christ, no! Wouldn't *that* be a smart move! He watched tautly, his body yearning toward his wife, and urged calm upon himself. Camille was in no danger, of course—not here and now, anyway. He wondered if Farrell had met her again in there and hoped he hadn't. Thomas couldn't really explain why . . . it was just—well, somehow he didn't like these two extremes of his life coming into actual contact. Yet they already had, hadn't they?

Thomas could not help but think back to the conversation he and his wife had had just a few evenings earlier, when Camille breezed in from the city bubbling. She paraded before her husband with the exaggerated languorous grace of a fashion model. "Camille Dubois, *couturière!* How does that sound, darling? Oh—you don't mind my using Dubois professionally, do you, love? It has such a continental flavor—*n'est-ce pas, mon chéri?*" she vamped.

"But of course," he mimicked back, forcing a smile. "But what—?"

"My benefactor. He's getting me together with his attorney to draw up incorporation papers—for my very own business! And then he wants to give a dinner party to celebrate our partnership! You'll *have* to come, Roy. Isn't it marvelous? I still can hardly believe it—I'm afraid I'll wake up any minute!"

"I almost wish you would," he said sourly.

She cut short her prancing to stare at him. "Now what does *that* mean?"

Thomas saw he'd taken the wrong tack, but now he felt committed. "I just don't know about all this. You happen to bump into this fat cat you haven't seen in years, and just like that he's setting you up in business? It just doesn't seem natural."

"Hey now," she flared, "if you're thinking what it sounds like—you can just cool it, mister!" She turned away from him, suddenly wounded and deflated.

"I'm sorry. I just can't help wondering what this guy is really after."

Her anger subsided. "This can be a marvelous opportunity for me, Roy," she explained. "This man is a businessman, smart, imaginative, and daring. He sees real potential in my ideas, and he's willing to back them up with money and time and influence." She gauged him. "Do you *really* doubt me?"

Thomas shook his head. "Of course not. But—well, hell, it does bother me . . . knowing other guys might even *think* like that about you."

She reached out and softly traced his face with her fingertips. "But you should know you're the only one." She sat back, smiling at him. "Anyway, Aaron happens to be a perfect gentleman."

Aaron. The sound of it stabbed him inside. It struck him then that in fact it was the first time she'd mentioned her munificent patron's name to him.

"Actually, I think you'll like him, Roy. You will come to the dinner?"

Fat chance, he was thinking, but he said with a shrug: "You know my hours. It's hard to say. . . ." Another disturbing idea crossed his mind. "Have you, uh, talked about me at all? To him or his friends?" Including one Tony Farrell, he thought.

"No . . . I don't think so. There hasn't been the occasion, really."

"It might not be a bad idea if you didn't mention what I do. That often turns people off, even honest people. I wouldn't want to be the cause of any problems, even indirectly."

She eyed him uncertainly. "Well of course, if you don't *want* me to . . ."

"I just think it would be better for you." He weighed his next remark. "For that matter, considering everything —'Camille Dubois, *couturière,*' and such—maybe you shouldn't even mention you've *got* an old man laying around the house."

She arched her brows at him. "Well, isn't *this* a different tune from a few minutes ago!"

He managed a thin smile. "Just trying to be continental. After all, you don't want to blow your French connection." Or put your head to the guillotine, Thomas had added to himself with a shiver. . . .

His dour musings were interrupted as another person he recognized came out of the building: Brothers' lawyer, Weissberg. A swine, but a damned sharp trial lawyer. If they did get the Giant into a courtroom, Weissberg would be the one Hartnett would have to deal with; and he knew all the angles, he would not be easy. Versatile was hardly an adequate word to categorize Arnold Weissberg. His client list had ranged an unlikely gamut from top corporate takeover artists to four-star mobsters to scruffy bomb-throwing radicals—the more newsworthy and/or notorious the better, it seemed. He took the big bucks from the high-powered hustlers and often worked for free for the rabble-rousers. Just where Weissberg really stood —where his true sympathies or convictions, if any, lay —nobody could quite figure out. It was said he'd originally built his success as the pet defender of Mafia "businessmen," but that they'd eventually soured on him because of the attention he kept attracting to himself defending hippie anarchists and surly Indians—"causes" that no doubt alienated his more bourgeois clientele as distastefully un-American. Now, on retainer to Aaron Luke Brothers and his growing conglomerate of interests, Weissberg probably considered himself as sharing the best of two possible worlds: serving yet another "oppressed minority," and carving himself a sizable chunk of the pie of the future. God help the oppressed *and* the future! thought the black federal agent with a grimace.

Thomas heaved a great sigh of relief when at last Farrell appeared. Alone. He stopped on the sidewalk to light a cigarette and looked up and down the street. Thomas did not move. He didn't want Farrell to spot him yet and head straight for the parked cab; somebody could be watching from inside. Let him get away from the building, in the opposite direction preferably, and Thomas would catch up with him.

In the next moment, he was doubly glad he'd waited. For as Farrell did turn and start walking at an easy pace east toward West End Avenue, out of a side door of the building slipped two black men, their gaze following Farrell. As he neared the next corner, one of the men crossed 104th Street, then the two of them, on opposite sidewalks, proceeded deliberately after him.

Thomas did not like the looks of it. Out of the frying pan—? He decided to head Farrell off. Starting the cab, he made a slow U-turn into 104th Street. Farrell was at the far corner now, peering up West End Avenue as though searching for a taxi. Coming right up, mister, thought Thomas grimly as he cruised through the block, passing between the pair trailing Farrell without glancing at either. He remembered to switch on the roof light signifying that the cab was available. But then, before he was halfway to West End, he saw another cab swerve to a stop at the corner ahead and Farrell get in. Damn! was the agent's reaction; he had to warn Farrell, as well as find out what was going on.

Farrell's cab pulled away, and Thomas, coming to a stop at the signal light on the corner, leaned forward to watch it down West End Avenue, memorizing the plate number. He was about to turn after it when his rear door opened and a man's voice drawled, getting into the cab, "Lose a fare, brother? You got another. Let's see where that cat goes to."

The door slammed shut. Two men had climbed in. Thomas didn't have to look around to know who they were. He protested: "I was just going off duty."

"Bull*shit!*" one of them growled. "We see you jes' turn on your light. Now you move it, 'fore you lose that mother!"

"Let's go, brother," the first said. "You don't wanna make us itchy."

Thomas made the turn onto West End. His passengers did not speak to him again, concentrating on the vehicle ahead. Thomas stole looks at them in his mirror: two stern, unlined faces, glistening heads, narrow, alert eyes. He marked them as qualified assassins. Farrell's taxi turned, east, taking them through Central Park, coming out at 79th Street and Fifth Avenue. After a few more blocks, Thomas guessed Farrell's destination was his apartment. Then what? Carefully he slid a hand inside his windbreaker and fingered the revolver in its holster. If these two *were* aiming to hit Farrell, he would have to make a move; at least they wouldn't be the only ones with the edge of surprise.

It was growing dusk as they turned into East 84th Street.

Thomas could feel the two in the back tense, peering ahead intently as the first cab's brake lights glowed and it eased to a stop in front of an apartment house.

"Keep goin'," one commanded hoarsely, "right on past. Take it nice 'n' slow."

Thomas's hand felt again for the butt of his gun. Scarcely breathing, he guided the vehicle toward the narrow lane left by the one double-parked outside Farrell's building. Coming alongside, gratefully he saw that the other cab provided a shield for Farrell, who had paid his fare and was crossing the sidewalk to the entrance. The Giant's men, keeping to the shadows, watched Farrell go inside as they passed. Thomas breathed out, his bound muscles loosening.

Almost at the corner, one of them said: "Pull over here." They had a quick murmuring huddle, then one got out. "Don't leave me here all fuckin' night," he said to the other before closing the door.

"Have fun, brother." The one still in the cab grinned through the window.

Where to now? thought Thomas with irritation. He had to get to Farrell. "Hey, mister," he said over his shoulder. "What's going on? You got where you wanted. I have to sign this heap in!"

"Don't give me your problems, man," retorted the other. "You wanna get paid? Take me back uptown."

"All the way back—? Hey, come on, give me a break! I'm overdue. There are plenty other cabs—"

The man leaned on the seat back. "Don't give me no trouble, nigger," he said with quiet menace.

Farrell was tired and preoccupied as he walked across the lobby of his apartment. It had been a long, emotionally draining day. From the D.A. . . . and poor Alison, and her father . . . to the Giant. He needed a respite to sort things out. Where had Thomas gone to—? He started at the glimpse of a figure rising from one of the vestibule chairs and approaching him.

"Michael! How long have you been here?"

"A while," his uncle said, unsmiling. He had a drawn look.

"Is anything wrong?" asked Farrell with concern.

Michael pressed the elevator button. "We'll talk upstairs," he said tonelessly.

Nothing was said on the way up. Farrell fumbled with his key opening the apartment door. It was dark inside, and he went to turn on some lights.

Michael shut the door deliberately and double-locked it. Turning to Farrell, his face was like granite. When he spoke, the words were measured as though squeezed one by one through the clenched teeth: "You've been ducking me, haven't you?"

"Hey, Michael—no! I've been meaning to get back to you, really. But every time—I've just been so tied up lately, it's—"

"Tied up with what?"

"Oh, you know—the place, mostly. . . ."

"The place." Michael's eyes burned into him. "Every time I call they tell me you're out somewhere. You don't seem to spend that much time there. You must have something else going you haven't told me about."

"No, I—you don't understand. . . ." Farrell fumbled, alarm rising in him. "See, there's a lot more to running a restaurant than just the inside. You've got to go out and deal with purveyors, make the rounds of the markets—"

"Nights as well as days, eh?" Michael cut in sharply. His mouth curled down. "Really keeps you hopping."

"It really does. But it's good. When it pays off like—"

"Balls."

"What?"

Michael came over to him and stared him full in the face. "I'm going to give you one chance to tell me something I heard is not true." It was though he'd dropped a gauntlet between them.

As much as he wanted it not to be, Farrell knew what he'd

dreaded was about to happen. But he had to play it out. "What is it, Michael?" he responded, adding hastily—and regretting the words even as he spoke them: "It's not about Linda, is it?"

Michael started, then his face darkened into a scowl. "Yeah, in a way it is, at that." He glared at Farrell a moment. "I heard what you're tied up with is a bunch of nigger scum, getting rich selling dope to kids like Linda!"

It was like a knife through Farrell's heart. He felt humiliated, suddenly both naked and helpless before the barely controlled rage of this one man who deserved the accountability he demanded. Michael knew. It would be pointless and cowardly either to attempt to lie his way out of it or to defend himself. But what could he possibly say—? "Oh God, Michael," he tried, voice cracking, "I—"

The older man's open hand flew out and slapped across Farrell's cheek like a whip, bringing tears to his eyes. "Scum!" Michael slapped him again, and again, becoming frenzied. "You filthy *scum!*"

Farrell reeled, face aflame, half blinded by smarting tears, instinctively trying to turn away from each stinging cuff yet not warding them off, as though acknowledging the righteousness of his punishment. Then he was jolted by a thumping blow high on his cheekbone that rattled his head and staggered him backward. Michael, releasing all his fury, was punching now.

"Rotten no-good bastard!" he bellowed, charging at Farrell. "I'll kill you myself!"

He threw a wild right that just caught the tip of Farrell's nose, bringing a spurt of blood, and had his left fist cocked when Farrell's hand shot out and clamped on his wrist. "Don't, Michael," he cried, "please don't!"

Michael struggled ferociously in Farrell's grip, spitting out a string of guttural obscenities in both English and Italian, and twisted around to fire the right hand again. Farrell, anticipating him, caught that wrist too, inches before the balled fist could slam into his mouth. Michael made a furious effort to free his hands, but Farrell's desperate grip was unbreakable.

The two of them stood locked together in rigid, straining immobility, gasping, perspiring in a head-to-head stalemate. "Please, Michael . . ." Farrell appealed once more, a sob catching in his throat, "this is no good. . . ."

A woman's scream from across the room startled both of them. "Tony! Michael! Oh my God, what are you *doing?*"

Liz flew at them, frantically trying to get between them. "What's the matter with you? Not *you* two! *Stop it!*"

Michael looked at her, and then, slowly, Farrell could feel the intensity ebbing out of the older man, and watched his livid face lose its color and turn to gray sadness, watched tears overflow his eyes and spill in rivulets down his cheeks. Michael looked back at Farrell and shook his head without speaking, and, the struggle over, Farrell gradually released his hold on him. Michael turned away from them and stood with his head bowed, motionless but for the heaving of his shoulders as he wept soundlessly.

Liz glanced from one to the other helplessly, as if unsure which needed more comforting. Farrell put his arm around her shoulders and drew her close, as, desolate, he watched Michael through a mist of his own now. And, in sudden resolve not to let his uncle go away thinking *only this* of him, he made a decision.

"Michael," he said in a hoarse whisper, "it's not just what you—there's more to it—a lot more. I want you to know. Please." Eyes on Michael, entreating him, Farrell went to the telephone and lifted the receiver, laying it aside. He wanted no calls now.

Michael listened to him, scornful at first, then in progressive stages of disbelief, wonderment, fascination and, finally, when he could visualize all of it as a whole, with great sadness.

When Farrell was finished, they sat looking bleakly at one another. There was nothing to discuss, no way now to undo what had been done or change what must be done.

They were silent again, absorbed in separate reflections on past, present and future . . . until Farrell asked quietly, "How *is* Linda?"

Michael's eyes turned hard for just an instant, then softened. "She's coming along real well," he said. He seemed to be looking through Farrell. "She always asks for you."

After Michael was gone, it never occurred to Farrell to ask himself how or where his uncle had found out about him. Alone, he and Liz just looked at each other blankly, both eyes and hearts barren. Finally, wearily, he slipped an arm around her and they started upstairs. Remembering the phone, he went back down and replaced the receiver. He'd hardly turned away before it rang with loud urgency. He looked toward her in abject futility. She continued up the stairs in silence.

"Yes?" he answered.

"Specs? Are you all right?" It was Blackman/Thomas.

"Yes," he said in a dead voice.

"I've been trying to get you. The line's been busy. I was getting worried."

"It was off the hook. I wanted a breather."

"Don't do that to me, man!" Thomas scolded. "I thought maybe— Nobody's been there? You've had no visitors?"

Farrell hesitated, then said: "No." He wasn't up to relating the confrontation with Michael.

"That's a relief. Now listen." Thomas told him about the two who'd trailed him from 104th Street. "It looks like they're going to keep you in their sights from now on. So far it's just surveillance, but— We'll have to watch every step now, think twice before every move. What happened back there?"

Farrell described the Giant's curiosity—and, maybe, his onset of suspicion. Then he remembered about Cheech. "He mentioned the deal is set, Cheech is on his way back. The first load could be moving right now. Another week, he said . . ." His voice trailed off as he contemplated. A week somehow had become as distant as a year.

"This is what we've been waiting for, working toward," the agent declared, trying to pump him up. "Can you make it?"

Farrell sighed heavily. "I've got nowhere else to go."

"Oh yes you do—*if* you can hold on just a while longer. And it could be sooner than you think!"

19

Four carefully selected JUST agents—two men and two women, cleared personally by Brendan Hartnett—had boarded the *SS Zaandam* at Port of Miami amongst several hundred other Caribbean-bound vacationers. Of the vessel's crew, only her captain, whose absolute integrity had been certified by the Holland-American Line, knew of the agents' presence on board, although even he did not know their purpose.

They were to watch and log every movement of two couples traveling separately: one pair from Camden, New Jersey, using the name Browne; the other from Towson, Maryland, under the name Johnson. Both couples were black, as were about a third of the passengers on this cruise.

On the morning of the second day out of Miami, the *Zaandam* put in at Port-au-Prince, Haiti. Most of the passengers went ashore, among them the Brownes and, somewhat later, the Johnsons. Two agents stayed with each. Neither pair appeared to follow any set pattern nor the same route; they moved around as aimlessly as any tourists—exploring, browsing, haggling over trinkets and knickknacks, sampling the local food, taking snapshots of each other, sunning at bazaars or outdoor cafes—except that each couple, at different times, did exactly the same thing just before returning to the ship: They stopped into a small back-street shop featuring handcrafted native artifacts and emerged some time later carrying gift-wrapped packages, in each instance their only substantial acquisitions.

Upon landing at San Juan the next day, an odd similarity of both couples' behavior was noted almost at once. Upon clearing the pier, each separately sought out a public telephone booth and placed a brief call; then, in each instance, they waited around the entrance to the pier, off to one side, apart from other passengers. Each had a large mesh shopping bag in which could be seen the gaily wrapped packages. Shortly, in each case, a taxi arrived to pick them up—evidently in response to the call. (But why *call* for a taxi when there was a cab line right in front of the pier, many still empty?) On both occasions the responding taxis were Prontos.

The first pair were followed to the Caribe Hilton, where they dismissed the cab. They wandered about the Hilton, then strolled down Ashford Avenue, along hotel row, stopping into several as it seemed to strike their fancy, having a leisurely drink or bite to eat here, browsing for postcards or souvenirs there. In late afternoon, they rode a bus back down to the harbor and the *Zaandam.*

The second couple left their cab in Old San Juan and spent the rest of the day exploring and sampling the charms of the restored original Spanish settlement. To return to the ship, they hailed a taxi at random—not a Pronto.

Later, in examining the results of the surveillance, the undercover agents agreed that on their respective excursions the Brownes and the Johnsons this time had done *two* things exactly alike: One, telephoning for a Pronto; and two, each couple leaving the cab at their destination *without* the wrapped gift packages from Haiti.

Each cab was tracked, of course—both to the central Pronto garage, where the drivers carried the mesh shopping bags inside. So they knew the *how,* at least the first part of it; now local investigators could get to work ferreting out the *who,* which would complete the picture. New York should be pleased.

Reboarding the *Zaandam* to stay with their subjects dutifully through the final leg of the voyage, the agents relaxed, hopeful that they might enjoy what was left of the cruise.

They would have been less easy had they realized that a certain pair of individuals, two young black men who'd traveled together from Miami, had not returned to the ship after the stopover at San Juan; the agents did not realize it because, absorbed in their surveillance, they'd simply never noticed the unobtrusive pair. These two, known only to Abou Jamal on instruction from the Giant, had been sent to covertly "watchdog" the Brownes and Johnsons from embarkation through delivery of their precious cargo in San Juan, keeping sharp eyes out for any unusual attention or misadventures the couples might encounter anywhere along the way. Finally, if all proceeded without hitch, they were to shepherd the merchandise back to New York.

And now, as they followed the apparently smooth transfer of the cocaine from Pronto Taxi to the designated couriers, the two watchdogs were vaguely troubled: A keen sense of alien presence had given them bad vibes. Especially in San Juan. Somehow, without being able to pinpoint exactly what was out of synch, they'd got the feeling that the flawless operation was being orchestrated by other forces.

Positive affirmation that the major targets had received the illegal goods was necessary, Brendan Hartnett insisted, to cap the case against them. Hartnett would settle for no less than eyewitness testimony to this effect. More conclusive, of course, would be to catch the ringleaders in actual possession of the stuff; but many circumstances, all unpredictable, would have to fall exactly in place to achieve that sort of coup, and the Giant had proved over the years that he was not so accident-prone.

In either case, the onus would lie solely with Tony Farrell. For Frank Casanova, the other informant amidst the conspirators, was now rated as less than trustworthy.

The rogue detective had provided JUST investigators with quite a bit of helpful information about what he knew of the day-to-day workings of the Brothers organization, some of which had already led to successful abortion of several choice criminal actions, including arrests of some lesser confederates of the Giant's and Cheech Donato's. But about the cocaine operation Casanova was playing it very cozy. He had volunteered no information about the scheme, although he'd been as much privy to the particulars as Farrell; and when nudged about so-called rumors in the street of something big about to go down, he'd acknowledged only that he too had heard such talk and promised to "keep my eyes and ears open."

Hartnett's people figured that any of three likely factors shaped Casanova's thinking about this: One, he was afraid to get himself any more ensnarled than he already was with them by further complicity in what stacked up as a top-drawer felony rap; two, he was slyly keeping it on ice for himself, should he finally need all possible leverage to wiggle off their hook; or three, he hoped somehow to cut into the enormous pie without detection on either side—unable to resist playing both ends against the middle, even on the brink of personal disaster. They could not challenge him about the cocaine deal, for that would suggest another intimate source of their information.

Thus it was up to Farrell alone to make the case. He had been waiting restlessly, counting days and hours for some word from Cheech or the Giant himself that the first shipment of coke had been negotiated successfully. He'd been equipped with another Kel transmitter, to be brought into play should the opportunity arise to coordinate with JUST ("It's been tested, and the batteries are fresh," Ed Stabler had assured him); but he'd locked the device in a drawer with a prayer that it wouldn't have to come to that.

Farrell had had little contact with Cheech in more than a week, since the latter's return from his negotiations with Santiago in Florida. Partly it was because Cheech had seemed to throw himself, with a singlemindedness noteworthy even for him, into personally looking after his bread-and-butter "businesses"; and also because Farrell, for his own part, had contrived to give his associate as wide a berth as he could at this time, short of pointedly avoiding him.

One reason—other than the suspicion and resentment he still harbored toward Cheech over Alison—was the sense that his every move might be under scrutiny now by God knew how many different arms of the law: D.A.'s investigators, narcotics dicks, private snoops of Fournier's, any of them surely would be more than interested to log him in close or frequent company with a known racketeer like Cheech Donato. At this critical stage, Farrell needed no more complications; so he had taken pains to devote all the time he could, with Liz, to the affairs of Anthony's, determined to remain as inconspicuous as possible until something broke.

But eight days had passed, the first cruise should already have returned, and yet Farrell had heard nothing. Had something gone wrong that JUST wasn't aware of? Thomas and Stabler swore that all their information was that everything had gone as planned—they were as anxious as he.

Edgily, he debated forcing the issue, seeking out Cheech in spite of himself to try to worm some clue out of him to what was happening. After all, he was supposed to be Cheech's partner. If this first shot had scored a hit, naturally he would expect they'd be buzzing now with plans to gear up for regular operation—hell, he'd half expected the Giant to throw a party to celebrate! And if they'd run into pitfalls, shouldn't he be put wise? But reflection brought him to a quandary: Maybe he was being kept in the dark for reasons he shouldn't be to eager to find out about! He decided all he could do was continue to wait.

Two hand-picked couriers had transported ten kilograms each of the cocaine in their hand luggage aboard separate flights

from San Juan to New York—one on an Eastern Airlines flight
via Atlanta to JFK, the other on an American jet direct to
Newark. Each was met at the airport by happy "relatives" who,
relieving them of their baggage, drove them off into the
obscurity of the great city.

The shipments were quickly divided into two-kilo lots and
delivered to several different locations in Brooklyn and the
Bronx for processing, packaging and storing preparatory to
distribution—all closely supervised by trusted aides of the
Giant's, who tolerated no allowance for waste, either from
spillage or pilferage. A specified quantity was set aside for the
Giant's personal disposition.

He was pleased with the quality of the narcotic and, at first,
elated by the apparent dispatch with which the plan had been
carried out—neither Frank Casanova having reported any
unusual stirrings within the local drug-enforcement establishment, nor his contacts in Washington any at Justice. But then his
enthusiasm had been deflated with the arrival of Abou Jamal's
two "watchdogs." Brothers was impatient with their inability to
document suspicion with anything more material than condi-
tioned intuition, but it was enough to disturb him—enough to
order a strict hold on any further movement of the cocaine,
while he gave attention to sounding out the depth of any trap he
might have fallen into.

It was early evening of the ninth day, and Farrell was preparing
to leave his apartment to relieve Liz at Anthony's, when the call
came from Cheech.

"What're you doin'?" he asked gruffly.

"Just on my way over to the place," Farrell responded, hope
flickering in him. "Why? Anything doing?"

"Yeah. Stick around. You're gonna have company."

"Here? Who?"

"Me. And somebody else wants to see you."

"Well, who, for Chrissake?" demanded Farrell, irritated at

the other's deviousness. "And why can't we meet at the restaurant?"

"Your joint's too public for this party. Just stick around," Cheech said and clicked off.

Farrell put down the phone, puzzled. Something seemed about to happen, and he had a rising presentiment that it might be unpleasant. Snatching up the receiver, he dialed Casualty Mutual.

To his dismay, the damn recorded voice answered. He recited the gist of Cheech's call. "I don't know what it means," he concluded, "but it doesn't sound right. One of you *please* get back to me as soon as you can." He thought a moment. "If I say it's a wrong number when you call, you'll know why."

He paced fretfully around the living room. All at once it came to him he did not want Liz home now. He grabbed for the phone again. He would try not to upset her, would just say a private meet had suddenly come up and it would be better if she stayed put. At least then, he told himself, she wouldn't be caught in the middle of . . . anything.

But Pete, who answered, said Liz had left a short while before—had some errands to do.

Frustrated, Farrell left a message for her to call if she returned—and not to come home yet.

He started prowling the room again, trying to identify what it was that had his gut in such a knot. Nothing he could put his finger on, just an instinct.

The phone rang. It was Stabler.

"Where are you when I need you?" he took it out on the policeman.

"Hey, get off your horse! I'm here. Is it okay if I go to the head once in a while?"

"Sorry. I just feel very alone all of a sudden."

"Sure. But wind down. We'll cover you. Maybe it's something, maybe not. You got the gizmo?"

He meant the Kel. Farrell squirmed. "Yes."

"Hook it up. Our friend's out in the car, probably close by.

I'll get him to plug in, and I'll be there myself in twenty minutes. If we hear anything—"

"You mean if it works this time."

"It'll work. And listen," Stabler cautioned, "if for any reason we do decide to bust in there, you don't know us, right? Don't let on *nothing*. Spit in our eye, even. You're still with *them*, remember?"

"Fucking fascist cops!" growled Farrell appropriately.

"That's the way. Stay cool."

Farrell reluctantly strapped on the miniature transmitter —hardly feeling "cool." Then he remembered the .38. He'd paid $350 for it from Cheech's contact uptown, and it had been in the pocket of his topcoat ever since. Would he finally need it tonight? He went to the closet by the apartment door and felt inside the topcoat— The doorbell jangled in his ear.

Through the peephole he could make out a magnified Cheech. No one was with him. Farrell unbolted the door.

"Where's the company?" Farrell asked.

"He'll be here," Cheech said, brushing past him. He looked around. "You alone?"

"Yeah."

"That's good." Cheech took off his coat and tossed it onto a chair. "What you got to drink?"

"Help yourself," Farrell said, indicating the sideboard. He watched Cheech pour himself half a highball glass of brandy, then sniff it as though he knew what he was doing. At last Farrell asked: "What is this, business or pleasure?"

"A little of both, maybe," said Cheech, slugging down the cognac. He looked across at Farrell with a glint in his eye.

"What the hell's going on? What about the big project? I haven't heard word one."

Cheech lowered his squarish frame into an armchair. "I'll tell ya, I was beginnin' to wonder myself—until today. I heard it went down just like it was supposed to, everything clicked in place, not a fuckin' hitch."

"So the stuff *is* in."

"Yeah . . ." The tone was qualified, like a door left ajar.

Farrell eyed him. "But . . . what?" he prodded.

"Well, it turns out there's a problem after all. A big one. He's gonna tell us all about it."

"He?"

"Himself. The Giant."

"He's coming here?"

"Should be any minute."

Farrell's skin was suddenly crawling. "I think I'll have a drink myself." He'd remembered the Kel. At the sideboard, his back to Cheech, he reached trembling fingers inside his shirt and switched it on. *Work, damn you, work!*

Farrell lit a cigarette and took a deep drag. Suddenly the doorbell rang, cutting through him like a knife. With an effort, Farrell stirred and went stiffly to the door. The huge form of Aaron Luke Brothers filled the peephole.

"Good evening, Tony!" he said heartily as he entered. "Thank you for making yourself available. I shan't keep you long." With complete assurance, he settled onto the divan and motioned Farrell to sit alongside. When Farrell turned to him, the dark face had turned somber.

"Tony," he began, not looking directly at him but just beyond, as though in distant reflection, "I should say it is a matter of some urgency. A disappointing matter that has caused me extended anxiety, and now, as it must be resolved . . . considerable regret." Farrell felt as though his hair stood straight up.

"Do you have a gun?" the Giant asked him abruptly.

"No," Farrell lied, flushing. He was beginning to wish he had it on him right now. It was still in his topcoat in the closet. He wondered if he could get to it if he had to.

"You didn't go see that guy uptown?" Cheech broke in.

Farrell looked at the dark, reproving face and tried to decide whether to risk extending the lie. "Well, I—" He stopped at a movement by Brothers . . . and his eyes widened at the pistol now leveled at him, held loosely, almost like a toy gun, in the great black hand.

"I have one here, as you can see," the Giant said quietly. "It hasn't been used in some time, but I assure you it's been kept in excellent working condition." Incomprehensibly, he smiled.

Farrell could only stare at him. His heart was pounding.

"Tony," the Giant said, "would it surprise you to know that we have learned of a traitor in our midst?" He held up his free hand to forestall any response. "A purely rhetorical question. Of course, *had* you suspected anything so despicable, you would have expressed your concern—isn't that so?" He smiled again. "Still more rhetoric.

"Sad to say, nevertheless, it's true." The smile was gone. "You see, recently we began to realize that some of our, ah, activities were falling prey to a succession of untimely setbacks. Odd, quirkish mishaps that were becoming increasingly disruptive, not to say confounding. It seemed that either we were being victimized by an incredible run of coincidental mischance, or . . ." he sighed heavily ". . . or that it was *not* coincidence but quite by design. Which, if that were the case, would indicate that someone had felt impelled to do us harm. And that, as surely you can appreciate, must be viewed as intolerable."

Farrell sat rigid, breathless as one staring at a coiled snake.

The Giant shook his head ruefully. "But who might the betrayer be? It could only be someone within our sphere of confidence, someone with access to intimate details of our various undertakings . . . and who was also in a position to establish a relationship with the police. There were several possibilities, individuals who for one reason or another seemed to give some of us 'bad vibes.' " He sighed. "I must say, when process of elimination brought us to our man, oddly he proved to be one I had hardly expected . . . although all evidence suggested I should not have been surprised."

He studied Farrell. "Have you the wildest notion of who it might be, Tony?"

Farrell's voice was frozen in his throat. He coughed. "Do I know him?" he managed to croak, his mind reaching out desperately to the topcoat in the closet. Was it already too late for that . . .?

Cheech guffawed. "Does he know him!"

"All too well, perhaps," the Giant grinned, fingering the pistol.

Farrell gauged the distance between them. To try to jump him was the only shot he'd have.

They were both looking at him with expressions of mean amusement.

"No idea at all, Tony?" asked the Giant again.

He shook his head dumbly and braced himself to lunge.

"Lieutenant Frank Casanova."

For a blinding instant Farrell teetered on the edge of consciousness, as when a sudden gust of wind snatches one's breath away. His head swam, and he had to gulp for air, but then the aftershock hit him like the first belt of an extra dry martini and made him shudder, and his senses came alive again, tingling. He swallowed his astonishment.

"Look't his face!" Cheech howled.

"Casanova—?" Farrell gasped finally.

"Unhappily," said the Giant.

"You're *sure* it's him?" Farrell persisted, grasping for unqualified assurance.

"Enough to take immediate preventive measures," the Giant said coolly. "To wit, it has come to our attention—and lest you doubt, we do keep more than one reliable source—that recently the presumed rogue lieutenant has had frequent covert meetings with certain confidential police operatives . . . significantly, all this following on the heels of our closed discussion of the Caribbean enterprise. Whereupon, subsequently, as if to confirm our fears, have come disquieting reports through various channels of—how shall I put it? peculiarities?—making themselves felt along virtually our entire—supposedly secret—route of supply. Some of our people suddenly have gotten the uneasy feeling of being silently stalked, of being closed in on. *Ergo*—?" He shrugged as if only one conclusion was reasonable from such a progression of circumstance.

Farrell nodded, partly to express agreement with the Giant's logic and partly, almost involuntarily, out of his own thankful sense of relief. But now he realized they had yet to reach the tag line of this scene.

He didn't want to ask it, but he knew it was expected: "You said 'preventive measures' . . . "

"Naturally." Brothers reached out and to Farrell's surprise, handed him the pistol.

It had a white ivory grip and seemed smaller and lighter than a .38, probably a .32. It was fully loaded. He looked up questioningly.

"A cherished memento of mine—from an old, departed associate." The Giant beamed at him. "*You* shall have the honors—you and, by all means, Francesco. I think it most fitting. Each of you might be said to have a personal score to settle with Lieutenant Casanova."

Shaken, Farrell squinted over at Cheech, who had the ravenous look of a lion creeping up on an unwary warthog.

He stared at the gun in his hand and then back to Brothers. "But—how? When . . . ?"

"I leave that to you two. I ask only that it be accomplished soon, and with absolute certainty." The Giant sat back with an air of satisfaction. "Actually, I must say I'm partial toward a conception of Francesco's. It has admirable flair. . . ." He grinned at Cheech, encouraging him.

Cheech licked his chops. "We just get ahold of Frank," he leered, "and take him out to the meat plant in Brooklyn. Like there's another big sitdown, see—only we don't let on nothin' like that *before,* 'cause then his pals'd be all over the place prob'ly. So we get him there nice and quiet . . . and then we stuff him in one of them machines, and he comes out chopped sausage! *Italian* sausage!"

Bile surged up into Farrell's throat and he had to gulp to keep it down. "Jesus!" he groaned.

"It makes you queasy, Tony?" The Giant gauged him. "I can appreciate your sensitivity. But weigh the alternative: Unchecked, Casanova can do us irreparable damage; thus there is no question of *whether* he must be eliminated—so you must reconcile yourself to that, at the least. Now, as to the proposal before us, that of course comes down merely to a question of style—of *taste,* one might even say." His eyes glinted with a humor that the appalled Farrell found macabre.

"Personally," Brothers continued, "I find singular merit in the idea: Handled properly, it guarantees removal of a danger- ous enemy with utter finality—leaving *not a trace* of his former existence! So much neater and less liable to later complications than, say, simply discarding a bullet-riddled corpse out in the wilds of the Bronx—don't you see?"

"Why don't we just shoot him up with 'H' and run his car into the bay?" Farrell bristled, glaring from Brothers to Cheech, who glowered back at him.

There was a long moment of heavy silence. Then the Giant, rising, said: "Whatever method you can agree upon. Just be sure it's *done.* And with no loose ends."

Cheech jumped up. "Don't worry about nothin'," he said, throwing Farrell a dark look. "We'll take care of it—you can count on it."

"I shall," Brothers said, collecting his things.

"I'll go with you," Cheech said. He turned back to Farrell with a scowl. "I'll work on this some more and we'll hash it out tomorrow."

Empty and sick, Farrell just nodded dismally. He let them out, scarcely conscious of the pistol dangling from his hand.

He didn't know how long it was after they'd gone—only minutes, probably, but it could have been an hour; time seemed to have stopped—that Liz hurried into the apartment. He was still standing there numbly holding the gun. She was startled, both at the sight of it and the look of him.

"Honey, what is it?" she cried.

He came out of it in slow motion, bringing her into focus before recognizing her fear. Looking down at the gun, he grimaced and flung it onto the divan. Then he went to Liz and put his arms tight around her.

"God, babe," he said into her hair, "I'm glad you didn't come any sooner."

She drew back to see his face. "I saw them leaving—Cheech and . . . that other one. Was that . . . *him?*"

Farrell nodded, his mouth set hard.

"Well, what was it?" she pleaded, her fingers straining at his shoulders. "What did they—why did *he* come here?"

Farrell saw the pain in her eyes. He kissed her forehead. "To tell me they'd figured out who the rat is. I was never so scared in my life."

Liz had blanched. "Oh my God, Tony!" she breathed.

"I don't know if he was trying to psyche me out, playing one of his cat-and-mouse numbers, or if it was just me . . . but he set me up to where I figured it had to be all over. I was about to—I just prayed *you* wouldn't walk in. . . . And then he let me off the hook. He enjoyed it. He really enjoyed it!"

Her eyes flooded with intermingled horror and pity. "Oh baby, how awful! *Was* it only a game, just to torment you . . . or—?"

"No. They finally told me who it is. And what's—to be done with him." Farrell drew in a long, quavering breath. "*I'm* supposed to—kill him. Cheech and I . . ."

Liz darted a frightened glance over at the white-handled pistol lying on the divan, and jerked her stricken face back to him.

"No way, Liz," he whispered fiercely, "no way in hell. We're out. Now."

Brendan Hartnett and his agents had not expected the dé-
nouement to come with quite such suddenness; but they were
prepared to adapt. The vacant house outside Danbury, Connecticut, had been readied long since, furnished and stocked with
food and other household necessities, to be occupied at any
time. If circumstances now dictated the time be sooner than
later, so be it.

Of course it was unthinkable that Farrell in any way
participate in the execution of Frank Casanova: It was too much
to expect, much less ask, of any but the most hopelessly
unreconstructed man—even an informer desperate to survive.
Moreover, analysis of all the evidence accumulated to date
suggested that Farrell's job, everything considered, could now
be viewed for the most part as done. They might have preferred
to gather a bit more for an added edge . . . but all in all,
Hartnett believed they had got enough to indict the Giant,
Cheech, and most of their top henchmen and then, with Farrell
the key witness, follow through with a strong, if not absolutely
invincible, case.

He'd fulfilled his end of the bargain and perhaps more. Now
they were bound to provide their "special employee" (and
themselves as well) every reasonable hope of harvesting the
fruit of his fearful labors—namely, at the very least, to keep
him alive.

What they had to do first was keep him from taking Liz and
running then and there. That's how he'd sounded when he
called. Roy Thomas had urgently told him to stand fast until a
sound course of action could be mapped out and they got back
to him. Farrell said he and Liz would climb the walls if they had
to just sit, waiting, in the apartment. Thomas then advised them
to go to Anthony's, as they might do on any ordinary night. He
would contact them at the restaurant later.

Farrell and Liz got to Anthony's just before nine—Farrell
having retrieved the .32 and secreted it in his coat pocket along
with the .38. Anthony's was beginning to fill up as the musicians

prepared to start the first set. Liz went behind the bar with Pete, and Farrell tried to behave as normally as he could in his usual role of host. Time passed torturously.

Around eleven, Farrell got a call on his office phone. It was Blackman.

"Any problems?" asked Thomas.

"Nothing I can see."

"Good. What time do you normally close up there?"

"It depends. Maybe two."

Blackman considered. "Can you hang on tonight till then?"

"We can try. Then what?"

"Go straight home. After that, you'll hear from us."

Farrell was disappointed: "That's *it?* Back up to the apartment to stew some more in our own juice?"

"Simmer a bit, maybe," said Blackman, "but I doubt it'll get as far as stew."

"I'll see you," muttered Farrell, hanging up. He turned to Liz, who'd been listening, and could not answer the question in her eyes.

They locked up the restaurant at twenty past two. Farrell stood at the curb, arm around Liz, looking over the darkened place, wondering if this might be the last time they would leave it, or see it. Then they started walking slowly up First Avenue, arms linked. The streets were quiet at that hour, with only an occasional pedestrian and a few cars and taxis passing. Keeping to their unhurried pace, talking little—as if to be able to detect every sound around them—it was almost three when they reached the apartment building. East 84th Street was utterly still. Weary, dispirited, they went upstairs. In the apartment, they slumped together on the divan without speaking. What next?

In a little while the telephone jangled. Farrell leaped to it. "Yes?"

"It's time to go," said a hollow voice at the other end.

"Who—?"

"It's your friendly insurance agent. Put on your coats and get ready to move out."

"Wait a minute," he began to protest, "we've got to pack and—" He stopped in mid-sentence, staring up the stairs of the duplex. Liz, startled, followed his gaze. A grinning Ed Stabler was lumbering down from their bedroom.

"Is that our Mr. Blackman?" asked the detective heartily. He came and took the receiver from the thunderstruck Farrell. "Blackman? All clear outside? Same here. We're on our way."

Hanging up, Stabler turned to the couple gaping at him. "Let's go, kiddies. The party's over. You don't want to turn into pumpkins."

Farrell came out of it at last. "Hey, take it easy! Let us get some things together."

"Uh-uh," Stabler shook his head firmly. "Nothing from here. You're leaving everything behind. You'll have all you need, just about, where we're going."

"My car—!" objected Farrell.

"Everything," repeated Stabler. "It's the only cushion you'll have—and we don't even know how long that'll last. You want to cut out of this life? You got to cut out clean. *Kaput.* Let's go."

PART · THREE

20

Later that day, around noon, Cheech Donato telephoned Farrell's apartment. When there was no answer, he rang Anthony's. The day manager said neither Farrell nor Miss Melville had come in yet, but they'd probably be in any minute.

Cheech waited an hour, then called the restaurant back. Still no sign of them. That fuckhead! he chafed. Farrell *knew* they had serious business to discuss! The Giant wanted fast action, and half a day had already been wasted!

In late afternoon, Cheech went to the restaurant himself. Pete told him he'd got a call from Farrell saying he and Liz were taking some time off for themselves.

"Didn't they say where the hell they were?" Cheech sputtered.

"No," Pete said, "just that they'd keep in touch."

Fuming, Cheech phoned their apartment once more. He let it ring a long time before slamming down the receiver, then stalked out of the restaurant, telling Pete to let him know if he heard from Farrell.

Farrell's apparent fade just at this time stirred an anxiety in Cheech that he was unaccustomed to. That night, accompanied by Ice Faccialati, who among his other assets was a skilled burglar, Cheech went to the apartment on East 84th Street. After insistent ringing of Farrell's bell from the vestibule went unanswered, Cheech pressed several other buttons until one tenant buzzed, and he and Ice got inside. Upstairs, by the deft use of a plastic credit card, Faccialati let them into the apartment.

Everything looked much as it had the night before. The liquor on the sideboard; the stack of records by the stereo; a newspaper tossed on the coffee table. In the kitchen, there was food in the refrigerator, milk, wine; a few dishes and a coffee cup were in the sink. In the bedroom, the bed was unmade, but nothing appeared out of the ordinary—the closets and dresser drawers were full of clothes, the vanity top held an array of Liz's cosmetics and scattered jewelry.

Cheech debated whether they should camp and wait, but decided that would be futile. There was a better chance of finding out something outside, asking around. Cheech was stumped. He didn't like it one bit—even if he still didn't know quite why.

Another also had been trying without success to reach Farrell. Michael Palmieri had picked up a bit of news he urgently wished to transmit: The Arthur Avenue council had formally determined to gear up for a serious assault on the organization of Aaron Luke Brothers and the key to the incursion continued to be the fortuitously positioned Tony Farrell. Michael had been able to stall them so far by insisting that the approach to his nephew had to be handled with great delicacy—which was true enough in any case but much more so than anyone understood, for Michael could not think how to explain to Tony his own involvement. But now the council was growing impatient, and unless Michael bestirred himself, Tony would be caught in the crossfire.

That Tony and Liz should have become suddenly inaccessible was especially disturbing to Michael, knowing their precarious situation. Had they fled, and if so for what reason? Or had they been withdrawn? And by which side: under protection, or under fire?

The same day Farrell and Liz went under cover, Frank Casanova, who had been free on bond in return for his "cooperation," was informed by JUST agents that he'd been targeted to be hit by the Giant (the identities of his proposed executioners being withheld). Under authorization from strike-force director Brendan Hartnett, the agents offered to retake the renegade lieutenant into protective custody. Though badly shaken, Casanova refused. He remembered all too many key informants over the years whose so-called protection had been disastrously breached; if someone like the Giant was out to get you, knowing who was harboring you was all that was needed —and then you were no better off than a stationary target. He would feel safer unrestricted, using his own experience and instincts to go underground while he sought help elsewhere.

For some time Casanova had also selectively negotiated his services to certain influential elements of the local Italian families, as a hedge against any sharp reversal in fortune, which he astutely had estimated could occur almost any time. His worth to Mafia entrepreneurs had been more in the nature of piecework, by comparison with his service to the Giant's operations; nonetheless, Casanova felt his periodic contributions had been of material value, and it seemed reasonable to him that they could not but honor their code and shelter one of their own blood in time of real need.

To his shock and horror, Casanova found he'd figured it wrong. Having made his approach through a street contact, he marked time out of sight waiting for the summons he anticipated. But what he finally got back was a shrug-off. He'd chosen to cast his lot with the coons, let him work it out with them. He was on his own.

Suddenly isolated, Casanova was seized by panic. For all his long-developed guile, he knew he could not bury himself indefinitely. There was no other choice: He *had* to go back to the police.

When Casanova's bond was revoked and he was returned to

246 · Edward Keyes ·

custody, attorney Arnold Weissberg soon learned of it. He duly informed his client, Aaron Luke Brothers. Brothers suggested that the lieutenant's civil rights appeared to have been violated, and that it was only proper that Weissberg file, as a public action, an appeal to have Casanova's bond reinstated and his freedom restored. The Giant would be pleased to advance all requisite costs, anonymously, of course.

By then almost a week had passed since anyone had seen or heard from Tony Farrell. At first, Brothers was merely annoyed. But as each day passed without him, the Giant's concern intensified. There simply was no "normal" explanation for Farrell—and his young woman—to have so abruptly severed all contact. There *were,* of course, explanations that the Giant had to consider: that some unaccounted trouble had befallen them; or that they'd had cause suddenly to flee the police; or . . . was it actually conceivable? . . . that they had bolted *to* the authorities!

Abou Jamal might readily ascribe to that last proposition —and Boo had often been uncanny in his instinctual assessments of others' behavioral probabilities—but the Giant was less quick to leap to vindictive judgment. Still, they had to know. The Giant thus began sending out word along his amorphous street network that he wanted to know at the earliest opportunity what had happened to Tony Farrell.

At the same time, moreover, he put through a private inquiry to someone in Washington, D.C., in the U.S. Department of Justice.

The house in the rural, thinly populated outskirts of Danbury, Connecticut, was small, scarcely as spacious overall as the duplex they'd left behind; but it was comfortably furnished and, as Ed Stabler had promised, well stocked with provisions. Even clothing had been provided.

Still, of course, it was an alien house, a way stop, that no reach of imagination or exertion of will could make feel like a home to them—not even in their virtually exclusive confinement within its walls. Farrell was not permitted to leave at all, beyond an occasional breather in a rear yard screened all around by a border of seven-foot-high privet hedges. Liz was granted, after a first week of similar restriction, the privilege of an excursion every week or so thereafter to a shopping mall some two miles distant, in the watchful escort of one of the two U.S. marshals indefinitely assigned to them. Thomas and Stabler were on the telephone to them almost daily from New York, and about once a week one or the other would drive out to spend a few hours with them. But it was the bodyguards, one a woman, who were responsible for them on a day-to-day basis.

The marshals were not intrusive, yet their hovering presence was a source of some annoyance. Most of the time, they were not even on the premises, stationing themselves by day in a rented cottage several hundred yards up the road, which commanded an unobstructed view of the house and all approaches to it.

Neither of the marshals was especially talkative, maintaining a distant all-business manner, so that Tony and Liz were able to learn little more about them than their names and a few details of their backgrounds: The male, J. W. Denny, was fortyish and wiry, a native of Connecticut, divorced, had been on the job some fifteen years, and had done this kind of duty twice before. The other, JoAnn Stephens, was around thirty, attractive in a hard-edged sort of way. She was from upstate New York, and was on the first such live-in assignment in her comparatively brief career. Beyond transmitting instructions or answering questions, however, the two, while unfailingly civil, were not given to casual exchange of observations or confidences.

Only at night would one of them come to stay with Farrell and Liz, taking over one of the small front bedrooms to keep armed vigil while they slept.

In any case, Farrell was not prepared to rely entirely on them for protection, and he'd brought two loaded revolvers with him. The ivory-handled .32 the Giant had given him would be for himself and the .38 for Liz. She had never handled any kind of firearm and was repelled by the thought of it. But they had to face reality: They might have to defend themselves by any means available. So, at times when they were sure the marshals were not nearby, Farrell would empty the chambers of the .38 and teach Liz the rudiments of firing a handgun.

When they'd been there almost two weeks, Thomas and Stabler arrived together one Friday afternoon with news that the Giant and his associates had become so concerned at Farrell's disappearance that they had initiated an intensive inquiry all over New York. The agents reported with satisfaction that Farrell was not yet suspected of having turned fink; it was apparently still a mystery as to what might have happened to him. That was good, because Brendan Hartnett needed a little more time before he would be fully armed to confront a special grand jury with his planned sweeping indictments, and security would be that much tougher once the Giant decided the circumstances were threatening enough to warrant a full-scale manhunt.

Stabler now had an idea how Farrell might forestall the search a bit longer.

"You put in a call to your buddy Cheech," the detective proposed. "Say it's the first chance you've had. You've gone underground because certain people are looking to settle a score with you—with extreme prejudice, like they say."

"What people?" asked Farrell.

"The Mafia—that always sounds believable. You took them off for something they wanted a lot. Suddenly you hear the word is out to make you dead, and *zap!* you split, down the deepest hole you can find."

Farrell considered. "And I'd have dragged Liz along?"

"That would be natural enough," Thomas put in. "Leave

her behind, and they could try to get at you through her."

"All right. And where are we supposed to be holed up?"

Stabler said, "Out of town. Far out. Only you don't say where, you can't risk it yet. You're taking a big chance even sticking your head up now, but you felt you had to at least tip your friends to what happened. But *nobody's* about to see you again until you're sure the heat's off. How's that sound?"

"If they buy it," Farrell said. "How long do you think I can stretch it out for?"

"Who knows?" shrugged Stabler. "Maybe not too long. Sooner or later they'll probably smell a rat . . . but that might be all the time we need."

"Okay. When do you want me to do it?"

"Why not right now?" said Thomas.

Farrell dialed the loft office where Cheech coordinated his loansharking activities. There was no answer. He thought a minute. It was too early for the casinos and late bars, and he didn't want to call every "health spa" in New York tracking the man down. There *was* one place. He dialed Randi Hollander's apartment.

She squealed "Lover!" when she recognized his voice. "Where have you *been,* tiger? People have been looking all over for you!"

"It's a long story," Farrell said. "Something came up suddenly, and I had to get lost for a while. Is Cheech around?"

"You got trouble, sugar?" She turned throaty. "You wanted to get lost, you should have come up here. I could've helped you . . . lose yourself."

I'll bet, thought Farrell. He said: "I wish I'd thought of it. I take it Cheech is not there?"

"I've hardly had a word from him in *days,*" she said, pouty now. "He's been in such a stew—"

He let out a long breath. "Look," he said, "will you try to get a message to him for me? It's important."

He told her, as rehearsed. When he was finished, she

exclaimed: "How *awful!* And you can't say when we'll see you again?"

"Not for a while. Just tell Cheech I'm okay. I'll be in touch when the coast looks clear."

"You poor darling," Randi cooed. "When you get back, you just be sure and let mama know, too, and we'll see if we can't find some way to help you forget *everything.*"

"Sounds good," Farrell said. "I'll see you." He hung up and looked around at the others. "She's all heart."

That same night, Michael Palmieri, frantic over his inability to unearth a clue to his nephew's eerie absence, remembered one last avenue he'd not thought to explore—the Club Royale, where Edgar Stelman had run afoul of Farrell. Michael knew, of course, that elements of the mob oversaw the Royale, and a telephone call gave him the names of a couple of the club's owners. Calling one, he received assurance that he would be permitted entry any time he wished.

Arriving at the Royale, Michael was admitted with noticeable deference. When he asked if Tony Farrell had been in, however, the warmth appeared to moderate somewhat. With eyes turned wary, the doorman said only "Not lately." Michael decided to browse upstairs anyway, in dim hopes of turning up something.

He had just reached the second-floor foyer when a flashy but stunning female with strawberry-red hair and a luscious figure came up the stairs. A floor captain was quickly at her side, smiling with a "Good evening, Miss Hollander" as he carefully took her wrap.

"Thanks, sugar," the redhead said without looking at him. She scanned the room impatiently. Then she turned to the captain: "Cheech isn't around?"

"Not yet, ma'am," he responded.

"If he comes in, tell him to find me," she ordered. "I got somethin' real important to tell him." She glided off into the gaming area.

Michael stood frozen, staring after her. She'd asked for Cheech. Of course; that would have to be Cheech Donato!

"Are you being taken care of, sir?" the captain was asking him.

"Everything's fine," Michael said. He added briskly: "I'm Michael Palmieri."

"Oh, yes, we were told . . ." the man said, brightening. "Anything I can do for you, sir?"

"Who's the movie star?" asked Michael, nodding toward the redhead.

"That's Miss Hollander—Randi Hollander."

"She come here much?"

"Mmmm, pretty often."

"Belong to anybody?"

"Well—she does have a gentleman friend, yes."

"Cheech Donato?"

The captain blinked. "Yes . . ."

"Thanks," Michael said. He looked toward the tables. "I think I'll try my luck."

He made his way through the room and came up alongside her watching the play at the blackjack table. Her eyes were bright and she moistened her lips expectantly as the dealer slid cards to each player. One woman, holding fourteen, deliberated taking another card. The dealer showed twelve. Michael leaned close to Randi and said quietly: "She should stand."

"No!" whispered Randi without taking her eyes from the board. "One more hit!"

The woman signaled hit. Six. The dealer drew. Seven. Randi sighed in vicarious satisfaction.

"You called it," Michael smiled to her, trying to be his most engaging.

She gave him a glance then. "You've got to take *some* chances if you want to make out."

"It's an exciting approach. I wonder how often it pays off?"

She turned back to him and looked him over. He thought he

detected a suggestion of awakening interest. Michael was aware that he still held attraction for a good many women despite his age, or perhaps because of it; they found him worldly-wise. He rarely disappointed them. "Why?" Randi countered with a mischievous smile. "You thinking of trying your luck?"

"Funny you should say that. I just finished saying to a fellow over there, 'I think I'll try my luck.' And here already I've met you."

"And you think that could be lucky?"

"As you say, one has to take chances." He smiled at her. "Actually, it's not pure luck. I intended it from the moment I saw you come in. I'm Michael Palmieri."

"Pretty sure of yourself, aren't you?" she said.

"All I'm absolutely sure of is that you are the most fascinating woman in this place . . . Randi Hollander."

"How'd you know my name?" she asked in surprise.

"I asked."

Her smile returned and slowly widened. "You're no gambler!"

"The only time to really gamble," Michael said, "is when you like the odds. Would you like a drink?"

She laughed. "What's to lose?"

They found a table out of the traffic flow and ordered cocktails. Michael noted that the floor captain was keeping a steady eye on them. Cheech Donato doubtless would hear of this. Possibly it was a recurring problem. The way Randi sat close to him, with her crossed leg in firm contact with his, he could hardly imagine otherwise.

They exchanged more banter. "I've got to come here more often," Michael said. "A friend of mine told me about this place, but I didn't realize how attractive it was . . . until now." He searched her face admiringly.

"A lot of people who come here find it habit-forming."

Michael took his eyes off her, and looked around again. As casually as he could, he said, "I'd been hoping *he* might be here tonight—my friend. Maybe you know him. Fellow named Tony Farrell?"

Randi stared at him in astonishment. "You're kidding!"

"You do know him," smiled Michael. "It figures—that handsome devil. Tony and I are old buddies. Only we seem to have lost touch lately." He eyed her lazily. "You haven't seen him around, by chance?"

"I heard from him just this evening," Randi blurted.

"Isn't that something! Well, what's the rascal been up to?" Michael asked, straining to keep his tone light.

"I really can't say. He's been out of town, but . . ." She was glancing about edgily now, searching for an escape route.

"Well, if you hear from him again, tell him I was asking for him, will you?" Michael felt he should back off. "How about another drink?"

"I don't know, I . . ." She halted abruptly, her attention fixed across the room. He followed her gaze to the foyer, where a chunky man wearing a dark leisure suit with a white shirt open at the throat and a golden chain around his neck had just arrived and was conversing with the floor captain. He looked unpleasant. "I better take a raincheck," Randi said.

"Someone you've been expecting?" Michael asked with a tilt of his head at the foyer. The man had to be Cheech.

"Yeah—more or less. And he's the jealous type." She got up and moved sinuously toward the foyer.

He stood up to go. Randi was with the newcomer now and obviously trying to explain herself as he glowered at her between dark glances in Michael's direction. Well, thought Michael, at least he knew Tony was still alive.

He passed the couple with a polite nod to Randi and a flicking glance at Donato. Descending the stairs, behind him he could hear the man: "You're *sure* he didn't say where he was, f'crissakes . . .?"

It sounded as though Donato, too, was looking for Tony. What was it all about? wondered Michael.

21

F arrell learned about Frank Casanova from the *Hartford Courant.* Liz had brought back the day-old copy of the newspaper, along with the previous Sunday's *New York Times,* from her weekly shopping expedition. The story was on an inside page. It was the headline that caught Farrell's attention:

DECORATED COP
SLAIN IN N.Y.

And a flick of the eye later, the name leaped out at him:

New York (AP)—A much-decorated New York City detective, himself a recent defendant on charges of alleged criminal activities, has been shot to death in apparent gangland fashion, the Bronx District Attorney's office disclosed today.

The body of Lieutenant Francis L. Casanova, a 22-year police veteran and recipient of several Departmental citations for extraordinary service, was found riddled with bullets in his parked car in the Pelham Bay section of the Bronx, according to District Attorney Vincent I. Margotta.

Lt. Casanova, 44, was discovered late Tuesday in the remote wooded area of the northeast Bronx, sprawled on the blood-soaked front seat of his late-model Oldsmobile Cutlass. He'd been shot six times, including at least twice from close range in the back of the head.

Lt. Casanova, a senior detective in the Narcotics Division, recently had been suspended from duty following his indictment on charges of criminal conspiracy with an unnamed organized-crime faction. Among specific counts was alleged trafficking in illegal narcotics seized in the course of his police work.

Just a week ago, Lt. Casanova had been released in $50,000 bond pending trial. The attorney who represented him, well-known criminal and civil rights lawyer Arnold Weissberg, said today he was "shocked and appalled" at the violent turn of events. . . .

Farrell read the story with a strange sense of resignation. He could appreciate why the agents had not told him. Yet it had not upset him; it could not make him any more fearful than he'd been from the beginning of this. But he decided not to tell Liz. He tore out the page with the Casanova story and burned it in the kitchen sink. Then he buried the rest of the *Courant* deep in the pile of discarded newspapers on the back porch.

He took the two revolvers from their hiding place in the living room bookshelf and—for the second time that day —examined each closely. They remained well-oiled, ready.

The Giant digested Cheech's report about Farrell's phone call with critical concern, assessing each nuance of the somewhat ambiguous message as thoughtfully as an epicure testing an unfamiliar dish. He wished he could feel satisfaction, but it eluded him. He could not quell an insistent misgiving that all might not be just as purported.

His contact in Washington had confirmed what had been long assumed, that the Department of Justice was determinedly fielding batteries of federal-local "task forces" whose mission was total war on major criminal organizations across the United States; that the Brothers organization was high on the list of targets; and that locally the joint command was under direction of the Assistant U.S. Attorney for the Southern District of New

York, Brendan Hartnett. Further, the word was that Hartnett might have succeeded in recruiting a high-level informant whose identity had been kept under the strictest security. With the elimination of Frank Casanova, the Giant had conceived that threat to have been disposed of; he had given little consideration to the probability that there may have been yet another subversive. That may have been a rare mistake —potentially a very serious one.

Casanova had been taken in as a calculated risk—worth the gamble, considering his position, for only so long as it had paid off. Once greed or peer pressure had put Casanova at odds with the best interests of Aaron Luke Brothers, there had been no compunction whatever about removing him—there would always be other amoral policemen to perform like services. But conversely, the Giant had to ask himself now, had he so misjudged Tony Farrell?

It simply did not ring true to him that Tony could have become so involved with the Italians as to have triggered their wrath as described. Donato himself, with his old ties, was not *that* close to them any more! Tony was clever, ambitious, aggressive; but in Brothers's view he was just not suited to voluntary affiliation with the Mafia. Nor was Donato's cautious probing of syndicate acquaintances producing any real substantiation of his story. Either nobody was talking about it, or it had never happened.

No, the Giant was bound to consider that there was perhaps something more threatening here than met the eye. It would be imprudent not to take into account the possibility that Tony Farrell, on whom he had lavished such trust, in fact had betrayed him. It was the only safe assumption, in fact, pending final clarification, to explain his sudden mysterious absence: He had withdrawn to the protection of the law. Which could only mean that he had completed his mission. Which meant that he must be found and neutralized before he could be put to destructive use.

But where to look?

Brothers once more contacted his man in Washington. He wanted to know as many locations as could be discreetly, and quickly, rooted out of secret Justice Department files of "safe houses" used to shelter important government witnesses. It would be an enormous task, but one that had to be undertaken, and with minimum delay. They would start with the northeast quadrant of the country and, if necessary, fan out from there.

The confusion and indecision resulting from Farrell's phone call had bought Brendan Hartnett the additional time needed to round out the presentation he was now prepared to make before a special grand jury. In Camden and Baltimore, both sets of couriers booked by Farrell to transport the first shipment of cocaine had been plucked up in swift, quiet swoops and vigorously interrogated. Confronted with sworn depositions by the surveilling agents, and promised the opportunity of generous plea-bargaining if they cooperated, they gave up enough information to help fill in what gaps had remained. Government agents in Puerto Rico were then able to complete their chart of the Pronto Taxi company, all but documenting the entire chain of conspiracy. The only principals in the movement of the narcotics to the U.S. mainland not yet positively identified were the terminal couriers who'd finally transported the contraband in by air. But it *was* known to have been received by representatives of the Giant's, and that was what mattered most.

The Assistant U.S. Attorney decided it was time at last to strike. He would empanel a grand jury secretly, present a detailed summary of his case, and seal it compellingly with the testimony of his key witness, co-conspirator (but not to be a co-defendant) Tony Farrell.

This meant slipping Farrell back into New York, and the timing and logistics of that had to be just right: He had to be in and out before anyone on the other side could be aware of it. Nothing must be left to chance now.

Farrell and Liz were mildly curious when both Roy Thomas and Ed Stabler showed up at the house on a Wednesday afternoon in separate automobiles, but nothing was made of it. The afternoon was passed in the usual fashion, with exchange of news and speculation.

Toward evening, Stabler went up to the cottage to confer with the marshals, and, as Liz repaired to the kitchen to fix something to eat for them, Thomas and Farrell were left together. Farrell studied Thomas for a moment. "What do *you* get out of all this?" he asked abruptly.

Thomas took a moment to answer. "I guess satisfaction, mostly. The old cops-and-robbers syndrome," he said with the trace of a smile, "seeing the bad guys pay for their crimes. By today's standards perhaps I was born a hundred years too late. I just still happen to believe in a couple of ageless principles: right and wrong. Does that seem simplistic?"

"I guess I would have thought it pretty square once. But, believe it or not, I can appreciate what you're saying, for a lot of reasons."

"I don't have to tell you about making your own bed, et cetera," the agent said. "And I know how you backed into this thing—but you're a guy with intelligence, who *could* distinguish right from wrong. Some things you did I can even understand. But the dope! Man, *everybody* can recognize pure filth!"

Farrell gazed past him. "What's really wrong and what's not? The whole idea of dope, heroin especially, always turned me off. Christ, as far as I was concerned, anybody hooked on that shit was hardly even human! And so, as long as I didn't have to see what they did to themselves—and I didn't think about it—it was like I was removed from the ugliness. Until—" He thought of Linda and had to swallow the lump suddenly in his throat.

Thomas regarded him quietly, then said: "Your sister Linda?"

Farrell started. "You know about her?"

"Yes. I know how hard it must have hit you."

With a sense of relief, Farrell began to unburden himself. He talked of Linda's entrapment in drugs, how it had devastated Michael, and how desperate he had been to keep his uncle from ever knowing about *him*. "Michael must be frantic now," he concluded: "first Linda, and then me dropping out of sight. I wish somehow I could let him know everything's all right. . . ."

"We've heard he's been asking around town about you," Thomas said. "We're sorry about that, but I'm afraid it would be too risky to—"

"I have to tell you," interrupted Farrell: "He knows."

The other's eyes widened in simultaneous surprise and concern.

"I don't know how exactly, but he found out about me and Cheech, even about the Giant. I had to give him *something* to hang onto, some hope."

Thomas looked bleak. "So. How long has he known?"

"Since just before we came out here. I didn't tell him all of it, not about this—and not the details, no names. Just—that I am trying to do something right to make up for everything. Don't worry: Michael understands the situation. He'll be cool."

"Hmmm," Thomas murmured, still frowning. "I just wish you'd told us sooner."

"Why? It was just between him and me. How much difference would it have made?"

"It's *not* just between you and him! It's *much* bigger. And we might have done things differently if—" Thomas clamped his mouth shut. "Well, never mind. We'll have to give this more thought."

They fell silent, strain having crept in.

Liz eased it somewhat: "Come and eat!" she called from the kitchen.

Stabler came down from the cottage, and he and Thomas conferred alone for a while. Then, when it was fully dark outside, the agents sprung it:

"Okay, kid, get your coat," Stabler announced to Farrell, "we're going for a ride."

"Where?"

"To the big city."

"Tonight?"

"You got a date first thing in the morning. The grand jury."

Farrell and Liz looked at one another without speaking.

"Don't worry, Liz," Thomas said gently. "We'll take care of him. He'll be back with you by tomorrow night." Then to Farrell he added simply: "The marshals will be here."

The lawmen waited just outside the front door as Tony and Liz held each other close in the living room. Liz raised her face to him, anxiety in her eyes. "I'd thought I was getting used to it," she said, "but I'm scared again."

"This is what it's been all about, babe." He nuzzled her. "We're one step closer to making it—think of it that way."

"Oh God, Tony, if we really could—!" She kissed him lightly. "I do love you."

He kissed her back. "We're going to make it." Releasing her, he went to the bookcase and extracted the plastic bag containing the pistols. Removing the ivory-handled one, he checked the magazine again before sliding it into his coat pocket, then rewrapped the other and returned it to its hiding place. Liz's face reflected a new stab of fear as he came back and put his arm around her.

"You won't need it," he said, "but you know where it is."

"And you?" she asked hoarsely, eyes flickering toward his coat.

"Just a precaution. Like taking Valium."

They walked arm in arm to the door. He smiled at her, "I'll see you tomorrow night—when I get home from work."

"And don't you dare be late." She tried to smile back.

22

Farrell rode with Stabler, Thomas following in his car. It was almost a two-hour drive to Stabler's apartment, where Farrell would stay for the night. They spoke little the whole way.

Stabler drove straight into the basement garage of his building, and he and Farrell took the freight elevator up from there. They reached the seventh-floor apartment without seeing anyone. It was small, but adequately comfortable, bachelor's quarters, furnished without much plan except for the bedroom, which contained a huge king-sized bed and an elaborate stereo system and was decorated in lush reds and blacks. "Make yourself at home," Stabler said, assigning his guest the bedroom.

In a little while, Roy Thomas phoned from outside to report no sign of their having attracted any attention. He said he was going home, and would be on tap to escort them again in the morning for the drive into Manhattan.

They had tuna sandwiches and a couple of beers, and silently watched the late news on television, weariness finally setting in. After the news, Stabler triple-locked the door and made up the convertible couch in the living room, as Farrell turned down the sheets in the bedroom.

It seemed to Farrell he'd just sunk deep into slumber when Stabler was shaking him awake. Looking at his watch, he was annoyed: It was only a little after five in the morning. "Is anything wrong?" he asked.

"Nah. We want to be sure we get the worm, right?" Stabler was already dressed. "Come on, roll out. I got coffee on. There's an electric razor in the bathroom."

Farrell dragged himself from the bed, ran a shower, then shaved and dressed. He felt a little better by the time he entered the kitchen, warm with the aroma of fresh-brewed coffee. Stabler looked up from the table with a quizzical eye. Alongside his half-empty cup was the ivory-handled .32. "Look what I found," he said.

Farrell eyed him with a tinge of embarrassment. He walked to the stove and poured himself coffee.

"Where'd you pick it up?" demanded Stabler.

Farrell stirred milk into his coffee before answering. "From the Giant," he said in a flat voice.

"I'll be damned!" exclaimed the detective. "Is that what you were supposed to use on Frank Casanova?"

"Yeh," said Farrell, "in case he balked about coming to the meat factory."

"Son of a gun!" Stabler turned the small revolver over in his fingers. Hefting it, he squeezed the trigger . . .

"Hey!" Farrell cried in alarm.

The hammer clicked sharply. Stabler opened his other hand, showing the cartridges.

"Just this side of a hair trigger," he noted. "Not too much fire-power, but efficient at close range." He inspected the muzzle. "Clean, and oiled. Not used recently."

"No . . ."

"But I'll bet it has been. Did he say it was his?"

"In fact, he said it was from an old associate. He didn't say who, but it was like he was doing me an honor."

"I think I can guess who it belonged to," Stabler said, "and the guy didn't get any older. He got blown away, more than likely by his nibs himself, though nobody's ever been able to pin it on him—like so many other things. Reuben Powell. Ever hear of him?"

"No."

"Before your time. He used to be tight with Brothers, I think as far back as Atlanta. Mean, ambitious boogie, only not as smart as his buddy. Then he got too ambitious, tried a power move to take over everything—and *wham,* he was gone. His personal trademark, I heard, was a little number just like this. It was never found." Stabler held the weapon up to the light. "A personal memento. The Giant's real sentimental."

A shiver went through Farrell. A dead man's gun. And he might have left it with Liz. . . .

"If it was Reuben Powell's," remarked Stabler, "it might just be one more nail in Brothers's coffin. Take good care of it."

"I'd planned to." Farrell eyed him. "You're going to let me keep it?"

"Not *keep.* You can hang on to it, till we need it more than you do. Like I said, it could be evidence."

"Fair enough. Thanks." Farrell reached for the .32.

"Uh-uh," Stabler shook his head. "You won't need it with the grand jury. We don't want to take a chance of embarrassing the boss. I'll hold it till after we're out of there."

The telephone rang. It was Thomas, outside. Stabler spoke briefly with him. Hanging up, he turned briskly to Farrell: "Okay, we're set to move. You ready?"

It was only 5:45 A.M.

The two cars glided through nearly empty streets in the pre-dawn darkness. They were crossing the Queensboro Bridge before the first suggestion of daylight appeared, creeping wanly down the still black towers of the Manhattan skyline ahead.

There was full gray light as Stabler and Thomas hustled him into the United States Courthouse in Foley Square through an underground entrance guarded by two uniformed marshals.

They took a private elevator upstairs, and only when safely within the inner offices of the U.S. Attorney did the three relax. Now they had time to kill. They made coffee on the office brewer and ate buttered rolls Thomas had brought in a white bakery bag, and made small talk. Brendan Hartnett would brief Farrell officially when he arrived.

The Assistant U.S. Attorney breezed in at 8:30. The grand jury had been summoned for 9:30. Thomas and Stabler sat in (for they, too, would be key witnesses, corroborating the prosecutor's charges and augmenting Farrell's dramatic and hopefully explosive testimony) as Hartnett outlined what he called "the scenario." He would make an oral and visual presentation of evidence—tapes, photographs, sworn depositions, and so on—calling for multi-felony indictments of Aaron Luke Brothers and eleven others, including Francis "Cheech" Donato, for conspiracy to violate, and *de facto* violation of, Sections 173 and 174 of Title 21 and Sections 4705(a) and 7337(b) of the United States Criminal Code. Other witnesses would be introduced, but the key one, the "convincer," as Hartnett put it, was Farrell—to be brought in near the end for the greatest possible impact. Until called, he was to remain in Hartnett's private office, with tight security outside. When his time came, he would be swiftly escorted down a back flight of stairs to the grand jury room.

Hartnett read through the series of questions he proposed to put to Farrell. "Answer directly, without hedging, exaggerating or coloring of any kind," he instructed. "Do not try to fudge your own complicity prior to your agreement to work for us. *I* will make sufficiently clear to the jurors the positive aspects of your cooperation. Remember, when the indictments are handed up, you will not be among those charged—so you need not be concerned about ingratiating yourself before the grand jury."

"This may sound stupid," Farrell said, "but just what does a grand jury do? I've never really understood it."

"It's a panel of citizens—customarily twenty-three—called to hear charges, most often of serious criminal offenses, major felonies, to decide whether there seems just cause to bring an accused to trial. There is no adversary proceeding—no cross-examination, no defense. Just the prosecutor, trying to persuade a majority of the panel that he has a valid case to indict."

"And what if they *don't* indict?"

The ruddy-faced prosecutor leaned back, locking his hands behind his white mane, and smiled. "There's scarcely any question of that, I daresay."

"So it's a setup," Farrell said. "Okay, then what?"

"In this case, the indictments will be 'sealed' until such time as it is deemed appropriate to issue warrants for the arrest of those accused—which is to say, when we're sure where they all are and can get to them. They will be arraigned, and trial dates will be set . . . whereupon, undoubtedly, they will post bonds, most of them, and then set about furiously to prepare a defense."

"And look for me."

"When they understand you are our key witness," said Hartnett, "that most certainly should be high on their list of priorities, yes—if it isn't already. By the same token, your continued safekeeping just as surely remains foremost among *our* priorities, pending the trial."

"Why can't you just use the evidence I give to the grand jury?" Farrell asked. "Why do I have to sweat out the trial? That could be months."

Hartnett shook his head. "In your case a mere deposition is not good enough. For maximum effect, you must testify openly before a trial jury and convince *them*—despite cross-examination, attempts to discredit your motives, all the legal flak the defense will throw at you. If you can do that—and it will be an ordeal for you, no question—we've got this crowd locked, I'm convinced. And incidentally, it may not mean months more of hiding. We shall press for the earliest possible trial . . . owing to, shall we say, the unusual circumstances involved here."

Farrell mulled that over. "If we win, what happens then? To them, I mean."

"*When* we win: Think positive. Each of them could draw anywhere from a low of fifteen years to as much as forty. I'll push for the maximum for the Giant and those closest to him—and I think I'll get it."

"And what about me? Liz and me?"

"We'll discuss that," said Hartnett with a glance at the two agents, "a bit farther down the road. Rest assured, we're formulating provisions for you and your lady—"

"I hope to hell you are," Farrell declared. "But I didn't mean just that. Even with them put away, what chance will we have? Are we going to be on the run forever?"

Hartnett appraised him frankly. "It could be touch and go, for a while at least. A strong thirst for revenge must be anticipated as an immediate response. But I suspect that could abate sooner than you fear. With the leaders out of circulation for so far into the future, their disciples might shortly lose the taste for a relentless, prolonged hunt. No guarantees, of course. But look at it this way: You'll be away, you *will* have a chance.

"Which, I might point out," he added wryly, "is assuredly more than you could have hoped for had you not accepted this opportunity."

"Yeah, maybe," Farrell retorted, "but as points go, that's pretty damned moot right now, isn't it?"

Farrell was not called until nearly two that afternoon, following the grand jury's lunch recess. By then he'd been in the prosecutor's office, alone much of the time, for close to seven and a half hours, growing more restive with each dragging hour. Preying more and more on his mind was the dread that once he left the sanctuary of this office he would expose himself to recognition by some of *them*. He didn't know how, he just felt it. And then—? Could he ever get out of the city again? He imagined them picking up his trail from the courthouse, following all the way to Connecticut . . . !

He was tight as a drum, damp with perspiration, when Stabler came for him.

"How you doing?" the detective asked quietly.

"Nobody even brought me lunch," complained Farrell, realizing at once how petty that sounded.

"Sorry. Maybe the boss didn't want to attract any attention, sending out for something when he's not here." Stabler noticed the empty coffee pot. "Ran out of jo, huh?"

"One more cup and I'd've turned into *El Exigente,*" cracked Farrell, making an effort to sound less snappish. "I'm down to my last couple of cigarettes, too."

"Butts I've got," Stabler said, tossing him a fresh pack. "And when we're through here, we'll buy you a steak. How do you feel otherwise?"

"Like five pounds of shit in a four-pound bag. When the hell *will* we be through? Nobody has told me anything!"

"That's why I'm here. You're on in about five minutes."

A chill raced through Farrell. "Okay," he said. His mouth was dry.

It was easier than he'd thought it would be. He'd envisioned a gloomy, forbidding courtroom setting out of the Inquisition. Instead he found himself in a large, sedately paneled chamber which, though windowless, was brightly lit and comfortably appointed. The jurors sat in two rows on one side of the room, Farrell at a long polished wood table facing them. Hartnett, on his feet, moving about, led him through his prepared questions briskly, tersely. Farrell responded coolly, in a clear, steady voice. His composure pleased him. And he sensed the panel was impressed. They all appeared middle-aged or older, more men than women by at least two to one, most of them dressed conservatively, the men wearing ties, the women pearls

—business people, merchants, housewives, grandmothers, re-
tirees. From time to time a juror would ask him a question,
pursuing some answer of his or statement of the prosecutor's,
and Farrell would first reply directly to that one and then
expand to include the entire panel. It was effective. He bared
himself without either breast-beating or self-justification—and
in so doing became vividly aware of how mercilessly he was
succeeding in branding his erstwhile confederates. Hartnett had
coached him well, but he also knew that his own performance
measured up to all that had been hoped of him.

Farrell testified for just under two hours. Then he was
excused and escorted back upstairs to Hartnett's inner office.
They encountered no one on the way. It scarcely crossed
Farrell's mind, he was so pumped up. All he could think now
was to get back to Liz and tell her about it—tell her how much
closer he felt they'd really come to deliverance.

In the office, Thomas and Stabler were jubilant. Hartnett
had phoned up from below to say it appeared certain they
would get the full indictments hoped for, and to congratulate
Farrell. The agents discussed the logistics of spiriting Farrell
back to Danbury, deciding to wait until dark before leaving the
courthouse. Hartnett's secretary, Sheila, telephoned out for
steak sandwiches, beer and soft drinks, and Stabler remembered then to call in to Casualty Mutual.

Farrell could tell something was wrong after Stabler completed his call. He couldn't tell if it had anything to do with him,
because Stabler neither looked at him nor said anything as he
motioned Thomas out into the other office. He wondered
almost disinterestedly what it was that had cut short their
exultation. Too bad for them, he thought, but *he* was going to
luxuriate in his own sense of accomplishment as long as he
could.

The empty house had been unbearable for Liz that day. By
early afternoon she had to get out. She went to JoAnn Stephens
and besought the marshal to drive with her to the shopping
mall—anything for a change of scene, to absorb the sight

and sounds of life going on "normally." After consultation with J. W. Denny, Stephens, uncertain but sympathetic, agreed.

The day was bright and crisp, the country air refreshing. Liz's spirits were given a further lift when she discovered the amateur art exhibit set out in the mall's fountained plaza. The watchful Stephens trailing along, Liz eagerly joined the meandering stream of shoppers browsing the easeled oils and watercolors, determined to lose herself in the splash and symmetry of color.

Neither she nor the marshal was aware of the sharp-eyed young black man observing them from across the plaza, careful not to be noticed. His presence would not have alarmed them. But his purpose, had they guessed it, most certainly would: He was a contract employee of the Giant's—a professional killer. And he'd been looking for them. . . .

The man was one of a number of free-lancers commissioned to prowl those localities of the Northeast in which it was known, via the Giant's secret contact in Washington, that the Justice Department maintained clandestine shelters for fugitive turncoats. The man was a specialist, with at least a half-dozen acknowledged hits, whose minimum fee was ten thousand dollars, with negotiable increments depending on the difficulties involved. He always anticipated problems—they came with such a job—and in fact he welcomed complexity, for that not only added a certain zest to the hunt, but also afforded opportunity to raise his price.

As it was, he was surprised that it was proving so easy. He had received from representatives of the Giant's three locations in the Danbury vicinity where the couple might be ensconced. And on only his second day out he'd zeroed in on the two cottages in the hilly, forested area some miles from Danbury proper.

On his first pass, the previous afternoon, two of three cars in one driveway bore New York plates. Parking his own car down the road, out of sight, he'd watched for a couple of hours, studying the layout. There had been no outward sign of activity until just before dusk, when a burly white man with sandy hair had emerged and ambled up the road to the other cottage. That one did not fit the description given of the man Farrell, but his very appearance had confirmed the location: He had "cop" written all over him.

Waiting until the beefy one returned, just before dark, he had decided to let up his vigil until morning. He had to consider the situation with care. There probably were at least two cops in the house, possibly others up the hill. He was not so foolish as to try to take them all on singlehanded. He would wait until circumstances broke his way. There was time. It had to be done right.

But today when he'd returned, the two New York cars were gone! Unsure whether to curse himself for complacency or to grasp the hope that actually he was in luck, that the profectors had been drawn away for some reason, he'd stayed doggedly and watched. And then, at last, the two women had come out and gotten into the car remaining in the driveway. He had not gotten a clear look at them from his distance, but one appeared of the general description of Farrell's girlfriend. He'd had to decide quickly: Should he wait for them to drive off and then reconnoiter the house (would Farrell be left behind alone?), or follow them first—perhaps find something about the girl that could be turned to effective use? If Farrell was *not* alone (and he must assume that), then barging in now in broad daylight could be ruinous. He'd elected to follow the women.

Now, having observed them closely at the shopping mall, he had no doubt that the young one was the Liz Melville he'd been looking for. The other, older, flintier-looking woman he pegged as fuzz, and no doubt armed. He would just keep tagging after them and see where it led him. . . .

Liz and Stephens lingered at the mall a couple of hours before the marshal at last prevailed on her to go. They drove back in good spirits; it had been a worthwhile outing. Liz made them tea, while Stephens checked in by phone with J. W.

Denny at the house above. He reported all quiet. No word yet from New York.

They talked some and listened to soft music on the stereo. About five fifteen, Liz suggested she fix supper and have J. W. down when it was ready—it would be the first time the three would have eaten together. Stephens got on the phone to J. W. Pleased, he said the only thing he'd noticed since they'd been back was a green Volkswagen that had driven past both houses twice, first in one direction and then the other, its driver and lone occupant a youngish light-skinned Negro wearing a white turtleneck and what appeared to be a suede jacket: Did that strike any familiar chord with Stephens? She said no. Well, J. W. said, it was probably nothing. Just give him a buzz when it was time to eat.

Just before six, Stephens took a bag of garbage out back. It was almost dark. She took a moment to drink in the crisp night air, grateful for the serenity all about. Then, suddenly, there was a rustle just behind her, and a metallic click; before she could react, a powerful arm was around her neck and a hand clamped roughly over her mouth. A cold razor-sharp blade bit into her throat.

"Don't you make *no* sound, mother!" a husky male voice growled into her ear.

Stephens froze every muscle—except for the fingers of her right hand, creeping toward the deep pocket of her skirt and the .38 there.

The man, breathing shallowly, remained still for several seconds, apparently listening for any response from inside the house. Then he released the pressure slightly on her mouth. "Now listen good," he rasped. "Don't mess with me—I'm *bad*. You don't say nothin', 'cept when I ask you. You hear?" He jabbed the point of the knife into her throat, and Stephens jumped, stifling a cry. She nodded emphatically. Her fingers were inside the pocket.

"I know the girl's in there," he said, "—Farrell's girl. But *he ain't.* Now, where's he at? When he comin' back?''

Stephens shook her head. "You've got it all wrong," she gasped, the words muffled by his hand. "We don't know any Farrell—"

He stuck her again, snarling: "I *told* you don't fuck with me, bitch! This ain't no soft-shoe we doin'! I'm gonna ask you one more time: Where's . . ."

The phone's ringing inside stopped him. He tensed. Stephens's hand plunged down into her pocket, grasping the revolver . . . He was too alert for her. Like a snake, the knife whipped down from her throat to her side and stabbed into her fist just as she withdrew it. Stephens yelped with pain, the gun flying to the ground. "Stupid slut!" he hissed. A punch exploded on the side of her head, blinding her and buckling her knees. He continued to hold her up, breathing harder now, as he bent for the gun. Stephens let her body go lifeless, as if she'd passed out, and he dumped her to the ground with a snort.

She lay still on the cool, moist grass, trying to regain her wits. She had to warn J. W.—he'd be on his way down for dinner! With the two of them disarmed, Farrell and the agents would walk straight into an ambush! Think! Should she cry out . . . ?

Then his rough hands were on her again, pulling her unsteadily to her feet. "Come on, now," he grunted, "we don't wanna leave you out here where you catch your death. We'll go inside where it's cozy—keep that poor li'l gal company . . . while we wait."

At knifepoint, he propelled Stephens to the back door. "Don't do *nothin'* make me stick you for real!"

Stephens opened the door into the bright kitchen, steamy and fragrant with food cooking. Liz was not there. "Call her," he whispered.

"Liz?" she called hoarsely. They waited, motionless. The marshal gritted her teeth. She had to do something *now!* Twisting suddenly, she jerked out of his grasp, the knife barely slashing her neck, and swung about, kicking viciously upward toward his groin. With a cry of fury he sidestepped, but her lunging foot caught his knife hand and sent the blade clattering across the room. He wasn't carrying the pistol!

His hand went for his pocket as he growled "You get yours now, pig!" She threw herself at him. He chopped at her with his other fist, staggering her; then he put his foot in her stomach and shoved her jarringly back against the sink.

All at once he stopped and stared past Stephens. His blazing eyes seemed to cool, and a mean little smile began to play around his mouth. "Well, *there* she is!" he exclaimed.

Liz stood stiffly in the doorway of the living room, eyes wide with terror, hands clasped tight behind her back.

The man retrieved his knife and straightened. "Ain't this nice, sugar?" he drawled to Liz. "We gonna have a little surprise party for . . . " His mouth dropped open and his eyes widened in a look of astonishment and fear.

An explosion rocked the room and Stephens saw the man's face fly apart in a burst of red. In the next instant she was staring down at a weightless pile of flesh thrown carelessly into a corner of the kitchen.

Finally she moved herself to spin around, ears ringing, eyes and nose smarting from the acrid fumes. Beyond the haze of gunsmoke stood Liz, rigid, arms still extended forward, both hands clutching a revolver, staring vacantly, her face a frozen mask of horror.

Stephens went over to Liz and carefully unlocked her fingers from the gun.

"Where did you get this?" she asked, incredulous. "Good God! And how . . .?"

"The phone . . ." Liz murmured. "I was coming to get you, and I saw him, the knife . . ." Her voice quavered. "I went back to get the gun. Tony told me they might—he showed me how . . ." She sagged, and Stephens caught her and led her to a chair.

The front door flew open as J. W. Denny burst in brandishing a shotgun, a holstered pistol on his hip. He stopped short at the sight. "What the hell . . .?"

Stephens displayed the gun and nodded at Liz. "Farrell," she said. They stood looking at the pitiable young woman, slumped in the chair, staring straight ahead. She might have been in a trance.

Thomas and Stabler had dreaded something like this. They said nothing to Farrell, for fear he might panic or revolt at the realization that the danger they faced had suddenly come so close to Liz.

A search of the would-be assassin's body had identified him as Bobby Claymore. The agents knew of him. It could have been no coincidence that he'd come upon the setup in Danbury: He'd had to be looking for Farrell, and it had to be on orders from the Giant. *How* he'd found them—how he'd known where to look—was disturbing. But for now that was of lesser consequence. The big question was: Had he had the time or opportunity to signal his employer? The only safe assumption was that he had. The only possible move, then, was to relocate the couple at once.

Leaving Farrell in Hartnett's inner office out of earshot, they manned the phones to hunt down the prosecutor, who had left earlier. Located at the Downtown Athletic Club, where he'd been about to enjoy a steam and massage, Hartnett dressed quickly and hurried back across lower Manhattan.

This could not be allowed to happen again. Hartnett felt they could no longer trust themselves to Justice's authorized hideaways—he was convinced now there had to be a serious leak out of Washington. But he knew of a place, a new one, that not even members of the JUST force were yet aware of: a beachfront condominium at Ocean City, Maryland, an area not frequented by many outsiders in the off season. He secured clearance for a small government jet allocated to the FBI to fly at once from Teterboro, in New Jersey, to Danbury, to wait at the municipal airport there for three passengers. The plane then was to proceed to the Marine Air Terminal at New York's LaGuardia, there to pick up two more passengers, and thence directly to the Maryland shore via Salisbury, the nearest equipped airport facility to Ocean City.

When the plans were complete, a final call was put through to Danbury. The marshals were to move Liz Melville out without delay. First, however, it would be advisable to remove Bobby Claymore's remains from the house. It would not be good for a bullet-riddled corpse somehow to be discovered on what was, after all, government property.

Stephens and Denny decided how to do it.

First, they carried the bloody, faceless corpse out to the assassin's green Volkswagen and stuffed it into the passenger side, taking care to replace the lethal switchblade in Claymore's jacket pocket. Liz remained listless and silent in the living room, unseeing as the marshals went about their preparations. They scoured clean the mess around the kitchen. Then Denny hurried back up to the other cottage to collect his gear, as Stephens, keeping one eye on Liz, did the same. Finally, with everything in order, they doused the light, locked up, and led Liz around back to their car. Denny eased her into the rear seat and put their baggage into the trunk, as Stephens settled behind the wheel. Then Denny went out to Claymore's car and started it up.

Stephens following in the sedan, Denny led the way up the hill, past the darkened lookout cottage, down and around onto a heavily wooded, little-traveled side road. The sky, what could be seen of it above the clumped trees, was completely black when he turned off onto a dirt path just wide enough for the VW; Stephens pulled over and waited.

Struggling with the dead weight, Denny pulled the body across to the driver's seat. Finally switching off the headlights, he strode back to the other car and got in without a word.

At the Danbury airport, while Stephens waited with Liz, Denny sought out the aircraft sent for them. After identifications and instructions had been cleared, he came and escorted the two women to the plane. Then he returned briefly to the small, almost deserted terminal. From an enclosed phone booth he dialed the state police.

"Never mind who this is," he said in a low, guttural voice, "but there's a dead rat in a green VW out off Claxton Road. Half his head is blowed off. Tell the papers it was an execution." Denny hung up and went to board the plane.

23

Aaron Luke Brothers heard about the special grand jury hearing less than twenty-four hours after it was held. The news came from his man at the Justice Department in Washington, who also gave him the first information of the damning statements previously taken from the people in Camden and Towson. Almost surely, the Giant was warned, large-scale indictments were imminent.

Neither shocked nor much surprised, he wasted no time on personal recrimination. There was much work to be done to offset these apparent setbacks. For it was hardly yet *finished*. Sights must be adjusted to concentrate primary energies on a counteroffensive. The errant couriers, for instance. They would be persuaded to recant . . . or they would be silenced permanently. Others would be made to understand their like options.

Then, close on the heels of this, from other sources came word of the violent death of Bobby Claymore near Danbury, Connecticut. Early details were sketchy, but it was being suggested that Claymore had been gunned down by some vengeful rival. Of course, that was always possible, considering the nature of such a one's profession. But Brothers was not inclined to accept it. The Danbury area was one of the locations to have been combed for a government safe-house. He'd had no report from Claymore, but the man's reputation was that of a thorough, unrelenting hunter. But perhaps *he* had been the one to be executed this time. By the guardians of law and order, Brothers contemplated ironically.

And if his speculation was correct, what were the immediate effects? Assuming government agents *had* been aware of the threat represented by Claymore, and thus had no recourse but to dispatch him, the hideaway at Danbury by now certainly should be abandoned; Farrell and his woman would have been moved elsewhere without a moment's delay. Brothers would, naturally, send others to scout Danbury to confirm his suppositions. But he doubted they would find anything hopeful. He believed the search must now begin anew.

The Giant felt almost a twinge of pity for Tony Farrell, who must now be realizing that he might never be fully out of reach. Ah, but such were the rewards of betrayal.

Cheech Donato's reaction to all this was somehow less reasoned. "Son of a motherfuckin' *bitch!*" he exploded. "I shoulda knew it, I just fuckin' shoulda *knew* it! I get ahold of that lousy scumbag—! I want him, I want him personal!"

But Cheech was more than enraged by Farrell's treachery. He was also fearful. Even as he bellowed fury, he'd begun calculating his chances of dissociating himself from Aaron Luke Brothers with the least damage to his own future. The only conclusion he could come to, however, after feverishly examining the question from all sides, was that contesting the law had to be preferable to attempting to forsake the Giant. So to smoke out Farrell became, by default, his sole obsession.

From the outset of Farrell's withdrawal, Cheech and his various henchmen also had been scurrying after some clue to their associate's unexplained whereabouts, casting feelers as far off as Florida and points west. They had harried Pete, the barman at Anthony's, who seemed as perplexed as anyone. Dan Mulcahy, at Farrell's one-time favorite watering hole, La Veranda, was also visited more than once by hard-faced, narrow-eyed strangers. By one means or another, anybody they knew to have had any relationship or dealings with Farrell had been observed and checked out, without result.

All but one. Michael Palmieri—Farrell's "buddy."

From the first, Cheech hadn't liked the feel of this Palmieri's turning up out of the blue at the Royale, calmly asking about Farrell when everybody else had been busting chops looking for him. What had bothered him above all was that he himself, who'd thought he knew as much about Farrell as anybody, had never once heard a mention of this "old pal."

Cheech had doubted Palmieri might be the law—aside from the fact he could make a cop practically in his sleep, and this guy had none of the markings—because Sam Costanza would never have signed his ticket. But when he'd asked Costanza about him, Cheech was surprised, and in fact a little miffed, to get something of a brushoff: Michael Palmieri was an old and valued acquaintance, period.

Cheech had not pressed Sam further. But he'd still not been satisfied, and had continued sifting elsewhere. And what he'd been able to piece together eventually surprised him: Farrell and this guy were family! Palmieri had practically raised him, in fact. He was some kind of financial consultant, pretty well off, and he had a wife and a couple of other kids and a house up in Westchester, where Farrell used to live with them.

Now, in deepening frustration as precious time diminished, Cheech's thoughts turned again to Michael Palmieri. Who would be closer to Farrell, after all, than his own family? Could that be where the key had been the whole time? There was nothing to lose, and everything to gain—he could see himself triumphantly presenting Farrell's balls on a platter to the Giant—by putting some heat on this Palmieri, Sam Costanza be fucked.

For once, Michael was less than enthusiastic about visiting his daughter at Valhalla. She appeared to be improving nicely now, both physically and psychologically, coming around to an acceptance of responsibility for her reckless behavior. These signs of reformation were much encouraging to Michael, naturally. But as her vitality and awareness returned, she also had become increasingly curious to know why she had not seen Tony for so long. Was anything wrong? Was he sick? Was her father keeping something from her—? Michael had managed to put her off, so far, explaining that Tony simply was away on business. But he was losing the will to continue feigning unconcern; he was beginning to fear that Linda must soon detect how troubled he was about Tony.

Linda surprised him when he arrived this day. She was bubbling. Before he could express his pleasure at this new animation, she handed him an envelope. "See who it's from!" she chirped.

The handwriting, firm and bold, made Michael's heart skip. The envelope bore no return address. With mixed emotions, he removed the letter. Unfolding the single sheet, his eyes raced to the signature at the bottom. *LuvYerGuts, Big Bro'.*

Michael looked up at her quickly and attempted an I-told-you-so smile. "And you were so worried." He had to force himself not to read what Tony had written to her—that would give away his own anxiety. It had to be all right, the way she was beaming.

"It's a nice letter," Linda smiled. "Not much about himself . . . and *verrry* serious, for Tony. Read it. He talks about you."

Michael first scanned the letter quickly for any clue to where Tony was and why. Nothing. Then he read more carefully. It was warm and caring, full of hope and enthusiasm; no rebukes for the past, only encouragement for Linda's future. At the end there was a message for Michael:

When you see him, say "hi" for me and tell him everything seems to be working out fine—you know how he worries. Cherish him, Linda. He's a super father, who worries about each of us because he CARES. It's his way of saying "I love you!"

Mine is, till I see you again, LuvYerGuts. . . .

Michael sat staring at the words. *He's trying to tell me he's all right.* That was some relief. But *where* was he, and *why?*

"You know, there *is* one funny thing about it," Linda broke into his thoughts. "Did you notice the postmark, Daddy? Tony says he's been away . . . but look at the postmark: New York, New York. Dated two days ago."

Linda handed Michael the envelope. "And you haven't heard from him at all?"

The rumors were all through the streets now: The Feds were about to land on Aaron Luke Brothers; his whole setup was headed for a major bust. How such arcane information got abroad could never be traced accurately, but it invariably did—and usually it was correct at least in essence. There were few details, although the most persistent conjecture had it that a recent big drug operation launched by the Giant had been infiltrated and blown. The one thing everybody seemed to have heard, and believed—for it was the one explanation that people who dwelt in such shadowy areas could relate to—was that at the bottom of it all was a rat, a *big* rat. And the desperate hunt was said to be on for whoever it was. And anybody who got in the Giant's way would find life suddenly as worthless as the informer's.

Was the anticipated crackdown a portent of the early demise of the powerful Brothers' organization? No one was reckless enough to posit this loudly, but the prospect was given much morbid speculation.

Already beginning to be felt, by the Giant and many with whom he and his confederates regularly dealt along his network, was a marked recession of activity and, as a most painful result, of revenues. A lot of people were pulling in their horns, laying back, finding shelter until they could make out which way things were going to fall. If it was the Giant who fell, they wanted to be standing clear; for if *he* came down, the crash would be mighty. The ripple effect was building into a tide.

Abou Jamal was all for barricading the building on West 104th Street and turning it in effect into a fortress. Preoccupation with locating Farrell aside, if it was up to him no honky pigs would be allowed to walk in and pick them apart without having to pay for the privilege!

In fact, the Giant had ordered security strengthened around the premises, although not to fight off the expected police, but rather to assure that other predators would be discouraged from trying to exploit the current uncertainty. Any rival who misjudged the situation as ripe now for plucking would be dealt with with severe prejudice.

For Aaron Luke Brothers himself was *not* so fatalistic about the situation facing them; although his mind was broad enough to conjure the possibility of defeat, he certainly did not anticipate it would turn out that way. He would weather this storm and emerge for the most part unscathed, and his dominance would continue and grow.

Until, of course, the next defection and threat. But that was only to be expected at the top.

Cheech decided to go back and take another look at Farrell's East 84th Street apartment. You never could tell, something might have been overlooked there the first time—something that could have seemed insignificant but maybe would provide a tipoff to where the prick had disappeared to. Just what it might be, Cheech had not the faintest notion; he could only hope if he spotted anything he would recognize it.

When he and Ice Faccialati again let themselves into the apartment, however, they were stopped dead in their tracks; all of Farrell's *and* the girl's personal belongings had been removed —closets, dressers and cabinets stripped bare! Every stitch of clothing was gone, all toiletry items, jewelry, books, recordings, even the booze! All that remained were dishes in the sink and the furniture, untouched and beginning to gather dust.

Shaking off his utter consternation, Cheech followed a

hunch. He and Ice raced to the garage on 69th Street where Farrell had kept his Audi. It, too, was gone! The attendant on duty thought it had been taken away some weeks ago—he wasn't sure, he hadn't been on at the time. At Cheech's menacing insistence, he looked it up. A man named Whitehead had come in with a note from Mr. Farrell and a check, authorizing him to pay up and cancel the rental and remove the vehicle. The attendant became frightened: What was the trouble, had the car been stolen?

Cheech stalked off without reassuring him.

So they'd come back for their things. Furiously, he wondered who it might have been. Farrell himself? Not likely. Cops, probably. "Whitehead" could be anybody—Cheech didn't believe names used in a situation like this. Or . . . the thought crept across his mind tantalizingly . . . maybe someone else real close to Farrell? Like his uncle?

Cheech had never given up on the notion that Palmieri and his family might somehow lead him to Farrell—or else serve as bait to lure the rat out. He'd learned where Palmieri lived in Manhattan, and from there had soon discovered the house in Westchester. And recently he'd found out about the daughter sweating out a drug bust up in Valhalla. He'd filed *that* for future consideration. . . .

Now it might be time to give it some really heavy thought.

24

Liz had mostly remained vacant-eyed and ashen during the flight to LaGuardia, and it was only when Farrell boarded the plane with Ed Stabler and cradled her in his arms that she began to exhibit the first signs of returning feeling. She wept softly for a long time, and Farrell held her until the jet landed at Salisbury, Maryland. Then on the thirty-mile drive to Ocean City, in the darkness of the car, she tried, haltingly, to tell him about it. And by the time they reached their new lodgings, she was able to sleep.

They were settled in a large, sumptuous suite on the top floor of a newly completed eighteen-story condominium apartment tower, as yet virtually unoccupied. It still had bugs to be ironed out before it would be entirely functional and presentable to show off in the spring to prospective summer buyers. They and the marshals next door were the only tenants on the floor. The suite had a terrace that overlooked a large swimming pool below, a broad, fine beach, and the unbroken expanse of ocean.

The security was tight—no more chances would be taken after the near-miss at Danbury. Tony and Liz could go nowhere outside their quarters. All meals were cooked in or else ordered out and brought in by a marshal from one of the restaurants along Ocean Highway. They felt like inmates in an opulent prison. There were other federal agents in the building, and in a motel across the road, and in cars periodically cruising Ocean Highway and the adjacent access roads to the beach. This time, anybody approaching the hideaway would be given very careful attention.

The mass arrests in New York got big play on the television news and hardly less in the next day's Baltimore and Washington papers.

**REPUTED BLACK CRIME LORD
ARRESTED IN MAJOR SWEEP
Brothers, Known as "Giant,"
And 11 Others Charged With
Widescale Drug Trafficking.**

There were pictures of the alleged "kingpins," Aaron Luke Brothers and Frank (Cheech) Donato, being escorted by arresting officers into the Manhattan federal courthouse. The Giant appeared composed, undaunted by the cameras; Cheech was trying to shield his face with a folded newspaper. On an inside page there was a layout of small head shots of many of those arrested—including, to Farrell's surprise, Cheech's wife, May. He hadn't thought Cheech spent enough time at home to implicate his wife in anything.

The stories reported that, following arraignment, the principals had posted bail (fifty thousand dollars each for Brothers and Donato, both represented by Attorney Arnold Weissberg), and were released with the imposition of specific limitations on their movements out of New York City. Prosecuting attorney Brendan Hartnett, representing the government, was described as "outraged" that bail had been set so low for "two of the most notorious racketeers in the Northeastern United States, who now are politely returned to society to continue their business of preying upon defenseless citizens."

Hartnett said he would seek to circumvent all "the usual, time-consuming red tape" and move for a trial at the earliest possible date. "We're ready to go right now," the Assistant U.S. Attorney was quoted as declaring.

So, Farrell thought, clasping Liz's hand tightly, it was almost time.

Stunned more than anyone, perhaps, by the arrest of Aaron Luke Brothers and his coterie was Camille Thomas. She could not believe she had been so gullible.

So many meetings and earnest discussions with the man, and she'd perceived not a hint of his other, obviously primary interests! The truth was, of course, she'd not been receptive to any thought about him beyond his exciting support of their mutual enterprise.

Couturière d'Afrique. All their plans had seemed to be going well. He had approved all her sketches, forms, mockups. She had found a location for a shop on West 66th Street, close to Lincoln Center, and Aaron had set out to negotiate a favorable lease for her. As promised, he had staged a lavish dinner party in her honor at an elegant French restaurant, among the selected guests a number of prominent purveyors in the fashion world. She had been about to give notice at the apparel firm to devote herself entirely to the new venture.

Camille had come to regard Brothers with growing affection, even with . . . yes, she had to admit it to herself, with warmth. Yet, although she'd sensed from time to time a desire in him, he had never been other than a gentleman—charming, considerate, amusing, deeply interested and always stimulating. With only twinges of guilt, sometimes she'd found herself wishing he might shed some of his almost courtly restraint. She'd almost felt it inevitable. How her abstract fantasy might finally meet with flesh-and-blood reality, she had not yet reconciled. . . .

But now—a *gangster!* Her husband could only think her the most incredible fool.

Roy Thomas had rushed to her as soon as the arrests were official in hopes of breaking the news gently. As he'd feared, she already knew. Her shock was not easily overcome. He tried to explain his excruciatingly awkward position. How it had ripped him apart inside; how he'd prayed that it would all be resolved before any harm could possibly come to her. Thank God, it *had* worked out! Imagine what might have happened had the Giant ever discovered who she was, whom she was married to!

"He does know about you," she said limply.

It was like the crack of a whip. "*What?*"

"Your name. That we're married."

"Jesus! When?"

"Not long ago—maybe a week. He'd found out—from somebody in Atlanta—that I was married, so I acknowledged it. It didn't seem anything to go out of my way to hide."

"How much did you tell him about me?"

"Just that you work for the government. I didn't say what branch. And he didn't ask. . . ."

Thomas's mind flew back to the arrest scene, the building on 104th Street. The milling about of officers and accused, the interminable formalities—verification of credentials, identifications, obligatory statements. Caught up in all that, he'd paid little attention to individual personalities or attitudes . . . until just at the end, when the prisoners at last were being herded out. The Giant, in passing, paused before him—quite deliberately—and, eye to eye for a moment, seemed to appraise him with particular interest. And then the slow, enigmatic smile, with its connotation of secret triumph . . . and finally a nod, as if in recognition, before striding on, his head held high. Thomas had looked after him in wonderment. It was almost as though the Giant had left him with a message—meant for him alone.

It had been merely puzzling then. Now, looking intently at his wife, a chill went through him. What did it mean?

Early in his reassociation with Millie Dubois, Aaron Luke Brothers, ever circumspect, had routinely initiated inquiries to Atlanta, wishing to bring himself up to date on her personal

history since they'd known one another there. Word had shortly
come back that for some time prior to her leaving Atlanta for
New York, Millie apparently had lived with a young man named
Thomas, who, there was some recollection, may have been
connected with the law in some way. In any case, so far as could
be learned, there seemed to be no one at the present time on
the local law-enforcement scene who fit either that name or the
man's description obtained. Possibly both he and the woman
had left Atlanta at around the same time. That much had not
disturbed the Giant. But as an afterthought he'd also bade his
contact in Washington to seek out any information in Department of Justice intelligence files about a former or current
operative in any federal agency, named Something Thomas or
Thomas Something, who had served recently in Atlanta.

It had been many weeks, and he and Millie meanwhile had
proceeded to develop their relationship of deepening mutual
respect, before Brothers had received any more definitive
information about her erstwhile lover—and then it *had* given
him pause: There was a special agent of the FBI named Roy
Thomas, who had been assigned to the Atlanta bureau during
the period in question, later transferred to New York. He was
black. He was thirty-four and married; his wife's given name
was Camille. Curiously, Thomas's performance record since
Atlanta had been withdrawn as "classified."

Armed with this information, the Giant then had deftly
probed his own sources within the New York law establishment.
There seemed to be some secrecy about Agent Thomas's
current activities; all that could be learned was that for an
indeterminate period of time he'd been detached from normal
duty on some sort of "special assignment." Off that, the Giant
could afford to assume no less than that this Thomas was among
the JUST force stalking him.

The clincher, that the agent was indeed Millie's Roy
Thomas, had been simple to confirm: Over luncheon one day,
he had whimsically sounded her out about the "secret life"

she'd not disclosed to him, and she had—without seeming guile or fluster, he'd noted—acknowledged Thomas as her husband. Extraordinary!

Thus, Brothers had been left with but one perplexity: Where Millie herself stood. He'd decided that, bizarre as it was, she really was unaware of the nature of Thomas's present assignment—just as, Brothers was persuaded, she had no conception that *he* was the one her husband pursued and why! Thomas, then, torn between wife and duty by an outrageous trick of fate, must have elected to tiptoe a perilous line between the two, and tell her nothing, for fear of risking disaster to both! If that were so, then each day must have been a torment for the FBI agent. So be it.

The Giant had drawn a trump card. Millie Thomas for Tony Farrell! A huge gamble, to be sure, which the Giant wished not to be forced to—not only because of the ramifications of seizing as hostage the wife of a federal officer, but because of his personal reluctance to make the estimable Millie a pawn in this violent game. So she would be held in reserve, up his sleeve as it were, to be thrown down for the final play only if Farrell could not be delivered by any other means.

It would then be for Roy Thomas to decide which held the greater ultimate value: His informer, or his wife. . . .

Cheech Donato had a plan of his own, which he was also keeping to himself. If it backfired, they'd really be up shit creek. But it was all or nothing now, and he'd decided it was the only way left. If he pulled it off, he'd be a fucking hero.

Cheech would get at Farrell through Michael Palmieri. And he would do that by snatching his daughter from the rehab center up in Valhalla. From all Cheech had been able to find out about the Palmieris and Farrell's relationship with them, the girl Linda apparently was special to him. Grab her, and the odds were at least even that it would draw Farrell out of the woodwork.

Cheech had considered that Michael Palmieri could be a
hardnose. So to soften him up, Cheech had determined to work
on his women. He would first harass them, systematically
intimidate them with threats of harm if Farrell did not show
himself. Stir *them* up, and Palmieri would get to stewing. And
when he was tender, Cheech would stick him with the girl. Even
if Palmieri might be one of those traditional Italian patriarchs
who would sooner die himself before bartering for any of his
family, Cheech figured it could be different where it came down
to a choice between natural daughter and adopted son.

Palmieri would go howling to the Feds. And then Farrell
would know. And then—

Michael was in an icy rage.

The filthy animals were sniffing around his family! Anony-
mous phone calls, asking for Tony, demanding to know his
whereabouts, intimating they would be in deep trouble if he did
not soon reveal himself. . . .

JoAnna had called him from Crestwood twice. "Where *is*
Tony? What do these people want with him? Why are they
calling here?"

Michael could guess, but he told his family none of his own
suspicions. He said he would look into it, but not to be
frightened—it probably was no more than a matter of unpaid
gambling debts. Whatever it was, he would straighten it all out.

But Michael was fearful as well as angry. Did they really
think they could get to Tony through his family? Were they *that*
desperate? Thank Heaven, he thought, at least Linda was out
of reach. But the others—he must move to protect them before
this went a step further.

He knew just where to begin. Cheech Donato.

He tried the Club Royale. As before, he was admitted
without delay—although, he thought, the courteous respect
shown him by the doorkeepers seemed a bit more reserved. He
asked if Cheech Donato had come in, and was told, guardedly,
not yet. He decided to wait.

The place was busy, as usual. He wandered the second floor impatiently, keeping an eye on the stairs. He did not have to wait long. After about twenty minutes, he spied Donato. Cheech crossed the second-floor foyer without pausing, followed by a sinewy hulk of a man, and climbed the stairs to the third floor. Michael hurried after them. Trotting up the stairs, he held a hand over his breast to keep the pistol in his inside jacket pocket from jiggling.

Donato's companion stood outside the closed office. Michael headed straight for the door. The man stepped in front of him. "Yeah?" he challenged.

Michael looked up at him and said, "I'm Palmieri."

"Yeah, and—?"

"And I want to see your boss!" Michael shot back, trying to reach around him to the doorknob.

"Wait a minute!" barked the watchdog. Powerful hands grasped Michael's shoulders and effortlessly spun him to face the wall. "Lean on it, hotshot! And spread out."

Michael placed his hands flat against the wall as the other, deftly for so ponderous a man, patted him up from ankles to armpits. Coming upon the gun, he removed it from the jacket pocket. With a contemptuous snort he propelled Michael to the door and shoved him inside.

It was a cubicle no larger than ten feet square, with a small desk fitted into one corner. Donato sat on a swivel chair partially turned away from them, a telephone to his ear. After a glance up at them, he returned to the phone, speaking in low grunts.

Finally hanging up, he swiveled around. "Yeah?" His hooded eyes looked Michael over without expression.

"Mister Palmieri," said the big man with a sneer. "He was carryin'."

Cheech raised an eyebrow at the gun. "Hold on to it, Goom'. He can have it back on his way out—*empty*." He looked at Michael with a twisted little smile. "So?"

"I want to talk to you—alone."

Cheech regarded him a moment, then said to Goomba: "Okay."

When the door clicked shut, Cheech leaned back and smirked at the man standing stiffly before him. "There ain't no other chair," he said.

"I won't be here long."

"Yeah? Okay. So, what's on your mind?"

"You know damned well what's on my mind!"

Cheech assumed a look of confounded innocence. "How could I? I don't even know you."

"You know who I am. Now you listen to this," Michael said, "I'm going to tell you just once: Donato, leave my family alone!"

"What family? What do I got to do with your family?"

"The phone calls to my house. I want them stopped!"

Cheech took on a pained expression. "Me? Why should I call your house? I got problems enough with my own."

"*Look*," fired Michael, "you've got some beef with Tony, and you're trying to find him. All right. That's between you and him. But keep the rest of us out of it! There's no way any of us can help you—or would if we could!"

Cheech shook his head, the smile gone, eyes hooded again. "Some people—who's ever makin' these phone calls, say —might think different. They might figure if Tony thought somethin' could happen to one of his family. . . ."

Michael lunged for him and lifted him bodily from the chair. "You stinking wop bastard!" he snarled and smashed his fist into Cheech's face. There was a splat of torn skin and cracking bone and Cheech groaned with the pain as he sagged in Michael's grip. But Michael held on to him and cocked his fist again. "I'm warning you, prick! You bug off, or you're going to get more trouble than you can ever handle!" Then he hit him once more, with all the strength he had left, and Cheech went hurtling across the little room, crashing in a heap at the foot of the desk.

The door burst open and Goomba charged in. He stopped in

his tracks, a monstrous startled animal coiled for an attack. Eyes flashing from one man to the other, he growled, "What the fuck is this?" He turned toward Michael.

"No!" croaked Cheech from the corner, halting Goomba. "Don't bust him up here—it's bad for the place." He breathed deep and grimaced. "And we need him in one piece—for a while."

Michael turned without a word and edged warily past the massive figure in the doorway. A knot of casino workers outside eyed him in silence. He paused as Cheech called out from the office: "Hey! Goom', give him back his piece. He might need it."

As Michael walked toward the stairs, he heard Cheech sing out again mockingly: "Take good care of your faaam-i-ly . . . !"

The Giant was, for once, flabbergasted. He could scarcely believe the greaser had done it. Penetrated the Westchester County prison-hospital and simply taken out the girl!

Donato had brought in a couple of professionals from the Midwest to do the job. He'd fixed them up with proper credentials as agents of the Drug Enforcement Administration, plus a forged note from Michael Palmieri, approving the agents' visit to his recuperating daughter.

It had worked out so easily Cheech almost had to laugh. Security in the rehabilitation section was loose, and once they were inside nobody looked twice at the two official-looking visitors. They bad no problem convincing the girl they were federal narcotics agents making a routine follow-up inquiry. Telling her they were taking her to another part of the compound to record a statement, they walked her out to their car—where one of them stuck a needle in her to keep her quiet in case she started getting suspicious, then covered her up with a blanket in the back—and just drove away. Now they had her at a house in Queens. So it was time to call in the markers on Tony Farrell!

The Giant was not overcome by Cheech's optimism. Indeed, he was beset by doubts. It left him with the uneasy impression of an action bold in concept but ill-thought-out as to its effects. But it was done; gears could not be switched in mid-flight. The best he could do, now that they were committed, was take the wheel himself and try to steer an unerring course.

At first it had seemed Linda had just walked out of the rehab center herself. JoAnna had got the call from Valhalla inquiring if her daughter had returned home. She had telephoned Michael in New York, and he'd sped up to Crestwood. They were together, waiting anxiously for word, when the state police came. They announced that it appeared she had left the hospital facility in the company of two men who'd gained admittance as federal narcotics investigators. Among other items of identification they had presented a note from Michael Palmieri.

The bogus note told Michael at once what had happened. Suddenly frantic, he cried *kidnap!* It appeared so, the troopers agreed. But for what purpose?

Michael couldn't tell them what he knew the price of ransom really would be.

The troopers left, saying they would do everything possible and advising the Palmieris to stay put in case there should be any message from their daughter or her abductors. An electronics team would be sent at once to install a monitoring system on the telephone.

The call came in from Michael's New York answering service. A woman, who'd identified herself as "Royale Red," wanted Mr. Palmieri to telephone her at the earliest opportunity. The operator had said as instructed that he was unavailable indefinitely; but she'd insisted it was urgent. And she'd given a strange message: "Don't challenge a dealer who's holding an eighteen."

Randi Hollander—it had to be. *Don't challenge a dealer . . . holding an eighteen!* Linda was eighteen. Cheech had Linda. So the swine *had* done it! And now came the brutal test.

Telling JoAnna the call might be a lead, but withholding the contents of the message and his own grim assumptions, Michael said he had to hurry back to town to check it out. He urged her not to say anything about this to the police until he had something definite to go on. He would be in touch as soon as he knew anything more.

He rang Randi from his apartment. "I just got your message," he said tensely.

"Please . . . you've got to come over here right away." She sounded keyed up.

"Tell me what it's about."

"You'll find out. Hurry!" She clicked off.

Michael went out at once and hailed a cab. He had to play it their way until the ground rules were all laid out. Then he'd see about making some moves of his own.

She lived in a highrise at 63rd and York, overlooking the East River. Her face was taut, pale, when she opened the twenty-second-floor apartment door to him. "I'm sorry," she said in a weak voice.

The place was done all in immaculate white. He looked past her to the squat figure standing alone in front of the picture window. Michael advanced into the room, eyes riveted on Donato. He took some satisfaction from the other's appearance: His mouth and the left side of his face still were bruised and discolored.

Cheech eyed him with a cruel satisfaction of his own. "How's the family?"

Fire leaped to Michael's temples; it was all he could do to keep from going for him again. "Don't fuck with me now, mister. Have your say, and—"

A movement to his right had caught his attention. A huge black man had lifted himself from a deep stuffed chair and stood now facing him. Elegantly attired, he exuded a power that effortlessly dominated the room. Michael guessed that this could only be the one called "the Giant."

"Mr. Palmieri," he said, his deep-throated voice at once as

impressive as his appearance and manner, "believe me when I tell you that I regret this most unhappy turn of events. Alas, we seem to have been caught up inextricably in a complex web not entirely of our own making."

It took Michael a moment to regain his bearings. "I appreciate your sensitivity," he managed at last, an edge to his tone. "Does that make you any better than *him?*" he challenged, nodding toward Cheech.

The Giant shrugged. "There are times we find our choices, whatever our personal tastes, are limited." He turned to Randi. "Miss Hollander, would you kindly leave us now?"

When she'd left the room, Michael demanded: "All right, where's my daughter?"

"I am reliably informed," said the Giant, "that the young lady is in capable hands and quite unharmed."

"I suppose it's pointless to remind you of the penalties for kidnapping."

" 'Kidnapping' is an extremely harsh interpretation," the Giant objected. "You see, Mr. Palmieri, this is hardly your classic 'kidnap' situation. Those who have, ah, assumed temporary custody of your daughter wish only to exchange a commodity of undoubted value for another of like worth. Now, in our considered view such a proposition is not terribly unreasonable."

"For Chrissake, tell me what you want!"

"They believe a fair value for a daughter would be an adopted son—such as your ward, Tony Farrell. In fact, they seem to feel they would be returning more of quality than they would receive."

Michael's fists clenched at his sides. "And that to you is 'fair'—when what you want from me is not in my power to give?"

"Ah, but that could be arranged."

"How? I don't even know where Tony *is,* much less—!"

"His precise location at this time," said the Giant, "would

seem no longer relevant. The only meaningful question now is whether he will be induced to reappear upon learning of your plight. Or, perhaps, I should say, Linda's . . ."

"But I don't know how to reach him." Michael was quivering with rage and frustration.

"I should think that a relatively simple matter. You would communicate with one Brendan Hartnett, Assistant United States Attorney here in New York, and advise him of the, ah, proposition that's been suggested to you. Then the responsibility would fall upon him."

Michael squinted at him. "Why couldn't *you* just do that?"

"Oh my, no! That could be misconstrued as offering *ourselves* as accessories to what might be regarded by some, I admit, in the nature of a capital offense! Naturally, we should prefer to avoid any direct implication. No, coming from you such an appeal would pose at least as much immediacy . . . and I daresay even greater poignancy."

Michael glowered at the smug black face. "What will you do to *him*, then?"

The other's eyes narrowed the slightest bit as his smile turned rueful. "Leave it that his debt is exceedingly great and cannot go unsatisfied."

Michael paused, clutched in a private agony. "And if I refuse to—? Linda—?"

The Giant glanced sideways at Donato before answering. "I can only leave that to your imagination," he said softly.

Michael steeled himself. "How do I know you even have —you can produce Linda?"

"You have my word on it," said the Giant gravely.

"How do I know what *that's* worth? Let me talk to her."

The Giant considered. "That can be arranged. When you leave here, return to your apartment and wait for a telephone call. Linda will speak with you for thirty seconds. Then—if you wish ever to hear her voice *again*—you will comply with our recommended course of action with a minimum of delay."

Michael grappled with uncertainty. "You have to give me a little time to think this out. This is an awful lot to get hit with all at once. . . ."

"No doubt," the Giant said not unsympathetically. "But there is little time. Twenty-four hours is your limit. If we have not heard from you before then . . . other steps may have to be taken."

With a dismal look, Michael nodded and walked to the door. Halting there, he turned back: "Say I go along with you, but I can't get through to this Hartnett?"

"Good point," agreed the Giant. Then a slow smile widened across his face, as if a pleasing idea had come to him. *"Should* you have difficulty reaching the prosecutor himself, ask for one of his chief investigators: Roy Thomas. I'm sure if you impress upon either of them the urgency—that it bears directly on Tony Farrell—you shall find a quick response."

25

Leaving the Giant and Donato, Michael taxied back to his apartment grappling with the dilemma. Of course he could not trade Tony for Linda; nor could he possibly abandon either. Yet the only resolution he could think of was so risky . . . if it worked, each might be saved; if not, both could be lost. It meant his calling in personal debts that he had let accumulate over the years. It was a way that he had taken pains to avoid for himself—his power was in figures, not muscle. But now he could think of no other choice.

Upstairs, he went straight to the desk in his office. Unlocking a shallow side drawer, be removed a small leather-bound address book and skimmed the pages for a certain telephone number. After hesitating briefly, he sighed and dialed it quickly.

The wire was answered by a gruff voice. Michael identified himself and asked for "the Butcher."

He needed a meeting of the council as soon as it could be set up. He had an urgent proposal, and there were less than twenty-four hours in which it could be acted upon.

The Butcher said he would get back to him.

The phone rang almost as soon as he'd put it down. "Daddy?" Linda's voice was hesitant.

"Baby? Are you all right?"

"Daddy, what's happening?" She sounded far away. Michael wondered where they had her.

"Linda, are you all right?" he repeated insistently. "Have they done anything to you?"

"I'm okay, I guess. I mean, they haven't hurt me. I'm a little woozy. They stuck me with something. . . ."

Doping her up again! *The pigs!* "Who are they?" he demanded.

"I don't know, just two—" Linda broke off as if abruptly muzzled. "I don't know . . ." she resumed weakly. "Daddy, I don't understand. Does this have something to do with Tony? They said—"

"Don't you think about that," Michael exhorted her. "You just hang in, do what they say. Everything's going to be all right. Okay?" She didn't respond, and he called, "Linda?" He realized the line had gone dead.

All doubts were expelled from his mind then. What he would propose *must* be done. There was no other way.

In a little while the call came. The Butcher told him the sitdown would be at twelve midnight at The Grotto on Arthur Avenue.

There was much talk through the night, some impassioned debate, and it was close to dawn before the council finally agreed. Then, quietly, grimly, over many cups of espresso and cappuccino, plans were outlined, responsibilities assigned. The wheels would start grinding at noon, and then there could be no turning back. . . .

Michael went home to change clothes, and refresh himself for the ordeal still ahead.

Late in the day of Linda Palmieri's disappearance, the local police had communicated with the Federal Bureau of Investigation, whose primary jurisdiction the matter would become if it was, as signs indicated, a planned abduction. The following morning, a summary from the FBI regional bureau was circulated in the Manhattan offices of the United States Attorney.

Brendan Hartnett almost passed it up amongst the mound of paperwork crossing his desk. Then the name of the suspected kidnapping victim caught his eye and he did a double-take. He called in Roy Thomas and Ed Stabler.

"Isn't that—?" he began as his investigators scanned the report together.

"Holy Christ!" exclaimed Stabler.

Thomas stared at Hartnett.

The prosecutor gauged the agents' thoughts. "You think they're making a move?"

"Sure smells funny to me," Stabler said. "Two dudes take her out, and the D.E.A. says it wasn't them. . . ."

"Let's hope it wasn't the Giant's friends," said Hartnett. "Because if *they* have her, we've got a problem."

"A deal," Stabler muttered: "Farrell for the kid."

"No question. Her father'll be in here screaming for us to save his little girl. *Then* which way do we go?"

"Except, if it was that," persisted Thomas, "wouldn't we have heard by now—from them or Palmieri himself?"

"Maybe not Palmieri," mused Stabler.

"You mean Palmieri might take it uptown?" said Hartnett.

"It wouldn't surprise me. When's the last time the wise guys came crawling to the *law* for help when one of their own got shit on? Especially from competition they can't stomach in the first place?"

Figuring the most direct conduit to the facts was from the source, they tried to reach Michael Palmieri. Several calls to Palmieri's Manhattan apartment went unanswered; and at the house in Crestwood, a sheriff's deputy on duty advised Stabler that Palmieri had not been seen there since he'd returned to the city the previous afternoon. No ransom demand had yet been received. JoAnna Palmieri and her mother, both in highly emotional states, had been ordered to bed under sedation. There had been no further developments.

They speculated on what to do next. Stabler decided to look

up a couple of his pet stools tuned in to the Mafia. Thomas, for want of a more original idea, idly tried Palmieri's apartment again. To his surprise, it was picked up on the second ring.

"Yes?" asked a hoarse voice.

"Michael Palmieri?"

"Yes," warily.

"This is Roy Thomas, special agent, FBI. We've been trying to reach you—"

"Yes? What about?" The man sounded ice cold.

"About your daughter, Linda."

"What about her?"

"Well, I was hoping I could talk with you about the situation."

"I've already spoken with the police. I can't tell you any more than that."

"Perhaps not. But it is an FBI matter now, and there are a few points I'd like to clarify. May I come up?"

Palmieri was hesitant. "I don't know. I'm kind of tied up . . ."

Thomas decided to gamble. "It could vitally concern Tony Farrell."

There was a sharp intake of breath at the other end. "What do you know about Tony?"

"I can be there in twenty minutes. We'll discuss it."

"What did you say your name was again?"

"Roy Thomas."

"Hmmm." Surprisingly, there seemed a tone of recognition. "All right. But I don't have much time."

The call from the FBI man had made Michael sit up. His first thought was that the last people he wanted hanging around were the FBI! They could only get in the way, screw things up. But the guy had brought Tony into it . . . and then his name had rung a bell, and Michael knew he had to meet this Roy Thomas. He had to get a feel of one of those, maybe *the* one, who had got the lock on Tony. Maybe at last he could get some information about the kid—was he really safe, was he well; was he hanging tough, or was he scared?

Michael showered and shaved and waited in a terrycloth robe for the FBI man. He didn't want to look as though he was about to rush off as soon as they were through talking. It was after eleven; he planned to be gone by noon.

The buzzer sounded, and Michael opened the door to a tall, well-built black man. "Mr. Palmieri? Roy Thomas," he said, producing his ID. Michael examined it and looked curiously at the agent. "May I come in?" Thomas asked.

"Oh, sure. Sorry."

"You indicated you were pressed for time . . ." Thomas eyed the casual robe and bare feet.

"This is my office, too," Michael explained. "One of the advantages is not having to dress for work. But time is still money, so let's get on with it. You mentioned Tony Farrell . . ."

"First your daughter," said Thomas. "She's been missing almost twenty-four hours. You say you've had no word at all?"

"Not a word."

Thomas studied him. "Excuse me for saying so, but you don't appear much concerned about it."

Michael looked the agent over. "Why are *you* so concerned about it?"

"You know the police feel it's a good possibility she was taken against her will."

Michael waved off the notion. "It's their job to think big. Why would anybody kidnap *her?*"

"I can think of one very plausible reason."

"Such as?"

"As bait—for someone else." Thomas searched his face for a reaction.

Michael did not waver. "Who would that be?" It was almost a challenge.

Thomas hesitated a long moment before going on. "Look
. . . suppose we level with each other. You know the spot Tony
got himself into. We *know* he told you, all right? That has to be
of tremendous concern to you, because you must realize that
certain vicious, unprincipled people would go to any extreme to
get their hands on him if ever they found out what he had done
to them. Well, they have found out. And to save themselves,
they've got to stop him." Thomas measured him. "Their
problem has been they haven't been able to get to him, bring
him out into the open. Until now. We think—"

"Where is he?" Michael asked sharply.

"Naturally I can't tell you that."

"But you do have him? He's not out there by himself?"

"We have him. He's safe and well, believe me. Liz Melville
is with him, and together they're strong. They're doing something pretty courageous. All they need is about one more
week—"

"What happens then?"

"That's when Tony comes forward and helps us put a whole
mob of very dangerous characters out of commission for a long,
long time."

"And *then* what's his life going to be worth?" For the first
time Michael could not keep emotion from his voice.

"The risk is high. But he's chosen to take it because it's his
only shot. And we'll see they get every possible chance. Unless
something happens in the meantime to queer it for them."

"Like what?"

"Like your daughter," said Thomas bluntly. "If she has
been taken by the people who're after Tony, to be offered for a
trade . . ."

Michael nodded, tight-lipped.

"What puzzles us, though," the agent went on, watching
him carefully, "is that there doesn't seem to have been any
ultimatum given yet. So far as *we* know. Unless . . . somebody
else may have received such an ultimatum . . . and has decided
to handle it his own way—through some third parties who are

known to react as violently as the other bunch. Which could just turn everything into a complete shambles—for Tony, Linda, everybody."

Michael stared at him. "What 'third parties'?"

"Mr. Palmieri," Thomas said deliberately, "we are aware of your syndicate connection. We don't know exactly how high up you go, but we can guess you've earned a fair measure of respect—and attention, when you go to them with a difficult situation."

"You must have me mixed up with somebody else."

"Come on, man, you're on file!"

Michael sighed. "I do know some people. I'll talk to them this afternoon." He looked at his wristwatch. "It's almost noon. Call me here after six and maybe I can give you what you're after."

Thomas peered at him. "Six hours to make a decision?"

"That's the way it is." They regarded one another in silence for a moment before Michael concluded: "Now you'd better go. I've got things to do."

At the door he asked Thomas: "Let me ask you one thing. Does Tony know—about me, what you said before?"

"Not from us. I don't think so. He's spoken of you only with the highest respect. With love."

"That's good. He's a hell of a kid." Michael looked searchingly at the FBI agent. "What do *you* think of him?"

"I've gained a lot of admiration for him. He's tough. But," Thomas added with emphasis, "everybody has his weak spot."

Michael nodded, tight-lipped.

Downstairs, Thomas walked quickly to a public telephone on the corner and dialed Casualty Mutual. Stabler answered. "Did you get anything from Palmieri?"

"I think I did—I'm just not sure what." He summarized their sparring. "How'd you do?"

"Not a helluva lot. There's some talk of a big hurry-up meet late last night, up in the Bronx, but I can't pin it down yet."

"Stay after that," Thomas said. "It might tie in. I have this feeling something might be coming off this afternoon. Just where or what, I couldn't tell you. I'm going to stick around here a while and see if Palmieri makes any kind of move."

Thomas returned to his car and sat behind the wheel, his eyes on the entrance to Palmieri's building. He could only hope the man would come out and lead him somewhere.

He sensed a fraction of a moment too late the presence alongside the car. "Don't look around, nigger!" a guttural voice commanded. "Don't move a fuckin' *muscle!*" Thomas froze as ordered . . . and in the next instant a thunderous blow to his temple sent clanging pain and blinding lights through his head and then it was pitch dark and soundless.

A second young, swarthy man on the curb side peered in at the inert form sprawled across the front seat. Nodding across at the other to put his gun away, he went into the vestibule of Palmieri's building and pressed the apartment buzzer. A disembodied voice squawked over the intercom: "Yes?"

"Mr. Palmieri, Vinnie Fusco. We come to bring you uptown. The street is clear now."

Cheech Donato had responded to the rare summons in stages: immediate annoyance at having been awakened so early; then surprise and a surge of excitement. All these years they give me the finger, and now, when I got my ass to the wall, they want to make up!

It was May's Uncle Nunzio—"The Lip" himself! (who usually treated Cheech like he was—yeah, a nigger), who had telephoned, a little after ten that morning. Ippolito was not warm (Cheech couldn't expect *that!*) but quietly businesslike. A council meeting had been hurriedly called in the Bronx to consider certain new matters that had come up, and Ippolito found he could not attend because of a prior commitment. He would be grateful if Cheech, as his "nephew," would fill in for him to represent the family's interests. The meeting was set for noon at The Grotto restaurant on Arthur Avenue. Could he make it? Cheech agreed without hesitation. May was excited for him.

He called Goomba and told him to pick him up. They would take the Lincoln to the Bronx, in style befitting the representative of Nunzio Ippolito. Cheech was dressed and waiting outside when Goomba arrived.

They made good time, pulling up in front of The Grotto only a little past noon. The gaudy pink Lincoln stood out among the other more somber gray and dark-colored sedans and limos already lining the street. Cheech instructed Goomba to stay with the car, and strutted into The Grotto.

"I'm here for The Lip," he said with an air of self-importance. "Cheech Donato."

The barman nodded toward an archway in the rear where curtains were drawn. Cheech sauntered back and came up short as he noticed the piranha glowering at him from the brightly lit tanks on either side of the archway. *Jesus!* he thought with a shiver, *they're ugly enough to get you off fish!* A muscular young man emerged from behind the curtains and planted himself in front of Cheech. "Yeah?" he challenged.

"Donato—Ippolito's man," Cheech announced.

"Inside." The sentry held open one side of the curtains. The dining room was deserted. Cheech was directed to a door in the rear.

In a square, windowless room, perhaps a dozen men sat around an oblong table. Boxes were stacked against the walls; evidently it was a storeroom. One overhead light illuminated the table and shadowed the faces of those silently turned toward Cheech. It was like arriving late at a wake. He heard the door snap shut behind him. There was a little stirring in the room; somebody coughed, but no one spoke.

Cheech found his voice. "Nunz asked me to sit in for him," he said.

The burly man at the head of the table acknowledged him. "It's Frank Donato, isn't it?"

"Right. But mostly it's Cheech."

"Sit down, Frank," the man directed, indicating a vacant chair at one end of the table.

Cheech went around to it, noticing one chair at the opposite end was unoccupied.

"We'll wait," the man said, "until everyone is here."

They sat. Cheech was getting itchy. He furtively searched the faces on either side of him. Most of them were older than he and strangers to him. He began to feel out of place. Why didn't anybody *talk?* He cleared his throat. "Look," he spoke out brightly to those on either side of him, "why don't everybody get to know each other?"

"That won't be necessary, Frank," the man in the center said in a flat voice.

There was a tap at the door—once . . . twice. Cheech waited with the rest as it was opened. In walked Michael Palmieri! Behind him came two young guys built like linebackers. The door closed.

Cheech stared at Palmieri in amazement. Then he thought, *I'll be damned—they're gonna put the squeeze on the fucker over Farrell! Ain't this hot shit!* He started to smile.

The smile faded almost at once as Palmieri moved directly to the remaining vacant chair and sat with no hesitancy. His husky escorts came around and stood somewhere behind Cheech. Palmieri turned to the man in the center, then said calmly, "Hello, Joseph. And thank you." He glanced around the table. "Thank you all."

His eyes fell on Cheech. "This is the man," he said.

Cheech stopped breathing as the recognition of what was happening struck him. His heart was pounding as though it would burst.

Michael despised Donato, but he also hated being a party to what was taking place.

It was a drumhead trial in a kangaroo court. Cheech was charged with a list of offenses and permitted no defense. It was as though the catalogue of complaints against the man had been long compiled and awaited only the withdrawal of Nunzio Ippolito's mantle of immunity to be executed.

He was accused first of having broken his natural ties and taken up with the detested blacks. Of having, moreover, in defiance of the currently accepted mood of disfavor among the families toward trafficking in hard drugs, flagrantly invested much of his enterprise in that direction. But it was the last indictment that was the most damning. He was guilty of engineering the kidnapping of one of their own—an inviolable female—as a means of saving his own neck.

Cheech pleaded he'd had no idea who Linda Palmieri's father really was. His eyes sought out Michael's, questioning beseechingly. Michael could return only pity mingled with disgust—and unwavering determination.

The verdict was self-evident: The girl must be returned, unharmed, no strings attached.

Cheech protested miserably that it was impossible to reverse. Others as involved as he, and far more powerful, would never permit it!

"They" wouldn't permit it? That black slime? They'd fucking well permit it! They'd *suck* for it!

Cheech, by then clearly wishing for nothing so much in his entire life, still could not see how.

Simple. *He* was how. He and his friends wanted a trade? Okay. Him for the girl.

Cheech squealed that they didn't know the Giant. He wouldn't bend for Cheech's sake—for anyone! He wanted Farrell. He'd kill the girl before—!

Michael stirred.

No, he wouldn't, said Giuseppe Bucceroni. He would give the girl over to them because they would have something more valuable to him than the girl, and maybe even Farrell, could ever be. More valuable than just Cheech himself. Cheech's

information. Cheech's detailed, first-person account of everything he and this black mob had been into together—everything
he knew about them and everybody connected with them! On
tape.

He couldn't do that! cried Cheech. He'd be a dead man!
They couldn't ask—!

Sure he could. And they weren't "asking." Bucceroni
nodded at the pair of linebackers.

They wore gloves and had what looked like hard rubber
truncheons, and they worked on his body first to soften him up.
Then, oblivious to Cheech's agonized screams, they went to his
joints—knees, elbows, wrists.

Michael couldn't stand it for long. He hurried outside after
they deliberately broke one of Cheech's pinkies. Several other
of the men at the council followed, faces white.

By late afternoon they had everything they wanted on three
ninety-minute cassettes. The beating had not lasted long; it had
taken only the first broken bone to convince Cheech to submit.
He was battered and suffering greatly, but they had not touched
his head. He could think, and speak, and he did. Council
members came and went during his lengthy interrogation, only
Bucceroni, Michael, and a third man, and of course the two
enforcers, staying with Cheech. Bucceroni had food sent in.
Michael could not look at it.

When he was satisfied, Bucceroni, with a glance of approval
at Michael, said to the exhausted Cheech: "What we got here is
a collector's item. The D.A., the goddamn Attorney General of
the United States, would give their left nuts for these tapes! I
guess they'll be worth at least a little girl to your friend. Have
some wine. Then we'll give him a call."

Cheech waggled his head no to the wine, and they dragged
him out to the kitchen where there was a wall telephone. Barely
able to hold the receiver—his little finger horribly discolored
and misshapen—he dialed jerkily.

After going through the usual intermediary buffers, he got the Giant on the line. "Aaron, Cheech. I got—bad news." His voice cracked with pain and fear. Bucceroni took the instrument from him.

"Mr. Brothers, this is Joe Bucceroni—a friend."

"Ah, 'the Butcher,' " was the cheerful response. "I've heard of you."

"I heard a lot about you, too." Bucceroni winked at those around him. "Your pal and me just spent the whole afternoon talking about you, in fact. Very interesting!"

There was a pause on the Giant's end. Then: "You're about to tell me something. Do I gather this will be the 'bad news' he mentioned?"

"It's all how you look at it. See, you got something that don't belong to you, that belongs to *us,* to tell you the truth, and we want to have it back."

"Something of yours?"

"Some*body*. A girl. Get it? Now, we're reasonable. We understand you didn't know who you had there. So there don't have to be no big fuss over it. . . ."

The Giant was clucking ironically. "My, my! It seems I completely underestimated Mr. Palmieri! I expect *he* is also with you?"

"That's not important. What counts is, your Mr. Donato is with us. And he ain't too happy—he'd love to get back to his *real* pals. But the thing is, to us he's been such entertaining company, we'd hate for him to go without getting somebody in return. See what I mean?"

"You want to trade Francesco for—?" The Giant chortled, incredulous. "I'm afraid that would hardly be an even trade. One must always weigh relative values, and I regret—for his sake—that on my scales the balance now is really quite against him. My deepest apologies, but it will be impossible to accommodate you."

"Maybe *Francesco* ain't worth much," retorted Bucceroni

with a mocking look at the bedraggled Cheech, "but what he give us sure as hell is."

"Oh, dear. Poor Francesco! But . . . as is so often true, the old saying still obtains: Talk is cheap."

"You think so? Listen." Bucceroni punched the play button on his recorder and held the receiver to the speaker. After a minute of Cheech's tortured recital, he stopped the machine and spoke again to Brothers. "Like I said—interesting, huh? And we got about four more hours of that on tape. Names, places, numbers—the works. *Now* what do you think's worth more to you?"

"I begin to appreciate your point." The Giant turned thoughtful. "You must give me a little time to consider."

"We don't gotta do shit! It's a take-it-or-leave-it deal. Take it and you still got problems, but nothing like you could have, if certain parties downtown got their mitts on this stuff. Which is just what'll happen if you don't come across. So?"

The Giant considered. "It would appear," he said quietly, "my options have been sharply reduced."

"Yeah, like to nothin'!" agreed Bucceroni, with a thumbs-up signal to his companions. "So let's talk about how we do it."

"The young lady for the tapes . . ."

"Oh, no. Her for *Donato!* We'll hang on to the tapes."

"Why, you honky motherfu—!" the Giant burst uncharacteristically. He took a moment to compose himself. "That changes everything. Without her, I certainly have no further need of *him!*"

"That's up to you. But if we give you him *and* the tapes, what's to stop you from pulling this same crap again? This is our security blanket. The tapes will stay locked up as long as you keep hands off."

"And how can I be sure of that—that you won't release them the minute the girl is returned?"

"I understand you put a high price on your word—your 'honor'?" Bucceroni said.

"I do."

"Well, so do we. You got *my* word."

The exchange was set for 7:00 P.M. at a remote section of the Bronx called Ferry Point Park. Michael went in a car with the two musclemen and Donato. (Coming out of The Grotto, Cheech looked around anxiously for Goomba, but his bodyguard had long since been removed from the area.) Cheech slunk in the corner of the rear seat like a whipped dog.

They sat in the car under the bridge without speaking. A few minutes after seven, another vehicle approached slowly and stopped, facing them, some fifty yards off. For several minutes there was no movement. Then Michael ordered Cheech: "Get out."

A moment later, a back door of the other car opened and Linda stepped out.

"Go ahead," one of the men in the front seat said to Cheech, "—slow and easy." The other, the driver, motioned from his window to Linda. After looking behind her questioningly, she started forward.

Then she was in the car with Michael, and he was holding her close. She was crying, and tears filled his eyes as well.

They waited until the other car, with Cheech Donato in it, pulled around and drove off before they started up.

When they got to the apartment, Michael checked the answering service. Among his calls were three from a Mr. Thomas, the last just before seven. He could imagine how irate the FBI man must be, if he'd been "the black fuck" the bruisers said they had decommissioned outside his building earlier. Michael was sorry about that, but if that was the worst price anybody would pay, then he had to feel it was richly worth it. Thomas was sure to ring again; this time, Michael would have good news for him. And for Tony.

Meanwhile, he sat Linda down and told her, as gently as he knew how, about her "big brother."

Roy Thomas and a large, stocky white man came to the apartment at 8:30. Thomas had a bandage on the left side of his head. He did not look pleased, but it was the other who was plainly angry.

"My partner, Ed Stabler," Thomas said as they entered. Stabler glared at Michael.

"Mr. Thomas, I had no idea anything like that would happen," Michael said with feeling. "Some friends of mine were concerned about me, and when they saw a black man—I didn't even know they were out there until later . . . and then it was too late."

"Goddamn Mafia punks!" growled Stabler.

"I can't say no harm done," said Thomas, fingering the bandage, "but right now I'm more interested in what happened after that. You were away all afternoon. What did you find out?"

Their attention was drawn to the bedroom door opening behind Michael. A young woman came out. She was pretty, but pale and somewhat haggard. Michael went to her, put an arm around her waist, and led her to his visitors. "This is my daughter—Linda," he smiled.

The agents stared at her and then at one another.

"I told you she'd turn up," said Michael.

"You mean she *wasn't*—?"

"She just went AWOL for a little while, you might say —right, baby?" Michael smiled, giving her a squeeze.

Linda looked at him uncertainly, and nodded.

"Now wait a minute—!" insisted Stabler.

"There's no more I can tell you," Michael said softly but firmly. "The important thing is she's here, safe. And she'll be all right now. Let's just leave it at that. Good night, gentlemen."

Thomas turned at the door. "There's one thing I'd like to ask you. When we first spoke earlier, when I told you who I was, you reacted as though the name was familiar to you."

"Well . . . yes, I guess I had heard it before."

"In what connection? With the FBI?"

"No. As one of the chief investigators for . . ." Michael caught himself as though realizing suddenly he might be saying too much.

"For the Attorney General's office?"

"Something like that."

Thomas studied him. The man was holding back, probably so as not to betray a source he did not want Thomas to know about. But no one on the outside was supposed to know of his special assignment to Brendan Hartnett. Where could—?

It hit him suddenly. The Giant! He had found out from Camille that her husband "worked for the government." He must have done some checking—more than likely had his own inside sources. The Giant had given Michael his name as one to contact about a proposed trade of Linda for Farrell!

Then he knew about Camille! That enigmatic smile the day of the arrest—oh, Jesus!

"Quick," he cried, grasping the startled Palmieri by the arm, "can I use the phone in your office?"

"Of course," the other said.

"What the hell's the matter, Roy?" called Stabler after him as Thomas hurried to the rear of the apartment.

"I hope nothing," he threw back over his shoulder.

The phone in New Rochelle rang a number of times, as he leaned over Palmieri's desk, fingers drumming with mounting anxiety. *Come on, babe, come on!* Finally it was picked up.

"Camille! Are you all right?"

"Roy? Yes . . . I'm fine. Why, is anything wrong?"

"I'll tell you when I get home. Have you noticed any-body—unusual . . . ?" He couldn't find the right words.

"Here?" She sounded baffled. "No . . . I don't know what you mean."

"Never mind now. Just listen. I want you to double-lock the door; chain it. And the window to the fire escape. Have you got that?"

"Roy, what *is* it?" He was getting her frightened now. It couldn't be helped.

"Do not open the door for anyone—I mean *anyone*—until I get there. Don't even answer the phone."

"Roy, does it have anything to do with . . . him?"

"Possibly. Just sit tight."

"There *was* a phone call, a little while ago," she said, almost in a whisper.

"From who?" he snapped.

"I don't know. No one spoke. They hung up. . . ."

"I'm on my way. It'll be all right."

26

Thomas made one more call, to the FBI office in New Rochelle. Then he and Stabler hurried from Palmieri's apartment to their car and sped up to Westchester. Thomas explained to the detective en route his sudden fear that the Giant—the scheme to ransom Linda Palmieri apparently having been foiled—might now actually have in mind repeating the attempt with Thomas's own wife! Stabler was speechless for once.

They reached New Rochelle in record time. On Pelham Road, Thomas cruised slowly past his apartment building, alert for the FBI surveillance car. He spotted it on the second pass, sitting at the front of the building's outdoor parking area, one agent behind the wheel. The agent, whom Thomas knew as Jack Henry, told him that his partner was upstairs keeping watch on the Thomases' apartment, just as they'd been directed. No suspicious persons of the type Thomas had suggested on the telephone had approached the building. But Henry thought at least two were around: a pair of young, tough-looking blacks, loitering a block apart across Pelham Road. The agent sensed that they were lookouts, but unless they made some overt attack there was little he could do. Suspicious loitering was not in the FBI's jurisdiction.

Thomas knew what to do. Leaving Stabler with the car, he walked quickly to a small restaurant adjacent to the parking lot and from the public telephone booth dialed the New Rochelle

Police, asking for a captain of detectives he'd worked with before. . . .

On his floor, the man sitting reading a newspaper in the elevator foyer tensed as Thomas got off. They didn't know one another, and Thomas, anticipating surprise as a black man suddenly emerged, already had his ID out. The agent said everything was quiet. Thomas strode down the corridor to his apartment and pressed the doorbell.

There was no response, and for a moment his heart froze. He rang again. Still no sound. One hand fingering his gun, he tapped the door urgently: "Camille, it's me!"

"Roy?" her soft voice filtered out from inside.

"Yes. You can open up now."

Two bolts were slid back, the door opened a crack, and she peered at him. Then it closed, the chain was released, and it was flung open wide, and her arms were around him.

"Are you okay?" he asked, hugging her.

"Yes, yes, now," she breathed.

"Any more phone calls?"

"No." She gazed up at him. "I thought of taking it off the hook . . . then I thought, no, if they tried again they'd think it was busy and know I was still here." She sagged wearily against him. "I guess I do need you around."

"Pretty soon you'll be sick of me, I'll be around so much," he said, nuzzling her ear. "But first, we've got to get you out of harm's way for a little while. Can you pack a couple of bags real quick?"

"Where are we going?"

"Just you. I'm taking you to my folks' over in Yonkers. And you're going to *stay* there till this is over!"

Camille had just finished her preparations when the telephone rang. She started, looking to her husband anxiously. He held up a hand. After only three rings it stopped. Then, moments later, it rang again. He picked it up at once.

"Yes? Right, Lloyd." Listening, Thomas smiled. "Beautiful.

We'll leave right away. Hey, I won't have time to stop now, but I want you to know how much I appreciate this. I'll catch up with you."

They took the elevator down to the garage, accompanied by the agent. Stabler's attention was all on Camille as they approached, and it occurred to Thomas again that the two had never met. He introduced them without ceremony.

"Mrs. Thomas," acknowledged Stabler, examining Camille with frank interest.

She looked him over just as critically. "Mr. Stabler." But then she smiled: "Ed."

"I'll drive," Thomas said, hurrying them into the car.

As they started up the ramp outside, he said: "Honey, just to be on the safe side, why don't you duck down out of sight until we clear the street. I'll let you know when it's okay."

They stopped for a red signal at the corner of Pelham Road. Looking up the block to his left, Thomas could see the flashing lights of two stopped patrol cars. Several officers were bunched about a pair of black men under a street lamp. Suspicious loitering *was* in their jurisdiction. The signal changed, and Thomas accelerated across Pelham Road and out of sight up a quiet residential street that would lead them to the parkway to Yonkers.

"Come on up for air, babe. We can breathe easy from here on in."

Thomas hoped he sounded more certain than he really was. What move would the desperate Giant make next?

The stunning news that broke the following day could have been taken as an answer to Roy Thomas's unspoken question.

Cheech Donato was dead.

Early that morning two Queens fishermen discovered the body of a man hanging by the neck from a tree on the edge of a boggy inlet off Little Neck Bay. Police identified the man as Frank "Cheech" Donato, a reputed gangland figure. It was estimated that he had been dead several hours. Based on the battered condition of the body—including partial mutilation —the police were inclined to view the death as an "execution."

The victim's wife, Mrs. May Donato, was unavailable for comment at the couple's Queens home. Friends of the family said she was in a state of shock and would remain in seclusion. Donato and his wife—a niece of alleged organized-crime "boss" Nunzio Ippolito—both had been among eleven defendants due to stand trial shortly in federal court on charges of international drug trafficking, the news media reported. Among the co-defendants was Aaron Luke Brothers, also known as "the Giant," said to be a major black crime figure. There was some speculation among informed sources that Donato might have decided recently to cooperate with federal authorities in exchange for "considerations." The United States Attorney's office in Manhattan had no comment.

No comment, indeed. Brendan Hartnett and his closest aides were too busy trying to assess the possible effects of this harsh development upon their case. If it scared off other witnesses, that could of course make things more difficult. But even with this, it still all came down to Tony Farrell.

Their own speculation was on the question of *who* had executed Cheech—the Giant, or the Mafia? They might never really know.

In Ocean City, Maryland, Farrell and Liz had sensed that their time was drawing near.

There'd been the increasing telephone calls, presumably from New York, and the subtly changing demeanor, the barely perceptible stiffening, of the marshals guarding them. Then there'd been two visits in a single week: first by Ed Stabler, whose purpose obviously was to buoy the flagging spirits of the occupants of Suite 1803; next, several days later, by Brendan Hartnett himself, accompanied by two young Justice Department aides from Washington, who re-briefed Farrell privately.

Hartnett said that jury selection had begun; it might be completed in a week's time.

Hartnett did not have to tell them about Cheech; it had been on the TV news and in the papers. The prosecutor seemed pleased at the way Farrell was handling it. While he conceded he was shaken, he was able to accommodate himself realistically to the dynamics of the situation he faced. Yes, he was afraid ("Wouldn't *you* be?" he put to Hartnett); but it was something he believed had to be done, and he felt committed. He was ready for whatever came.

Hartnett said nothing of the Palmieris, or of Roy Thomas's wife.

The *voir dire* took, surprisingly, only four days. A jury was empaneled on a Friday, the trial set to open the following Tuesday.

Late Sunday afternoon, the marshals in Ocean City received the word from New York: Move him out!

Tony and Liz kept their farewell short. Neither wanted to prolong it as though it were a last time. It would be only a temporary interlude apart. They held each other close. "I'll see you," Farrell said.

"Soon."

"Do you realize," he began, "the next time we're together —"

She put a finger over his lips. "It's all I think about. I'm afraid I'll jinx it."

Their mouths came together in a long, tender kiss. Then he withdrew, smiled, "Later," and left her.

He knew Liz would cry after he was gone. God, let me come back to her! he thought.

Farrell and two marshals drove to the Salisbury Airport, where they boarded a small jet for the short flight to Teterboro in New Jersey. There a Dodge van, with dark, opaque windows and

READY Business Machines—Newark, N. J. stenciled on the sides, waited on the apron, two men in work clothes up front. The three arrivals jumped into the back, which contained a large wooden crate and a dolly, and the van drove away toward New York. The crate was his entree to the Federal Courthouse. He looked at it gloomily: It didn't really resemble a coffin, but still . . .

It was almost nightfall as they neared Foley Square. Farrell's stomach began to knot. But before he could think too much he was given the signal to proceed as instructed. With some difficulty he managed to squeeze his long frame into the empty crate, lying on its side lengthwise. The lid was closed over him and nailed shut. He had a flash of panic in the sudden, stifling darkness, until he made out the airholes spaced along the length of the box. But his heart continued to thump, and in the stillness it began to sound to him like a pounding disco beat.

The van backed up to the courthouse. Farrell heard the doors opening, and men's low voices and shuffling of feet, the clang of metal; then the crate was being lifted and lowered carefully, his feet to the bottom; he felt himself being wheeled at a backward angle across pavement, bumped down several steps, then wheeled smoothly once more until there was a full stop and he was almost upright. He could hear the hum and clank of an elevator approaching, the doors swooshing open; tilted again, wheeled some more, stop, upright; the sensation of rolling down a long corridor; stop, being lowered to full length. Voices; a hammer wrenching at nails. The lid was lifted, and he blinked at the bright light, unable immediately to make out the faces peering down at him.

"Enjoy your nap?" a voice asked.

Farrell sat up slowly. "Good evening," he said in a Bela Lugosi dialect. "I've come for your blood."

The two "workmen" left, to return to their colleagues waiting below inside the van, surveilling the courthouse basement for any intruders from behind their opaque glass shield. Now Farrell was left with Brendan Hartnett, Roy Thomas and Ed Stabler. Pizzas had been brought in, and beer and soft drinks. As they munched, slouched about Hartnett's office, the prosecutor explained his strategy.

He'd brought Farrell in early to catch the opposition off guard. The trial would not begin until the day after next. The defense almost surely would not expect Farrell to appear until late in the proceedings, to be introduced as the prosecution's clincher. So, in all probability, the Giant's forces would not be mounted to try to intercept Farrell before the end of the trial's first week at the earliest.

"And I have another surprise for them," the prosecutor said. "I'm calling you the second or third day!"

"Leading off with the cleanup hitter," drawled Stabler.

"Not *quite* leading off. After my opening statement, we'll put some fast men on the bases first—a few strong establishing witnesses, depositions, material evidence. But no long, calculated buildup. After Tony socks it to them, we'll work backward from there with corroboration. But quickly. I plan this to be a bang-bang operation."

"Which comes out to what, timewise—as far as I'm concerned?" Farrell inquired.

"To a great extent," said Hartnett, "that should depend on how much time they put into cross-examination. I expect they'll concentrate on you—trying to rebut your testimony, but most of all discrediting you, *and* your motivation." He regarded Farrell with great seriousness. "They're going to cut and slash at you, try to tear you apart. You'll need every bit of that cool of yours—if *you* blow, the whole thing could sink under all of us.

"Remember this: Do not deny anything they accuse you of—no matter how vicious they make it—if it's true. Straightforwardness is your only watchword. The jury must be made to believe without any doubt that you are *not* intrinsically bad and to your credit have been able to rediscover yourself . . . while these other people are totally evil and will never change. And I might say, speaking for each of us here"—glancing at his two investigators—"I happen to believe that is the truth." Thomas and Stabler each nodded in agreement.

"Thanks for that," Farrell said. "So when *they're* through with me, what then?"

"As I said, we go on to build our case from the top down. Then, of course, after I rest, the defense has its turn. Frankly, I can't see how they can offer much of a positive defense. Their main strategy undoubtedly will be to counter whatever we've produced. . . ."

"How long could *that* take?"

"There's no telling," shrugged Hartnett. The prosecutor thought how to frame his words. "We still may have to keep you on ice a while longer. You see, it's just possible, if they're really desperate, they might decide to call you back as a rebuttal witness. And we'd have to make you available. But five minutes after they say 'no more questions of this witness,' you're gone."

"And then . . . ?" asked Farrell hopefully.

"Have we made you any specific promises?"

"Not yet."

"And I won't now, either. They're sure to make a big thing of that when you're up there. I want you to be *completely* truthful!"

Farrell considered that with some disappointment. Hartnett, looking at the others, said, "For now, though, let's get you settled in here."

Hartnett had a private lavatory with a stall shower adjacent to his office, and beyond a door on the other side of that was a small room, the only access to which was through the lavatory. This was where Farrell was to live as long as he was needed here. It had one window that looked out on an airshaft of solid wall. They had outfitted the room with a cot, television set, table and chair, and a deck of playing cards. Any books,

magazines and newspapers he wanted would be delivered to
him, and all his meals brought in by a marshal or Hartnett's
personal secretary, Sheila. Except when summoned downstairs
to testify, he was not to go outside this room, other than to the
lavatory; the door between was to be locked on his side at all
other times. A small red light on his wall would indicate when
the lavatory was in use, as would another on Hartnett's office
side.

Home. Farrell could only guess how many others had
"lived" here before him.

Security was tight at the courthouse Tuesday morning. Armed
marshals and federal officers recruited from other agencies
were posted inside the courtroom and patrolled the corridors
outside. Everyone entering the chamber, male and female
alike, was subjected to a thorough body search, and the women
had to display the contents of their handbags as well.

The visitors' benches were filled to capacity as the trial was
gaveled into session. Of the eleven originally indicted, two were
missing: Cheech Donato, of course, and now his wife. Following her husband's violent demise, May Donato's attorneys had
moved for her separation from the others on both legal and
humanistic grounds, and their plea had been granted.

Hartnett's opening argument was a scathing denunciation of
the defendants as leaders of one of the nation's most powerful,
vicious and dangerous criminal networks. The defense, spear-
headed by Arnold Weissberg, contended that the government's
case was the product of illegal entrapment—just the latest
frightening example of police-state methods that increasingly
threatened the civil liberties of unwary citizens. The battle lines
were clearly drawn.

The Assistant U.S. Attorney led into his presentation
smartly, as planned, painting in deft, crisp strokes a graphic
outline of the exploitative terrorism practiced by the accused.
When court was adjourned, Hartnett was pleased as he

reviewed the performance with Farrell and his chief investigators.

"I think we did well with the jury," he said. To Farrell he explained: "There are seven men and five women. We wanted as many women as we could get, and middle-class professional types among the men. They got three blacks in, but I'd say the edge is in our favor. They seemed impressed today—starting to get a sense of what kind of horror show they're in for."

"A few of them were starting to squirm, all right," agreed Stabler. He and Thomas, who would not testify until later, had been in and out of the courtroom throughout the day. "And some of the bad guys, too."

"Not the Giant," noted his partner. "God, he's a cool one! Sitting there as though he's attending a concert."

"Yeah, but did you catch his number-one boy, Jamal? Man, is he sizzling! Give him a gun, he'd jump up and wipe out the whole joint! *Boom, boom!*"

"There are enough of the brothers around to do just that," Thomas remarked soberly, "in *and* outside the building. Do we have enough security, Bren? If they ever got restless enough to start something . . ."

"We have all the personnel down there that are available. We *have* to keep a few up here," Hartnett said with a nod toward Farrell.

"I noticed some of their people starting to fan out around the courthouse already," said Thomas. "We didn't get him in here any too soon."

"The moment of truth will come when Tony makes his appearance," Hartnett said, looking at Farrell. "How're you holding up?"

Farrell grimaced. "Scared shitless. But don't sweat it: I won't cop out on you."

"You'll be fine," Hartnett said confidently. "And I'm not going to leave you dangling. I think I can put you on by tomorrow afternoon."

Farrell slept little that night. He fought the still darkness, angrily trying to will himself to sleep and of course only aggravating his fretfulness. And then just when, out of exhaustion, he felt himself beginning to drift off, the frightening sensation of suddenly dropping into space jolted him awake again. Finally he gave up and blearily watched a succession of old late movies on Channel 2. His head was heavy and his stomach queasy in the morning, and the only food he could take was a glass of milk and many cups of coffee.

They'd brought him a set of fresh clothes from among those retrieved from his apartment. For the most "sincere" appearance possible before the jury, he'd asked for his navy blue suit, a white shirt and regimental tie, dark knee-length hose and polished black oxfords. By the time Hartnett came upstairs at the noon recess, Farrell was neatly dressed and combed, almost the image again, despite his extreme uneasiness, of the assured, on-his-way-up junior executive.

"You'll do," the prosecutor said. "I'll be calling you soon after we resume—about two." He eyed Farrell. "Try to relax. Have something to eat."

Farrell swallowed drily and shook his head. "Later, maybe."

"Later we'll drink. All right, now I've finished with other witnesses for the present. When the marshals bring you down to the witness room, you'll be the only one. There's nothing to worry about. Today it'll be just you and I—no cross yet. I'll lead and you follow. We tell it just like it was. When you're through they'll hustle you straight back up here. Clear?"

Farrell nodded, still trying to displace the crusty lump in his throat.

Just before two o'clock, three marshals came for him and led him to the witness room. One went in with him, locking the door behind. "Sit down," the marshal said flatly; "it'll be a few minutes." He walked across the room to a door opposite and went out, closing it softly behind him, and Farrell was alone.

He paced about, trying to quell the fearful urge to run. He

kept wiping his palms down the sides of his trousers. Moisture trickled into the small of his back.

Then the door swung open and the marshal nodded to him. Drawing a deep breath, Farrell moved stiffly toward the door, feeling as an actor must when cued to appear before a great throng. But as he forced himself across that threshold onto the stage of the courtroom, something astonishing happened to him.

His eyes fell straight on Aaron Luke Brothers, seated in the first row of benches, regally dwarfing those around him. The powerful figure peered back at him, and a smile began to play at the corners of his mouth—a smile of irony, perhaps, or of contempt. And in that instant Farrell's mind was swept sparkling clean. The overbearing weight had flown. He felt fit and ready.

"Mr. Farrell," he heard the judge clearly, "please step into the witness box."

"Raise your right hand . . . " began the clerk opposite. His hand was steady.

Hartnett's questions led him carefully through his middle-class suburban upbringing after his being tragically orphaned as a child. Then his ambitious but risky plunge into the restaurant field—"following the familiar and laudable American dream of succeeding on one's own." And then, through uncontrollable misfortune and rash judgment, falling into the inescapable clutches of a notorious and ruthless loan shark.

The prosecutor pulled no punches, and Farrell did not attempt to dodge any of the thrusts. Together, the two catalogued step-by-step, phase-by-phase, his slippage into illegal activities. And from that base they launched into the details of his participation and rising favor in the widespread criminal organization headed by Aaron Luke Brothers. . . .

Farrell's testimony was devastating. Only once did he glance toward the jury. Nor did he again look at the Giant, keeping his gaze directly on Hartnett or on some abstract point toward the rear of the courtroom.

Even so, he could almost feel the hot fury of one pair of eyes out there, and he didn't have to look to know whose *they* were. Abou Jamal's.

Hartnett's timing was precise. By adjournment that afternoon, he'd brought Farrell just up to the point where the Brothers organization was about to embark on its sweeping cocaine scheme—the main charge against them in this case. The prosecutor wanted the jurors to wrestle overnight with all the other disturbing data heaped on them, then start them off fresh the next day with the *coup de grâce.*

There was restrained confidence in Hartnett's offices, as over sandwiches and drinks they savored the proceedings to date and prepped for the following day. When all had left, after seeing that the assigned marshals were at their posts immediately outside, Farrell locked himself in his room off the lavatory, weary but soothed by a sense of accomplishment that he'd not enjoyed in a long while. That night he slept.

Farrell was in the witness box all the next morning, his detailed account of the cocaine operation's conception and of each of the defendants' parts in it—including his own—scoring what Stabler would later put as "a grand slam home run."

By noon, he'd about touched all the bases; yet Hartnett did not release his witness at the recess, indicating he intended to continue with him in the afternoon session. Actually his intent, as he explained to Farrell during the break, was to throw the defense a little off stride, giving them less time to prepare their cross-examination than if they'd had the entire lunch period to think about it. For now he did have to turn Farrell over to them—"and this is where the going will get rough," he warned again. "Just remember: Don't let them get under your skin."

When Arnold Weissberg finally got his shot at him, the lawyer allowed no doubt about his contempt for the witness. "Where do you live?" he asked first. Farrell gave him the address where he had lived. "Isn't that quite a high-rent building?" Farrell guessed so. "What was your rent?" Farrell told him; it was high. "A duplex, wasn't it?" Yes. "And you own an expensive imported automobile?" Farrell supposed the Audi cost a bit more than some American cars. "You also kept a young woman in that fancy duplex apartment of yours?" Farrell blazed at him for an instant, but controlled himself and said he and the young woman he intended to marry had shared the apartment, yes.

"From what you say, you do not reside there any longer —you or your *fiancée*," Weissberg noted, with a sneering emphasis on the last word. "Where do you live now?"

"Recently I've—been on the move," Farrell said hesitantly.

"You mean hiding out?"

"I guess you could say that."

"Under the auspices—and at the expense—of the United States Government?"

"Yes."

"And dragging this woman, your intended bride, from hole to hole with you?"

"Not dragging," Farrell retorted. "We just wanted to be together."

"Touching. She must be an . . . unusual young woman."

The attorney switched abruptly to a discussion of Farrell's restaurant—its usual volume, income, net return. The numbers suggested a profitable business that would afford its proprietor a better than comfortable living—but nothing so extravagant, as Weissberg then went on to establish, as the level of monetary return that Farrell had come to enjoy from his "obviously willful and even enthusiastic submergence into illegal activities." With deliberate relish, the lawyer recounted again the glossary of Farrell's admitted illicit involvements.

"It is not unfair, then, is it, to categorize you as much a 'criminal' as these defendants you accuse?" Weissberg concluded.

"Objection!" interrupted Hartnett matter-of-factly. "Such characterization has already been established quite openly. I see no purpose—"

"I think it is a point of material issue," his opponent cut back in, "that in this case cannot be made clear enough, Your Honor."

"Overruled," said the judge.

"Now," continued Weissberg, "isn't it true that even now you have pending against you a charge of assault with a deadly weapon on a police officer in the performance of his duty? And that in fact this came about as you were trying to salvage a blown narcotics transaction that you yourself had set up—without any knowledge or implication of the defendants here on trial?"

"Objection!" cried Hartnett, more vigorously this time. "Counsel has made a charge against the witness that is not on record!"

"Sustained. Confine your cross-examination to recorded testimony, Mr. Weissberg."

Farrell then volunteered: "I don't know if the assault charge is still pending or what the status is now." He eyed the lawyer squarely. "For one thing, the police officer in question isn't around any more to press the charge."

"Oh? Can you tell us why not?" Weissberg seemed genuinely surprised.

"Yes. Somebody shot him in the head. It was Frank Casanova—the one I later was told to kill because they," he nodded toward the Giant, "thought he was betraying them!"

Weissberg looked stunned. He turned to the Giant, who was frowning.

"As I said earlier, that was when I split," Farrell added. "I'm not a killer. I was long gone when—"

The defense lawyer recovered belatedly. "Objection, your honor! The witness was not asked—"

"Strike the witness's last remark," the judge ordered.

Weissberg consulted with his clients, then returned. "All right, now tell us what it was . . . all the soul-searching circumstances . . . that brought you to discover the error of your ways?"

"You can be sarcastic if you want," said Farrell evenly, not rising to the bait, "but there *was* plenty of soul-searching."

"Come off it!" barked the attorney. "Isn't it the plain and simple—and shameless—truth that you were offered a *deal?* The government wanted these defendants so desperately that they said to you, Turn on them, help us convict them of whatever sordid crimes a jury is willing to believe, and we'll see that you—what? Haven't you fabricated everything you've told us for the purpose of saving your own neck? What *did* they offer you?"

Hartnett objected: Counsel was badgering the witness. The judge sustained.

Farrell collected his thoughts. "They *promised* me nothing. They never have. All they gave me was a hope—my fiancée and me—that if I got out of it then, and honestly tried to help them, there might be a *chance,* some day, for us to have any kind of life again . . . and that it could be our only chance. But we still don't know what's going to happen after . . ."

The jurors were being affected, and Weissberg knew it. "You expect this jury to believe in such nobility from—from such a one as you? You lived a lie. How easy it would be now to invent lies to fit the government's requirements, for your own selfish ends!"

"Believe it or not; everything I've said here is true, for better or worse. And I'll tell you," he added, raising his voice as Weissberg was about to speak, "it's *not* easy—living each day in fear."

"In fear? You've had threats upon your life?" pounced Weissberg quickly. "Are you accusing any of these defendants —?" He could practically taste a mistrial.

"Not directly," Farrell said. "They haven't had the chance."

"Well, then—"

"But I do know what happened to Frank Casanova. And Cheech Donato . . ."

The judge gaveled. It was time to adjourn for the day. The cross-examination would be continued tomorrow—if the defense wished.

This time the optimism ran high during the recap in Hartnett's office. The prosecutor was pleased; Farrell had scored points even when under the gun. His investigators were impressed. And Farrell himself felt a great new strength: He felt he'd withstood the worst. He was even eager to return to the battle in the morning.

The trial was to resume at 9:30 A.M. Farrell was ready well ahead of time, refreshed by another good rest and a solid breakfast. But there was a delay. Roy Thomas brought him the news at 9:45. The agent's mood was sharply different from the night before: He seemed upset.

"Abou Jamal is missing," he declared.

"Missing? What does that mean?"

"He may have bailed out. He hasn't shown in court yet."

"So what's happening?"

"The judge'll give him until ten, then put out a warrant," Thomas said. "It's crawling with their people down there, and they're acting itchy. I don't like what I feel."

"What?"

"Trouble, maybe. You stay secured here till we see what develops. Somebody will keep you posted."

Farrell locked the door after him and, throwing off his suit jacket and loosening his tie, slumped at the table with the *Times*. He felt more let down than anxious over possible trouble brewing downstairs.

The disturbance was well orchestrated. Followers of Aaron Luke Brothers abruptly surged through the corridors outside the courtroom, spilling out into the lobby of the building, demanding justice and an end to racism. Spectators and security guards alike were caught up in the melee. Marshals from all over the courthouse raced to the scene, hands on pistols, to try to restore order.

Unnoticed in the confusion was a trim black man wearing a gray suit and soft hat and carrying a trenchcoat over his arm,

334 • Edward Keyes •

who ducked in through the main entrance and hurried to the deserted bank of elevators.

At that moment, the receptionist at the U.S. Attorney's offices on the eighth floor was taking an urgent call: "Are the marshals still up there—at Hartnett's office?" an excited male voice asked.

"Yes . . ." the startled woman replied.

"Mr. Hartnett wants them down to the first floor right away. There's a riot starting up!"

"But—!"

"Tell Hartnett's secretary. A city detective will be there in a few minutes to stand in for the marshals."

The receptionist, befuddled, rang Sheila Carbone. Moments later, the three marshals scurried out and went down in the elevator.

The man in the gray suit and hat had gone to the ninth floor, then walked down the fire stairs one flight. From the doorway to the eighth-floor corridor he watched the marshals disappear into the elevator. Emerging, he strode to the receptionist's desk, reaching into his jacket pocket and flipping open an ID case as he confronted her.

"Johnson, NYPD," he smiled.

She examined the ID carefully. It was well-worn and no doubt authentic: Larvell Johnson, No. 7611, Det. 1st Grade, Det. Squad 1st Precinct. She looked up at him inquiringly.

"They told me to go to"—he fumbled in a side pocket and withdrew a slip of paper—"Mr. Hartnett's office."

The receptionist rose and led him down a long corridor to a door marked *Asst. United States Atty.* Sheila was at her desk alone, looking apprehensive.

"Detective Johnson," the receptionist said, as she led him in. Then she turned and closed the door.

"I don't know exactly what it's all about," the man said ingratiatingly to Sheila, "so you can tell me what to do. They say you got somebody here needs protection?"

Sheila looked at him, uncertain of how much to say. "Why don't you just take a seat, officer. It shouldn't be long. You are armed?"

"Oh, yes." Dropping the coat from his arm, he leveled a pistol at her. It had a silencer attached to the muzzle. "Where is he?" he snapped.

Sheila recoiled, then lunged for a button on the side of her desk. He was too quick, bringing the butt of the gun down viciously on her wrist, pinning her. She cried out in pain, and he clamped his free hand over her mouth.

"Bitch!" he spat. "Tell me *where.*"

Sheila shook her head against the pressure of his hand. "No?" He put the gun to her nose.

She stared at him, eyes goggling. Then she closed them tight and shook her head again.

"Then I'll just have to find him myself." He gave her a short chop to the side of her throat, and Sheila crumpled to the floor.

Locking the outer door, he went to the door of Hartnett's inner office and opened it slowly, revolver poised. Empty. He stepped inside and looked around. There seemed nowhere to hide. *The motherfucker!*

Peering around an ornamental screen, he discovered two other doors. Crouching, he tried one. A closet. He swore to himself again. Suddenly he heard the sound of a toilet flushing. It came from behind the other door! He froze, every sense alert. Then a little red light on the wall alongside went off, and he waited, gun aimed at the door. But a moment later he could hear another, farther door clicking shut and a lock sliding into place.

He pressed his ear to the door. There was silence beyond it, except for the last trickling of the commode. He tapped very lightly and heard nothing. With great care he opened the door a crack. It was dark inside. He reached in, feeling for the light switch. It flipped on, revealing a carpeted washroom. Opposite him was another door. He tiptoed over to it and listened. A radio or TV was playing on the other side. He drew himself up, lowering the gun behind his right leg, and knocked.

"Mr. Farrell?" he called. "You all right in there?"

Farrell was stretched out with the TV on, waiting impatiently to be called.

"Who is it?" he called back, sitting up.

"The marshal. It's time to go."

Farrell got up with a sigh of relief. "It's about time." He unlatched the door. "Did they find Jamal . . . ?"

The tall black man standing there bared his teeth in a grin. "No, Mr. Rat, he found *you.*" The gun was raised to Farrell's chest. With the pistol Jamal shoved him back into the room. He looked around. "Nice little hole. A real rat's nest." The window drew his attention, and the mean grin returned. "Open it," he ordered. "You gonna take a trip."

Farrell's insides were going haywire, but he couldn't move. He thought he might faint. *Please, God!*

Jamal whipped the pistol barrel across the side of his face, staggering him. "Open it!"

Hands shaking, Farrell tugged at the lower sash and managed to raise it. He turned back to Jamal to make a last appeal—and past the other's shoulder saw another black face appear suddenly in the lavatory behind him. Roy Thomas!

"Go ahead!" commanded Jamal. "Climb out there. You can pray all the way down!"

"Jamal!" shouted Thomas from just inside the lavatory. He was crouched in a firing position, arms straight out holding his revolver not four feet from Jamal's head. "Twitch and you're dead!"

Jamal's eyes widened, staring at Farrell. Then they narrowed quickly, and Farrell sensed rather than saw the tensing of the man's muscles. Just as Jamal started to spin around, Farrell swung and caught him with his full arm across the chest. Jamal's bullet whined into the wall above Thomas's head as he lurched backward. Farrell lunged for the gun. Jamal, off balance, fell heavily against the window. Glass and rotted wood shattered outward and, dropping the gun, with a cry of sudden fright, Jamal groped frantically to hold himself upright. But his hands found nothing, and he teetered on the sill, eyes screaming, and then he was gone. His long, despairing cry echoing up the airshaft was terrifying.

The trial was discontinued while the circumstances leading to Abou Jamal's death were investigated. The preliminary report, submitted later that day in judge's chambers, was Accident/Self Defense: The deceased defendant had clearly set out to do harm to the government's material witness and had been repelled.

The following day, the trial resumed with augmented security throughout the courthouse. The air was thick with some brooding murmurings and discontent among the supporters of Aaron Luke Brothers, but no new disturbances arose. There was a feeling almost of anticlimax pervading the trial now.

It reached even to defense counsel. Weissberg, who was to have renewed cross-examination of Farrell, instead rose and said, "No more questions of this witness, Your Honor," and sat down wearily. It was as though the spirit for battle had been taken out of them, or that they saw it was meaningless, in the circumstances, to carry on an exposed charade. The judge (prepped beforehand by prosecutor Hartnett) then asked: "Does counsel propose to recall the witness at a future time for purposes of rebuttal?"

Weissberg leaned across to confer with his chief client. Brothers, while somber now, remained composed. Farrell's heart skipped, waiting. At last the lawyer straightened and half rose toward the bench: "No, sir."

"Then the witness may be excu—"

"Your honor." Hartnett was on his feet. "With all respect, may I ask the court to keep the witness under oath? The

government may see fit to recall him at some later point."
Farrell's heart sank, and he looked sharply at Hartnett, who
ignored him.

"So ordered. This witness is excused for now," the judge
amended. "Have you any other witnesses at this time, Mr.
Hartnett?"

"Yes, indeed, sir. But if we could have a short recess to get
ourselves organized . . . ?"

The judge rapped his gavel. "The court will recess for ten
minutes."

Rising, disheartened, Farrell gazed bleakly out over the
courtroom he'd been sure he was seeing for the last time.
Damn! What was Hartnett up to?

His eye was caught by a face seeming to reach out to him
from the last row of spectator benches. Michael! How much had
he heard? His face was seamed with anxiety and yet flushed
with—what? Encouragement? Farrell smiled at him and
winked. Michael's face broke into a wide grin and he nodded
firmly. He was saying he was *proud!*

One of the marshals flanking him at the witness box touched
his arm and Farrell threw his uncle a last warm look before
turning to go.

Hartnett was waiting in the witness room, along with
Thomas and Stabler. "What kept you?" he said to Farrell. "I
still have a lot of work to do. And you've got to go."

"Go?"

"Go. Goodbye," the prosecutor smiled. "You've done all
you can here."

"But in there—"

"That was for their benefit. So they think you'll be around a
while yet. Gives you a small head start. I won't need you
again." He turned to his agents. "Is everything ready?"

"Just about," Stabler said. "By the time we get downstairs
it should be."

"Before you leave," Hartnett said to Farrell, "I have some

papers for you to sign." He took some documents from his briefcase and spread them on the table.

"What are these?" asked Farrell.

"Mostly government requirements. But this one"—he separated a sheaf—"should be of special interest."

Farrell scanned the pages. They included his authorization to designate power of attorney, a blank bill of sale, and a filled-out application to place Anthony's in receivership. "That's good." He smiled.

"We'll see you get whatever proceeds may come of it," Hartnett told him as he scrawled his signature on each of the forms.

"I trust you," Farrell said. When he had finished signing, he looked at them. "Okay, now what? Do I crawl back in my box?"

"Not this time," said Thomas. "We're going to be a bit more civilized. We just stroll out."

Stabler explained: "Because they don't expect you to be leaving yet, they won't be looking for you outside just now. But to be safe, we've got the local cops blocking off a street on one side of the courthouse, and an armored van is about to back up to the ground-floor door on that side—lots of security all around. That should attract their attention. So will Bren, when he hurries out the front entrance. And while all this is going on, me and Roy and you just slip in a car on the other side of the building and take off!"

Farrell shook his head. "Christ, it was harder getting *in* here than out!"

"Let's hope," said Thomas.

"Let's get this show on the road," put in Hartnett briskly. Smiling, he clasped Farrell's hand. "You've done all we could have hoped for. I thank you, on behalf of the Justice Department as well as myself. I just hope *you* will find it's been worthwhile. Let me wish you well now—you and your lady. I doubt we'll see each other again. In fact, I hope not. They'll explain everything to you as you go," Hartnett said. "All I have time for now is . . . Godspeed."

The three rode down in the freight elevator and walked through the basement to a side door of the courthouse, where Farrell's three guardian marshals waited. Outside, two sedans were parked. Farrell and Thomas got into the rear of one, Stabler up front, one of the marshals behind the wheel; the other two marshals climbed into the car behind. And they simply drove off, in the opposite direction from the street that had been sealed so portentously by the police.

They'd gone several blocks when a marshal in the following vehicle radioed: "Clean as a whistle!"

Only then did they relax. Thomas said they were going to the Wall Street heliport. An Army helicopter was there to take Farrell, accompanied by two of the marshals, to Kennedy Airport. Liz should be there by the time he arrived—under tight security in the VIP lounge of Aer Lingus, the Irish airline. Brendan Hartnett had arranged it all. Liz would have all the necessary papers: air tickets, passports and visas (Thomas did not know what their new identities were), and a complete assortment of documents profiling a newlywed couple. "Your flight leaves in a little over an hour," Thomas said.

"Ireland!" Farrell exclaimed. "Just like that!"

"Your visitors' permits are for an indefinite period," the agent added. "A house has been rented for six months. Sorry, I understand it rains there most of the time. But it's away from the mainstream of tourists."

"Six months . . ." mused Farrell. "And then?"

"It's up to you," said Thomas. "Stay, or move on. You two will have to make your own life from there. All we can do is give you the start. You might open a pub. . . ."

"I'll tell you what he ought to do," Stabler offered from the front. "Once he gets settled, he ought to think about going to work for the government—you know, like in Europe or someplace. I think he'd be good at it."

Thomas grinned at Farrell. "You'll never know what a compliment that is—coming from him. And he may be right, too, for a change."

"It is a thought," Farrell said quietly.

An hour and a half later, he and Liz huddled close together aboard the Aer Lingus Boeing, scarcely believing what was happening to them even as they peered down at the indistinct fingers of eastern Long Island disappearing into the sea.

They had credentials and some money. Liz had been given an envelope containing ten thousand dollars in cash, which represented *per diem* payments to a "Special Employee" of the government amounting to fifty dollars a day for a period of six months, plus "unusual expenses." It was not a lot but, as Thomas had said, a "start."

There had been no emotional farewells when Farrell left Thomas and Stabler at the heliport. The three men, who had been closer in their peculiarly remote way than many ever get, had just shaken hands firmly and wished one another well. There was no talk of the future, what might be or might have been. It was enough—at least for Farrell—that in the eyes of each there had been mutual respect.

His thoughts had skipped to the Giant and his gang when he tensed and his skin suddenly crawled. A black man with gleaming, hairless skull was making his way down the aisle toward them. Farrell looked up stiffly. The man passed by with no apparent recognition. Farrell breathed out, his taut muscles relaxing. So that was how it was going to be, he thought. He glanced over at Liz. She had not noticed, adrift in her own reverie.

"Is everything all right?" a cheery female voice asked off Farrell's right shoulder.

Farrell looked up to a smiling, pink-faced young flight attendant. "So far, so good—thank you."

The attendant glanced at a manifest she was holding. "Let's

see, now, Mr. and Mrs. Murray. Will you be having drinks once we're aloft?"

"We will that. Have you any champagne? We're on our honeymoon, you know."

"God keep you both," she beamed. "You'll have all the champagne you want!"

She went off along the aisle, and Farrell smiled to himself, aware that already his own speech was taking on an Irish lilt. He looked self-consciously toward Liz. His "wife," Patricia Mary. Wife of Michael Daniel Murray. The new identity warmed him all at once. Michael. He could not help but think of the other, the only Michael in his life to now. In that he could be content. Whatever happened from here on out, at least he'd left Michael pleased with him.

One week later, as Michael and Patricia Murray were starting to reorder their lives in a small cottage outside a village near Galway Bay, a New York jury returned a verdict of Guilty against nine criminal conspirators. The foremost among them, Aaron Luke Brothers, would be sentenced to the maximum penalty under the law: thirty years in prison. He would be eligible for parole in one fourth that time.

Scarcely was the feared gang leader removed to Attica Prison (pending appeal), than others moved in to take his place in the illicit markets he'd dominated.

But even if put out of active commission, the Giant had lost none of his finely honed sense of perspective. Life would go on. His life. Others might be less secure. Michael Palmieri, for one. And of course Tony Farrell. Were he ever to be found. . . .